CELL

By Stephen King and published by
Hodder & Stoughton

FICTION:

Carrie
'Salem's Lot
The Shining
Night Shift
The Stand
Christine
The Talisman *(with Peter Straub)*
Pet Sematary
It
Misery
The Tommyknockers
The Dark Half
Four Past Midnight
Needful Things
Gerald's Game
Dolores Claiborne
Nightmares and Dreamscapes
Insomnia
Rose Madder
Desperation
Bag of Bones
The Girl Who Loved Tom Gordon
Hearts in Atlantis
Dreamcatcher
Everything's Eventual
From a Buick 8
The Dark Tower I: The Gunslinger
The Dark Tower II: The Drawing of the Three
The Dark Tower III: The Waste Lands
The Dark Tower IV: Wizard and Glass
The Dark Tower V: Wolves of the Calla
The Dark Tower VI: Song of Susannah
The Dark Tower VII: The Dark Tower

By Stephen King as Richard Bachman

Thinner
The Running Man
The Bachman Books
The Regulators

NON-FICTION:

On Writing (A Memoir of the Craft)

STEPHEN KING

CELL

A Novel

HODDER &
STOUGHTON

Copyright © 2006 by Stephen King

First published in Great Britain in 2006 by Hodder and Stoughton
A division of Hodder Headline

The right of Stephen King to be identified as the Author
of the Work has been asserted by him in accordance with the
Copyright, Designs and Patents Act 1988

First Edition

A CIP catalogue record for this title is
available from the British Library

ISBN 0 340 92144 7

Typeset in Bembo by
Palimpsest Book Production Limited, Polmont, Stirlingshire

Printed and bound by Clays Ltd, St Ives plc

Hodder Headline's policy is to use papers that are natural,
renewable and recyclable products and made from wood grown
in sustainable forests. The logging and manufacturing processes
are expected to conform to the environmental regulations
of the country of origin

Hodder and Stoughton
A division of Hodder Headline
338 Euston Road
London NW1 3BH

For Richard Matheson and George Romero

The id will not stand for a delay in gratification. It always feels the tension of the unfulfilled urge.

SIGMUND FREUD

Human aggression is instinctual. Humans have not evolved any ritualised aggression-inhibiting mechanisms to ensure the survival of the species. For this reason man is considered a very dangerous animal.

KONRAD LORENZ

Can you hear me now?

VERIZON

CELL

Civilization slipped into its second dark age on an unsurprising track of blood, but with a speed that could not have been foreseen by even the most pessimistic futurist. It was as if it had been waiting to go. On October 1, God was in His heaven, the stock market stood at 10,140, and most of the planes were on time (except for those landing and taking off in Chicago, and that was to be expected). Two weeks later the skies belonged to the birds again and the stock market was a memory. By Halloween, every major city from New York to Moscow stank to the empty heavens and the world as it had been was a memory.

THE PULSE

1

The event that came to be known as The Pulse began at 3:03 p.m., eastern standard time, on the afternoon of October 1. The term was a misnomer, of course, but within ten hours of the event, most of the scientists capable of pointing this out were either dead or insane. The name hardly mattered, in any case. What mattered was the effect.

At three o'clock on that day, a young man of no particular importance to history came walking – almost *bouncing* – east along Boylston Street in Boston. His name was Clayton Riddell. There was an expression of undoubted contentment on his face to go along with the spring in his step. From his left hand there swung the handles of an artist's portfolio, the kind that closes and latches to make a traveling case. Twined around the fingers of his right hand was the drawstring of a brown plastic shopping bag with the words **small treasures** printed on it for anyone who cared to read them.

Inside the bag, swinging back and forth, was a small round object. A present, you might have guessed, and you would have been right. You might further have guessed that this Clayton Riddell was a young man seeking to commemorate some small (or perhaps even not so small) victory with a **small treasure**, and you would have been right again. The item inside the bag was a rather expensive glass paperweight with a gray haze of dandelion fluff caught in its center.

He had bought it on his walk back from the Copley Square Hotel to the much humbler Atlantic Avenue Inn where he was staying, frightened by the ninety-dollar pricetag on the paperweight's base, somehow even more frightened by the realisation that he could now afford such a thing.

Handing his credit card over to the clerk had taken almost physical courage. He doubted if he could have done it if the paperweight had been for himself; he would have muttered something about having changed his mind and scuttled out of the shop. But it was for Sharon. Sharon liked such things, and she still liked him – *I'm pulling for you, baby,* she'd said the day before he left for Boston. Considering the shit they'd put each other through over the last year, that had touched him. Now he wanted to touch her, if that was still possible. The paperweight was a small thing (a **small treasure**), but he was sure she'd love that delicate gray haze deep down in the middle of the glass, like a pocket fog.

2

Clay's attention was attracted by the tinkle of an ice cream truck. It was parked across from the Four Seasons Hotel (which was even grander than the Copley Square) and next to the Boston Common, which ran along Boylston for two or three blocks on this side of the street. The words MISTER SOFTEE were printed in rainbow colors over a pair of dancing ice cream cones. Three kids were clustered around the window, bookbags at their feet, waiting to receive goodies. Behind them stood a woman in a pants suit with a poodle on a leash and a couple of teenage girls in lowrider jeans with iPods and earphones that were currently slung around their necks so they could murmur together – earnestly, no giggles.

Clay stood behind them, turning what had been a little group into a short line. He had bought his estranged wife a present; he would stop at Comix Supreme on the way home and buy his son the new issue of *Spider-Man*; he might as well treat himself, as well. He was bursting to tell Sharon his news, but she'd be out of reach until she got home, three forty-five or so. He thought he would hang around the Inn at least until he talked to her, mostly pacing the confines of his small room and looking at his latched-up portfolio. In the meantime, Mister Softee made an acceptable diversion.

The guy in the truck served the three kids at the window, two Dilly Bars and a monster chocolate-and-vanilla swirl sof'-serve cone for the big spender in the middle, who was apparently paying for all of them. While he fumbled a rat's nest of dollar bills from the pocket of his fashionably baggy jeans, the woman with the poodle and the power suit dipped into her shoulder bag, came out with her cell phone — women in power suits would no more leave home without their cell phones than without their AmEx cards — and flipped it open. Behind them, in the park, a dog barked and someone shouted. It did not sound to Clay like a happy shout, but when he looked over his shoulder all he could see were a few strollers, a dog trotting with a Frisbee in its mouth (weren't they supposed to be on leashes in there, he wondered), acres of sunny green and inviting shade. It looked like a good place for a man who had just sold his first graphic novel — *and* its sequel, both for an amazing amount of money — to sit and eat a chocolate ice cream cone.

When he looked back, the three kids in the baggies were gone and the woman in the power suit was ordering a sundae. One of the two girls behind her had a peppermint-colored phone clipped to her hip, and the woman in the power suit had hers screwed into her ear. Clay thought, as he almost always did on one level of his mind or another when he saw a variation of this behavior, that he was watching an act which would once have been considered almost insufferably rude — yes, even while engaging in a small bit of commerce with a total stranger — becoming a part of accepted everyday behavior.

Put it in Dark Wanderer, *sweetheart,* Sharon said. The

version of her he kept in his mind spoke often and was bound to have her say. This was true of the real-world Sharon as well, separation or no separation. Although not on his cell phone. Clay didn't own one.

The peppermint-colored phone played the opening notes of that Crazy Frog tune that Johnny loved – was it called 'Axel F'? Clay couldn't remember, perhaps because he had blocked it out. The girl to whom the phone belonged snatched it off her hip and said, 'Beth?' She listened, smiled, then said to her companion, 'It's Beth.' Now the other girl bent forward and they both listened, nearly identical pixie haircuts (to Clay they looked almost like Saturday-morning cartoon characters, the Powerpuff Girls, maybe) blowing together in the afternoon breeze.

'Maddy?' said the woman in the power suit at almost exactly the same time. Her poodle was now sitting contemplatively at the end of its leash (the leash was red, and dusted with glittery stuff), looking at the traffic on Boylston Street. Across the way, at the Four Seasons, a doorman in a brown uniform – they always seemed to be brown or blue – was waving, probably for a taxi. A Duck Boat crammed with tourists sailed by, looking high and out of place on dry land, the driver bawling into his loudhailer about something historic. The two girls listening to the peppermint-colored phone looked at each other and smiled at something they were hearing, but still did not giggle.

'Maddy? Can you hear me? *Can you*—'

The woman in the power suit raised the hand holding the leash and plugged a long-nailed finger into her free ear. Clay winced, fearing for her eardrum. He imagined drawing her: the dog on the leash, the power suit, the fashionably short hair . . . and one small trickle of blood from around the finger in her ear. The Duck Boat just exiting the frame and the doorman in the background, those things somehow lending the sketch its verisimilitude. They would; it was just a thing you knew.

CELL

'Maddy, you're breaking *up*! I just wanted to tell you I got my hair done at that new . . . my *hair*? . . . *MY* . . .'

The guy in the Mister Softee truck bent down and held out a sundae cup. From it rose a white Alp with chocolate and strawberry sauce coursing down its sides. His beard-stubbly face was impassive. It said he'd seen it all before. Clay was sure he had, most of it twice. In the park, someone screamed. Clay looked over his shoulder again, telling himself that had to be a scream of joy. At three o'clock in the afternoon, a sunny afternoon on the Boston Common, it pretty much *had* to be a scream of joy. Right?

The woman said something unintelligible to Maddy and flipped her cell phone closed with a practiced flip of the wrist. She dropped it back into her purse, then just stood there, as if she had forgotten what she was doing or maybe even where she was.

'That's four-fifty,' said the Mister Softee guy, still patiently holding out the ice cream sundae. Clay had time to think how fucking *expensive* everything was in the city. Perhaps the woman in the power suit thought so, too — that, at least, was his first surmise — because for a moment more she still did nothing, merely looked at the cup with its mound of ice cream and sliding sauce as if she had never seen such a thing before.

Then there came another cry from the Common, not a human one this time but something between a surprised yelp and a hurt yowl. Clay turned to look and saw the dog that had been trotting with the Frisbee in its mouth. It was a good-sized brown dog, maybe a Labrador, he didn't really know dogs, when he needed to draw one he got a book and copied a picture. A man in a business suit was down on his knees beside this one and had it in a necklock and appeared to be — *surely I'm not seeing what I think I'm seeing,* Clay thought — chewing on its ear. Then the dog howled again and tried to spurt away. The man in the business suit held it firm, and yes, that was the dog's ear in the man's mouth, and

7

as Clay continued to watch, the man tore it off the side of the dog's head. This time the dog uttered an almost human scream, and a number of ducks which had been floating on a nearby pond took flight, squawking.

'Rast!' someone cried from behind Clay. It sounded like *rast*. It might have been *rat* or *roast,* but later experience made him lean toward *rast*: not a word at all but merely an inarticulate sound of aggression.

He turned back toward the ice cream truck in time to see Power Suit Woman lunge through the serving window in an effort to grab Mister Softee Guy. She managed to snag the loose folds at the front of his white tunic, but his single startle-step backwards was enough to break her hold. Her high heels briefly left the sidewalk, and he heard the rasp of cloth and the clink of buttons as the front of her jacket ran first up the little jut of the serving window's counter and then back down. The sundae tumbled from view. Clay saw a smear of ice cream and sauce on Power Suit Woman's left wrist and forearm as her high heels clacked back to the sidewalk. She staggered, knees bent. The closed-off, well-bred, out-in-public look on her face — what Clay thought of as your basic on-the-street-no-face look — had been replaced by a convulsive snarl that shrank her eyes to slits and exposed both sets of teeth. Her upper lip had turned completely inside out, revealing a pink velvet lining as intimate as a vulva. Her poodle ran into the street, trailing its red leash with the hand-loop in the end. A black limo came along and ran the poodle down before it got halfway across. Fluff at one moment; guts at the next.

Poor damn thing was probably yapping in doggy heaven before it knew it was dead, Clay thought. He understood in some clinical way he was in shock, but that in no way changed the depth of his amazement. He stood there with his portfolio hanging from one hand and his brown shopping bag hanging from the other and his mouth hanging open.

Somewhere — it sounded like maybe around the corner on Newbury Street — something exploded.

CELL

The two girls had exactly the same haircut above their iPod headphones, but the one with the peppermint-colored cell phone was blond and her friend was brunette; they were Pixie Light and Pixie Dark. Now Pixie Light dropped her phone on the sidewalk, where it shattered, and seized Power Suit Woman around the waist. Clay assumed (so far as he was capable of assuming anything in those moments) that she meant to restrain Power Suit Woman either from going after Mister Softee Guy again or from running into the street after her dog. There was even a part of his mind that applauded the girl's presence of mind. Her friend, Pixie Dark, was backing away from the whole deal, small white hands clasped between her breasts, eyes wide.

Clay dropped his own items, one on each side, and stepped forward to help Pixie Light. On the other side of the street — he saw this only in his peripheral vision — a car swerved and bolted across the sidewalk in front of the Four Seasons, causing the doorman to dart out of the way. There were screams from the hotel's forecourt. And before Clay could begin helping Pixie Light with Power Suit Woman, Pixie Light had darted her pretty little face forward with snakelike speed, bared her undoubtedly strong young teeth, and battened on Power Suit Woman's neck. There was an enormous jet of blood. The pixie-girl stuck her face in it, appeared to bathe in it, perhaps even drank from it (Clay was almost sure she did), then shook Power Suit Woman back and forth like a doll. The woman was taller and had to outweigh the girl by at least forty pounds, but the girl shook her hard enough to make the woman's head flop back and forth and send more blood flying. At the same time the girl cocked her own blood-smeared face up to the bright blue October sky and howled in what sounded like triumph.

She's mad, Clay thought. *Totally mad.*

Pixie Dark cried out, 'Who are you? *What's happening?*'

At the sound of her friend's voice, Pixie Light whipped

her bloody head around. Blood dripped from the short dagger-points of hair overhanging her forehead. Eyes like white lamps peered from blood-dappled sockets.

Pixie Dark looked at Clay, her eyes wide. 'Who are you?' she repeated . . . and then: 'Who am *I*?'

Pixie Light dropped Power Suit Woman, who collapsed to the sidewalk with her chewed-open carotid artery still spurting, then leaped at the girl with whom she had been chummily sharing a phone only a few moments before.

Clay didn't think. If he had thought, Pixie Dark might have had her throat opened like the woman in the power suit. He didn't even look. He simply reached down and to his right, seized the top of the **small treasures** shopping bag, and swung it at the back of Pixie Light's head as she leaped at her erstwhile friend with her outstretched hands making claw-fish against the blue sky. If he missed—

He didn't miss, or even hit the girl a glancing blow. The glass paperweight inside the bag struck the back of Pixie Light's head dead-on, making a muffled *thunk*. Pixie Light dropped her hands, one bloodstained, one still clean, and fell to the sidewalk at her friend's feet like a sack of mail.

'What the *hell*?' Mister Softee Guy cried. His voice was improbably high. Maybe shock had given him that high tenor.

'I don't know,' Clay said. His heart was hammering. 'Help me quick. This other one's bleeding to death.'

From behind them, on Newbury Street, came the unmistakable hollow bang-and-jingle of a car crash, followed by screams. The screams were followed by another explosion, this one louder, concussive, hammering the day. Behind the Mister Softee truck, another car swerved across three lanes of Boylston Street and into the courtyard of the Four Seasons, mowing down a couple of pedestrians and then plowing into the back of the previous car, which had finished with its nose crumpled into the revolving doors. This second crash shoved the first car further into the revolving doors, bending them askew. Clay couldn't see if anyone was trapped in there – clouds of steam were rising from the first car's breached radiator – but the agonized shrieks from the shadows suggested bad things. Very bad.

Mister Softee Guy, blind on that side, was leaning out his serving window and staring at Clay. 'What's going on over there?'

'I don't know. Couple of car wrecks. People hurt. Never mind. Help me, man.' He knelt beside Power Suit Woman in the blood and the shattered remnants of Pixie Light's pink cell phone. Power Suit Woman's twitches had now become weak, indeed.

'Smoke from over on Newbury,' observed Mister Softee Guy, still not emerging from the relative safety of his ice cream wagon. 'Something blew up over there. I mean bigtime. Maybe it's terrorists.'

As soon as the word was out of his mouth, Clay was sure he was right. 'Help me.'

'*WHO AM I?*' Pixie Dark suddenly screamed.

Clay had forgotten all about her. He looked up in time to see the girl smack herself in the forehead with the heel of her hand, then turn around rapidly three times, standing almost on the toes of her tennies to do it. The sight called up a memory of some poem he'd read in a college lit class – *Weave a circle round him thrice.* Coleridge, wasn't it? She staggered, then ran rapidly down the sidewalk and directly into a lamppost. She made no attempt to avoid it or even put up her hands. She struck it face-first, rebounded, staggered, then went at it again.

'*Stop that!*' Clay roared. He shot to his feet, started to run toward her, slipped in Power Suit Woman's blood, almost fell, got going again, tripped on Pixie Light, and almost fell again.

Pixie Dark looked around at him. Her nose was broken and gushing blood down her lower face. A vertical contusion was puffing up on her brow, rising like a thunderhead on a summer day. One of her eyes had gone crooked in its socket.

11

She opened her mouth, exposing a ruin of what had probably been expensive orthodontic work, and laughed at him. He never forgot it.

Then she ran away down the sidewalk, screaming.

Behind him, a motor started up and amplified bells began tinkling out the *Sesame Street* theme. Clay turned and saw the Mister Softee truck pulling rapidly away from the kerb just as, from the top floor of the hotel across the way, a window shattered in a bright spray of glass. A body hurtled out into the October day. It fell to the sidewalk, where it more or less exploded. More screams from the forecourt. Screams of horror; screams of pain.

'*No!*' Clay yelled, running alongside the Mister Softee truck. '*No, come back and help me! I need some help here, you son of a bitch!*'

No answer from Mister Softee Guy, who maybe couldn't hear over his amplified music. Clay could remember the words from the days when he'd had no reason not to believe his marriage wouldn't last forever. In those days Johnny watched *Sesame Street* every day, sitting in his little blue chair with his sippy cup clutched in his hands. Something about a sunny day, keepin' the clouds away.

A man in a business suit came running out of the park, roaring wordless sounds at the top of his lungs, his coattails flapping behind him. Clay recognized him by his dogfur goatee. The man ran into Boylston Street. Cars swerved around him, barely missing him. He ran on to the other side, still roaring and waving his hands at the sky. He disappeared into the shadows beneath the canopy of the Four Seasons forecourt and was lost to view, but he must have gotten up to more dickens immediately, because a fresh volley of screams broke out over there.

Clay gave up his chase of the Mister Softee truck and stood with one foot on the sidewalk and the other planted in the gutter, watching as it swerved into the center lane of Boylston Street, still tinkling. He was about to turn back to the unconscious girl and dying woman when another Duck Boat appeared, this one not loafing but roaring at top speed and yawing crazily from port to starboard. Some of the passengers were tumbling back and forth and howling – *pleading* – for the driver to stop. Others simply clung to the metal struts running up the open sides of the ungainly thing as it made its way up Boylston Street against the flow of traffic.

A man in a sweatshirt grabbed the driver from behind, and Clay heard another of those inarticulate cries through the Duck Boat's primitive amplification system as the driver threw the guy off with a mighty backward shrug. Not *'Rast!'* this time but something more guttural, something that sounded like *'Gluh!'* Then the Duck Boat driver saw the Mister Softee truck – Clay was sure of it – and changed course, aiming for it.

'Oh God please no!' a woman sitting near the front of the tourist craft cried, and as it closed in on the tinkling ice cream truck, which was approximately one-sixth its size, Clay had a clear memory of watching the victory parade on TV the year the Red Sox won the World Series. The team rode in a slow-moving procession of these same Duck Boats, waving to the delirious multitudes as a cold autumn drizzle fell.

'God please no!' the woman shrieked again, and from beside Clay a man said, almost mildly: 'Jesus Christ.'

The Duck Boat hit the ice cream truck broadside and flipped it like a child's toy. It landed on its side with its own amplification system still tinkling out the *Sesame Street* theme music and went skidding back toward the Common, shooting up friction-generated bursts of sparks. Two women who had been watching dashed to get out of the way, holding hands, and just made it. The Mister Softee truck bounced onto the sidewalk, went briefly airborne, then hit the wrought-iron fence surrounding the park and came to rest. The music hiccuped twice, then stopped.

The lunatic driving the Duck Boat had, meanwhile, lost

whatever marginal control he might have had over his vehicle. It looped back across Boylston Street with its freight of terrified, screaming passengers clinging to the open sides, mounted the sidewalk across and about fifty yards down from the point where the Mister Softee truck had tinkled its last, and ran into the low brick retaining wall below the display window of a toney furniture shop called Citylights. There was a vast unmusical crash as the window shattered. The Duck Boat's wide rear end (*Harbor Mistress* was written on it in pink script) rose perhaps five feet in the air. Momentum wanted the great waddling thing to go end-over-end; mass would not allow. It settled back to the sidewalk with its snout poked among the scattered sofas and expensive living room chairs, but not before at least a dozen people had gone shooting forward, out of the Duck Boat and out of sight.

Inside Citylights, a burglar alarm began to clang.

'Jesus Christ,' said the mild voice from Clay's right elbow a second time. He turned that way and saw a short man with thinning dark hair, a tiny dark mustache, and gold-rimmed spectacles. 'What's going on?'

'I don't know,' Clay said. Talking was hard. Very. He found himself almost having to push words out. He supposed it was shock. Across the street, people were running away, some from the Four Seasons, some from the crashed Duck Boat. As he watched, a Duck Boat run-awayer collided with a Four Seasons escapee and they both went crashing to the sidewalk. There was time to wonder if he'd gone insane and was hallucinating all this in a madhouse somewhere. Juniper Hill in Augusta, maybe, between Thorazine shots. 'The guy in the ice cream truck said maybe terrorists.'

'I don't see any men with guns,' said the short man with the mustache. 'No guys with bombs strapped to their backs, either.'

Neither did Clay, but he *did* see his little **small treasures** shopping bag and his portfolio sitting on the sidewalk, and he saw that the blood from Power Suit Woman's opened throat – *ye gods,* he thought, *all that blood* – had almost reached the portfolio. All but a dozen or so of his drawings for *Dark Wanderer* were in there, and it was the drawings his mind seized on. He started back that way at a speed-walk, and the short man kept pace. When a second burglar alarm (*some* kind of alarm, anyway) went off in the hotel, joining its hoarse bray to the clang of the Citylights alarm, the little guy jumped.

'It's the hotel,' Clay said.

'I know, it's just that . . . oh my *God.*' He'd seen Power Suit Woman, now lying in a lake of the magic stuff that had been running all her bells and whistles – what? Four minutes ago? Only two?

'She's dead,' Clay told him. 'At least I'm pretty sure she is. That girl . . .' He pointed at Pixie Light. 'She did it. With her teeth.'

'You're joking.'

'I wish I was.'

From somewhere up Boylston Street there was another explosion. Both men cringed. Clay realised he could now smell smoke. He picked up his **small treasures** bag and his portfolio and moved them both away from the spreading blood. 'These are mine,' he said, wondering why he felt the need to explain.

The little guy, who was wearing a tweed suit – quite dapper, Clay thought – was still staring, horrified, at the crumpled body of the woman who had stopped for a sundae and lost first her dog and then her life. Behind them, three young men pelted past on the sidewalk, laughing and hurrahing. Two had Red Sox caps turned around backward. One was carrying a carton clutched against his chest. It had the word **panasonic** printed in blue on the side. This one stepped in Power Suit Woman's spreading blood with his right sneaker and left a fading one-foot trail behind him as he and his mates ran on toward the east end of the Common and Chinatown beyond.

3

Clay dropped to one knee and used the hand not clutching his portfolio (he was even more afraid of losing it after seeing the sprinting kid with the **panasonic** carton) to pick up Pixie Light's wrist. He got a pulse at once. It was slow but strong and regular. He felt great relief. No matter what she'd done, she was just a kid. He didn't want to think he had bludgeoned her to death with his wife's gift paperweight.

'Look out, look out!' the little guy with the moustache almost sang. Clay had no time to look out. Luckily, this call wasn't even close. The vehicle – one of those big OPEC-friendly SUVs – veered off Boylston and into the park at least twenty yards from where he knelt, taking a snarl of the wrought-iron fence in front of it and coming to rest bumper-deep in the duck-pond.

The door opened and a young man floundered out, yelling gibberish at the sky. He fell to his knees in the water, scooped some of it into his mouth with both hands (Clay had a passing thought of all the ducks that had happily shat in that pond over the years), then struggled to his feet and waded to the far side. He disappeared into a grove of trees, still waving his hands and bellowing his nonsense sermon.

'We need to get help for this girl,' Clay said to the man with the mustache. 'She's unconscious but a long way from dead.'

'What we need to *do* is get off the street before we get run over,' said the man with the mustache, and as if to prove this point, a taxi collided with a stretch limo not far from the wrecked Duck Boat. The limo had been going the wrong way but the taxi got the worst of it; as Clay watched from where he still knelt on the sidewalk, the taxi's driver flew through his suddenly glassless windshield and landed in the street, holding up a bloody arm and screaming.

The man with the mustache was right, of course. Such

rationality as Clay could muster – only a little managed to find its way through the blanket of shock that muffled his thinking – suggested that by far the wisest course of action would be to get the hell away from Boylston Street and under cover. If this was an act of terrorism, it was like none he had ever seen or read about. What he – *they* – should do was get down and stay down until the situation clarified. That would probably entail finding a television. But he didn't want to leave this unconscious girl lying on a street that had suddenly become a madhouse. Every instinct of his mostly kind – and certainly civilized – heart cried out against it.

'You go on,' he told the little man with the mustache. He said it with immense reluctance. He didn't know the little man from Adam, but at least he wasn't spouting gibberish and throwing his hands in the air. Or going for Clay's throat with his teeth bared. 'Get inside somewhere. I'll . . .' He didn't know how to finish.

'You'll what?' the man with the mustache asked, then hunched his shoulders and winced as something else exploded. That one came from directly behind the hotel, it sounded like, and now black smoke began to rise over there, staining the blue sky before it got high enough for the wind to pull away.

'I'll call a cop,' Clay said, suddenly inspired. 'She's got a cell phone.' He cocked his thumb at Power Suit Woman, now lying dead in a pool of her own blood. 'She was using it before . . . you know, just before the shit . . .'

He trailed off, replaying exactly what *had* happened just before the shit hit the fan. He found his eyes wandering from the dead woman to the unconscious girl and then on to the shards of the unconscious girl's peppermint-colored cell phone.

Warbling sirens of two distinctly different pitches rose in the air. Clay supposed one pitch belonged to police cars, the other to fire trucks. He supposed you could tell the difference if you lived in this city, but he didn't, he lived in Kent Pond, Maine, and he wished with all his heart that he were there right now.

What happened just before the shit hit the fan was that Power Suit Woman had called her friend Maddy to tell her she'd gotten her hair done, and one of Pixie Light's friends had called *her*. Pixie Dark had listened in to this latter call. After that all three of them had gone crazy.

You're not thinking—

From behind them, to the east, came the biggest explosion yet: a terrific shotgun-blast of sound. Clay leaped to his feet. He and the little man in the tweed suit looked wildly at each other, then toward Chinatown and Boston's North End. They couldn't see what had exploded, but now a much larger, darker plume of smoke was rising above the buildings on that horizon.

While they were looking at it, a Boston PD radio-car and a hook-and-ladder fire truck pulled up in front of the Four Seasons across the street. Clay glanced that way in time to see a second jumper set sail from the top story of the hotel, followed by another pair from the roof. To Clay it looked as if the two coming from the roof were actually brawling with each other on the way down.

'Jesus Mary and Joseph NO!' a woman screamed, her voice breaking. *'Oh NO, no MORE, no MORE!'*

The first of the suicidal trio hit the rear of the police car, splattering the trunk with hair and gore, shattering the back window. The other two hit the hook and ladder as firemen dressed in bright yellow coats scattered like improbable birds.

'NO!' the woman shrieked. *'No MORE! No MORE! Dear GOD, no MORE!'*

But here came a woman from the fifth or sixth floor, tumbling like a crazy acrobat, striking a policeman who was peering up and surely killing him even as she killed herself.

From the north there came another of those great roaring explosions – the sound of the devil firing a shotgun in hell – and once again Clay looked at the little man, who was looking anxiously back up at him. More smoke was rising in the sky, and in spite of the brisk breeze, the blue over there was almost blotted out.

'They're using planes again,' the little man said. 'The dirty bastards are using planes again.'

As if to underline the idea, a third monstrous explosion came rolling to them from the city's northeast.

'But . . . that's Logan over there.' Clay was once again finding it hard to talk, and even harder to think. All he really seemed to have in his mind was some sort of half-baked joke: *Did you hear the one about the* [insert your favourite ethnic group here] *terrorists who decided to bring America to its knees by blowing up the airport?*

'So?' the little man asked, almost truculently.

'So why not the Hancock Building? Or the Pru?'

The little man's shoulders slumped. 'I don't know. I only know I want to get off this street.'

As if to emphasize his point, half a dozen more young people sprinted past them. Boston was a *city* of young people, Clay had noticed – all those colleges. These six, three men and three women, were running lootless, at least, and they most assuredly weren't laughing. As they ran, one of the young men pulled out his cell phone and stuck it to his ear.

Clay glanced across the street and saw that a second black-and-white unit had pulled up behind the first. No need to use Power Suit Woman's cell phone after all (which was good, since he'd decided he really didn't want to do that). He could just walk across the street and talk to them . . . except he wasn't sure that he dared to cross Boylston Street just now. Even if he did, would they come over *here* to look at one unconscious girl when they had God knew how many casualties over *there*? And as he watched, the firemen began piling back on board their hook-and-ladder unit; it looked like they were heading someplace else. Over to Logan Airport, quite likely, or—

'Oh my God-Jesus, watch out for this one,' said the little man with the mustache, speaking in a low, tight voice. He was looking west along Boylston, back toward downtown, in the direction Clay had been coming from when his major object in life had been reaching Sharon on the phone. He'd even known how he was going to start: *Good news, hon – no matter how it comes out between us, there'll always be shoes for the kid.* In his head it had sounded light and funny – like the old days.

There was nothing funny about this. Coming toward them – not running but walking in long, flat-footed strides – was a man of about fifty, wearing suit pants and the remains of a shirt and tie. The pants were gray. It was impossible to tell what color the shirt and tie had been, because both were now shredded and stained with blood. In his right hand the man held what looked like a butcher knife with an eighteen-inch blade. Clay actually believed he had seen this knife, in the window of a shop called Soul Kitchen, on his walk back from his meeting at the Copley Square Hotel. The row of knives in the window (**SWEDISH STEEL!** the little engraved card in front of them proclaimed) had shone in the cunning glow of hidden downlighters, but this blade had done a good deal of work since its liberation – or a bad deal of it – and was now dull with blood.

The man in the tattered shirt swung the knife as he closed in on them with his flat-footed strides, the blade cutting short up–and–down arcs in the air. He broke the pattern only once, to slash at himself. A fresh rill of blood ran through a new rip in his tattered shirt. The remains of his tie flapped. And as he closed the distance he hectored them like a back-woods preacher speaking in tongues at the moment of some divine godhead revelation.

'*Eyelah!*' he cried. '*Eeelah-eyelah-a-babbalah naz! A-babbalah why? A-bunnaloo coy? Kazzalah! Kazzalah-CAN! Fie! SHY-fie!*' And now he brought the knife back to his right hip and then beyond it, and Clay, whose visual sense was overdeveloped, at once saw the sweeping stroke that would follow. The gutting stroke, made even as he continued his nuthouse march to nowhere through the October afternoon in those flat-footed declamatory strides.

'*Look out!*' the little guy with the mustache screamed, but *he* wasn't looking out, not the little guy with the mustache; the little guy with the mustache, the first *normal* person with whom Clay Riddell had spoken since this craziness began — who had, in fact, spoken to *him,* which had probably taken some courage, under the circumstances — was frozen in place, his eyes bigger than ever behind the lenses of his gold-rimmed spectacles. And was the crazy guy going for him because of the two men, the one with the mustache was smaller and looked like easier prey? If so, maybe Mr Speaking-in-Tongues wasn't *completely* crazy, and suddenly Clay was mad as well as scared, mad the way he might have been if he'd looked through a schoolyard fence and seen a bully getting ready to tune up on a smaller, younger kid.

'*LOOK OUT!*' the little man with the mustache almost wailed, still not moving as his death swept toward him, death liberated from a shop called Soul Kitchen where Diner's Club and Visa were no doubt accepted, along with Your Personal Check If Accompanied By Bank Card.

Clay didn't think. He simply picked up his portfolio again by its double handle and stuck it between the oncoming knife and his new acquaintance in the tweed suit. The blade went all the way through with a hollow *thuck,* but the tip stopped four inches short of the little man's belly. The little man finally came to his senses and cringed aside, toward the Common, shrieking for help at the top of his lungs.

The man in the shredded shirt and tie — he was getting a bit jowly in the cheek and heavy in the neck, as if his personal equation of good meals and good exercise had stopped balancing about two years ago — abruptly ceased his nonsense peroration. His face took on a look of vacuous perplexity that stopped short of surprise, let alone amazement.

What Clay felt was a species of dismal outrage. That blade had gone through all of his *Dark Wanderer* pictures (to him they were always pictures, never drawings or illustrations), and it seemed to him that the *thuck* sound might as well have been the blade penetrating a special chamber of his heart. That was stupid when he had repros of everything, including the four color splash-pages, but it didn't change how he felt. The madman's blade had skewered Sorcerer John (named after his own son, of course), the Wizard Flak, Frank and the Posse Boys, Sleepy Gene, Poison Sally, Lily Astolet, Blue Witch, and of course Ray Damon, the Dark Wanderer himself. His own fantastic creatures, living in the cave of his imagination and poised to set him free from the drudgery of teaching art in a dozen rural Maine schools, driving thousands of miles a month and practically living out of his car.

He could swear he had heard them moan when the madman's Swedish blade pierced them where they slept in their innocency.

Furious, not caring about the blade (at least for the moment), he drove the man in the shredded shirt rapidly backward, using the portfolio as a kind of shield, growing angrier as it bent into a wide V-shape around the knife-blade.

'Blet!' the lunatic hollered, and tried to pull his blade back. It was caught too firmly for him to do so. *'Blet ky-yam doe-ram kazzalah a-babbalah!'*

'I'll a-babbalah *your* a-kazzalah, you fuck!' Clay shouted, and planted his left foot behind the lunatic's backpedaling legs. It would occur to him later that the body knows how to fight when it has to. That it's a secret the body keeps, just as it does the secrets of how to run or jump a creek or throw a fuck or – quite likely – die when there's no other choice. That under conditions of extreme stress it simply takes over and does what needs doing while the brain stands off to one side, unable to do anything but whistle and tap its foot and look up at the sky. Or contemplate the sound a knife makes going through the portfolio your wife gave you for your twenty-eighth birthday, for that matter.

The lunatic tripped over Clay's foot just as Clay's wise

body meant him to do and fell to the sidewalk on his back. Clay stood over him, panting, with the portfolio still held in both hands like a shield bent in battle. The butcher knife still stuck out of it, handle from one side, blade from the other.

The lunatic tried to get up. Clay's new friend scurried forward and kicked him in the neck, quite hard. The little fellow was weeping loudly, the tears gushing down his cheeks and fogging the lenses of his spectacles. The lunatic fell back on the sidewalk with his tongue sticking out of his mouth. Around it he made choking sounds that sounded to Clay like his former speaking-in-tongues babble.

'He tried to kill us!' the little man wept. 'He tried to *kill* us!'

'Yes, yes,' Clay said. He was aware that he had once said *yes, yes* to Johnny in exactly the same way back when they'd still called him Johnny-Gee and he'd come to them up the front walk with his scraped shins or elbows, wailing *I got BLOOD!*

The man on the sidewalk (who had plenty of blood) was on his elbows, trying to get up again. Clay did the honors this time, kicking one of the guy's elbows out from under him and putting him back down on the pavement. This kicking seemed like a stopgap solution at best, and a messy one. Clay grabbed the handle of the knife, winced at the slimy feel of half-jellied blood on the handle – it was like rubbing a palm through cold bacon-grease – and pulled. The knife came a little bit, then either stopped or his hand slipped. He fancied he heard his characters murmuring unhappily from the darkness of the portfolio, and he made a painful noise himself. He couldn't help it. And he couldn't help wondering what he meant to do with the knife if he got it out. Stab the lunatic to death with it? He thought he could have done that in the heat of the moment, but probably not now.

'What's wrong?' the little man asked in a watery voice. Clay, even in his own distress, couldn't help being touched by the concern he heard there. 'Did he get you? You had him blocked out for a few seconds and I couldn't see. Did he get you? Are you cut?'

'No,' Clay said. 'I'm all r—'

There was another gigantic explosion from the north, almost surely from Logan Airport on the other side of Boston Harbor. Both of them hunched their shoulders and winced.

The lunatic took the opportunity to sit up and was scrambling to his feet when the little man in the tweed suit administered a clumsy but effective sideways kick, planting a shoe squarely in the middle of the lunatic's shredded tie and knocking him back down. The lunatic roared and snatched at the little man's foot. He would have pulled the little guy over, then perhaps into a crushing embrace, had Clay not seized his new acquaintance by the shoulder and pulled him away.

'*He's got my shoe!*' the little man yelped. Behind them, two more cars crashed. There were more screams, more alarms. Car alarms, fire alarms, hearty clanging burglar alarms. Sirens whooped in the distance. '*Bastard got my sh—*'

Suddenly a policeman was there. One of the responders from across the street, Clay assumed, and as the policeman dropped to one blue knee beside the babbling lunatic, Clay felt something very much like love for the cop. That he'd take the time to come over here! That he'd even noticed!

'You want to be careful of him,' the little man said nervously. 'He's—'

'I know what he is,' the cop replied, and Clay saw the cop had his service automatic in his hand. He had no idea if the cop had drawn it after kneeling or if he'd had it out the whole time. Clay had been too busy being grateful to notice.

The cop looked at the lunatic. Leaned close to the lunatic. Almost seemed to *offer* himself to the lunatic. 'Hey, buddy, how ya doin?' he murmured. 'I mean, what the haps?'

The lunatic lunged at the cop and put his hands on the

cop's throat. The instant he did this, the cop slipped the muzzle of his gun into the hollow of the lunatic's temple and pulled the trigger. A great spray of blood leaped through the graying hair on the opposite side of the lunatic's head and he fell back to the sidewalk, throwing both arms out melo-dramatically: *Look, Ma, I'm dead.*

Clay looked at the little man with the mustache and the little man with the mustache looked at him. Then they looked back at the cop, who had holstered his weapon and was taking a leather case from the breast pocket of his uniform shirt. Clay was glad to see that the hand he used to do this was shaking a little. He was now frightened of the cop, but would have been more frightened still if the cop's hands had been steady. And what had just happened was no isolated case. The gunshot seemed to have done something to Clay's hearing, cleared a circuit in it or something. Now he could hear other gunshots, isolated cracks punctuating the escalating cacophony of the day.

The cop took a card – Clay thought it was a business card – from the slim leather case, then put the case back in his breast pocket. He held the card between the first two fingers of his left hand while his right hand once more dropped to the butt of his service weapon. Near his highly polished shoes, blood from the lunatic's shattered head was pooling on the sidewalk. Close by, Power Suit Woman lay in another pool of blood, which was now starting to congeal and turn a darker shade of red.

'What's your name, sir?' the cop asked Clay.

'Clayton Riddell.'

'Can you tell me who the president is?'

Clay told him.

'Sir, can you tell me today's date?'

'It's the first of October. Do you know what's—'

The cop looked at the little man with the mustache. 'Your name?'

'I'm Thomas McCourt, 140 Salem Street, Malden. I—'

'Can you name the man who ran against the president in the last election?'

Tom McCourt did so.

'Who is Brad Pitt married to?'

McCourt threw up his hands. 'How should *I* know? Some movie star, I think.'

'Okay.' The cop handed Clay the card he'd been holding between his fingers. 'I'm Officer Ulrich Ashland. This is my card. You may be called on to testify about what just happened here, gentlemen. What happened was you needed assistance, I rendered it, I was attacked, I responded.'

'You wanted to kill him,' Clay said.

'Yes, sir, we're putting as many of them out of their misery as fast as we can,' Officer Ashland agreed. 'And if you tell any court or board of inquiry that I said that, I'll deny it. But it has to be done. These people are popping up everywhere. Some only commit suicide. Many others attack.' He hesitated, then added: 'So far as we can tell, *all* the others attack.' As if to underline this, there was another gunshot from across the street, a pause, then three more, in rapid succession, from the shadowed forecourt of the Four Seasons Hotel, which was now a tangle of broken glass, broken bodies, crashed vehicles, and spilled blood. 'It's like the fucking *Night of the Living Dead*.' Officer Ulrich Ashland started back toward Boylston Street with his hand still on the butt of his gun. 'Except these people aren't dead. Unless we help them, that is.'

'Rick!' It was a cop on the other side of the street, calling urgently. 'Rick, we gotta go to Logan! All units! Get over here!'

Officer Ashland checked for traffic, but there was none. Except for the wrecks, Boylston Street was momentarily deserted. From the surrounding area, however, came the sound of more explosions and automotive crashes. The smell of smoke was getting stronger. He started across the street, got halfway, then turned back. 'Get inside somewhere,' he said.

'Get under cover. You've been lucky once. You may not be lucky again.'

'Officer Ashland,' Clay said. 'Your guys don't use cell phones, do you?'

Ashland regarded him from the center of Boylston Street – not, in Clay's opinion, a safe place to be. He was thinking of the rogue Duck Boat. 'No, sir,' he said. 'We have radios in our cars. And these.' He patted the radio in his belt, hung opposite his holster. Clay, a comic-book fiend since he could read, thought briefly of Batman's marvellous utility belt.

'Don't use them,' Clay said. 'Tell the others. *Don't use the cell phones.*'

'Why do you say that?'

'Because *they* were.' He pointed to the dead woman and the unconscious girl. 'Just before they went crazy. And I'll bet you anything that the guy with the knife—'

'*Rick!*' the cop on the other side shouted again. '*Hurry the fuck up!*'

'Get under cover,' Officer Ashland repeated, and trotted to the Four Seasons side of the street. Clay wished he could have repeated the thing about the cell phones, but on the whole he was just glad to see the cop out of harm's way. Not that he believed anyone in Boston really was, not this afternoon.

4

'What are you doing?' Clay asked Tom McCourt. 'Don't touch him, he might be, I don't know, contagious.'

'I'm not going to touch him,' Tom said, 'but I need my shoe.'

The shoe, lying near the splayed fingers of the lunatic's left hand, was at least away from the exit-spray of blood. Tom hooked his fingers delicately into the back and pulled it to him. Then he sat down on the kerb of Boylston Street – right where the Mister Softee truck had been parked in what now seemed to Clay like another lifetime – and slipped his foot into it. 'The laces are broken,' he said. 'That damn nutball broke the laces.' And he started crying again.

'Do the best you can,' Clay said. He began working the butcher knife out of the portfolio. It had been slammed through with tremendous force, and he found he had to wiggle it up and down to free it. It came out reluctantly, in a series of jerks, and with ugly scraping sounds that made him want to cringe. He kept wondering who inside had gotten the worst of it. That was stupid, nothing but shock-think, but he couldn't help it. 'Can't you tie it down close to the bottom?'

'Yeah, I think s—'

Clay had been hearing a mechanical mosquito whine that now grew to an approaching drone. Tom craned up from his place on the kerb. Clay turned around. The little caravan of BPD cars pulling away from the Four Seasons halted in front of Citylights and the crashed Duck Boat with their gumballs flashing. Cops leaned out the windows as a private plane – something midsize, maybe a Cessna or the kind they called a Twin Bonanza, Clay didn't really know planes – came cruising slowly over the buildings between Boston Harbour and the Boston Common, dropping fast. The plane banked drunkenly over the park, its lower wing almost brushing the top of one autumn-bright tree, then settled into the canyon of Charles Street, as if the pilot had decided that was a runway. Then, less than twenty feet above the ground, it tilted left and the wing on that side struck the façade of a gray stone building, maybe a bank, on the corner of Charles and Beacon. Any sense that the plane was moving slowly, almost gliding, departed in that instant. It spun around on the caught wing as savagely as a tetherball nearing the end of its rope, slammed into the redbrick building standing next to the bank, and disappeared in bright petals of red-orange fire. The shock-wave hammered across the park. Ducks took wing before it.

Clay looked down and saw he was holding the butcher knife in his hand. He had pulled it free while he and Tom

McCourt were watching the plane crash. He wiped it first one way and then the other on the front of his shirt, taking pains not to cut himself (now *his* hands were shaking). Then he slipped it – very carefully – into his belt, all the way down to the handle. As he did this, one of his early comic-book efforts occurred to him . . . a bit of juvenilia, actually.

'Joxer the Pirate stands here at your service, my pretty one,' he murmured.

'What?' Tom asked. He was now beside Clay, staring at the boiling inferno of the airplane on the far side of Boston Common. Only the tail stuck out of the fire. On it Clay could read the number LN6409B. Above it was what looked like some sports team's logo.

Then that was gone, too.

He could feel the first waves of heat begin to pump gently against his face.

'Nothing,' he told the little man in the tweed suit. 'Leave us boogie.'

'Huh?'

'Let's get out of here.'

'Oh. Okay.'

Clay started to walk along the southern side of the Common, in the direction he'd been heading at three o'clock, eighteen minutes and an eternity ago. Tom McCourt hurried to keep up. He really was a *very* short man. 'Tell me,' he said, 'do you often talk nonsense?'

'Sure,' Clay said. 'Just ask my wife.'

5

'Where are we going?' Tom asked. 'I was headed for the T.' He pointed to a green-painted kiosk about a block ahead. A small crowd of people were milling there. 'Now I'm not sure being underground is such a hot idea.'

'Me, either,' Clay said. 'I've got a room at a place called the Atlantic Avenue Inn, about five blocks further up.'

Tom brightened. 'I think I know it. On Louden, actually, just *off* Atlantic.'

'Right. Let's go there. We can check the TV. And I want to call my wife.'

'On the room phone.'

'The room phone, check. I don't even *have* a cell phone.'

'I have one, but I left it home. It's broken. Rafe − my cat − knocked it off the counter. I was meaning to buy a new one this very day, but . . . listen. Mr Riddell—'

'Clay.'

'Clay, then. Are you sure the phone in your room will be safe?'

Clay stopped. He hadn't even considered this idea. But if the landlines weren't okay, what *would* be? He was about to say this to Tom when a sudden brawl broke out at the T station up ahead. There were cries of panic, screams, and more of that wild babbling − he recognised it for what it was now, the signature scribble of madness. The little knot of people that had been milling around the gray stone pillbox and the steps going below-ground broke up. A few of them ran into the street, two with their arms around each other, snatching looks back over their shoulders as they went. More − most − ran into the park, all in different directions, which sort of broke Clay's heart. He felt better somehow about the two with their arms around each other.

Still at the T station and on their feet were two men and two women. Clay was pretty sure it was they who had emerged from the station and driven off the rest. As Clay and Tom stood watching from half a block away, these remaining four fell to fighting with each other. This brawl had the hysterical, killing viciousness he had already seen, but no discernible pattern. It wasn't three against one, or two against two, and it certainly wasn't the boys against the girls; in fact, one of the 'girls' was a woman who looked to be in her middle sixties, with a stocky body and a no-nonsense haircut that made Clay think of several women teachers he'd known who were nearing retirement.

They fought with feet and fists and nails and teeth, grunting and shouting and circling the bodies of maybe half a dozen people who had already been knocked unconscious, or perhaps killed. One of the men stumbled over an outstretched leg and went to his knees. The younger of the two women dropped on top of him. The man on his knees swept something up from the pavement at the head of the stairs – Clay saw with no surprise whatever that it was a cell phone – and slammed it into the side of the woman's face. The cell phone shattered, tearing the woman's cheek open and showering a freshet of blood onto the shoulder of her light jacket, but her scream was of rage rather than pain. She grabbed the kneeling man's ears like a pair of jughandles, dropped her own knees into his lap, and shoved him back-wards into the gloom of the T's stairwell. They went out of sight locked together and thrashing like cats in heat.

'Come on,' Tom murmured, twitching Clay's shirt with an odd delicacy. 'Come on. Other side of the street. Come on.'

Clay allowed himself to be led across Boylston Street. He assumed that either Tom McCourt was watching where they were going or he was lucky, because they got to the other side okay. They stopped again in front of Colonial Books (Best of the Old, Best of the New), watching as the unlikely victor of the T station battle went striding into the park in the direction of the burning plane, with blood dripping onto her collar from the ends of her zero-tolerance gray hair. Clay wasn't a bit surprised that the last one standing had turned out to be the lady who looked like a librarian or Latin teacher a year or two away from a gold watch. He had taught with his share of such ladies, and the ones who made it to that age were, more often than not, next door to indestructible.

He opened his mouth to say something like this to Tom – in his mind it sounded quite witty – and what came out was a watery croak. His vision had come over shimmery, too. Apparently Tom McCourt, the little man in the tweed suit, wasn't the only one having trouble with his waterworks. Clay swiped an arm across his eyes, tried again to talk, and managed no more than another of those watery croaks.

'That's okay,' Tom said. 'Better let it come.'

And so, standing there in front of a shop window filled with old books surrounding a Royal typewriter hailing from long before the era of cellular communications, Clay did. He cried for Power Suit Woman, for Pixie Light and Pixie Dark, and he cried for himself, because Boston was not his home, and home had never seemed so far.

6

Above the Common Boylston Street narrowed and became so choked with cars – both those wrecked and those plain abandoned – that they no longer had to worry about kamikaze limos or rogue Duck Boats. Which was a relief. From all around them the city banged and crashed like New Year's Eve in hell. There was plenty of noise close by, as well – car alarms and burglar alarms, mostly – but the street itself was for the moment eerily deserted. *Get under cover,* Officer Ulrich Ashland had said. *You've been lucky once. You may not be lucky again.*

But, two blocks east of Colonial Books and still a block from Clay's not-quite-fleabag hotel, they *were* lucky again. Another lunatic, this one a young man of perhaps twenty-five with muscles that looked tuned by Nautilus and Cybex, bolted from an alley just in front of them and went dashing across the street, hurdling the locked bumpers of two cars, foaming out an unceasing lava-flow of that nonsense-talk as he went. He held a car aerial in each hand and stabbed them rapidly back and forth in the air like daggers as he cruised his lethal course. He was naked except for a pair of what looked like brand-new Nikes with bright red swooshes. His cock swung from side to side like the pendulum of a grand-father clock on speed. He hit the far sidewalk and sidewheeled west, back towards the Common, his butt clenching and unclenching in fantastic rhythm.

Tom McCourt clutched Clay's arm, and hard, until this latest lunatic was gone, then slowly relaxed his grip. 'If he'd seen us—' he began.

'Yeah, but he didn't,' Clay said. He felt suddenly, absurdly happy. He knew that the feeling would pass, but for the moment he was delighted to ride it. He felt like a man who has successfully drawn to an inside straight with the biggest pot of the night lying on the table in front of him.

'I pity who he *does* see,' Tom said.

'I pity who sees *him*,' Clay said. 'Come on.'

7

The doors of the Atlantic Avenue Inn were locked.

Clay was so surprised that for a moment he could only stand there, trying to turn the knob and feeling it slip through his fingers, trying to get the idea through his head: locked. The doors of his hotel, locked against him.

Tom stepped up beside him, leaned his forehead against the glass to cut the glare, and peered in. From the north – from Logan, surely – came another of those monster explosions, and this time Clay only twitched. He didn't think Tom McCourt reacted at all. Tom was too absorbed in what he was seeing.

'Dead guy on the floor,' he announced at last. 'Wearing a uniform, but he really looks too old to be a bellhop.'

'I don't want anyone to carry my fucking luggage,' Clay said. 'I just want to go up to my room.'

Tom made an odd little snorting sound. Clay thought maybe the little guy was starting to cry again, then realised that sound was smothered laughter.

The double doors had **ATLANTIC AVENUE INN** printed on one glass panel and a blatant lie – **BOSTON'S FINEST ADDRESS** – printed on the other. Tom slapped the flat of his hand on the glass of the lefthand panel, between **BOSTON'S FINEST ADDRESS** and a row of credit card decals.

Now Clay was peering in, too. The lobby wasn't very big. On the left was the reception desk. On the right was a pair of elevators. On the floor was a turkey-red rug. The old guy in the uniform lay on this, facedown, with one foot up on a couch and a framed Currier & Ives sailing-ship print on his ass.

Clay's good feelings left in a rush, and when Tom began to hammer on the glass instead of just slap, he put his hand over Tom's fist. 'Don't bother,' he said. 'They're not going to let us in, even if they're alive and sane.' He thought about that and nodded. '*Especially* if they're sane.'

Tom looked at him wonderingly. 'You don't get it, do you?'

'Huh? Get what?'

'Things have changed. They can't keep us out.' He pushed Clay's hand off his own, but instead of hammering, he put his forehead against the glass again and shouted. Clay thought he had a pretty good shouting voice on him for a little guy. *'Hey! Hey, in there!'*

A pause. In the lobby nothing changed. The old bellman went on being dead with a picture on his ass.

'Hey, if you're in there, you better open the door! The man I'm with is a paying guest of the hotel and I'm his guest! Open up or I'm going to grab a kerbstone and break the glass! You hear me?'

'A *curb*stone?' Clay said. He started to laugh. 'Did you say *curb*stone? Jolly *good*.' He laughed harder. He couldn't help it. Then movement to his left caught his eye. He looked around and saw a teenage girl standing a little way farther up the street. She was looking at them out of haggard blue disaster-victim eyes. She was wearing a white dress, and there was a vast bib of blood on the front of it. More blood was crusted beneath her nose, on her lips and chin. Other than the bloody nose she didn't look hurt, and she didn't look crazy at all, just shocked. Shocked almost to death.

'Are you all right?' Clay asked. He took a step toward her and she took a corresponding step back. Under the circumstances, he couldn't blame her. He stopped but held a hand up to her like a traffic cop: *Stay put.*

Tom glanced around briefly, then began to hammer on the door again, this time hard enough to rattle the glass in its old wooden frame and make his reflection shiver. *'Last chance, then we're coming in!'*

Clay turned and opened his mouth to tell him that masterful shit wasn't going to cut it, not today, and then a bald head rose slowly from behind the reception desk. It was like watching a periscope surface. Clay recognised that head even before it got to the face; it belonged to the clerk who'd checked him in yesterday and stamped a validation on his parking-lot ticket for the lot a block over, the same clerk who'd given him directions to the Copley Square Hotel this morning.

For a moment he still lingered behind the desk, and Clay held up his room key with the green plastic Atlantic Avenue Inn fob hanging down. Then he also held up his portfolio, thinking the desk clerk might recognize it.

Maybe he did. More likely he just decided he had no choice. In either case, he used the pass-through at the end of the desk and crossed quickly to the door, detouring around the body. Clay Riddell believed he might be witnessing the first reluctant scurry he had ever seen in his life. When the desk clerk reached the other side of the door, he looked from Clay to Tom and then back to Clay again. Although he did not appear particularly reassured by what he saw, he produced a ring of keys from one pocket, flicked rapidly through them, found one, and used it on his side of the door. When Tom reached for the handle, the bald clerk held his hand up much as Clay had held his up to the bloodstained girl behind them. The clerk found a second key, used this one in another lock, and opened the door.

'Come in,' he said. 'Hurry.' Then he saw the girl, lingering at a little distance and watching. '*Not* her.'

'Yes, her,' Clay said. 'Come on, honey.' But she wouldn't, and when Clay took a step toward her, she whirled and took off running, the skirt of her dress flying out behind her.

8

'She could die out there,' Clay said.

'Not my problem,' the desk clerk said. 'Are you coming in or not, Mr Riddle?' He had a Boston accent, not the blue-collar-Southie kind Clay was most familiar with from Maine, where it seemed that every third person you met was a Massachusetts expat, but the fussy I-wish-I-were-British one.

'It's Riddell.' He was coming in all right, no way this guy was going to keep him out now that the door was open, but he lingered a moment longer on the sidewalk, looking after the girl.

'Go on,' Tom said quietly. 'Nothing to be done.'

And he was right. Nothing to be done. That was the exact hell of it. He followed Tom in, and the desk clerk once more double-locked the doors of the Atlantic Avenue Inn behind them, as if that were all it would take to keep them from the chaos of the streets.

9

'That was Franklin,' said the desk clerk as he led the way around the uniformed man lying facedown on the floor.

He looks too old to be a bellhop, Tom had said, peering in through the window, and Clay thought he certainly did. He was a small man, with a lot of luxuriant white hair. Unfortunately for him, the head on which it was probably still growing (hair and nails were slow in getting the word, or so he had read somewhere) was cocked at a terrible crooked angle, like the head of a hanged man. 'He'd been with the Inn for thirty-five years, as I'm sure he told every guest he ever checked in. Most of them twice.'

That tight little accent grated on Clay's frayed nerves. He thought that if it had been a fart, it would have been the kind that comes out sounding like a party-horn blown by a kid with asthma.

'A man came out of the elevator,' the desk clerk said, once more using the pass-through to get behind the desk. Back there was apparently where he felt at home. The overhead light struck his face and Clay saw he was very pale. 'One of the crazy ones. Franklin had the bad luck to be standing right there in front of the doors—'

'I don't suppose it crossed your mind to at least take the damn picture off his ass,' Clay said. He bent down, picked up the Currier & Ives print, and put it on the couch. At the same time, he brushed the dead bellman's foot off the cushion where it had come to rest. It fell with a sound Clay knew very well. He had rendered it in a great many comic books as **CLUMP**.

'The man from the elevator only hit him with one punch,' the desk clerk said. 'It knocked poor Franklin all the way against the wall. I think it broke his neck. In any case, that was what dislodged the picture, Franklin striking the wall.'

In the desk clerk's mind, this seemed to justify everything.

'What about the man who hit him?' Tom asked. 'The crazy guy? Where'd he go?'

'Out,' the desk clerk said. 'That was when I felt locking the door to be by far the wisest course. After he went out.' He looked at them with a combination of fear and prurient, gossipy greed that Clay found singularly distasteful. 'What's *happening* out there? How bad has it gotten?'

'I think you must have a pretty good idea,' Clay said. 'Isn't that why you locked the door?'

'Yes, but—'

'What are they saying on TV?' Tom asked.

'Nothing. The cable's been out—' He glanced at his watch. 'For almost half an hour now.'

'What about the radio?'

The desk clerk gave Tom a prissy *you-must-be-joking* look. Clay was starting to think this guy could write a book – *How to Be Disliked on Short Notice*. 'Radio in *this* place? In *any* downtown hotel? You must be joking.'

From outside came a high-pitched wail of fear. The girl in the bloodstained white dress appeared at the door again and began pounding on it with the flat of her hand, looking over her shoulder as she did so. Clay started for her, fast.

'No, he locked it again, remember?' Tom shouted at him.

Clay hadn't. He turned to the desk clerk. 'Unlock it.'

'No,' the desk clerk said, and crossed both arms firmly over his narrow chest to show how firmly he meant to oppose this course of action. Outside, the girl in the white dress looked over her shoulder again and pounded harder. Her blood-streaked face was tight with terror.

Clay pulled the butcher knife out of his belt. He had almost forgotten it and was sort of astonished at how quickly, how naturally, it returned to mind. 'Open it, you sonofabitch,' he told the desk clerk, 'or I'll cut your throat.'

10

'No time!' Tom yelled, and grabbed one of the high-backed, bogus Queen Anne chairs that flanked the lobby sofa. He ran it at the double doors with the legs up.

The girl saw him coming and cringed away, raising both of her hands to protect her face. At the same instant the man who had been chasing her appeared in front of the door. He was an enormous construction-worker type with a slab of a gut pushing out the front of his yellow T-shirt and a greasy salt-and-pepper ponytail bouncing up and down on the back of it.

The chair-legs hit the panes of glass in the double doors, the two legs on the left shattering through **ATLANTIC AVENUE INN** and the two on the right through **BOSTON'S FINEST ADDRESS**. The ones on the right punched into the construction-worker type's meaty, yellow-clad left shoulder just as he grabbed the girl by the neck. The underside of the chair's seat fetched up against the solid seam where the two doors met and Tom McCourt went staggering backward, dazed.

The construction-worker guy was roaring out that speaking-in-tongues gibberish, and blood had begun to course down the freckled meat of his left biceps. The girl managed to pull free of him, but her feet tangled together and she went down in a heap, half on the sidewalk and half in the gutter, crying out in pain and fear.

Clay was standing framed in one of the shattered glass door-panels with no memory of crossing the room and only the vaguest one of raking the chair out of his way. 'Hey dick-weed!' he shouted, and was marginally encouraged when the big man's flood of crazy-talk ceased for a moment and he froze in his tracks. 'Yeah, you!' Clay shouted. 'I'm talking to you!' And then, because it was the only thing he could think of: 'I fucked your mama, and she was one dry hump!'

The large maniac in the yellow shirt cried out something that sounded eerily like what the Power Suit Woman had cried out just before meeting her end – eerily like *Rast!* – and whirled back toward the building that had suddenly grown teeth and a voice and attacked him. Whatever he saw, it couldn't have been a grim, sweaty-faced man with a knife in his hand leaning out through a rectangular panel that had lately held glass, because Clay had to do no attacking at all. The man in the yellow shirt leaped *onto* the jutting blade of the butcher knife. The Swedish steel slid smoothly into the hanging, sunburned wattle beneath his chin and released a red waterfall. It doused Clay's hand, amazingly hot – almost hot as a freshly poured cup of coffee, it seemed – and he had to fight off an urge to pull away. Instead he pushed forward, at last feeling the knife encounter resistance. It hesitated, but there was no buckle in that baby. It ripped through gristle, then came out through the nape of the big man's neck. He fell forward – Clay couldn't hold him back with one arm, no way in hell, the guy had to go two-sixty, maybe even two-ninety – and for a moment leaned against the door like a drunk against a lamppost, brown eyes bulging, nicotine-stained tongue hanging from one corner of his mouth, neck spewing. Then his knees came unhinged and he went down. Clay held on to the handle of the knife and was amazed at how easily it came back out. Much easier than pulling it back through the leather and reinforced particleboard of the portfolio.

With the lunatic down he could see the girl again, one knee on the sidewalk and the other in the gutter, screaming through the curtain of hair hanging across her face.

'Honey,' he said. 'Honey, don't.' But she went on screaming.

11

Her name was Alice Maxwell. She could tell them that much. And she could tell them that she and her mother had come into Boston on the train – from Boxford, she said – to do some shopping, a thing they often did on Wednesday, which she called her 'short day' at the high school she attended. She said they'd gotten off the train at South Station and grabbed a cab. She said the cabdriver had been wearing a blue turban. She said the blue turban was the last thing she could remember until the bald desk clerk had finally unlocked the shattered double doors of the Atlantic Avenue Inn and let her in.

Clay thought she remembered more. He based this on the way she began to tremble when Tom McCourt asked her if either she or her mother had been carrying a cell phone. She claimed not to remember, but Clay was sure one or both of them had been. Everyone did these days, it seemed. He was just the exception that proved the rule. And there was

Tom, who might owe his life to the cat that had knocked his off the counter.

They conversed with Alice (the conversation consisted for the most part of Clay asking questions while the girl sat mutely, looking down at her scraped knees and shaking her head from time to time) in the hotel lobby. Clay and Tom had moved Franklin's body behind the reception desk, dismissing the bald clerk's loud and bizarre protest that 'it will just be under my feet there.' The clerk, who had given his name simply as Mr Ricardi, had since retired to his inner office. Clay had followed him just long enough to ascertain that Mr Ricardi had been telling the truth about the TV being out of commish, then left him there. Sharon Riddell would have said Mr Ricardi was brooding in his tent.

The man hadn't let Clay go without a parting shot, however. 'Now we're open to the world,' he said bitterly. 'I hope you think you've accomplished something.'

'Mr Ricardi,' Clay said, as patiently as he could, 'I saw a plane crash-land on the other side of Boston Common not an hour ago. It sounds like more planes – big ones – are doing the same thing at Logan. Maybe they're even making suicide runs on the terminals. There are explosions all over downtown. I'd say that this afternoon all of Boston is open to the world.'

As if to underline this point, a very heavy thump had come from above them. Mr Ricardi didn't look up. He only flapped a *begone* hand in Clay's direction. With no TV to look at, he sat in his desk chair and looked severely at the wall.

12

Clay and Tom moved the two bogus Queen Anne chairs against the door, where their high backs did a pretty good job of filling the shattered frames that had once held glass. While Clay was sure that locking the hotel off from the street offered flimsy or outright false security, he thought that blocking the *view* from the street might be a good idea, and Tom had concurred. Once the chairs were in place, they lowered the sun-blind over the lobby's main window. That dimmed the room considerably and sent faint prison-bar shadows marching across the turkey-red rug.

With these things seen to, and Alice Maxwell's radically abridged tale told, Clay finally went to the telephone behind the desk. He glanced at his watch. It was 4:22 p.m., a perfectly logical time for it to be, except any ordinary sense of time seemed to have been canceled. It felt like hours since he'd seen the man biting the dog in the park. It also seemed like no time at all. But there *was* time, such as humans measured it, anyway, and in Kent Pond, Sharon would surely be back by now at the house he still thought of as home. He needed to talk to her. To make sure she was all right and tell her he was, too, but those weren't the important things. Making sure Johnny was all right, that was important, but there was something even more important than that. Vital, really.

He didn't have a cell phone, and neither did Sharon, he was almost positive of that. She might have picked one up since they'd separated in April, he supposed, but they still lived in the same town, he saw her almost every day, and he thought if she'd picked one up, he would have known. For one thing, she would have given him the number, right? Right. But—

But Johnny had one. Little Johnny-Gee, who wasn't so little anymore, twelve wasn't so little, and that was what he'd wanted for his last birthday. A red cell phone that played the theme music from his favorite TV program when it rang. Of course he was forbidden to turn it on or even take it out of his backpack when he was in school, but school hours were over now. Also, Clay and Sharon actually *encouraged* him to take it, partly because of the separation. There might be emergencies, or minor inconveniences such as a missed bus. What Clay had to hang on to was how Sharon had said she'd look into Johnny's room lately and more often than not see the cell lying forgotten on his desk or the windowsill beside his bed, off the charger and dead as dogshit.

Still, the thought of John's red cell phone ticked away in his mind like a bomb.

Clay touched the landline phone on the hotel desk, then withdrew his hand. Outside, something else exploded, but this one was distant. It was like hearing an artillery shell explode when you were well behind the lines.

Don't make that assumption, he thought. *Don't even assume there* are *lines.*

He looked across the lobby and saw Tom squatting beside Alice as she sat on the sofa. He was murmuring to her quietly, touching one of her loafers and looking up into her face. That was good. *He* was good. Clay was increasingly glad he'd run into Tom McCourt . . . or that Tom McCourt had run into him.

The landlines were probably all right. The question was whether probably was good enough. He had a wife who was still sort of his responsibility, and when it came to his son there was no sort-of at all. Even thinking of Johnny was dangerous. Every time his mind turned to the boy, Clay felt a panic-rat inside his mind, ready to burst free of the flimsy cage that held it and start gnawing anything it could get at with its sharp little teeth. If he could make sure Johnny and Sharon were okay, he could keep the rat in its cage and plan what to do next. But if he did something stupid, he wouldn't be able to help anyone. In fact, he would make things worse for the people here. He thought about this a little and then called the desk clerk's name.

When there was no answer from the inner office, he called again. When there was still no answer, he said, 'I know you hear me, Mr Ricardi. If you make me come in there and get you, it'll annoy me. I might get annoyed enough to consider putting you out on the street.'

'You can't do that,' Mr Ricardi said in a tone of surly instruction. 'You are a *guest* of the *hotel.*'

Clay thought of repeating what Tom had said to him while they were still outside – *things have changed*. Something made him keep silent instead.

'What,' Mr Ricardi said at last. Sounding more surly than ever. From overhead came a louder thump, as if someone had dropped a heavy piece of furniture. A bureau, maybe. This time even the girl looked up. Clay thought he heard a muffled shout – or maybe a howl of pain – but if so, there was no follow-up. What was on the second floor? Not a restaurant, he remembered being told (by Mr Ricardi himself, when Clay checked in) that the hotel didn't have a restaurant, but the Metropolitan Café was right next door. *Meeting rooms,* he thought. *I'm pretty sure it's meeting rooms with Indian names.*

'What?' Mr Ricardi asked again. He sounded grouchier than ever.

'Did you try to call anyone when all this started happening?'

'Well of *course!*' Mr Ricardi said. He came to the door between the inner office and the area behind the reception desk, with its pigeonholes, security monitors, and its bank of computers. There he looked at Clay indignantly. 'The fire alarms went off – I got *them* stopped, Doris said it was a wastebasket fire on the third floor – and I called the Fire Department to tell them not to bother. The line was busy! *Busy,* can you imagine!'

'You must have been very upset,' Tom said.

Mr Ricardi looked mollified for the first time. 'I called the police when things outside started . . . you know . . . to go downhill.'

'Yes,' Clay said. *To go downhill* was one way of putting it, all right. 'Did you get an answer?'

'A man told me I'd have to clear the line and then hung up on me,' Mr Ricardi said. The indignation was creeping back into his voice. 'When I called again – this was after the crazy man came out of the elevator and killed Franklin – a woman answered. She said . . .' Mr Ricardi's voice had begun

44

to quiver and Clay saw the first tears running down the narrow defiles that marked the sides of the man's nose. '. . . said . . .'

'What?' Tom asked, in that same tone of mild sympathy. 'What did she say, Mr Ricardi?'

'She said if Franklin was dead and the man who killed him had run away, then I didn't have a problem. It was she who advised me to lock myself in. She also told me to call the hotel's elevators to lobby level and shut them off, which I did.'

Clay and Tom exchanged a look that carried a wordless thought: *Good idea.* Clay got a sudden vivid image of bugs trapped between a closed window and a screen, buzzing furiously but unable to get out. This picture had something to do with the thumps they'd heard coming from above them. He wondered briefly how long before the thumper or thumpers up there would find the stairs.

'Then *she* hung up on me. After that, I called my wife in Milton.'

'You got through to her,' Clay said, wanting to be clear on this.

'She was very frightened. She asked me to come home. I told her I had been advised to stay inside with the doors locked. Advised by the police. I told her to do the same thing. Lock up and keep a, you know, low profile. She *begged* me to come home. She said there had been gunshots on the street, and an explosion a street over. She said she had seen a naked man running through the Benzycks' yard. The Benzycks live next door to us.'

'Yes,' Tom said mildly. Soothingly, even. Clay said nothing. He was a bit ashamed at how angry he'd been at Mr Ricardi, but Tom had been angry, too.

'She said she believed the naked man might – *might,* she only said *might* – have been carrying the body of a . . . mmm . . . nude child. But possibly it was a doll. She begged me again to leave the hotel and come home.'

Clay had what he needed. The landlines were safe. Mr Ricardi was in shock but not crazy. Clay put his hand on the telephone. Mr Ricardi laid his hand over Clay's before Clay could pick up the receiver. Mr Ricardi's fingers were long and pale and very cold. Mr Ricardi wasn't done. Mr Ricardi was on a roll.

'She called me a son of a bitch and hung up. I know she was angry with me, and of course I understand why. But the police told me to lock up and stay put. The police told me to keep off the streets. The police. The *authorities*.'

Clay nodded. 'The authorities, sure.'

'Did you come by the T?' Mr Ricardi asked. 'I always use the T. It's just two blocks down the street. It's very convenient.'

'It wouldn't be convenient this afternoon,' Tom said. 'After what we just saw, you couldn't get me down there on a bet.'

Mr Ricardi looked at Clay with mournful eagerness. 'You see?'

Clay nodded again. 'You're better off in here,' he said. Knowing that he meant to get home and see to his boy. Sharon too, of course, but mostly his boy. Knowing he would let nothing stop him unless something absolutely did. It was like a weight in his mind that cast an actual shadow on his vision. 'Much better off.' Then he picked up the phone and punched 9 for an outside line. He wasn't sure he'd get one, but he did. He dialled 1, then 207, the area code for all of Maine, and then 692, which was the prefix for Kent Pond and the surrounding towns. He got three of the last four numbers – almost to the house he still thought of as home – before the distinctive three-tone interrupt. A recorded female voice followed. 'We're sorry. All circuits are busy. Please try your call again later.'

On the heels of this came a dial tone as some automated circuit disconnected him from Maine . . . if that was where the robot voice had been coming from. Clay let the handset

46

drop to the level of his shoulder, as if it had grown very heavy. Then he put it back in the cradle.

13

Tom told him he was crazy to want to leave.

For one thing, he pointed out, they were relatively safe here in the Atlantic Avenue Inn, especially with the elevators locked down and lobby access from the stairwell blocked off. This they had done by piling boxes and suitcases from the luggage room in front of the door at the end of the short corridor beyond the elevator banks. Even if someone of extraordinary strength were to push against that door from the other side, he'd only be able to shift the pile against the facing wall, creating a gap of maybe six inches. Not enough to get through.

For another, the tumult in the city beyond their little safe haven actually seemed to be increasing. There was a constant racket of conflicting alarms, shouts and screams and racing engines, and sometimes the panic-tang of smoke, although the day's brisk breeze seemed to be carrying the worst of that away from them. *So far,* Clay thought, but did not say aloud, at least not yet – he didn't want to frighten the girl any more than she already was. There were explosions that never seemed to come singly but rather in spasms. One of those was so close that they all ducked, sure the front window would blow in. It didn't, but after that they moved to Mr Ricardi's inner sanctum.

The third reason Tom gave for thinking Clay was crazy to even *think* about leaving the marginal safety of the Inn was that it was now quarter past five. The day would be ending soon. He argued that trying to leave Boston in the dark would be madness.

'Just take a gander out there,' he said, gesturing to Mr Ricardi's little window, which looked out on Essex Street. Essex was crowded with abandoned cars. There was also at least one body, that of a young woman in jeans and a Red Sox sweatshirt. She lay facedown on the sidewalk, both arms outstretched, as if she had died trying to swim. VARITEK, her sweatshirt proclaimed. 'Do you think you're going to drive your car? If you do, you better think again.'

'He's right,' Mr Ricardi said. He was sitting behind his desk with his arms once more folded across his narrow chest, a study in gloom. 'You're in the Tamworth Street Parking Garage. I doubt if you'd even succeed in securing your keys.'

Clay, who had already given his car up as a lost cause, opened his mouth to say he wasn't planning to drive (at least to start with), when another thump came from overhead, this one heavy enough to make the ceiling shiver. It was accompanied by the faint but distinctive shiver-jingle of breaking glass. Alice Maxwell, who was sitting in the chair across the desk from Mr Ricardi, looked up nervously and then seemed to shrink further into herself.

'What's up there?' Tom asked.

'It's the Iroquois Room directly overhead,' Mr Ricardi replied. 'The largest of our three meeting rooms, and where we keep all of our supplies – chairs, tables, audiovisual equipment.' He paused. 'And, although we have no restaurant, we arrange for buffets or cocktail parties, if clients request such service. That last thump . . .'

He didn't finish. As far as Clay was concerned, he didn't need to. That last thump had been a trolley stacked high with glassware being upended on the floor of the Iroquois Room, where numerous other trolleys and tables had already been tipped over by some madman who was rampaging back and forth up there. Buzzing around on the second floor like a bug trapped between the window and the screen, something without the wit to find a way out, something that could only run and break, run and break.

Alice spoke up for the first time in nearly half an hour, and without prompting for the first time since they'd met her. 'You said something about someone named Doris.'

'Doris Gutierrez.' Mr Ricardi was nodding. 'The head housekeeper. Excellent employee. Probably my best. She was on three, the last time I heard from her.'

'Did she have——?' Alice wouldn't say it. Instead she made a gesture that had become almost as familiar to Clay as the index finger across the lips indicating *Shh*. Alice put her right hand to the side of her face with the thumb close to her ear and the pinkie in front of her mouth.

'No,' Mr Ricardi said, almost primly. 'Employees have to leave them in their lockers while they're on the job. One violation gets them a reprimand. Two and they can be fired. I tell them this when they're taken on.' He lifted one thin shoulder in a half-shrug. 'It's management's policy, not mine.'

'Would she have gone down to the second floor to investigate those sounds?' Alice asked.

'Possibly,' Mr Ricardi said. 'I have no way of knowing. I only know that I haven't heard from her since she reported the wastebasket fire out, and she hasn't answered her pages. I paged her twice.'

Clay didn't want to say *You see, it isn't safe here, either* right out loud, so he looked past Alice at Tom, trying to give him the basic idea with his eyes.

Tom said, 'How many people would you say are still upstairs?'

'I have no way of knowing.'

'If you had to guess.'

'Not many. As far as the housekeeping staff goes, probably just Doris. The day crew leaves at three, and the night crew doesn't come on until six.' Mr Ricardi pressed his lips tightly together. 'It's an economy gesture. One cannot say *measure* because it doesn't work. As for guests . . .'

He considered.

'Afternoon is a slack time for us, very slack. Last night's guests have all checked out, of course – checkout time at the Atlantic Inn is noon – and tonight's guests wouldn't begin

49

checking in until four o'clock or so, on an ordinary afternoon. Which this most definitely is not. Guests staying several days are usually here on business. As I assume *you* were, Mr Riddle.'

Clay nodded without bothering to correct Ricardi on his name.

'At midafternoon, business people are usually out doing whatever it was that brought them to Boston. So you see, we have the place almost to ourselves.'

As if to contradict this, there came another thump from above them, more shattering glass, and a faint feral growl. They all looked up.

'Clay, listen,' Tom said. 'If the guy up there finds the stairs . . . I don't know if these people are capable of thought, but—'

'Judging by what we saw on the street,' Clay said, 'even calling them people might be wrong. I've got an idea that guy up there is more like a bug trapped between a window and a screen. A bug trapped like that might get out – if it found a hole – and the guy up there might find the stairs, but if he does, I think it'll be by accident.'

'And when he gets down and finds the door to the lobby blocked, he'll use the fire-door to the alley,' Mr Ricardi said with what was, for him, eagerness. 'We'll hear the alarm – it's rigged to ring when anyone pushes the bar – and we'll know he's gone. One less nut to worry about.'

Somewhere south of them something big blew up, and they all cringed. Clay supposed he now knew what living in Beirut during the 1980s had been like.

'I'm trying to make a point here,' he said patiently.

'I don't think so,' Tom said. 'You're going anyway, because you're worried about your wife and son. You're trying to persuade us because you want company.'

Clay blew out a frustrated breath. 'Sure I want company, but that's not why I'm trying to talk you into coming. The smell of smoke's stronger, but when's the last time you heard a siren?'

None of them replied.

'Me either,' Clay said. 'I don't think things are going to get better in Boston, not for a while. They're going to get worse. If it *was* the cell phones—'

'She tried to leave a message for Dad,' Alice said. She spoke rapidly, as if wanting to make sure she got all the words out before the memory flew away. 'She just wanted to make sure he'd pick up the dry cleaning because she needed her yellow wool dress for her committee meeting and I needed my extra uni for the away game on Saturday. This was in the cab. And then we crashed! *She choked the man and she bit the man and his turban fell off and there was blood on the side of his face and we crashed!*'

Alice looked around at their three staring faces, then put her own face in her hands and began to sob. Tom moved to comfort her, but Mr Ricardi surprised Clay by coming around his desk and putting one pipestemmy arm around the girl before Tom could get to her. 'There-there,' he said. 'I'm sure it was all a misunderstanding, young lady.'

She looked up at him, her eyes wide and wild. *'Misunderstanding?'* She indicated the dried bib of blood on the front of her dress. 'Does this look like a *misunderstanding*? I used the karate from the self-defence classes I took in junior high. I used karate on my own mother! I broke her nose, I think . . . I'm *sure* . . .' Alice shook her head rapidly, her hair flying. 'And still, if I hadn't been able to reach behind me and get the door open . . .'

'She would have killed you,' Clay said flatly.

'She would have killed me,' Alice agreed in a whisper. 'She didn't know who I was. My own mother.' She looked from Clay to Tom. 'It was the cell phones,' she said in that same whisper. 'It was the cell phones, all right.'

14

'So how many of the damn things are there in Boston?' Clay asked. 'What's the market penetration?'

'Given the large numbers of college students, I'd say it's got to be huge,' Mr Ricardi replied. He had resumed his seat behind his desk, and now he looked a little more animated. Comforting the girl might have done it, or perhaps it was being asked a business-oriented question. 'Although it goes much further than affluent young people, of course. I read an article in *Inc.* only a month or two ago that claimed there's now as many cell phones in mainland China as there are people in America. Can you imagine?'

Clay didn't want to imagine.

'All right.' Tom was nodding reluctantly. 'I see where you're going with this. Someone – some terrorist outfit – rigs the cell phone signals somehow. If you make a call or take one, you get some kind of a . . . what? . . . some kind of a subliminal message, I guess . . . that makes you crazy. Sounds like science fiction, but I suppose fifteen or twenty years ago, cell phones as they now exist would have seemed like science fiction to most people.'

'I'm pretty sure it's something like that,' Clay said. 'You can get enough of it to screw you up righteously if you even *overhear* a call.' He was thinking of Pixie Dark. 'But the insidious thing is that when people see things going wrong all around them—'

'Their first impulse is to reach for their cell phones and try to find out what's causing it,' Tom said.

'Yeah,' Clay said. 'I saw people doing it.'

Tom looked at him bleakly. 'So did I.'

'What all this has to do with you leaving the safety of the hotel, especially with dark coming on, I don't know,' Mr Ricardi said.

As if in answer, there came another explosion. It was

followed by half a dozen more, marching off to the south-east like the diminishing footsteps of a giant. From above them came another thud, and a faint cry of rage.

'I don't think the crazy ones will have the brains to leave the city any more than that guy up there can find his way to the stairs,' Clay said.

For a moment he thought the look on Tom's face was shock, and then he realised it was something else. Amazement, maybe. And dawning hope. 'Oh, Christ,' he said, and actually slapped the side of his face with one hand. '*They* won't leave, I never thought of that.'

'There might be something else,' Alice said. She was biting her lip and looking down at her hands, which were working together in a restless knot. She forced herself to look up at Clay. 'It might actually be *safer* to go after dark.'

'Why's that, Alice?'

'If they can't see you – if you can get behind something, if you can hide – they forget about you almost right away.'

'What makes you think that, honey?' Tom asked.

'Because I hid from the man who was chasing me,' she said in a low voice. 'The guy in the yellow shirt. This was just before I saw you. I hid in an alley. Behind one of those Dumpster thingies? I was scared, because I thought there might not be any way back out if he came in after me, but it was all I could think of to do. I saw him standing at the mouth of the alley, looking around, *walking* around and around – walking the worry-circle, my grampa would say – and at first I thought he was playing with me, you know? Because he *had* to've seen me go into the alley, I was only a few feet ahead of him . . . just a few feet . . . almost close enough to grab . . .' Alice began to tremble. 'But once I was in there, it was like . . . I dunno . . .'

'Out of sight, out of mind,' Tom said. 'But if he was that close, why did you stop running?'

'Because I couldn't anymore,' Alice said. 'I just couldn't. My legs were like rubber, and I felt like I was going to shake myself apart from the inside. But it turned out I didn't have to run, anyway. He walked the worry-circle a few more times, muttering that crazy talk, and then just walked off. I could hardly believe it. I thought he had to be trying to fake me out . . . but at the same time I knew he was too crazy for anything like that.' She glanced briefly at Clay, then back down at her hands again. 'My problem was running into him again. I should have stuck with you guys the first time. I can be pretty stupid sometimes.'

'You were sca—' Clay began, and then the biggest explosion yet came from somewhere east of them, a deafening *KER-WHAM!* that made them all duck and cover their ears. They heard the window in the lobby shatter.

'My . . . *God,*' Mr Ricardi said. His wide eyes underneath that bald head made him look to Clay like Little Orphan Annie's mentor, Daddy Warbucks. 'That might have been the new Shell superstation they put in over on Kneeland. The one all the taxis and the Duck Boats use. It was the right direction.'

Clay had no idea if Ricardi was right, he couldn't smell burning gasoline (at least not yet), but his visually trained mind's eye could see a triangle of city concrete now burning like a propane torch in the latening day.

'Can a modern city burn?' he asked Tom. 'One made mostly of concrete and metal and glass? Could it burn the way Chicago did after Mrs O'Leary's cow kicked over the lantern?'

'That lantern-kicking business was nothing but an urban legend,' Alice said. She was rubbing the back of her neck as if she were getting a bad headache. 'Mrs Myers said so, in American History.'

'Sure it could,' Tom said. 'Look what happened to the World Trade Center, after those airplanes hit it.'

'Airplanes full of jet fuel,' Mr Ricardi said pointedly.

As if the bald desk clerk had conjured it, the smell of burning gasoline began to come to them, wafting through the shattered lobby windows and sliding beneath the door to the inner office like bad mojo.

'I guess you were on the nose about that Shell station,' Tom remarked.

Mr Ricardi went to the door between his office and the lobby. He unlocked it and opened it. What Clay could see of the lobby beyond already looked deserted and gloomy and somehow irrelevant. Mr Ricardi sniffed audibly, then closed the door and locked it again. 'Fainter already,' he said.

'Wishful thinking,' Clay said. 'Either that or your nose is getting used to the aroma.'

'I think he might be right,' Tom said. 'That's a good west wind out there – by which I mean the air's moving towards the ocean – and if what we just heard was that new station they put in on the corner of Kneeland and Washington, by the New England Medical Center—'

'That's the one, all right,' Mr Ricardi said. His face registered glum satisfaction. 'Oh, the protests! The smart money fixed *that,* believe you m—'

Tom overrode him. '—then the hospital will be on fire by now . . . along with anybody left inside, of course . . .'

'*No,*' Alice said, then put a hand over her mouth.

'I think yes. And the Wang Center's next in line. The breeze may drop by full dark, but if it doesn't, everything east of the Mass Pike is apt to be so much toasted cheese by ten p.m.'

'We're *west* of there,' Mr Ricardi pointed out.

'Then we're safe enough,' Clay said. 'At least from *that* one.' He went to Mr Ricardi's little window, stood on his toes, and peered out onto Essex Street.

'What do you see?' Alice asked. 'Do you see people?'

'No . . . yes. One man. Other side of the street.'

'Is he one of the crazy ones?' she asked.

'I can't tell.' But Clay thought he was. It was the way he ran, and the jerky way he kept looking back over his shoulder. Once, just before he went around the corner and onto Lincoln Street, the guy almost ran into a fruit display in front of a grocery store. And although Clay couldn't hear him, he could see the man's lips moving. 'Now he's gone.'

'No one else?' Tom asked.

'Not at the moment, but there's smoke.' Clay paused. 'Soot and ash, too. I can't tell how much. The wind's whipping it around.'

'Okay, I'm convinced,' Tom said. 'I've always been a slow learner but never a no-learner. The city's going to burn and nobody's going to stand pat but the crazy people.'

'I think that's right,' Clay said. And he didn't think this was true of just Boston, but for the time being, Boston was all he could bear to consider. In time he might be able to widen his view, but not until he knew Johnny was safe. Or maybe the big picture was always going to be beyond him. He drew small pictures for a living, after all. But in spite of everything, the selfish fellow who lived like a limpet on the underside of his mind had time to send up a clear thought. It came in colors of blue and dark sparkling gold. *Why did it have to happen today, of all days? Just after I finally made a solid strike?*

'Can I come with you guys, if you go?' Alice asked.

'Sure,' Clay said. He looked at the desk clerk. 'You can, too, Mr Ricardi.'

'I shall stay at my post,' Mr Ricardi said. He spoke loftily, but before they shifted away from Clay's, his eyes looked sick.

'I don't think you'll get in Dutch with the management for locking up and leaving under these circumstances,' Tom said. He spoke in the gentle fashion Clay was so much coming to like.

'I shall stay at my post,' he said again. 'Mr Donnelly, the day manager, went out to make the afternoon deposit at the bank and left me in charge. If he comes back, perhaps then . . .'

'Please, Mr Ricardi,' Alice said. 'Staying here is no good.'

But Mr Ricardi, who had once more crossed his arms over his thin chest, only shook his head.

15

They moved one of the Queen Anne chairs aside, and Mr Ricardi unlocked the front doors for them. Clay looked out. He could see no people moving in either direction, but it was hard to tell for sure because the air was now full of fine dark ash. It danced in the breeze like black snow.

'Come on,' he said. They were only going next door to start with, to the Metropolitan Café.

'I'm going to relock the door and put the chair back in place,' Mr Ricardi said, 'but I'll be listening. If you run into trouble – if there are more of those . . . *people* . . . hiding in the Metropolitan, for instance – and you have to retreat, just remember to shout, "Mr Ricardi, Mr Ricardi, we need you!" That way I'll know it's safe to open the door. Is that understood?'

'Yes,' Clay said. He squeezed Mr Ricardi's thin shoulder. The desk clerk flinched, then stood firm (although he showed no particular sign of pleasure at being so saluted). 'You're all right. I didn't think you were, but I was wrong.'

'I hope I do my best,' the bald man said stiffly. 'Just remember—'

'We'll remember,' Tom said. 'And we'll be over there maybe ten minutes. If anything goes wrong over here, *you* give a shout.'

'All right.' But Clay didn't think he would. He didn't know why he thought that, it made no sense to think a man wouldn't give a shout to save himself if he was in trouble, but Clay *did* think it.

Alice said, '*Please* change your mind, Mr Ricardi. It's not safe in Boston, you must know that by now.'

Mr Ricardi only looked away. And Clay thought, not without wonder, *This is how a man looks when he's deciding that the risk of death is better than the risk of change.*

'Come on,' Clay said. 'Let's make some sandwiches while we've still got electricity to see by.'

'Some bottled water wouldn't hurt, either,' Tom said.

16

The electricity failed just as they were wrapping the last of their sandwiches in the Metropolitan Café's tidy, white-tiled little kitchen. By then Clay had tried three more times to get through to Maine: once to his old house, once to Kent Pond Elementary, where Sharon taught, and once to Joshua Chamberlain Middle School, which Johnny now attended. In no case did he get further than Maine's 207 area code.

When the lights in the Metropolitan went out, Alice screamed in what at first seemed to Clay like total darkness. Then the emergency lights came on. Alice was not much comforted. She was clinging to Tom with one arm. In the other she was brandishing the bread-knife she'd used to cut the sandwiches with. Her eyes were wide and somehow flat.

'Alice, put that knife down,' Clay said, a little more harshly than he'd intended. 'Before you cut one of us with it.'

'Or yourself,' Tom said in that mild and soothing voice of his. His spectacles glinted in the glare of the emergency lights.

She put it down, then promptly picked it up again. 'I want it,' she said. 'I want to take it with me. You have one, Clay. I want one.'

'All right,' he said, 'but you don't have a belt. We'll make you one from a tablecloth. For now, just be careful.'

Half the sandwiches were roast beef and cheese, half ham and cheese. Alice had wrapped them in Saran Wrap. Under the cash register Clay found a stack of sacks with DOGGY BAG written on one side and PEOPLE BAG written on the other. He and Tom tumbled the sandwiches into a pair of these. Into a third bag they put three bottles of water.

The tables had been made up for a dinner-service that was never going to happen. Two or three had been tumbled over but most stood perfect, with their glasses and silver shining in the hard light of the emergency boxes on the walls. Something about their calm orderliness hurt Clay's heart. The cleanliness of the folded napkins, and the little electric lamps on each table. Those were now dark, and he had an idea it might be a long time before the bulbs inside lit up again.

He saw Alice and Tom gazing about with faces as unhappy as his felt, and a desire to cheer them up – almost manic in its urgency – came over him. He remembered a trick he used to do for his son. He wondered again about Johnny's cell phone and the panic-rat took another nip out of him. Clay hoped with all his heart the damned phone was lying forgotten under Johnny-Gee's bed among the dust-kitties, with its battery flat-flat-flat.

'Watch this carefully,' he said, setting his bag of sandwiches aside, 'and please note that at no time do my hands leave my wrists.' He grasped the hanging skirt of a tablecloth.

'This is hardly the time for parlour tricks,' Tom said.

'I want to see,' Alice said. For the first time since they'd met her, there was a smile on her face. It was small but it was there.

'We need the tablecloth,' Clay said, 'it won't take a second, and besides, the lady wants to see.' He turned to Alice. 'But you have to say a magic word. *Shazam* will do.'

'*Shazam!*' she said, and Clay pulled briskly with both hands.

He hadn't done the trick in two, maybe even three years, and it almost didn't work. And yet at the same time, his mistake – some small hesitation in the pull, no doubt – actually added to the charm of the thing. Instead of staying where they were while the tablecloth magically disappeared from beneath them, all the place-settings on the table moved about four inches to the right. The glass nearest to where Clay was standing actually wound up with its circular base half on and half off the table.

Alice applauded, now laughing. Clay took a bow with his hands held out.

'Can we go now, O great Vermicelli?' Tom asked, but even Tom was smiling. Clay could see his small teeth in the emergency lights.

'Soon's I rig this,' Clay said. 'She can carry the knife on one side and a bag of sandwiches on the other. You can tote the water.' He folded the tablecloth over into a triangle shape, then rolled it quickly into a belt. He slipped a bag of sandwiches onto this by the bag's carrier handles, then put the tablecloth around the girl's slim waist, having to take a turn and a half and tie the knot in back to make the thing secure. He finished by sliding the serrated bread-knife home on the right side.

'Say, you're pretty handy,' Tom said.

'Handy is dandy,' Clay said, and then something else blew up outside, close enough to shake the café. The glass that had been standing half on and half off the table lost its balance, tumbled to the floor, and shattered. The three of them looked at it. Clay thought to tell them he didn't believe in omens, but that would only make things worse. Besides, he did.

17

Clay had his reasons for wanting to go back to the Atlantic Avenue Inn before they set off. One was to retrieve his portfolio, which he'd left sitting in the lobby. Another was to see if they couldn't find some sort of makeshift scabbard for Alice's knife – he reckoned even a shaving kit would do, if it was long enough. A third was to give Mr Ricardi another chance to join them. He was surprised to find he wanted this even more than he wanted the forgotten portfolio of drawings. He had taken an odd, reluctant liking to the man.

When he confessed this to Tom, Tom surprised him by nodding. 'It's the way I feel about anchovies on pizza,' he said. 'I tell myself there's something disgusting about a combination of cheese, tomato sauce, and dead fish . . . but sometimes that shameful urge comes over me and I can't stand against it.'

A blizzard of black ash and soot was blowing up the street and between the buildings. Car alarms warbled, burglar alarms brayed, and fire alarms clanged. There seemed to be no heat in the air, but Clay could hear the crackle of fire to the south and east of them. The smell of burning was stronger, too. They heard voices shouting, but these were back towards the Common, where Boylston Street widened.

When they got next door to the Atlantic Avenue Inn, Tom helped Clay push one of the Queen Anne chairs away from one of the broken glass door-panels. The lobby beyond was now a pool of gloom in which Mr Ricardi's desk and the sofa were only darker shadows; if Clay hadn't already been in there, he would have had no idea what those shadows represented. Above the elevators a single emergency light guttered, the boxed battery beneath it buzzing like a horsefly.

'Mr Ricardi?' Tom called. 'Mr Ricardi, we came back to see if you changed your mind.'

There was no reply. After a moment, Alice began carefully to knock out the glass teeth that still jutted from the windowframe.

'Mr Ricardi!' Tom called again, and when there was still no answer, he turned to Clay. 'You're going in there, are you?'

'Yes. To get my portfolio. It's got my drawings in it.'

'You don't have copies?'

'Those are the originals,' Clay said, as if this explained everything. To him it did. And besides, there was Mr Ricardi. He'd said, *I'll be listening.*

'What if Thumper from upstairs got him?' Tom asked.

'If that had happened, I think we'd have heard him thumping around down here,' Clay said. 'For that matter, he would have come running at the sound of our voices, babbling like the guy who tried to carve us up back by the Common.'

'You don't know that,' Alice said. She was gnawing at her lower lip. 'It's way too early for you to think you know all the rules.'

Of course she was right, but they couldn't stand around out here discussing it, that was no good, either.

'I'll be careful,' he said, and put a leg over the bottom of the window. It was narrow, but plenty wide enough for him to climb through. 'I'll just poke my head into his office. If he's not there, I won't go hunting around for him like a chick in a horror movie. I'll just grab my portfolio and we'll boogie.'

'Keep yelling,' Alice said. 'Just say "Okay, I'm okay," something like that. The whole time.'

'All right, but if I stop yelling, just *go*. Don't come in after me.'

'Don't worry,' she said, unsmiling. 'I saw all those movies, too. We've got Cinemax.'

18

'I'm okay,' Clay shouted, picking up his portfolio and then putting it down on the reception desk. *Good to go,* he thought. But not quite yet.

He looked over his shoulder as he went around the desk and saw the one unblocked window glimmering, seeming to float in the thickening gloom, with two silhouettes cut into the day's last light. 'I'm okay, still okay, just going in to check his office now, still okay, still o—'

'Clay?' Tom's voice was alarmed, but for a moment Clay couldn't respond and set Tom's mind at rest. There was an overhead light fixture in the middle of the inner office's high ceiling. Mr Ricardi was hanging from it by what looked like a drape-cord. There was a white bag pulled down over his head. Clay thought it was the kind of plastic bag the hotel gave you to put your dirty laundry and dry cleaning in. 'Clay, are you all right?'

'Clay?' Alice sounded shrill, ready to be hysterical.

'Okay,' he heard himself say. His mouth seemed to be operating itself, with no help from his brain. 'Still right here.' He was thinking of how Mr Ricardi had looked when he said *I shall stay at my post.* The words had been lofty, but the eyes had been scared and somehow humble, the eyes of a small raccoon driven into a corner of the garage by a large and angry dog. 'I'm coming out now.'

He backed away, as if Mr Ricardi might slip his home-made drape-cord noose and come after him the second he turned his back. He was suddenly more than afraid for Sharon and Johnny; he was homesick for them with a depth of feeling that made him think of his first day at school, his mother leaving him at the playground gate. The other parents had walked their kids inside. But his mother said, *You just go in there, Clayton, it's the first room, you'll be fine, boys should do this part alone.* Before he did what she told him he had watched her going away, back up Cedar Street. Her blue coat. Now, standing here in the dark, he was renewing acquaintance with the knowledge that the second part of homesick was *sick* for a reason.

Tom and Alice were fine, but he wanted the people he loved.

Once he was around the reception desk, he faced the street and crossed the lobby. He got close enough to the long broken window to see the frightened faces of his new friends, then remembered he had forgotten his fucking portfolio again and had to go back. Reaching for it, he felt certain that Mr Ricardi's hand would steal out of the gathering darkness behind the desk and close over his. That didn't happen, but from overhead came another of those thumps. Something still up there, something still blundering around in the dark. Something that had been human until three o'clock this afternoon.

This time when he was halfway to the door, the lobby's single battery-powered emergency light stuttered briefly, then went out. *That's a Fire Code violation,* Clay thought. *I ought to report that.*

He handed out his portfolio. Tom took it.

'Where is he?' Alice asked. 'Wasn't he there?'

'Dead,' Clay said. It had crossed his mind to lie, but he didn't think he was capable. He was too shocked by what he had seen. How did a man hang himself? He didn't see how it was even possible. 'Suicide.'

Alice began to cry, and it occurred to Clay that she didn't know that if it had been up to Mr Ricardi, she'd probably be dead herself now. The thing was, he felt a little like crying himself. Because Mr Ricardi had come around. Maybe most people did, if they got a chance.

From west of them on the darkening street, back towards the Common, came a scream that seemed too great to have issued from human lungs. It sounded to Clay almost like the trumpeting of an elephant. There was no pain in it, and no joy. There was only madness. Alice cringed against him, and he put an arm around her. The feel of her body was like the feel of an electrical wire with a strong current passing through it.

'If we're going to get out of here, let's do it,' Tom said. 'If we don't run into too much trouble, we should be able to get as far north as Malden, and spend the night at my place.'

'That's a hell of a good idea,' Clay said.

Tom smiled cautiously. 'You really think so?'

'I really do. Who knows, maybe Officer Ashland's already there.'

'Who's Officer Ashland?' Alice asked.

'A policeman we met back by the Common,' Tom said. 'He . . . you know, helped us out.' The three of them were now walking east toward Atlantic Avenue, through the falling ash and the sound of alarms. 'We won't see him, though. Clay's just trying to be funny.'

'Oh,' she said. 'I'm glad somebody's trying to be.' Lying

on the pavement by a littler barrel was a blue cell phone with a cracked casing. Alice kicked it into the gutter without breaking stride.

'Good one,' Clay said.

Alice shrugged. 'Five years of soccer,' she said, and at that moment the streetlights came on, like a promise that all was not yet lost.

MALDEN

1

Thousands of people stood on the Mystic River Bridge and watched as everything between Comm Ave and Boston Harbor took fire and burned. The wind from the west remained brisk and warm even after the sun was down and the flames roared like a furnace, blotting out the stars. The rising moon was full and ultimately hideous. Sometimes the smoke masked it, but all too often that bulging dragon's eye swam free and peered down, casting a bleary orange light. Clay thought it a horror-comic moon, but didn't say so.

No one had much to say. The people on the bridge only looked at the city they had so lately left, watching as the flames reached the pricey harborfront condos and began engulfing them. From across the water came an interwoven tapestry of alarms – fire alarms and car alarms, mostly, with several whooping sirens added for spice. For a while an amplified voice had told citizens to GET OFF THE STREETS, and then another had begun advising them to LEAVE THE CITY ON FOOT BY MAJOR ARTERIES WEST AND NORTH. These two contradictory pieces of advice had competed with each other for several minutes, and then GET OFF THE STREETS had ceased. About five minutes later, LEAVE THE CITY ON FOOT had also quit. Now there was only the hungry roar of the wind-driven fire, the alarms, and a steady low crumping sound that Clay thought must be windows imploding in the enormous heat.

He wondered how many people had been trapped over there. Trapped between the fire and the water.

'Remember wondering if a modern city could burn?' Tom McCourt said. In the light of the fire, his small, intelligent face looked tired and sick. There was a smudge of ash on one of his cheeks. 'Remember that?'

'Shut up, come on,' Alice said. She was clearly distraught, but like Tom, she spoke in a low voice. *It's like we're in a library,* Clay thought. And then he thought, *No – a funeral home.* 'Can't we please go? Because this is kicking my ass.'

'Sure,' Clay said. 'You bet. How far to your place, Tom?'

'From here, less than two miles,' he said. 'But it's not all behind us, I'm sorry to say.' They had turned north now, and he pointed ahead and to the right. The glow blooming there could almost have been orange-tinted arc-sodium streetlights on a cloudy night, except the night was clear and the street-lights were now out. In any case, streetlights did not give off rising columns of smoke.

Alice moaned, then covered her mouth as if she expected someone among the silent multitude watching Boston burn might reprimand her for making too much noise.

'Don't worry,' Tom said with eerie calm. 'We're going to Malden and that looks like Revere. The way the wind's blowing, Malden should still be all right.'

Stop right there, Clay urged him silently, but Tom did not. 'For now,' he added.

2

There were several dozen abandoned cars on the lower deck of the span, and a fire truck with EAST BOSTON lettered on its avocado-green side that had been sideswiped by a cement truck (both were abandoned), but mostly this level of the bridge belonged to the pedestrians. *Except now you probably have to call them refugees,* Clay thought, and then realised there was no *them* about it. Us. *Call us refugees.*

There was still very little talk. Most people just stood and watched the city burn in silence. Those who *were* moving went slowly, looking back frequently over their shoulders. Then, as they neared the far end of the bridge (he could see *Old Ironsides* – at least he thought it was *Old Ironsides* – riding at anchor in the Harbor, still safe from the flames), he noticed an odd thing. Many of them were also looking at Alice. At first he had the paranoid idea that people must think he and Tom had abducted the girl and were spiriting her away for God knew what immoral purposes. Then he had to remind himself that these wraiths on the Mystic Bridge were in shock, even more uprooted from their normal lives than the Hurricane Katrina refugees had been – those unfortunates had at least had some warning – and were unlikely to be capable of considering such fine ideas. Most were too deep in their own heads for moralizing. Then the moon rose a little higher and came out a little more strongly, and he got it: she was the only adolescent in sight. Even Clay himself was young compared to most of their fellow refugees. The majority of people gawking at the torch that had been Boston or plodding slowly toward Malden and Danvers were over forty, and many looked eligible for the Golden Ager discount at Denny's. He saw a few people with little kids, and a couple of babies in strollers, but that was pretty much it for the younger set.

A little farther on, he noticed something else. There were cell phones lying discarded in the roadway. Every few feet they passed another one, and none was whole. They had either been run over or stomped down to nothing but wire and splinters of plastic, like dangerous snakes that had been destroyed before they could bite again.

3

'What's your name, dear?' asked a plump woman who came angling across to their side of the highway. This was about five minutes after they had left the bridge. Tom said another fifteen would bring them to the Salem Street exit, and from there it was only four blocks to his house. He said his cat would be awfully glad to see him, and that had brought a wan smile to Alice's face. Clay thought wan was better than nothing.

Now Alice looked with reflexive mistrust at the plump woman who had detached herself from the mostly silent groups and little lines of men and women – hardly more than shadows, really, some with suitcases, some carrying shopping bags or wearing backpacks – that had crossed the Mystic and were walking north on Route One, away from the great fire to the south and all too aware of the new one taking hold in Revere, off to the northeast.

The plump woman looked back at her with sweet interest. Her graying hair was done in neat beauty-shop curls. She wore cat's-eye glasses and what Clay's mother would have called a 'car coat.' She carried a shopping bag in one hand and a book in the other. There seemed to be no harm in her. She certainly wasn't one of the phone-crazies – they hadn't seen a single one of those since leaving the Atlantic Avenue Inn with their sacks of grub – but Clay felt himself go on point, just the same. To be approached as if they were at a get-acquainted tea instead of fleeing a burning city didn't seem normal. But under these circumstances, just what was? He was probably losing it, but if so, Tom was, too. He was also watching the plump, motherly woman with go-away eyes.

'Alice?' Alice said at last, just when Clay had decided the girl wasn't going to reply at all. She sounded like a kid trying to answer what she fears may be a trick question in a class that's really too tough for her. 'My name is Alice Maxwell?'

'Alice,' the plump woman said, and her lips curved in a maternal smile as sweet as her look of interest. There was no reason that smile should have set Clay on edge more than he already was, but it did. 'That's a lovely name. It means "blessed of God".'

'Actually, ma'am, it means "of the royalty" or "regally born",' Tom said. 'Now could you excuse us? The girl has just lost her mother today, and—'

'We've *all* lost someone today, haven't we, Alice?' the plump woman said without looking at Tom. She kept pace with Alice, her beauty-shop curls bouncing with every step. Alice was eyeing her with a mixture of unease and fascination. Around them others paced and sometimes hurried and often plodded with their heads down, little more than wraiths in this unaccustomed darkness, and Clay still saw nobody young except for a few babies, a few toddlers, and Alice. No adolescents because most adolescents had cell phones, like Pixie Light back at the Mister Softee truck. Or like his own son, who had a red Nextel with a ring-tone from *The Monster Club* and a teacher workamommy who might be with him or might be just about anyw—

Stop it. Don't you let that rat out. That rat can do nothing but run, bite, and chase its own tail.

The plump woman, meanwhile, kept nodding. Her curls bounced along. 'Yes, we've all lost someone, because this is the time of the great Tribulation. It's all in here, in Revelation.' She held up the book she was carrying, and of course it was a Bible, and now Clay thought he was getting a better look at the sparkle in the eyes behind the plump woman's cat's-eye glasses. That wasn't kindly interest; that was lunacy.

'Oh, that's it, everybody out of the pool,' Tom said. In his voice Clay heard a mixture of disgust (at himself, for letting the plump woman bore in and get close to begin with, quite likely) and dismay.

The plump woman took no notice, of course; she had fixed Alice with her stare, and who was there to pull her away? The police were otherwise occupied, if there were any left. Here there were only the shocked and shuffling refugees, and they could care less about one elderly crazy lady with a Bible and a beauty-shop perm.

'The Vial of Insanity has been poured into the brains of

the wicked, and the City of Sin has been set afire by the cleansing torch of Yee-*ho*-vah!' the plump lady cried. She was wearing red lipstick. Her teeth were too even to be anything but old-fashioned dentures. 'Now you see the unrepentant flee, yea, verily, even as maggots flee the burst belly of—'

Alice put her hands over her ears. 'Make her stop!' she cried, and still the ghost-shapes of the city's recent residents filed past, only a few sparing a dull, incurious glance before looking once more into the darkness where somewhere ahead New Hampshire lay.

The plump woman was starting to work up a sweat, Bible raised, eyes blazing, beauty-shop curls nodding and swaying. 'Take your hands down, girl, and hear the Word of God before you let these men lead you away and fornicate with you in the open doorway of Hell itself! "For I saw a star blaze in the sky, and it was called Wormwood, and those that followed it followed upon Lucifer, and those that followed upon Lucifer walked downward into the furnace of—"'

Clay hit her. He pulled the punch at the last second, but it was still a solid clip to the jaw, and he felt the impact travel all the way up to his shoulder. The plump woman's glasses rose off her pug nose and then settled back. Behind them, her eyes lost their glare and rolled up in their sockets. Her knees came unhinged and she buckled, her Bible tumbling from her clenched fist. Alice, still looking stunned and horrified, nevertheless dropped her hands from her ears fast enough to catch the Bible. And Tom McCourt caught the woman under her arms. The punch and the two subsequent catches were so neatly done they could have been choreographed.

Clay was suddenly closer to undone than at any time since things had started going wrong. Why this should have been worse than the throat-biting teenage girl or the knife-wielding businessman, worse than finding Mr Ricardi hanging from a light fixture with a bag over his head, he didn't know, but it was. He had kicked the knife-wielding businessman, Tom had, too, but the knife-wielding businessman had been a different kind of crazy. The old lady with the beauty-shop curls had just been a . . .

'Jesus,' he said. 'She was just a nut, and I coldcocked her.' He was starting to shake.

'She was terrorizing a young girl who lost her mother today,' Tom said, and Clay realized it wasn't calmness he heard in the small man's voice but an extraordinary coldness. 'You did exactly the right thing. Besides, you can't keep an old iron horse like this down for long. She's coming around already. Help me get her over to the side of the road.'

4

They had reached the part of Route One – sometimes called the Miracle Mile, sometimes Sleaze Alley – where limited-access highway yielded to a jostle of liquor marts, cut-rate clothing stores, sporting-goods outlets, and eateries with names like Fuddruckers. Here the six lanes were littered, if not quite choked, with vehicles that had either been piled up or just abandoned when their operators panicked, tried their cell phones, and went insane. The refugees wove their various courses silently among the remains, reminding Clay Riddell more than a little of ants evacuating a hill that has been demolished by the careless passing boot-stride of some heed-less human.

There was a green reflectorized sign reading MALDEN SALEM ST EXIT 1/4 MI at the edge of a low pink building that had been broken into; it was fronted by a jagged skirting of broken glass, and a battery-powered burglar alarm was even now in the tired last stages of running down. A glance at the dead sign on the roof was all Clay needed to tell him what had made the place a target in the aftermath of the day's disaster: MISTER BIG'S GIANT DISCOUNT LIQUOR.

He had one of the plump woman's arms. Tom had the other, and Alice supported the muttering woman's head as they eased her to a sitting position with her back against one of the exit sign's legs. Just as they got her down, the plump woman opened her eyes and looked at them dazedly.

Tom snapped his fingers in front of her eyes, twice, briskly. She blinked, then turned her eyes to Clay. 'You . . . hit me,' she said. Her fingers rose to touch the rapidly puffing spot on her jaw.

'Yes, I'm sor—' Clay began.

'He may be, but I'm not,' Tom said. He spoke with that same cold briskness. 'You were terrorizing our ward.'

The plump woman laughed softly, but tears were in her eyes. *'Ward!* I've heard a lot of words for it, but never that one. As if I don't know what men like you want with a tender girl like this, especially in times like these. "They repented not their fornications, nor their sodomies, nor their—"'

'Shut up,' Tom said, 'or I'll hit you myself. And unlike my friend, who was I think lucky enough not to grow up among the holy Hannahs and thus does not recognize you for what you are, I won't pull my punch. Fair warning – one more word.' He held his fist before her eyes, and although Clay had already concluded that Tom was an educated man, civilized, and probably not much of a puncher under ordinary circumstances, he could not help feeling dismay at the sight of that small, tight fist, as if he were looking at an omen of the coming age.

The plump lady looked and said nothing. One large tear spilled down her rouged cheek.

'That's enough, Tom, I'm okay,' Alice said.

Tom dropped the plump lady's shopping bag of possessions into her lap. Clay hadn't even realised Tom had salvaged it. Then Tom took the Bible from Alice, picked up one of the plump lady's be-ringed hands, and smacked the Bible into it, spine first. He started away, then turned back.

'Tom, that's enough, let's go,' Clay said.

Tom ignored him. He bent towards the woman sitting with her back against the sign's leg. His hands were on his

76

knees, and to Clay the two of them — the plump, spectacled woman looking up, the small, spectacled man bending over with his hands on his knees — looked like figures in some lunatic's parody of the early illustrations from the Charles Dickens novels.

'Some advice, sister,' Tom said. 'The police will no longer protect you as they did when you and your self-righteous, holy-rolling friends marched on the family planning centers or the Emily Cathcart Clinic in Waltham—'

'That abortion mill!' she spat, and then raised her Bible, as if to block a blow.

Tom didn't hit her, but he was smiling grimly. 'I don't know about the Vial of Insanity, but there's certainly *beaucoup* crazy making the rounds tonight. May I be clear? The lions are out of their cages, and you may well find that they'll eat the mouthy Christians first. Somebody canceled your right of free speech around three o'clock this afternoon. Just a word to the wise.' He looked from Alice to Clay, and Clay saw that the upper lip beneath the mustache was trembling slightly. 'Shall we go?'

'Yes,' Clay said.

'Wow,' Alice said, once they were walking toward the Salem Street ramp again, Mister Big's Giant Discount Liquor falling behind them. 'You grew up with someone like that?'

'My mother and both of her sisters,' Tom said. 'First N.E. Church of Christ the Redeemer. They took Jesus as their personal savior, and the church took them as its personal pigeons.'

'Where is your mother now?' Clay asked.

Tom glanced at him briefly. 'Heaven. Unless they rooked her on that one, too. I'm pretty sure the bastards did.'

5

Near the stop sign at the foot of the ramp, two men were fighting over a keg of beer. If forced to guess, Clay would have said it had probably been liberated from Mister Big's Giant Discount Liquor. Now it lay forgotten against the guardrails, dented and leaking foam, while the two men – both brawny and both bleeding – battered each other with their fists. Alice shrank against him, and Clay put his arm around her, but there was something almost reassuring about these brawlers. They were angry – enraged – but not crazy. Not like the people back in the city.

One of them was bald and wearing a Celtics jacket. He hit the other a looping overhand blow that mashed his opponent's lips and knocked him flat. When the man in the Celtics jacket advanced on the downed man, the downed man scrambled away, then got up, still backing off. He spat blood. 'Take it, ya fuck!' he yelled in a thick, weepy Boston accent. 'Hope it chokes ya!'

The bald man in the Celtics jacket made as if to charge him, and the other went running up the ramp toward Route One. Celtics Jacket started to bend down for his prize, registered Clay, Alice, and Tom, and straightened up again. It was three to one, he had a black eye, and blood was trickling down the side of his face from a badly torn earlobe, but Clay saw no fear in that face, although he had only the diminishing light of the Revere fire to go by. He thought his grandfather would have said the guy's Irish was up, and certainly that went with the big green shamrock on the back of his jacket.

'The fuck you lookin at?' he asked.

'Nothing – just going by you, if that's all right,' Tom said mildly. 'I live on Salem Street.'

'You can go to Salem Street or hell, far as I'm concerned,' the bald man in the Celtics jacket said. 'Still a free country, isn't it?'

'Tonight?' Clay said. 'Too free.'

The bald man thought it over and then laughed, a humorless double ha-ha. 'The fuck happened? Any-a youse know?'

Alice said, 'It was the cell phones. They made people crazy.'

The bald man picked up the keg. He handled it easily, tipping it so the leak stopped. 'Fucking things,' he said. 'Never cared to own one. Rollover minutes. The fuck're those?'

Clay didn't know. Tom might've – he'd owned a cell phone, so it seemed possible – but Tom said nothing. Probably didn't want to get into a long discussion with the bald man, and probably a good idea. Clay thought the bald man had some of the characteristics of an unexploded grenade.

'City burning?' the bald man asked. 'Is, isn't it?'

'Yes,' Clay said. 'I don't think the Celtics will be playing at the Fleet this year.'

'They ain't shit, anyway,' the man said. 'Doc Rivers couldn't coach a PAL team.' He stood watching them, the keg on his shoulder, blood running down the side of his face. Yet now he seemed peaceable enough, almost serene. 'Go on,' he said. 'But I wouldn't stay this close to the city for long. It's gonna get worse before it gets better. There's gonna be a lot more fires, for one thing. You think everybody who hightailed it north remembered to turn off the gas stove? I fuckin doubt it.'

The three of them started walking, then Alice stopped. She pointed to the keg. 'Was that yours?'

The bald man looked at her reasonably. 'Ain't no was at times like this, sweetie pie. Ain't no was left. There's just now and maybe-tomorrow. It's mine now, and if there's any left it'll be mine maybe-tomorrow. Go on now. The fuck out.'

'Seeya,' Clay said, and raised one hand.

'Wouldn't want to be ya,' the bald man replied, unsmiling, but he raised his own hand in return. They had passed the stop sign and were crossing to the far side of what Clay assumed was Salem Street when the bald man called after them again: 'Hey, handsome!'

Both Clay and Tom turned to look, then glanced at each other, amused. The bald guy with the keg was now only a dark shape on the rising ramp; he could have been a caveman carrying a club.

'Where are the loonies now?' the bald guy asked. 'You're not gonna tell me they're all dead, are ya? Cause I don't fuckin believe it.'

'That's a very good question,' Clay said.

'You're fuckin-A right it is. Watch out for the little sweetie pie there.' And without waiting for them to reply, the man who'd won the battle of the beer keg turned and merged with the shadows.

6

'This is it,' Tom said no more than ten minutes later, and the moon emerged from the wrack of cloud and smoke that had obscured it for the last hour or so as if the little man with the spectacles and the mustache had just given the Celestial Lighting Director a cue. Its rays – silver now instead of that awful infected orange – illuminated a house that was either dark blue, green, or perhaps even gray; without the street-lights to help, it was hard to tell for sure. What Clay *could* tell for sure was that the house was trim and handsome, although maybe not as big as your eye first insisted. The moonlight aided in that deception, but it was mostly caused by the way the steps rose from Tom McCourt's well-kept lawn to the only pillared porch on the street. There was a fieldstone chimney on the left. From above the porch, a dormer looked down on the street.

'Oh, Tom, it's *beautiful*!' Alice said in a too-rapturous voice. To Clay she sounded exhausted and bordering on hysteria. He himself didn't think it beautiful, but it certainly looked like the home of a man who owned a cell phone and all the other twenty-first-century bells and whistles. So did the rest of the houses on this part of Salem Street, and Clay doubted if many of the residents had had Tom's fantastic good luck. He looked around nervously. All the houses were dark

– the power was out now – and they might have been deserted, except he seemed to feel eyes, surveying them.

The eyes of crazies? Phone-crazies? He thought of Power Suit Woman and Pixie Light; of the lunatic in the gray pants and the shredded tie; the man in the business suit who had bitten the ear right off the side of the dog's head. He thought of the naked man jabbing the car aerials back and forth as he ran. No, *surveying* was not in the phone-crazies' repertoire. They just came at you. But if there were normal people holed up in these houses – *some* of them, anyway – where *were* the phone-crazies?

Clay didn't know.

'I don't know if I'd exactly call it beautiful,' Tom said, 'but it's still standing, and that's good enough for me. I'd pretty well made up my mind that we'd get here and find nothing but a smoking hole in the ground.' He reached in his pocket and brought out a slim ring of keys. 'Come on in. Be it ever so humble, and all that.'

They started up the walk and had gone no more than half a dozen steps when Alice cried, *'Wait!'*

Clay wheeled around, feeling both alarm and exhaustion. He thought he was beginning to understand combat fatigue a little. Even his adrenaline felt tired. But no one was there – no phone-crazies, no bald man with blood flowing down the side of his face from a shredded ear, not even a little old lady with the talkin apocalypse blues. Just Alice, down on one knee at the place where Tom's walk left the sidewalk.

'What is it, honey?' Tom asked.

She stood up, and Clay saw she was holding a very small sneaker. 'It's a Baby Nike,' she said. 'Do you—'

Tom shook his head. 'I live alone. Except for Rafe, that is. He thinks he's the king, but he's only the cat.'

'Then who left it?' She looked from Tom to Clay with wondering, tired eyes.

Clay shook his head. 'No telling, Alice. Might as well toss it.'

But Clay knew she would not; it was déjà vu at its disorienting worst. She still held it in her hand, curled against her
waist, as she went to stand behind Tom, who was on the steps,
picking slowly through his keys in the scant light.

Now we hear the cat, Clay thought. *Rafe.* And sure enough,
there was the cat that had been Tom McCourt's salvation,
waowing a greeting from inside.

7

Tom bent down and Rafe or Rafer – both short for Rafael
– leaped into his arms, purring loudly and stretching his head
up to sniff Tom's carefully trimmed mustache.

'Yeah, missed you, too,' Tom said. 'All is forgiven, believe
me.' He carried Rafer across the enclosed porch, stroking the
top of his head. Alice followed. Clay came last, closing the
door and turning the knob on the lock before catching up
to the others.

'Follow along down to the kitchen,' Tom said when they
were in the house proper. There was a pleasant smell of furniture polish and, Clay thought, leather, a smell he associated
with men living calm lives that did not necessarily include
women. 'Second door on the right. Stay close. The hallway's
wide, and there's nothing on the floor, but there are tables on
both sides and it's as black as your hat. As I think you can see.'

'So to speak,' Clay said.

'Ha-ha.'

'Have you got flashlights?' Clay asked.

'Flashlights and a Coleman lantern that should be even
better, but let's get in the kitchen first.'

They followed him down the hallway, Alice walking
between the two men. Clay could hear her breathing rapidly,
trying not to let the unfamiliar surroundings freak her out,
but of course it was hard. Hell, it was hard for him.
Disorienting. It would have been better if there had been
even a little light, but—

CELL

His knee bumped one of the tables Tom had mentioned, and something that sounded all too ready to break rattled like teeth. Clay steeled himself for the smash, and for Alice's scream. That she *would* scream was almost a given. Then whatever it was, a vase or some knickknack, decided to live a little longer and settled back into place. Still, it seemed like a very long walk before Tom said, 'Here, okay? Hard right.'

The kitchen was nearly as black as the hall, and Clay had just a moment to think of all the things he was missing and Tom must be missing more: a digital readout on the microwave oven, the hum of the fridge, maybe light from a neighboring house coming in through the window over the kitchen sink and making highlights on the faucet.

'Here's the table,' Tom said. 'Alice, I'm going to take your hand. Here's a chair, okay? I'm sorry if I sound like we're playing blindman's bluff.'

'It's all r—' she began, then gave a little scream that made Clay jump. His hand was on the haft of his knife (now he thought of it as his) before he even realised he'd reached for it.

'What?' Tom asked sharply. *'What?'*

'Nothing,' she said. 'Just . . . nothing. The cat. His tail . . . on my leg.'

'Oh. I'm sorry.'

'It's all right. *Stupid,*' she added with self-contempt that made Clay wince in the dark.

'No,' he said. 'Let up on yourself, Alice. It's been a tough day at the office.'

'Tough day at the office!' Alice repeated, and laughed in a way Clay didn't care for. It reminded him of her voice when she'd called Tom's house beautiful. He thought, *That's going to get away from her, and then what do I do? In the movies the hysterical girl gets a slap across the chops and it always brings her around, but in the movies you can see where she* is.

He didn't have to slap her, shake her, or hold her, which was what he probably would have tried first. She heard what

83

was in her own voice, maybe, got hold of it, and bulldogged it down: first to a choked gargle, then to a gasp, then to quiet.

'Sit,' Tom said. 'You have to be tired. You too, Clay. I'll get us some light.'

Clay felt for a chair and sat down to a table he could hardly see, although his eyes had to be fully adjusted to the dark by now. There was a whisper of something against his pants leg, there and gone. A low miaow. Rafe.

'Hey, guess what?' he said to the dim shape of the girl as Tom's footsteps receded. 'Ole Rafer just put a jump in me, too.' Although he hadn't, not really.

'We have to forgive him,' she said. 'Without that cat, Tom would be just as crazy as the rest of them. And that would be a shame.'

'It would.'

'I'm so scared,' she said. 'Do you think it will get better tomorrow, in the daylight? The being scared part?'

'I don't know.'

'You must be worried sick about your wife and little boy.'

Clay sighed and rubbed his face. 'The hard part is trying to come to grips with the helplessness. We're separated, you see, and—' He stopped and shook his head. He wouldn't have gone on if she hadn't reached out and taken his hand. Her fingers were firm and cool. 'We separated in the spring. We still live in the same little town, what my own mother would have called a grass marriage. My wife teaches at the elementary school.'

He leaned forward, trying to see her face in the dark.

'You want to know the hell of it? If this had happened a year ago, Johnny would have been with her. But this September he made the jump to middle school, which is almost five miles away. I keep trying to figure if he would have been home when things went nuts. He and his friends ride the bus. I *think* he would have been home. And I think he would have gone right to her.'

Or pulled his cell phone out of his backpack and called her!
the panic-rat suggested merrily . . . then *bit*. Clay felt himself
tightening his fingers down on Alice's and made himself stop.
But he couldn't stop the sweat from springing out on his
face and arms.

'But you don't know,' she said.

'No.'

'My daddy runs a framing and print shop in Newton,'
she said. 'I'm sure he's all right, he's very self-reliant, but he'll
be worried about me. Me and my. My you-know.'

Clay knew.

'I keep wondering what he did about supper,' she said.
'I know that's crazy, but he can't cook a lick.'

Clay thought about asking if her father had a cell phone
and something told him not to. Instead he asked, 'Are you
doing all right for now?'

'Yes,' she said, and shrugged. 'What's happened to him
has happened. I can't change it.'

He thought: *I wish you hadn't said that.*

'My kid has a cell phone, did I tell you that?' To his own
ears, his voice sounded as harsh as a crow's caw.

'You did, actually. Before we crossed the bridge.'

'Sure, that's right.' He was gnawing at his lower lip and
made himself stop. 'But he didn't always keep it charged.
Probably I told you that, too.'

'Yes.'

'I just have no way of knowing.' The panic-rat was out
of its cage, now. Running and biting.

Now both of her hands closed over both of his. He didn't
want to give in to her comfort – it felt hard to let go of his
grip on himself and give in to her comfort – but he did it,
thinking she might need to give more than he needed to
take. They were holding on that way, hands linked next to
the pewter salt and pepper shakers on Tom McCourt's little
kitchen table, when Tom came back from the cellar with four
flashlights and a Coleman lantern that was still in its box.

85

8

The Coleman gave off enough light to make the flashlights unnecessary. It was harsh and white, but Clay liked its brilliance, the way it drove away every single shadow save for their own and the cat's – which went leaping fantastically up the wall like a Halloween decoration cut from black crepe paper – into hiding.

'I think you should pull the curtains,' Alice said.

Tom was opening one of the plastic sacks from the Metropolitan Café, the ones with DOGGY BAG on the side and PEOPLE BAG on the other. He stopped and looked at her curiously. 'Why?'

She shrugged and smiled. Clay thought it the strangest smile he had ever seen on the face of a teenage girl. She'd cleaned the blood off her nose and chin, but there were dark weary-circles under her eyes, the Coleman lamp had bleached the rest of her face to a corpselike pallor, and the smile, showing the tiniest twinkle of teeth between trembling lips from which all the lipstick had now departed, was disorienting in its adult artificiality. He thought Alice looked like a movie actress from the late 1940s playing a socialite on the verge of a nervous breakdown. She had the tiny sneaker in front of her on the table. She was spinning it with one finger. Each time she spun it, the laces flipped and clicked. Clay began to hope she would break soon. The longer she held up, the worse it would be when she finally let go. She had let some out, but not nearly enough. So far he'd been the one to do most of the letting-out.

'I don't think people should see we're in here, that's all,' she said. She flicked the sneaker. What she had called a Baby Nike. It spun. The laces flipped and clicked on Tom's highly polished table. 'I think it might be . . . bad.'

Tom looked at Clay.

'She could be right,' Clay said. 'I don't like us being the only lit-up house on the block, even if the light's at the back.'

Tom got up and closed the curtains over the sink without another word. There were two other windows in the kitchen, and he pulled those curtains, too. He started back to the table, then changed course and closed the door between the kitchen and the hall. Alice spun the Baby Nike in front of her on the table. In the harsh, unsparing glow of the Coleman lantern, Clay could see it was pink and purple, colors only a child could love. Around it went. The laces flew and clicked. Tom looked at it, frowning, as he sat down, and Clay thought: *Tell her to take it off the table. Tell her she doesn't know where it's been and you don't want it on your table. That should be enough to set her off and then we can start getting this part out of the way. Tell her. I think she wants you to. I think that's why she's doing it.*

But Tom only took sandwiches out of the bag – roast beef and cheese, ham and cheese – and doled them out. He got a pitcher of iced tea from the fridge ('Still cold as can be,' he said), and then set down the remains of a package of raw hamburger for the cat.

'He deserves it,' he said, almost defensively. 'Besides, it would only go over with the electricity out.'

There was a telephone hanging on the wall. Clay tried it, but it was really just a formality and this time he didn't even get a dial tone. The thing was as dead as . . . well, as Power Suit Woman, back there by Boston Common. He sat back down and worked on his sandwich. He was hungry but didn't feel like eating.

Alice put hers down after only three bites. 'I can't,' she said. 'Not now. I guess I'm too tired. I want to go to sleep. And I want to get out of this dress. I guess I can't wash up – not very well, anyway – but I'd give anything to throw this fucking dress away. It stinks of sweat and blood.' She spun the sneaker. It twirled beside the crumpled paper with her barely touched sandwich lying on top of it. 'I can smell my mother on it, too. Her perfume.'

For a moment no one said anything. Clay was at a complete loss. He had a momentary picture of Alice subtracted from her dress, in a white bra and panties, with her staring, hollowed-out eyes making her look like a paper-doll. His artist's imagination, always facile and always obliging, added tabs at the shoulders and lower legs of the image. It was shocking not because it was sexy but because it wasn't. In the distance – very faint – something exploded with a dim *foomp*.

Tom broke the silence, and Clay blessed him for it.

'I'll bet a pair of my jeans would just about fit you, if you rolled up the bottoms to make cuffs.' He stood up. 'You know what, I think you'd even look cute in em, like Huck Finn in a girls' school production of *Big River*. Come upstairs. I'm going to put out some clothes for you to wear in the morning and you can spend the night in the guest room. I've got plenty of pajamas, a plague of pajamas. Do you want the Coleman?'

'Just . . . I guess just a flashlight will be okay. Are you sure?'

'Yes,' he said. He took one flashlight and gave her another. He looked ready to say something about the small sneaker when she picked it up, then seemed to think better of it. What he said was, 'You can wash, too. There may not be a lot of water, but the taps will probably draw some even with the power out, and I'm sure we can spare a basinful.' He looked over the top of her head at Clay. 'I always keep a case of bottled drinking water in the cellar, so we're not short there.'

Clay nodded. 'Sleep well, Alice,' he said.

'You too,' she said vaguely, and then, more vaguely still: 'Nice meeting you.'

Tom opened the door for her. Their flashlights bobbed, and then the door shut again. Clay heard their footsteps on the stairs, then overhead. He heard running water. He waited for the chug of air in the pipes, but the flow of water stopped before the air started. A basinful, Tom had said, and that was what she'd gotten. Clay also had blood and dirt on him he wanted to wash off – he imagined Tom did, too – but he guessed there must be a bathroom on this floor, too, and if Tom was as neat about his personal habits as he was about his person, the water in the toilet bowl would be clean. And there was the water in the tank as well, of course.

Rafer jumped up on Tom's chair and began washing his paws in the white light of the Coleman lantern. Even with the lantern's steady low hiss, Clay could hear him purring. As far as Rafe was concerned, life was still cool.

He thought of Alice twirling the small sneaker and wondered, almost idly, if it was possible for a fifteen-year-old girl to have a nervous breakdown.

'Don't be stupid,' he told the cat. 'Of course it is. Happens all the time. They make movies of the week about it.'

Rafer looked at him with wise green eyes and went on licking his paw. *Tell me more,* those eyes seemed to say. *Vere you beaten as a child? Did you have ze sexual thoughts about your mother?*

I can smell my mother on it. Her perfume.

Alice as a paper-doll, with tabs sticking out of her shoulders and legs.

Don't be zilly, Rafer's green eyes seemed to say. *Ze tabs go on ze clothes, not on ze doll. Vut kind of artist are you?*

'The out-of-work kind,' he said. 'Just shut up, why don't you?' He closed his eyes, but that was worse. Now Rafer's green eyes floated disembodied in the dark, like the eyes of Lewis Carroll's Cheshire cat: *We're all mad here, dear Alice.* And under the steady hiss of the Coleman lamp, he could still hear it purring.

9

Tom was gone fifteen minutes. When he came back, he brushed Rafe out of his chair without ceremony and took a large, convincing bite from his sandwich. 'She's asleep,' he said. 'Got into a pair of my pajamas while I waited in the hall, and then we dumped the dress in the trash together. I think she was out forty seconds after her head hit the pillow. Throwing the dress away was what sealed the deal, I'm convinced of it.' A slight pause. 'It did indeed smell bad.'

'While you were gone,' Clay said, 'I nominated Rafe president of the United States. He was elected by acclamation.'

'Good,' Tom said. 'Wise choice. Who voted?'

'Millions. Everyone still sane. They sent in thought-ballots.' Clay made his eyes very wide and tapped his temple. 'I can read *miiiyyynds*.'

Tom's chewing stopped, then began again . . . but slowly. 'You know,' he said, 'under the circumstances, that's not really all that funny.'

Clay sighed, sipped some iced tea, and made himself eat a little more of his sandwich. He told himself to think of it as body gasoline, if that was what it took to get it down. 'No. Probably not. Sorry.'

Tom tipped his own glass to him before drinking. 'It's all right. I appreciate the effort. Say, where's your portfolio?'

'Left it on the porch. I wanted both hands free while we negotiated Tom McCourt's Hallway of Death.'

'*That's* all right, then. Listen, Clay, I'm sorry as hell about your family—'

'Don't be sorry yet,' Clay said, a little harshly. 'There's nothing to be sorry about yet.'

'—but I'm really glad I ran into you. That's all I wanted to say.'

'Same goes back,' Clay said. 'I appreciate the quiet place to spend the night, and I'm sure Alice does, too.'

'As long as Malden doesn't get loud and burn down around our ears.'

Clay nodded, smiling a little. 'As long as. Did you get that creepy little shoe away from her?'

'No. She took it to bed with her like . . . I don't know, a teddy bear. She'll be a lot better tomorrow if she sleeps through tonight.'

'Do you think she will?'

'No,' Tom said. 'But if she wakes up scared, I'll spend the night with her. Crawl in with her, if that's what it takes. You know I'm safe with her, right?'

'Yes.' Clay knew that he would have been safe with her, too, but he understood what Tom was talking about. 'I'm going to head north tomorrow morning as soon as it's light. It would probably be a good idea if you and Alice came with me.'

Tom thought about this briefly, then asked, 'What about her father?'

'She says he's, quote, "very self-reliant." Her biggest stated worry on his behalf was what he rolled himself for dinner. What I heard under that is that she isn't ready to know. Of course we'll have to see how she feels about it, but I'd rather keep her with us, and I *don't* want to head west into those industrial towns.'

'You don't want to head west at all.'

'No,' Clay admitted.

He thought Tom might argue the point, but he didn't. 'What about tonight? Do you think we should stand a watch?'

Clay hadn't even considered this until now. He said, 'I don't know how much good it would do. If a crazed mob comes down Salem Street waving guns and torches, what can *we* do about it?'

'Go down cellar?'

Clay thought it over. Going down cellar seemed awfully final to him – the Bunker Defence – but it was always possible the hypothetical crazed mob under discussion would think the house deserted and go sweeping by. Better than being slaughtered in the kitchen, he supposed. Maybe after watching Alice get gang-raped.

It won't come to that, he thought uneasily. *You're getting lost among the hypotheticals, that's all. Freaking in the dark. It won't come to that.*

Except Boston was burning to the ground behind them.

Liquor stores were being looted and men were beating each other bloody over aluminum kegs of beer. It had already come to that.

Tom, meanwhile, was watching him, letting him work it through . . . which meant that maybe Tom already had. Rafe jumped into his lap. Tom put his sandwich down and stroked the cat's back.

'Tell you what,' Clay said. 'If you've got a couple of comforters I can bundle up in, why don't I spend the night out there on your porch? It's enclosed, and it's darker than the street. Which means that I'd likely see anyone coming long before they saw me watching. Especially if the ones coming were phone-crazies. They didn't impress me as being into stealth.'

'Nope, not the creep-up-on-you type. What if people came from around in back? That's Lynn Avenue just a block over.'

Clay shrugged, trying to indicate that they couldn't defend against everything – or even very much – without saying so right out loud.

'All right,' Tom said, after eating a little more of his sandwich and feeding a scrap of ham to Rafe. 'But you could come get me around three. If Alice hasn't woken up by then, she might sleep right through.'

'Why don't we just see how it goes,' Clay said. 'Listen, I think I know the answer to this, but you don't have a gun, do you?'

'No,' Tom said. 'Not even a lonely can of Mace.' He looked at his sandwich and then put it down. When he raised his eyes to Clay's, they were remarkably bleak. He spoke in a low voice, as people do when discussing secret things. 'Do you remember what the cop said just before he shot that crazy man?'

Clay nodded. *Hey, buddy, how ya doin? I mean, what the haps?* He would never forget it.

'I knew it wasn't like in the movies,' Tom said, 'but I never suspected the enormous *power* of it, or the sudden-

92

ness . . . and the sound when the stuff . . . the stuff from his head . . .'

He leaned forward suddenly, one small hand curled to his mouth. The movement startled Rafer, and the cat leaped down. Tom made three low, muscular urking sounds, and Clay steeled himself for the vomiting that was almost sure to follow. He could only hope he wouldn't start vomiting himself, but he thought he might. He knew he was close, only a feather-tickle away. Because he knew what Tom was talking about. The gunshot, then the wet, ropy splatter on the cement.

There was no vomiting. Tom got control of himself and looked up, eyes watering. 'I'm sorry,' he said. 'Shouldn't have gone there.'

'You don't need to be sorry.'

'I think if we're going to get through whatever's ahead, we'd better find a way to put our finer sensibilities on hold. I think that people who can't do that . . .' He stopped, then started again. 'I think that people who can't do that . . .' He stopped a second time. The third time he was able to finish. 'I think that people who can't do that may die.'

They stared at each other in the white glare of the Coleman lamp.

10

'Once we left the city, I didn't see *anyone* with a gun,' Clay said. 'At first I wasn't really looking, and then I was.'

'You know why, don't you? Except maybe for California, Massachusetts has got the toughest gun law in the country.'

Clay remembered seeing billboards proclaiming that at the state line a few years ago. Then they'd been replaced by ones saying that if you got picked up for driving under the influence, you'd have to spend a night in jail.

Tom said, 'If the cops find a concealed handgun in your car – meaning like in the glove compartment with your registration and insurance card – they can put you

93

away for I think seven years. Get stopped with a loaded rifle in your pickup, even in hunting season, and you could get slapped with a ten-thousand-dollar fine and two years of community service.' He picked up the remains of his sandwich, inspected it, put it back down again. 'You can own a handgun and keep it in your home if you're not a felon, but a licence to carry? Maybe if you've got Father O'Malley of the Boys' Club to cosign, but maybe not even then.'

'No guns might have saved some lives, coming out of the city.'

'I agree with you completely,' Tom said. 'Those two guys fighting over the keg of beer? Thank *God* neither of them had a .38.'

Clay nodded.

Tom rocked back in his chair, crossed his arms on his narrow chest, and looked around. His glasses glinted. The circle of light thrown by the Coleman lantern was brilliant but small. 'Right now, however, I wouldn't mind having a pistol. Even after seeing the mess they make. And I consider myself a pacifist.'

'How long have you lived here, Tom?'

'Almost twelve years. Long enough to see Malden go a long way down the road to Shitsville. It's not there yet, but boy, it's going.'

'Okay, so think about it. Which of your neighbours is apt to have a gun or guns in their house?'

Tom answered promptly. 'Arnie Nickerson, across the street and three houses up. NRA bumper sticker on his Camry – along with a couple of yellow ribbon decals and an old Bush-Cheney sticker—'

'Goes without saying—'

'And *two* NRA stickers on his pickup, which he equips with a camper cap in November and takes hunting up in your part of the world.'

'And we're happy to have the revenue his out-of-state

hunting licence provides,' Clay said. 'Let's break into his house tomorrow and take his guns.'

Tom McCourt looked at him as though he were mad. 'The man isn't as paranoid as some of those militia types out in Utah – I mean, he *does* live in Taxachusetts – but he's got one of those burglar alarm signs on his lawn that basically says DO YOU FEEL LUCKY, PUNK, and I'm sure you must be familiar with the NRA's stated policy as to just when their guns will be taken away from them.'

'I think it has something to do with prying their cold dead fingers—'

'That's the one.'

Clay leaned forward and stated what to him had been obvious from the moment they'd come down the ramp from Route One: Malden was now just one more fucked-up town in the Unicel States of America, and that country was now out of service, off the hook, so sorry, please try your call again later. Salem Street was deserted. He had felt that as they approached . . . hadn't he?

No. Bullshit. You felt watched.

Really? And even if he had, was that the sort of intuition that could be relied upon, *acted* upon, after a day like this one? The idea was ridiculous.

'Tom, listen. One of us'll walk up to this guy Nackleson's house tomorrow, after it's full daylight—'

'It's Nickerson, and I don't think that's a very smart idea, especially since Swami McCourt sees him kneeling inside his living room window with a fully automatic rifle he's been saving for the end of the world. Which seems to have rolled around.'

'I'll do it,' Clay said. 'And I *won't* do it if we hear any gunshots from the Nickerson place tonight or tomorrow morning. I *certainly* won't do it if I see any bodies on the guy's lawn, with or without gunshot wounds. I watched all those old *Twilight Zone* episodes, too – the ones where civilization turns out to be nothing more than a thin layer of shellac.'

'If that,' Tom said gloomily. 'Idi Amin, Pol Pot, the pros-ecution rests.'

'I'll go with my hands raised. Ring the doorbell. If someone answers, I'll say I just want to talk. What's the worst that can happen? He tells me to get lost.'

'No, the worst that can happen is he can shoot you dead on his fucking welcome mat and leave me with a mother-less teenage girl,' Tom said sharply. 'Smart off about old *Twilight Zone* episodes all you want, just don't forget those people you saw today, fighting outside the T station in Boston.'

'That was . . . I don't know *what* it was, but those people were clinically insane. You can't doubt that, Tom.'

'What about Bible-Thumping Bertha? And the two men fighting over the keg? Were they insane?'

No, of course they hadn't been, but if there was a gun in that house across the street, he still wanted it. And if there was more than one, he wanted Tom and Alice each to have one, too.

'I'm thinking about going north over a hundred miles,' Clay said. 'We might be able to boost a car and drive some of it, but we might have to walk the whole way. Do you want to go with just knives for protection? I'm asking you as one serious man to another, because some of the people we run into *are* going to have guns. I mean, you *know* that.'

'Yes,' Tom said. He ran his hands through his neatly trimmed hair, giving it a comic ruffle. 'And I know that Arnie and Beth are probably not home. They were gadget-nuts as well as gun-nuts. He was always gabbing on his cell phone when he went by in that big Dodge Ram Detroit phallus of his.'

'See? There you go.'

Tom sighed. 'All right. Depending on how things look in the morning. Okay?'

'Okay.' Clay picked up his sandwich again. He felt a little more like eating now.

'Where did they go?' Tom asked. 'The ones you call the phone-crazies. Where did they go?'

'I don't know.'

'I'll tell you what I think,' Tom said. 'I think they crawled into the houses and the buildings around sundown and died.'

Clay looked at him doubtfully.

'Look at it reasonably and you'll see I'm right,' Tom said. 'This was almost certainly some sort of terrorist act, would you agree?'

'That seems the most likely explanation, although I'll be damned if I know how any signal, no matter how subversive, could have been programmed to do what this one did.'

'Are you a scientist?'

'You know I'm not. I'm an artist.'

'So when the government tells you they can guide computerised smart-bombs through bunker doors in the floor of the desert from aircraft carriers that are maybe two thousand miles away, all you can do is look at the photos and accept that the technology exists.'

'Would Tom Clancy lie to me?' Clay asked, unsmiling.

'And if *that* technology exists, why not accept this one, at least on a provisional basis?'

'Okay, spell it out. Small words, please.'

'At about three o'clock this afternoon, a terrorist organisation, maybe even a tinpot government, generated some sort of signal or pulse. For now we have to assume that this signal was carried by every cell phone operating in the entire world. We'll hope that wasn't the case, but for now I think we *have* to assume the worst.'

'Is it over?'

'I don't know,' Tom said. 'Do you want to pick up a cell phone and find out?'

'Touchy,' Clay said. 'That's how my little boy says *touché.' And please, God, how he's still saying it.*

'But if this group could transmit a signal that would send everyone hearing it insane,' Tom said, 'isn't it possible that the signal could also contain a directive for those receiving it to kill themselves five hours later? Or perhaps to simply go to sleep and stop breathing?'

'I would say that's impossible.'

'I would have said a madman coming at me with a knife across from the Four Seasons Hotel was impossible,' Tom said. 'Or Boston burning flat while the city's entire population – that part of it lucky enough not to have cell phones, that is – left by the Mystic and the Zakim.'

He leaned forward, looking at Clay intently. *He wants to believe this,* Clay thought. *Don't waste a lot of time trying to talk him out of it, because he really, really wants to.*

'In a way, this is no different from the bioterrorism the government was so afraid of after nine-eleven,' he said. 'By using cell phones, which have become the dominant form of communication in our daily lives, you simultaneously turn the populace into your own conscript army – an army that's literally afraid of nothing, because it's insane – and you break down the infrastructure. Where's the National Guard tonight?'

'Iraq?' Clay ventured. 'Louisiana?'

It wasn't much of a joke and Tom didn't smile. 'It's nowhere. How do you use a homeland force that now depends almost entirely on the cellular network to even *mobilize*? As for airplanes, the last one I've seen flying was the little one that crashed on the corner of Charles and Beacon.' He paused, then went on, looking straight across the table into Clay's eyes. 'All this they did . . . whoever *they* is. They looked at us from wherever it is they live and worship their gods, and what did they see?'

Clay shook his head, fascinated by Tom's eyes, shining behind his spectacles. They were almost the eyes of a visionary.

'They saw we had built the Tower of Babel all over again . . . and on nothing but electronic cobwebs. And in a space of seconds, they brushed those cobwebs aside and our Tower fell. All this they did, and we three are like bugs that happened, by dumb dim luck alone, to have avoided the fall of a giant's foot. All this they did, and you think they could not have encoded a signal telling the affected ones to simply fall asleep and stop breathing five hours later? What's that trick, compared to the first one? Not much, I'd say.'

Clay said, 'I'd say it's time we got some sleep.'

For a moment Tom remained as he was, hunched across the table a little, looking at Clay as if unable to understand what Clay had said. Then he laughed. 'Yeah,' he said. 'Yeah, you've got a point. I get wound up. Sorry.'

'Not at all,' Clay said. 'I hope you're right about the crazies being dead.' He paused, then said: 'I mean . . . unless my boy . . . Johnny-Gee . . .' He couldn't finish. Partly or maybe mostly because if Johnny had tried to use his phone this afternoon and had gotten the same call as Pixie Light and Power Suit Woman, Clay wasn't sure he wanted his son to still be alive.

Tom reached across the table to him and Clay took the other man's delicate, long-fingered hand in both of his. He saw this happening as if he were outside his body, and when he spoke, he didn't seem to be the one speaking, although he could feel his mouth moving and the tears that had begun to fall from his eyes.

'I'm so scared for him,' his mouth was saying. 'I'm scared for both of them, but mostly for my kid.'

'It'll be all right,' Tom said, and Clay knew he meant well, but the words struck terror into his heart just the same, because it was just one of those things you said when there was really nothing else. Like *You'll get over it* or *He's in a better place.*

11

Alice's shrieks woke Clay from a confused but not unpleasant dream of being in the Bingo Tent at the Akron State Fair. In the dream he was six again – maybe even younger but surely no older – and crouched beneath the long table where his mother was seated, looking at a forest of lady-legs and smelling sweet sawdust while the caller intoned, 'B-12, players, B-12! It's the *sunshine* vitamin!'

There was one moment when his subconscious mind tried to integrate the girl's cries into the dream by insisting he was hearing the Saturday noon whistle, but only a moment. Clay had let himself go to sleep on Tom's porch after an hour of watching because he was convinced that nothing was going to happen out there, at least not tonight. But he must have been equally convinced that Alice wouldn't sleep through, because there was no real confusion once his mind identified her shrieks for what they were, no groping for where he was or what was going on. At one moment he was a small boy crouching under a bingo table in Ohio; at the next he was rolling off the comfortably long couch on Tom McCourt's enclosed front porch with the comforter still wrapped around his lower legs. And somewhere in the house, Alice Maxwell, howling in a register almost high enough to burst crystal, articulated all the horror of the day just past, insisting with one scream after another that such things surely could not have happened and must be denied.

Clay tried to rid his lower legs of the comforter and at first it wouldn't let go. He found himself hopping toward the inside door and pulling at it in a kind of panic while he looked out at Salem Street, sure that lights would start going on up and down the block even though he knew the power was out, sure that someone – maybe the gun-owning, gadget-loving Mr Nickerson from up the street – would come out on his lawn and yell for someone to for chrissake shut that kid up. *Don't make me come down there!* Arnie Nickerson would yell. *Don't make me come down there and shoot her!*

Or her screams would draw the phone-crazies like moths to a bug-light. Tom might think they were dead, but Clay believed it no more than he believed in Santa's workshop at the North Pole.

But Salem Street – their block of it, anyway, just west of the town center and below the part of Malden Tom had called Granada Highlands – remained dark and silent and without movement. Even the glow of the fire from Revere seemed to have diminished.

Clay finally rid himself of the comforter and went inside and stood at the foot of the stairs, looking up into the blackness. Now he could hear Tom's voice – not the words, but the tone, low and calm and soothing. The girl's chilling shrieks began to be broken up by gasps for breath, then by sobs and inarticulate cries that became words. Clay caught one of them, *nightmare*. Tom's voice went on and on, telling lies in a reassuring drone: everything was all right, she would see, things would look better in the morning. Clay could picture them sitting side by side on the guestroom bed, each dressed in a pair of pajamas with **TM** monograms on the breast pockets. He could have drawn them like that. The idea made him smile.

When he was convinced she wasn't going to resume screaming, he went back to the porch, which was a bit chilly but not uncomfortable once he was wrapped up snugly in the comforter. He sat on the couch, surveying what he could see of the street. To the left, east of Tom's house, was a business district. He thought he could see the traffic light marking the entrance into the town square. The other way – which was the way they'd come – more houses. All of them still in this deep trench of night.

'Where are you?' he murmured. 'Some of you headed north or west, and still in your right minds. But where did the rest of you go?'

No answer from the street. Hell, maybe Tom was right – the cell phones had sent them a message to go crazy at three and drop dead at eight. It seemed too good to be true, but he remembered feeling the same way about recordable CDs.

Silence from the street in front of him; silence from the house behind him. After a while, Clay leaned back on the couch and let his eyes close. He thought he might doze, but doubted he would actually go to sleep again. Eventually, however, he did, and this time there were no dreams. Once, shortly before first light, a mongrel dog came up Tom McCourt's front walk, looked in at him as he lay snoring in his cocoon of comforter, and then moved on. It was in no hurry; pickings were rich in Malden that morning and would be for some time to come.

12

'Clay. Wake up.'

A hand, shaking him. Clay opened his eyes and saw Tom, dressed in a pair of blue jeans and a gray work-shirt, bending over him. The front porch was lit by strong pale light. Clay glanced at his wristwatch as he swung his feet off the couch and saw it was twenty past six.

'You need to see this,' Tom said. He looked pale, anxious, and grizzled on both sides of his mustache. The tail of his shirt was untucked on one side and his hair was still standing up in back.

Clay looked at Salem Street, saw a dog with something in its mouth trotting past a couple of dead cars half a block west, saw nothing else moving. He could smell a faint smoky funk in the air and supposed it was either Boston or Revere. Maybe both, but at least the wind had died. He turned his gaze to Tom.

'Not out here,' Tom said. He kept his voice low. 'In the backyard. I saw when I went in the kitchen to make coffee before I remembered coffee's out, at least for the time being. Maybe it's nothing, but . . . man, I don't like this.'

'Is Alice still sleeping?' Clay was groping under the comforter for his socks.

'Yes, and that's good. Never mind your socks and shoes, this ain't dinner at the Ritz. Come on.'

He followed Tom, who was wearing a pair of comfort-able-looking scuffs, down the hall to the kitchen. A half-finished glass of iced tea was standing on the counter.

Tom said, 'I can't get started without some caffeine in the morning, you know? So I poured myself a glass of that stuff – help yourself, by the way, it's still nice and cold – and I pushed back the curtain over the sink to take a look out at my garden. No reason, just wanted to touch base with the outside world. And I saw . . . but look for yourself.'

Clay peered out through the window over the sink. There was a neat little brick patio behind the house with a gas grill on it. Beyond the patio was Tom's yard, half-grass and half-garden. At the back was a high board fence with a gate in it. The gate was open. The bolt holding it closed must have been shot across because it now hung askew, looking to Clay like a broken wrist. It occurred to him that Tom could have made coffee on the gas grill, if not for the man sitting in his garden beside what had to be an ornamental wheel-barrow, eating the soft inside of a split pumpkin and spitting out the seeds. He was wearing a mechanic's coverall and a greasy cap with a faded letter *B* on it. Written in faded red script on the left breast of his coverall was *George*. Clay could hear the soft smooching sounds his face made every time he dived into the pumpkin.

'Fuck,' Clay said in a low voice. 'It's one of them.'

'Yes. And where there's one there'll be more.'

'Did he break the gate to get in?'

'Of course he did,' Tom said. 'I didn't see him do it, but it was locked when I left yesterday, you can depend on that. I don't have the world's best relationship with Scottoni, the guy who lives on the other side. He has no use for "fellas like me," as he's told me on several occasions.' He paused, then went on in a lower voice. He had been speaking quietly to begin with, and now Clay had to lean toward him to hear him. 'You know what's crazy? I *know* that guy. He works at Sonny's Texaco, down in the Center. It's the only gas station in town that still does repairs. Or did. He replaced a radiator hose for me once. Told me about how he and his brother made a trip to Yankee Stadium last year, saw Curt Schilling beat the Big Unit. Seemed like a nice enough guy. Now look at him! Sitting in my garden eating a raw pumpkin!'

'What's going on, you guys?' Alice asked from behind them.

Tom turned around, looking dismayed. 'You don't want to see this,' he said.

'That won't work,' Clay said. 'She's got to see it.'

He smiled at Alice, and it wasn't that hard to smile. There was no monogram on the pocket of the pajamas Tom had loaned her, but they were blue, just as he had imagined, and she looked most dreadfully cute in them, with her feet bare and the pants legs rolled up to her shins and her hair tousled with sleep. In spite of her nightmares, she looked better rested than Tom. Clay was willing to bet she looked better rested than he did, too.

'It's not a car wreck, or anything,' he said. 'Just a guy eating a pumpkin in Tom's backyard.'

She stood between them, putting her hands on the lip of the sink and rising up on the balls of her feet to look out. Her arm brushed Clay's, and he could feel the sleep-warmth still radiating from her skin. She looked for a long time, then turned to Tom.

'You said they all killed themselves,' she said, and Clay couldn't tell if she was accusing or mock scolding. *She probably doesn't know herself,* he thought.

'I didn't say for sure,' Tom replied, sounding lame.

'You sounded pretty sure to me.' She looked out again. At least, Clay thought, she wasn't freaking out. In fact he thought she looked remarkably composed − if a little Chaplinesque − in her slightly outsize pajamas. 'Uh . . . guys?'

'What?' they said together.

'Look at the little wheelbarrow he's sitting next to. Look at the wheel.'

Clay had already seen what she was talking about − the litter of pumpkin-shell, pumpkin-meat, and pumpkin seeds.

'He smashed the pumpkin on the wheel to break it

open and get to what's inside,' Alice said. 'I guess he's one of them—'

'Oh, he's one of them, all right,' Clay said. George the mechanic was sitting in the garden with his legs apart, allowing Clay to see that since yesterday afternoon he'd forgotten all his mother had taught him about dropping trou before you did number one.

'—but he used that wheel as a *tool*. That doesn't seem so crazy to me.'

'One of them was using a knife yesterday,' Tom said. 'And there was another guy jabbing a couple of car aerials.'

'Yes, but . . . this seems different, somehow.'

'More peaceful, you mean?' Tom glanced back at the intruder in his garden. 'I wouldn't want to go out there and find out.'

'No, not that. I don't mean peaceful. I don't know exactly how to explain it.'

Clay thought he had an idea of what she was talking about. The aggression they had witnessed yesterday had been a blind, forward-rushing thing. An anything-that-comes-to-hand thing. Yes, there had been the businessman with the knife and the muscular young guy jabbing the car aerials in the air as he ran, but there had also been the man in the park who'd torn off the dog's ear with his teeth. Pixie Light had also used her teeth. This seemed a lot different, and not just because it was about eating instead of killing. But like Alice, Clay couldn't put his finger on just *how* it was different.

'Oh God, two more,' Alice said.

Through the open back gate came a woman of about forty in a dirty gray pants suit and an elderly man dressed in jogging shorts and a T-shirt with GRAY POWER printed across the front. The woman in the pants suit had been wearing a green blouse that now hung in tatters, revealing the cups of a pale green bra beneath. The elderly man was limping badly, throwing his elbows out in a kind of buck-and-wing with

105

each step to keep his balance. His scrawny left leg was caked with dried blood, and that foot was missing its running shoe. The remains of an athletic sock, grimed with dirt and blood, flapped from his left ankle. The elderly man's longish white hair hung around his vacant face in a kind of cowl. The woman in the pants suit was making a repetitive noise that sounded like *'Goom! Goom!'* as she surveyed the yard and the garden. She looked at George the Pumpkin Eater as though he were of no account at all, then strode past him toward the remaining cucumbers. Here she knelt, snatched one from its vine, and began to munch. The old man in the GRAY POWER shirt marched to the edge of the garden and then only stood there awhile like a robot that has finally run out of juice. He was wearing tiny gold glasses – reading glasses, Clay thought – that gleamed in the early light. He looked to Clay like someone who had once been very smart and was now very stupid.

The three people in the kitchen crowded together, staring out the window, hardly breathing.

The old man's gaze settled on George, who threw away a piece of pumpkin-shell, examined the rest, and then ploughed his face back in and resumed his breakfast. Far from behaving aggressively toward the newcomers, he seemed not to notice them at all.

The old man limped forward, bent, and began to tug at a pumpkin the size of a soccer ball. He was less than three feet from George. Clay, remembering the pitched battle outside the T station, held his breath and waited.

He felt Alice grasp his arm. All the sleep-warmth had departed her hand. 'What's he going to do?' she asked in a low voice.

Clay only shook his head.

The old man tried to bite the pumpkin and only bumped his nose. It should have been funny but wasn't. His glasses were knocked askew and he pushed them back into place. It was a gesture so normal that for a brief moment Clay felt all but positive that *he* was the one who was crazy.

'*Goom!*' cried the woman in the tattered blouse, and threw away her half-eaten cucumber. She had spied a few late tomatoes and crawled toward them with her hair hanging in her face. The seat of her pants was badly soiled.

The old man had spied the ornamental wheelbarrow. He took his pumpkin to it, then seemed to register George, sitting there beside it. He looked at him, head cocked. George gestured with one orange-coated hand at the wheelbarrow, a gesture Clay had seen a thousand times.

'Be my guest,' Tom murmured. 'I'll be damned.'

The old man fell on his knees in the garden, a movement that obviously caused him considerable pain. He grimaced, raised his lined face to the brightening sky, and uttered a chuffing grunt. Then he lifted the pumpkin over the wheel. He studied the line of descent for several moments, elderly biceps trembling, and brought the pumpkin down, smashing it open. It fell in two meaty halves. What happened next happened fast. George dropped his own mostly eaten pumpkin in his lap, rocked forward, grabbed the old man's head in his big, orange-stained hands, and twisted it. They heard the crack of the old man's breaking neck even through the glass. His long white hair flew. His small spectacles disappeared into what Clay thought were beets. His body spasmed once, then went limp. George dropped it. Alice began to scream and Tom covered her mouth with his hand. Her eyes, bulging with terror, peered over the top of it. Outside in the garden, George picked up a fresh chunk of pumpkin and began calmly to eat.

The woman in the shredded blouse looked around for a moment, casually, then plucked another tomato and bit into it. Red juice ran from her chin and trickled down the dirty line of her throat. She and George sat there in Tom McCourt's backyard garden, eating vegetables, and for some reason the name of one of his favourite paintings popped into Clay's mind: *The Peaceable Kingdom.*

He didn't realize he'd spoken aloud until Tom looked at him bleakly and said: 'Not anymore.'

13

The three of them were still standing there at the kitchen window five minutes later when an alarm began to bray at some distance. It sounded tired and hoarse, as though it would run down soon.

'Any idea what that might be?' Clay asked. In the garden, George had abandoned the pumpkins and dug up a large potato. This had brought him closer to the woman, but he showed no interest in her. At least not yet.

'My best guess would be that the generator at the Safeway in the Center just gave up,' Tom said. 'There's probably a battery-powered alarm in case that happens, because of all the perishables. But that's only a guess. For all I know, it's the First Malden Bank and T—'

'Look!' Alice said.

The woman stopped in the act of plucking another tomato, got up, and walked toward the east side of Tom's house. George got to his feet as she passed, and Clay was sure he meant to kill her as he had the old man. He winced in anticipation and saw Tom reaching for Alice, to turn her away. But George only followed the woman, disappearing around the corner of the house behind her.

Alice turned and hurried toward the kitchen door.

'Don't let them see you!' Tom called in a low, urgent voice, and went after her.

'Don't worry,' she said.

Clay followed, worrying for all of them.

They reached the dining room door in time to watch the woman in her filthy pants suit and George in his even filthier coverall pass beyond the dining room window, their bodies broken into segments by venetian blinds which had been dropped but not closed. Neither of them glanced toward the house, and now George was so close behind the woman that he could have bitten the nape of her neck. Alice, followed by Tom and Clay, moved up the hall to Tom's little office. Here the blinds *were* closed, but Clay saw the projected shadows of the two outside pass swiftly across them. Alice went on up the hall, toward where the door to the enclosed porch stood open. The comforter lay half on and half off the couch, as Clay had left it. The porch was flooded with brilliant morning sunshine. It seemed to burn on the boards.

'Alice, be careful!' Clay said. 'Be—'

But she had stopped. She was just looking. Then Tom was standing beside her, almost exactly the same height. Seen that way, they could have been brother and sister. Neither of them took any pains at all to avoid being seen.

'Holy fucking shit,' Tom said. He sounded as if the wind had been knocked out of him. Beside him, Alice began to cry. It was the sort of out-of-breath weeping a tired child might make. One who is becoming used to punishment.

Clay caught up. The woman in the pants suit was cutting across Tom's lawn. George was still behind her, matching her stride for stride. They were almost in lockstep. That broke a little bit at the curb when George swung out to her left, becoming her wingman instead of her back door.

Salem Street was full of crazy people.

Clay's first assessment was that there might be a thousand or more. Then the observer part of him took over – the coldhearted artist's eye – and he realized that was a wild over-estimate, prompted by surprise at seeing anyone at all on what he had expected would be an empty street, and shock at realizing they were all *them*. There was no mistaking the vacant faces, the eyes that seemed to look beyond everything, the dirty, bloody, disheveled clothing (in several cases no clothing at all), the occasional cawing cry or jerky gesture. There was the man dressed only in tighty-whity undershorts and a polo shirt who seemed to be saluting repeatedly; the heavyset woman whose lower lip was split and hung in two beefy flaps, revealing all of her lower teeth; the tall teenage boy in blue jeans shorts who walked up the center of Salem Street carrying what looked like a blood-caked tire-iron in one hand; an Indian or Pakistani gentleman who passed Tom's house wriggling his jaw from side to side and simultaneously chattering his teeth; a boy – dear God, a boy Johnny's age – who walked with absolutely no sign of pain although one arm was flapping below the knob of his dislocated shoulder; a pretty young woman in a short skirt and a shell top who appeared to be eating from the red stomach of a crow. Some moaned, some made vocal noises that might once have been words, and all were moving east. Clay had no idea if they were being drawn by the braying alarm or the smell of food, but they were all walking in the direction of Malden Center.

'Christ, it's zombie heaven,' Tom said.

Clay didn't bother answering. The people out there weren't exactly zombies, but Tom was pretty close, just the same. *If any of them looks over here, sees us and decides to come after us, we're done. We won't have a hope in hell. Not even if we barricade ourselves in the cellar. And getting those guns across the street? You can forget that.*

The idea that his wife and son might be – very likely *were* – having to deal with creatures such as these filled him with dread. But this was no comic book and he was no hero: he was helpless. The three of them might be safe in the house, but as far as the immediate future was concerned, it didn't look like he and Tom and Alice were going anywhere.

14

'They're like birds,' Alice said. She wiped the tears from her cheeks with the heels of her hands. 'A flock of birds.'

Clay saw what she meant at once and gave her an impulsive hug. She had put her finger on something that had first struck him as he'd watched George the mechanic follow the woman instead of killing her, as he had the old man. The two of them clearly vacant in the upper story, yet seeming to go out front by some unspoken agreement.

'I don't get it,' Tom said.

'You must have missed *March of the Penguins*,' Alice said.

'Actually, I did,' Tom said. 'When I want to see someone waddle in a tuxedo, I go to a French restaurant.'

'But haven't you ever noticed the way birds are, especially in the spring and fall?' Clay asked. 'You must have. They'll all light in the same tree or along the same telephone wire—'

'Sometimes so many they make it sag,' Alice said. 'Then they all fly at once. My dad says they must have a group leader, but Mr Sullivan in Earth Science – back in middle school, this was – told us it was a flock-mind thing, like ants all going out from a hill or bees from a hive.'

'The flock swoops right or left, all at the same time, and the individual birds never hit each other,' Clay said. 'Sometimes the sky's black with them and the noise is enough to drive you nuts.' He paused. 'At least out in the country, where I live.' He paused again. 'Tom, do you . . . do you recognize any of those people?'

'A few. That's Mr Potowami, from the bakery,' he said, pointing to the Indian man who was wriggling his jaw and chattering his teeth. 'That pretty young woman . . . I believe she works in the bank. And do you remember me mentioning Scottoni, the man who lives on the other side of the block from me?'

Clay nodded.

Tom, now very pale, pointed to a visibly pregnant woman dressed only in a food-stained smock that came down to her upper thighs. Blond hair hung against her pimply cheeks, and a stud gleamed in her nose. 'That's his daughter-in-law,' he said. 'Judy. She has gone out of her way to be kind to me.' He added in a dry, matter-of-fact tone: 'This breaks my heart.'

From the direction of the town center there came a loud gunshot. Alice cried out, but this time Tom didn't have to cover her mouth; she did it herself. None of the people in the street glanced over, in any case. Nor did the report – Clay thought it had been a shotgun – seem to disturb them. They just kept walking, no faster and no slower. Clay waited for another shot. Instead there was a scream, very brief, there and gone, as if cut off.

The three standing in the shadows just beyond the porch went on watching, not talking. All of the people who passed were going east, and although they did not precisely walk in formation, there was an unmistakable order about them. For Clay it was best expressed not in his view of the phone-crazies themselves, who often limped and sometimes shambled, who gibbered and made odd gestures, but in the silent, ordered passage of their shadows on the pavement. They made him think of World War II newsreel footage he'd seen, where wave after wave of bombers flew across the sky. He counted two hundred and fifty before giving up. Men, women, teenagers. Quite a few children Johnny's age, too. Far more children than old people, although he saw only a few kids younger than ten. He didn't like to think of what must have happened to the little guys and gals who'd had no one to take care of them when the Pulse occurred.

Or the little guys and gals who'd been in the care of people with cell phones.

As for the vacant-eyed children he could see, Clay wondered how many now passing before him had pestered their parents for cell phones with special ring-tones last year, as Johnny had.

'One mind,' Tom said presently. 'Do you really believe that?'

'*I* sort of do,' Alice said. 'Because . . . like . . . what mind do they have on their own?'

'She's right,' Clay said.

The migration (once you'd seen it that way it was hard to think of it as anything else) thinned but didn't stop, even after half an hour; three men would pass walking abreast –

one in a bowling shirt, one in the remains of a suit, one with his lower face mostly obliterated in a cake of dried gore – and then two men and a woman walking in a half-assed conga line, then a middle-aged woman who looked like a librarian (if you ignored one bare breast wagging in the wind, that was) walking in tandem with a half-grown, gawky girl who might have been a library aide. There would be a pause and then a dozen more would come, seeming almost to form a kind of hollow square, like a fighting unit from the Napoleonic Wars. And in the distance Clay began to hear warlike sounds – a sporadic rattle of rifle- or pistol-fire and once (and close, maybe from neighboring Medford or right here in Malden) the long, ripping roar of a large-caliber automatic weapon. Also, more screams. Most were distant, but Clay was pretty sure that was what they were.

There were still other sane people around these parts, plenty of them, and some *had* managed to get their hands on guns. Those people were very likely having themselves a phoner-shoot. Others, however, had not been lucky enough to have been indoors when the sun came up and the crazies came out. He thought of George the mechanic gripping the old man's head in his orange hands, the twist, the snap, the little reading glasses flying into the beets where they would stay. And stay. And stay.

'I think I want to go into the living room and sit down,' Alice said. 'I don't want to look at them anymore. Listen, either. It makes me sick.'

'Sure,' Clay said. 'Tom, why don't you—?'

'No,' Tom said. 'You go. I'll stay here and watch for a while. I think one of us *ought* to watch, don't you?'

Clay nodded. He did.

'Then, in an hour or so, you can spell me. Turn and turn about.'

'Okay. Done.'

As they started back down the hall, Clay with his arm around Alice's shoulders, Tom said: 'One thing.'

They looked back at him.

'I think we all ought to try and get as much rest as possible today. If we're still planning on going north, that is.'

Clay looked at him closely to make sure Tom was still in his right mind. He appeared to be, but—

'Have you been seeing what's going on out there?' he asked. 'Hearing the shooting? The . . .' He didn't want to say *the screams* with Alice there, although God knew it was a little late to be trying to protect her remaining sensibilities. '. . . the yelling?'

'Of course,' Tom said. 'But the nutters went inside *last* night, didn't they?'

For a moment neither Clay nor Alice moved. Then Alice began to pat her hands together in soft, almost silent applause. And Clay began to smile. The smile felt stiff and unfamiliar on his face, and the hope that went with it was almost painful.

'Tom, you might just be a genius,' he said.

Tom did not return the smile. 'Don't count on it,' he said. 'I never broke a thousand on the SATs.'

15

Clearly feeling better – and that had to be a good thing, Clay reckoned – Alice went upstairs to poke around in Tom's clothes for daywear. Clay sat on the couch, thinking about Sharon and Johnny, trying to decide what they would have done and where they would have gone, always supposing they'd been fortunate enough to get together. He fell into a doze and saw them clearly at Kent Pond Elementary, Sharon's school. They were barricaded in the gym with two or three dozen others, eating sandwiches from the cafeteria and drinking those little cartons of milk. They—

Alice roused him, calling from upstairs. He looked at his wristwatch and saw he'd been sleeping on the couch for almost twenty minutes. He'd drooled on his chin.

'Alice?' He went to the foot of the stairs. 'Everything okay?' Tom, he saw, was also looking.

'Yes, but can you come for a second?'

'Sure.' He looked at Tom, shrugged, then went upstairs.

Alice was in a guest bedroom that looked like it hadn't seen many guests, although the two pillows suggested that Tom had spent most of the night here with her, and the rumpled look of the bedclothes further suggested very bad rest. She had found a pair of khakis that almost fit and a sweatshirt with CANOBIE LAKE PARK written across the front below the outline of a roller coaster. On the floor was the sort of large portable sound system that Clay and his friends had once lusted after the way Johnny-Gee had lusted after that red cell phone. Clay and his friends had called such systems ghetto blasters or boomboxes.

'It was in the closet and the batteries look fresh,' she said. 'I thought of turning it on and looking for a radio station, but then I was afraid.'

He looked at the ghetto blaster sitting there on the guest room's nice hardwood floor, and he was afraid, too. It could have been a loaded gun. But he felt an urge to reach out and turn the selector-knob, now pointed at CD, to FM. He imagined Alice had felt the same urge, and that was why she'd called him. The urge to touch a loaded gun would have been no different.

'My sister gave me that two birthdays ago,' Tom said from the doorway, and they both jumped. 'I loaded it up with batteries last July and took it to the beach. When I was a kid we all used to go to the beach and listen to our radios, although I never had one that big.'

'Me either,' Clay said. 'But I wanted one.'

'I took it up to Hampton Beach in New Hampshire with a bunch of Van Halen and Madonna CDs, but it wasn't the same. Not even close. I haven't used it since. I imagine all the stations are off the air, don't you?'

'I bet some of them are still on,' Alice said. She was biting at her lower lip. Clay thought if she didn't stop soon, it would begin to bleed. 'The ones my friends call the robo-eighties stations. They have friendly names like BOB and FRANK, but they all come from some giant radio-computer in Colorado and then get beamed down by satellite. At least that's what my friends say. And . . .' She licked at the place she had been biting. It was shiny with blood just under the surface. 'And that's the same way cell phone signals get routed, isn't it? By satellite.'

'I don't know,' Tom said. 'I guess the long-distance ones might . . . and the transatlantic ones for sure . . . and I suppose the right genius could hack the wrong satellite signal into all those microwave towers you see . . . the ones that boost the signals along . . .'

Clay knew the towers he was talking about, steel skeletons with dishes stuck all over them like gray suckers. They had popped up everywhere over the last ten years.

Tom said, 'If we could pick up a local station, we might be able to get news. Some idea about what to do, where to go—'

'Yes, but what if it's on the radio, too?' Alice said. 'That's what *I'm* saying. What if you tune into whatever my –' She licked her lips again, then resumed nibbling— 'my mother heard? And my dad? Him, too, oh yes, he had a brand-new cell phone, all the bells and whistles – video, autodial, Internet connection – he *loved* that puppy!' She gave a laugh that was both hysterical and rueful, a dizzy combination. 'What if you tune into whatever *they* heard? My folks and them out there? Do you want to risk that?'

At first Tom said nothing. Then he said – cautiously, as if testing the idea – '*One* of us could risk it. The other two could leave and wait until—'

'No,' Clay said.

'*Please* no,' Alice said. She was almost crying again. 'I want you *both*. I need you *both*.'

They stood around the radio, looking at it. Clay found

himself thinking of science fiction novels he'd read as a teenager (sometimes at the beach, listening to Nirvana instead of Van Halen on the radio). In more than a few of them, the world ended. And then the heroes built it back up again. Not without struggles and setbacks, but yes, they used the tools and the technology and they built it back up again. He couldn't remember anywhere the heroes just stood around in a bedroom looking at a radio. *Sooner or later someone is going to pick up a tool or turn on a radio,* he thought, *because someone will have to.*

Yes. But not this morning.

Feeling like a traitor to something larger than he could understand, he picked up Tom's ghetto blaster, put it back in the closet, and closed the door.

16

An hour or so later, the orderly migration to the east began to collapse. Clay was on watch. Alice was in the kitchen, eating one of the sandwiches they'd brought out of Boston – she said they had to finish the sandwiches before they ate any of the canned stuff in Tom's closet-sized pantry, because none of them knew when they'd get fresh meat again – and Tom was sleeping in the living room, on the couch. Clay could hear him snoring contentedly away.

He noticed a few people wandering against the general easterly flow, then sensed a kind of slackening in the order out there in Salem Street, something so subtle that his brain registered what his eye saw only as an intuition. At first he dismissed it as a falsity caused by the few wanderers – even more deranged than the rest – who were heading west instead of east, and then he looked down at the shadows. The neat herringbone patterns he had observed earlier had begun to distort. And soon they weren't patterns at all.

More people were now heading west, and some of them were gnawing on food that had been liberated from a grocery store, probably the Safeway Tom had mentioned. Mr Scottoni's daughter-in-law, Judy, was carrying a gigantic tub of melting chocolate ice cream, which had covered the front of her smock and coated her from knees to nose-stud; her chocolate-lathered face made her look like Mrs Bones in a minstrel show. And any vegetarian beliefs Mr Potowami might once have held were gone now; he strolled along noshing from a great double handful of raw hamburger meat. A fat man in a dirty suit had what looked like a partially defrosted leg of lamb, and when Judy Scottoni tried to take it from him, the fat man hit her a vicious clip in the center of the forehead with it. She fell as silently as a poleaxed steer, pregnant belly first, on top of her mostly crushed tub of Breyers chocolate.

There was a great deal of milling now, and a good deal of violence to go with it, but no return to the all-out viciousness of the afternoon before. Not here, in any case. In Malden Center, the alarm, tired-sounding to begin with, had long since run down. In the distance, gunfire continued to pop sporadically, but there had been nothing close since that single shotgun blast from the center of town. Clay watched to see if any of the crazies would try breaking into any of the houses, but although they occasionally walked on the lawns, they showed no signs of graduating from trespass to burglary. What they did mostly was wander around, occasionally trying to grab one another's food, sometimes fighting or biting one another. Three or four – the Scottoni woman, for one – lay in the street, either dead or unconscious. Most of those who had passed Tom's house earlier were still in the town square, Clay guessed, having a street dance or maybe the First Annual Malden Raw Meat Festival, and thank God for that. It was strange, though, how that sense of purpose – that sense of *flocking* – had seemed to loosen and fall apart.

After noon, when he began to feel seriously sleepy, he went into the kitchen and found Alice dozing at the kitchen table with her head in her arms. The little sneaker, the one she had called a Baby Nike, was loosely clasped in one hand.

When he woke her, she looked at him groggily and clasped it to the breast of her sweatshirt, as if afraid he would try to take it away.

He asked if she could watch from the end of the hallway for a while without falling asleep again or being seen. She said she could. Clay took her at her word and carried a chair for her. She paused for a moment at the door to the living room. 'Check it out,' she said.

He looked in over her shoulder and saw the cat, Rafe, was sleeping on Tom's belly. He grunted in amusement.

She sat where he put the chair, far enough inside the door so someone who glanced at the house wouldn't see her. After a single look she said, 'They're not a flock anymore. What happened?'

'I don't know.'

'What time is it?'

He glanced at his watch. 'Twenty past twelve.'

'What time did we notice they *were* flocking?'

'I don't know, Alice.' He was trying to be patient with her but he could hardly keep his eyes open. 'Six-thirty? Seven? I don't know. Does it matter?'

'If we could chart them, it might matter a lot, don't you think?'

He told her that he'd think about that when he'd had some sleep. 'Couple of hours, then wake me or Tom,' he said. 'Sooner, if something goes wrong.'

'It couldn't go much wronger,' she said softly. 'Go on upstairs. You look really wasted.'

He went upstairs to the guest bedroom, slipped off his shoes, and lay down. He thought for a moment about what she'd said: *If we could chart them.* She might have something there. Odds against, but maybe—

It was a pleasant room, very pleasant, full of sun. You lay in a room like this and it was easy to forget there was a radio in the closet you didn't dare turn on. Not so easy to forget your wife, estranged but still loved, might be dead and your son – not just loved but adored – might be crazy. Still, the body had its imperatives, didn't it? And if there had ever been a room for an afternoon nap, this was the one. The panic-rat twitched but didn't bite, and Clay was asleep almost as soon as he closed his eyes.

17

This time Alice was the one who shook him awake. The little purple sneaker swung back and forth as she did it. She had tied it around her left wrist, turning it into a rather creepy talisman. The light in the room had changed. It was going the other way, and diminished. He had turned on his side and he had to urinate, a reliable sign that he had slept for some time. He sat up in a hurry and was surprised – almost appalled – to see it was quarter of six. He had slept for over five hours. But of course last night hadn't been his first night of broken rest; he'd slept poorly the night before, as well. Nerves, on account of his presentation to the Dark Horse comics people.

'Is everything all right?' he asked, taking her by the wrist. 'Why'd you let me sleep so long?'

'Because you needed it,' she said. 'Tom slept until two and I slept until four. We've been watching together since then. Come down and look. It's pretty amazing.'

'Are they flocking again?'

She nodded. 'But going the other way this time. And that's not all. Come and see.'

He emptied his bladder and hurried downstairs. Tom and Alice were standing in the doorway to the porch with their arms around each other's waist. There was no question of being seen, now; the sky had clouded over and Tom's porch was already thick with shadows. Only a few people were left on Salem Street, anyway. All of them were moving west, not quite running but going at a steady clip. A group of four went past in the street itself, marching over a sprawl of bodies and a litter of discarded food, which included the leg of lamb, now gnawed down to the bone, a great many torn-open cellophane bags and cardboard boxes, and a scattering of discarded fruits and vegetables. Behind them came a group of six, the ones on the end using the sidewalks. They didn't look at each other but were still so perfectly together that when they passed Tom's house they seemed for an instant to be only a single man, and Clay realized even their arms were swinging in unison. After them came a youth of maybe fourteen, limping along, bawling inarticulate cow-sounds, and trying to keep up.

'They left the dead and the totally unconscious ones,' Tom said, 'but they actually helped a couple who were stirring.'

Clay looked for the pregnant woman and didn't see her. 'Mrs Scottoni?'

'She was one of the ones they helped,' Tom said.

'So they're acting like people again.'

'Don't get that idea,' Alice said. 'One of the men they tried to help couldn't walk, and after he fell down a couple of times, one of the guys who'd been lifting him got tired of being a Boy Scout and just—'

'Killed him,' Tom said. 'Not with his hands, either, like the guy in the garden. With his teeth. Tore out his throat.'

'I saw what was going to happen and looked away,' Alice said, 'but I heard it. He . . . *squealed*.'

'Easy,' Clay said. He squeezed her arm gently. 'Take it easy.'

Now the street was almost entirely empty. Two more stragglers came along, and although they moved more or less side by side, both were limping so badly there was no sense of unison about them.

'Where are they going?' Clay asked.

'Alice thinks maybe inside,' Tom said, and he sounded excited. 'Before it gets dark. She could be right.'

'Where? *Where* are they going in? Have you seen any of them going into houses along this block?'

'No.' They said it together.

'They didn't all come back,' Alice said. 'No way did as many come back *up* Salem Street as went down this morning. So a lot are still in Malden Center, or beyond. They may have gravitated toward public buildings, like school gymnasiums . . .'

School gymnasiums. Clay didn't like the sound of that.

'Did you see that movie, *Dawn of the Dead*?' she asked.

'Yes,' Clay said. 'You're not going to tell me someone let *you* in to see it, are you?'

She looked at him as if he were nuts. Or old. 'One of my friends had the DVD. We watched it at a sleepover back in eighth grade.' *Back when the Pony Express still rode and the plains were dark with buffalo,* her tone said. 'In that movie, all the dead people – well, not all, but a lot – went back to the mall when they woke up.'

Tom McCourt goggled at her for a second, then burst out laughing. It wasn't a little laugh, either, but a long series of guffaws, laughter so hard he had to lean against the wall for support, and Clay thought it wise to shut the door between the hall and the porch. There was no telling how well the things straggling up the street might hear; all he could think of at the moment was that the hearing of the lunatic narrator in Poe's 'The Tell-Tale Heart' had been extremely keen.

'Well they *did*,' Alice said, putting her hands on her hips. The baby sneaker flopped. 'Straight to the mall.' Tom laughed even harder. His knees buckled and he oozed slowly down to the hall floor, howling and flapping his hands against his shirt.

'They *died* . . .' he gasped, '. . . and came *back* . . . to go to the *mall*. Jesus Christ, does Jerry F-*Falwell* . . .' He went off into another gale. Tears were now running down his cheeks in clear streams. He brought himself under control enough to finish, 'Does Jerry Falwell know heaven's the Newcastle Mall?'

Clay also began to laugh. So did Alice, although Clay thought she was a little bit pissed off that her reference had been greeted not with interest or even mild good humor but outright howls. Still, when people started laughing, it was hard not to join in. Even when you were pissed.

They had almost stopped when Clay said, apropos of nothing, 'If heaven ain't a lot like Dixie, I don't want to go.'

That set them off again, all three. Alice was still laughing when she said, 'If they're flocking, then roosting for the night in gyms and churches and malls, people could machine-gun them by the hundreds.'

Clay stopped laughing first. Then Tom stopped. He looked at her, wiping moisture out of his neat little mustache.

Alice nodded. The laughter had brought high color to her cheeks, and she was still smiling. She had, at least for the moment, careened past pretty and into genuine beauty. 'By the thousands, maybe, if they're all going to the same place.'

'Jesus,' Tom said. He took off his glasses and began to wipe them, too. 'You don't fool around.'

'It's survival,' Alice said matter-of-factly. She looked down at the sneaker tied to her wrist, then up at the men. She nodded again. 'We ought to chart them. Find out *if* they're flocking and *when* they're flocking. *If* they're roosting and *where* they're roosting. Because if they can be charted—'

18

Clay had led them out of Boston, but when the three of them left the house on Salem Street some twenty-four hours later, fifteen-year-old Alice Maxwell was unquestionably in charge. The more Clay thought about it, the less it surprised him.

Tom McCourt didn't lack for what his British cousins called bottle, but he was not and never would be a natural leader. Clay had some leadership qualities, but that evening Alice had an advantage beyond her intelligence and desire to survive: she had suffered her losses and begun to move on. In leaving the house on Salem Street, both men were dealing with new ones. Clay had begun to suffer a rather frightening depression that at first he thought was just the result of his decision – unavoidable, really – to leave his portfolio behind. As the night went on, however, he realised it was a profound dread of what he might find if and when he got to Kent Pond.

For Tom, it was simpler. He hated to leave Rafe.

'Prop the door open for him,' Alice said – the new and harder Alice, who seemed more decisive by the minute. 'He'll almost certainly be okay, Tom. He'll find plenty of forage. It'll be a long time before the cats starve or the phone-crazies work their way down the food-chain to cat-meat.'

'He'll go feral,' Tom said. He was sitting on the living room couch, looking stylish and miserable in a belted rain-coat and trilby hat. Rafer was on his lap, purring and looking bored.

'Yeah, that's what they do,' Clay said. 'Think of all the dogs – the little ones and the oversized ones – that are just going to flat die.'

'I've had him for a long time. Since he was a kitten, really.' He looked up and Clay saw the man was on the verge of tears. 'Also, I guess I see him as my luck. My mojo. He saved my life, remember.'

'Now we're your mojo,' Clay said. He didn't want to point out that he himself had almost certainly saved Tom's life once already, but it was true. 'Right, Alice?'

'Yep,' she said. Tom had found a poncho for her, and she wore a knapsack on her back, although there currently was nothing in it but batteries for the flashlights . . . and, Clay was quite sure, that creepy little sneaker, which was at least no longer tied to her wrist. Clay was also carrying batteries in his pack, along with the Coleman lantern. They had nothing else, at Alice's suggestion. She said there was no reason for them to carry what they could pick up along the way. 'We're the Three Musketeers, Tom – all for one and one for all. Now let's go over to the Nicklebys' house and see if we can get some muskets.'

'Nickerson.' He was still stroking the cat.

She was smart enough – and compassionate enough, maybe that, too – not to say something like *Whatever,* but Clay could see she was getting low in the patience department. He said, 'Tom. Time to go.'

'Yeah, I suppose.' He started to put the cat aside, then picked it up and kissed it firmly between the ears. Rafe bore it with no more than a slight narrowing of the eyes. Tom put it down on the sofa and stood. 'Double rations in the kitchen by the stove, kiddo,' he said. 'Plus a big bowl of milk, with the rest of the half 'n' half poured in for good measure. Back door's open. Try to remember where home is, and maybe . . . hey, maybe I'll see you.'

The cat jumped down and walked out of the room toward the kitchen with its tail up. And, true to its kind, it never looked back.

Clay's portfolio, bent and with a horizontal wrinkle running both ways from the knife-slash in the middle, leaned against the living room wall. He glanced at it on the way by and resisted an urge to touch it. He thought briefly of the people inside he'd lived with so long, both in his little studio and in the much wider (or so he liked to flatter himself) reaches of his imagination: Wizard Flak, Sleepy Gene, Jumping Jack Flash, Poison Sally. And the Dark Wanderer, of course. Two days ago he'd thought that maybe they were going to be stars. Now they had a hole running through them and Tom McCourt's cat for company.

He thought of Sleepy Gene leaving town on Robbie the Robo-Cayuse, saying *S-So l-long b-boys! Meb-Meb-Mebbe I'll b-be back this w-w-way again!*

'So long, boys,' he said out loud – a little self-conscious but not very. It was the end of the world, after all. As farewells went, it wasn't much, but it would have to do . . . and as

Sleepy Gene might also have said, *It sh-sh-sure beats a p-poke in the eye with a ruh-ruh-rusty b-brandin'-arn.*

Clay followed Alice and Tom out onto the porch, into the sound of soft autumn rain.

19

Tom had his trilby, there was a hood on Alice's poncho, and Tom had found Clay a Red Sox cap that would keep his head dry for a while, at least, if the light rain didn't get heavier. And if it did . . . well, forage shouldn't be a problem, as Alice had pointed out. That would surely include foul-weather gear. From the slight elevation of the porch they could see roughly two blocks of Salem Street. It was impossible to be sure in the failing light, but it appeared completely deserted except for a few bodies and the food-litter the crazies had left behind.

Each of them was wearing a knife seated in scabbards Clay had made. If Tom was right about the Nickersons, they would soon be able to do better. Clay hoped so. He might be able to use the butcher knife from Soul Kitchen again, but he still wasn't sure he would be able to use it in cold blood.

Alice held a flashlight in her left hand. She looked to make sure Tom had one, too, and nodded. 'Okay,' she said. 'You take us to the Nickerson house, right?'

'Right,' Tom said.

'And if we see someone on our way there, we stop right away and put our lights on them.' She looked at Tom, then Clay, with some anxiety. They had been over this before. Clay guessed she probably obsessed the same way before big tests . . . and of course this was a very big one.

'Right,' Tom said. 'We say, "Our names are Tom, Clay, and Alice. We're normal. What are your names?"'

Clay said, 'If they have flashlights like us, we can almost assume—'

'We can't *assume* anything,' she said restlessly, querulously. 'My father says *assume* makes an ass out of you *and* me. Get it, *u* and—'

'I get it,' Clay said.

Alice brushed at her eyes, although whether to wipe away rain or tears Clay wasn't sure. He wondered, briefly and painfully, if Johnny was somewhere crying for him, right now. Clay hoped he was. He hoped his son was still capable of tears. Of memory.

'If they can answer, if they can say their names, they're fine, and they're probably safe,' Alice said. 'Right?'

'Right,' Clay said.

'Yeah,' Tom agreed, a little absently. He was looking at the street where there were no people and no bobbing flashlight beams, near or far.

Someplace in the distance, gunshots popped. They sounded like fireworks. The air stank of burning and char and had all day. Clay thought they were smelling it more strongly now because it was wet. He wondered how long before the smell of decaying flesh turned the fug hanging over greater Boston into a reek. He supposed it depended on how warm the days ahead turned out to be.

'If we meet normal people and they ask us what we're doing or where we're going, remember the story,' she said.

'We're looking for survivors,' Tom said.

'That's right. Because they're our friends and neighbours. Any people we meet will just be passing through. They'll want to keep moving. Later on we'll probably want to hook up with other normal people, because there's safety in numbers, but right now—'

'Right now we'd like to get to those guns,' Clay said. 'If there are any guns to get. Come on, Alice, let's do this.'

She looked worriedly at him. 'What's wrong? What am I missing? You can tell me, I know I'm just a kid.'

Patiently – as patiently as he could with nerves that felt like overtuned guitar-strings – Clay said, 'There's nothing wrong with it, honey. I just want to get rolling. I don't think we're going to see anyone, anyway. I think it's too soon.'

'I hope you're right,' she said. 'My hair's a mess and I've chipped a nail.'

They looked at her silently for a moment, then laughed. After that it was better among them, and stayed better until the end.

20

'No,' Alice said. She made a gagging sound. 'No. No, I can't.' A louder gagging sound. Then: 'I'm going to throw up. I'm sorry.'

She plunged out of the Coleman's glare and into the gloom of the Nickersons' living room, which adjoined the kitchen via a wide arch. Clay heard a soft thump as she went to her knees on the carpet, then more gagging. A pause, a gasp, and then she was vomiting. He was almost relieved.

'Oh Christ,' Tom said. He pulled in a long, gasping breath and this time spoke in a wavering exhalation that was nearly a howl. 'Oh *Chriiiiiist*.'

'Tom,' Clay said. He saw how the little man was swaying on his feet and understood he was on the verge of fainting. Why not? These bloody leavings had been his neighbours.

'*Tom!*' He stepped between Tom and the two bodies on the kitchen floor, between Tom and most of the splattered blood, which looked as black as India ink in the Coleman's unforgiving white glare. He tapped the side of Tom's face with his free hand. '*Don't pass out!*' And when he saw Tom steady on his feet, he dropped his voice a little. 'Go on in the other room and take care of Alice. I'll take care of the kitchen.'

'Why would you want to go in there?' Tom asked. 'That's Beth Nickerson with her brains . . . her b-brains all over . . .' He swallowed. There was an audible click in his throat. 'Most of her face is gone, but I recognize the blue jumper with the white snowflakes on it. And that's Heidi on the floor by the center island. Their daughter. I recognize *her*, even with . . .' He shook his head, as if to clear it, then repeated: 'Why would you *want* to?'

'I'm pretty sure I see what we came for,' Clay said. He was astounded by how calm he sounded.

'In the *kitchen*?'

Tom tried to look past him and Clay moved to block his view. 'Trust me. You see to Alice. If she can, you two start looking around for more guns. Shout if you hit paydirt. And be careful, Mr Nickerson may be here, too. I mean, we could assume he was at work when all this went down, but as Alice's dad says—'

'Assume makes an ass out of you *and* me,' Tom said. He managed a sickly smile. 'Gotcha.' He started to turn away, then turned back. 'I don't care where we go, Clay, but I don't want to stay here any longer than we have to. I didn't exactly love Arnie and Beth Nickerson, but they were my neighbors. And they treated me a hell of a lot better than that idiot Scottoni from around the block.'

'Understood.'

Tom snapped on his flashlight and went into the Nickerson living room. Clay heard him murmuring to Alice, comforting her.

Steeling himself, Clay walked into the kitchen with the Coleman lantern held up, stepping around the puddles of blood on the hardwood floor. It had dried now, but he still didn't want to put his shoes in any more of it than he had to.

The girl lying on her back by the center island had been tall, but both her pigtails and the angular lines of her body suggested a child two or three years younger than Alice. Her head was cocked at a strenuous angle, almost a parody of interrogation, and her dead eyes bulged. Her hair had been broomstraw-blond, but all of it on the left side of her head – the side that had taken the blow which had killed her – was now the same dark maroon as the stains on the floor.

Her mother reclined below the counter to the right of the stove, where the handsome cherrywood cabinets came together to form a corner. Her hands were ghost-white with flour and her bloody, bitten legs were indecorously splayed. Once, before starting work on a limited-run comic called *Battle Hell,* Clay had accessed a selection of fatal-gunshot photos on the Web, thinking there might be something he could use. There was not. Gunshot wounds spoke a terrible blank language of their own, and here it was again. Beth Nickerson was mostly spray and gristle from her left eye on up. Her right eye had drifted into the upper orbit of its socket, as if she had died trying to look into her own head. Her back hair and a good deal of her brain-matter was caked on the cherrywood cabinet against which she had leaned in her brief moments of dying. A few flies were buzzing around her.

Clay began to gag. He turned his head and covered his mouth. He told himself he had to control himself. In the other room Alice had stopped vomiting – in fact he could hear her and Tom talking together as they moved deeper into the house – and he didn't want to get her going again.

Think of them as dummies, props in a movie, he told himself, but he knew he could never do that.

When he looked back, he looked at the other things on the floor instead. That helped. The gun he had already seen. The kitchen was spacious and the gun was all the way on the other side, lying between the fridge and one of the cabinets with the barrel sticking out. His first impulse on seeing the dead woman and the dead girl had been to avert his eyes; they'd happened on the gun-barrel purely by accident.

But maybe I would have known there had to be a gun.

He even saw where it had been: a wall-mounted clip between the built-in TV and the industrial-size can-opener. *They were gadget-nuts as well as gun-nuts,* Tom had said, and a wall-mounted pistol in your kitchen just waiting to leap into your hand . . . why, if that wasn't the best of both worlds, what was?

'Clay?' That was Alice. Coming from some distance.

'What?'

There followed the sound of feet quickly ascending a set of stairs, then Alice called from the living room. 'Tom said you wanted to know if we hit paydirt. We just did. There must be a dozen guns downstairs in the den. Rifles and pistols both. They're in a cabinet with an alarm-company sticker on it, so we'll probably get arrested . . . that's a joke. Are you coming?'

'In a minute, hon. Don't come out here.'

'Don't worry. Don't *you* stay there and get grossed out.'

He was beyond grossed out, far beyond. There were two other objects lying on the bloody hardwood floor of the Nickerson kitchen. One was a rolling pin, which made sense. There was a pie tin, a mixing bowl, and a cheery yellow canister marked FLOUR sitting on the center island. The other object on the floor, this one lying not too distant from one of Heidi Nickerson's hands, was a cell phone only a teenager could love, blue with big orange daisy decals plastered all over it.

Clay could *see* what had happened, little as he wanted to. Beth Nickerson is making a pie. Does she know something awful has started to happen in greater Boston, in America, maybe in the world? Is it on TV? If so, the TV didn't send her a crazygram, Clay was sure of that.

Her daughter got one, though. Oh yes. And Heidi attacked her mother. Did Beth Nickerson try to reason with her daughter before driving her to the floor with a blow from the rolling pin, or did she just strike? Not in hate, but in pain and fear? In any case, it wasn't enough. And Beth wasn't wearing pants. She was wearing a jumper, and her legs were bare.

Clay pulled down the dead woman's skirt. He did it

gently, covering the plain working-at-home underwear that she had soiled at the end.

Heidi, surely no older than fourteen and perhaps only twelve, must have been growling in that savage nonsense-language they seemed to learn all at once after they got a full dose of Sane-B-Gone from their phones, saying things like *rast* and *eelah* and *kazzalah-CAN!* The first blow from the rolling pin had knocked her down but not out, and the madgirl had begun to work on her mother's legs. Not little nips, either, but deep, searing bites, some that had driven all the way to the bone. Clay could see not only toothmarks but ghostly tattoos that must have been left by young Heidi's braces. And so – probably screaming, undoubtedly in agony, almost certainly not aware of what she was doing – Beth Nickerson had struck again, this time much harder. Clay could almost hear the muffled crack as the girl's neck broke. Beloved daughter, dead on the floor of the state-of-the-art kitchen, with braces on her teeth and her state-of-the-art cell phone by one outstretched hand.

And had her mother stopped to consider before popping the gun from its clip between the TV and the can-opener, where it had been waiting who knew how long for a burglar or rapist to appear in this clean, well-lighted kitchen? Clay thought not. Clay thought there would have been no pause, that she would have wanted to catch up with her daughter's fleeing soul while the explanation for what she had done was still fresh on her lips.

Clay went to the gun and picked it up. From a gadget-boy like Arnie Nickerson he would have expected an automatic – maybe even one with a laser sight – but this was a plain old Colt .45 revolver. He supposed it made sense. His wife might feel more comfortable with this kind of gun; no nonsense about making sure it was loaded if the gun was needed (or wasting time fishing a clip out from behind the spatulas or spices if it wasn't), then racking the slide to make sure there was a hot one in the chamber. No, with this old whore you just had to swing the barrel out, which Clay did with ease. He'd drawn a thousand variations of this very gun for Dark Wanderer. As he'd expected, only one of the six chambers was empty. He shook out one of the other loads, knowing just what he would find. Beth Nickerson's .45 was loaded with highly illegal cop-killer bullets. Fraggers. No wonder the top of her head was gone. The wonder was that she had any left at all. He looked down at the remains of the woman leaning in the corner and began to cry.

'Clay?' That was Tom, coming up the stairs from the basement. 'Man, Arnie had *everything*! There's an automatic weapon that would have gotten him a stretch in Walpole, I bet . . . Clay? Are you all right?'

'I'm coming,' Clay said, wiping his eyes. He safetied the revolver and stuck it in his belt. Then he took off the knife and laid it on Beth Nickerson's counter, still in its homemade scabbard. It seemed they were trading up. 'Give me two more minutes.'

'Yo.'

Clay heard Tom clumping back to Arnie Nickerson's downstairs armoury and smiled in spite of the tears still running down his face. Here was something he would have to remember: give a nice little gay guy from Malden a roomful of guns to play with, he starts to say *yo* just like Sylvester Stallone.

Clay started going through drawers. In the third one he tried, he found a heavy red box marked **AMERICAN DEFENDER** .45 CALIBER **AMERICAN DEFENDER** 50 ROUNDS. It was under the dishtowels. He put the box in his pocket and went to join Tom and Alice. He wanted to get out of here now, and as quickly as possible. The trick would be getting them to go without trying to take Arnie Nickerson's entire gun collection along.

Halfway through the arch he paused and glanced back, holding the Coleman lantern high, looking at the bodies.

Pulling down the skirt of the woman's jumper hadn't helped much. They were still just corpses, their wounds as naked as Noah when his son had come upon him in liquor. He could find something to cover them with, but once he started covering bodies, where would it end? Where? With Sharon? With his son?

'God forbid,' he whispered, but he doubted that God would simply because he asked. He lowered the lantern and followed the dancing glow of flashlights downstairs to Tom and Alice.

21

They both wore belts with large-caliber handguns in the holsters, and these *were* automatics. Tom had also slung an ammunition bandolier over his shoulder. Clay didn't know whether to laugh or start crying again. Part of him felt like doing both at the same time. Of course if he did that, they would think he was having hysterics. And of course they would be right.

The plasma TV mounted on the wall down here was the big – very big – brother of the one in the kitchen. Another TV, only slightly smaller, had a multibrand videogame hookup Clay would, once upon a time, have loved to examine. To fawn over, maybe. As if to balance it off, a vintage Seeberg jukebox stood in the corner next to the Nickersons' Ping-Pong table, all its fabulous colors dark and dead. And of course there were the gun cabinets, two of them, still locked but with their glass fronts broken.

'There were locking-bars, but he had a toolbox in his garage,' Tom said. 'Alice used a wrench to break them off.'

'They were cookies,' Alice said modestly. 'This was in the garage behind the toolbox, wrapped in a piece of blanket. Is it what I think it is?' She picked it up off the Ping-Pong table, holding it carefully by the wire stock, and carried it over to Clay.

'Holy shit,' he said. 'This is . . .' He squinted at the embossing above the trigger-guard. 'I think it's Russian.'

'I'm sure it is,' Tom said. 'Do you think it's a Kalashnikov?'

'You got me. Are there bullets that match it? In boxes that match the printing on the gun, I mean?'

'Half a dozen. *Heavy* boxes. It's a machine gun, isn't it?'

'You might as well call it that, I guess.' Clay flicked a lever. 'I'm pretty sure one of these positions is single shot and the other is autofire.'

'How many rounds does it fire a minute?' Alice asked.

'I don't know,' Clay said, 'but I think it's rounds per *second.*'

'*Whoa.*' Her eyes got round. 'Can you figure out how to shoot it?'

'Alice – I'm pretty sure they teach sixteen-year-old farmboys how to shoot these. Yes, I can figure it out. It might take a box of ammo, but I can figure it out.' *Please God don't let it blow up in my hands,* he thought.

'Is something like that legal in Massachusetts?' she asked.

'It is now, Alice,' Tom said, not smiling. 'Is it time to go?'

'Yes,' she said, and then – perhaps still not entirely comfortable being the one to make the decisions – she looked at Clay.

'Yes,' he said. 'North.'

'Fine with me,' Alice said.

'Yeah,' Tom said. 'North. Let's do it.'

GAITEN ACADEMY

1

When rainy daylight arose the next morning, Clay, Alice, and Tom were camped in the barn adjacent to an abandoned horse-farm in North Reading. They watched from the door as the first groups of crazyfolk began to appear, flocking southwest on Route 62 in the direction of Wilmington. Their clothes looked uniformly soaked and shabby. Some were without shoes. By noon they were gone. Around four, as the sun broke through the clouds in long, spoking rays, they began flocking back in the direction from which they had come. Many were munching as they walked. Some were helping those who were having a hard time walking on their own. If there were acts of murder today, Clay, Tom, and Alice did not see any.

Perhaps half a dozen of the crazies were lugging large objects that looked familiar to Clay; Alice had found one in the closet of Tom's guest bedroom. The three of them had stood around it, afraid to turn it on.

'Clay?' Alice asked. 'Why are some of them carrying boomboxes?'

'I don't know,' he said.

'I don't like it,' Tom said. 'I don't like the flocking behavior, I don't like them helping each other, and I like seeing them with those big portable sound-systems least of all.'

'There's only a few with—' Clay began.

'Check her out, right there,' Tom interrupted, pointing

to a middle-aged woman who was staggering up Highway 62 with a radio/CD player the size of a living room hassock cradled in her arms. She held it against her breasts as though it were a sleeping toddler. Its power-cord had come out of the little storage compartment in back and dragged beside her on the road. 'And you don't see any of them carrying lamps or toasters, do you? What if they're programmed to set up battery-powered radios, turn them on, and start broadcasting that tone, pulse, subliminal message, whatever-it-is? What if they want to get the ones they missed the first time?'

They. The ever-popular paranoid *they.* Alice had produced her little sneaker from somewhere and was squeezing it in her hand, but when she spoke, her voice was calm enough. 'I don't think that's it,' she said.

'Why not?' Tom asked.

She shook her head. 'I can't say. Just that it doesn't feel right.'

'Woman's intuition?' He was smiling, but he wasn't sneering.

'Maybe,' she said, 'but I think one thing's obvious.'

'What's that, Alice?' Clay asked. He had an idea what she was going to say, and he was right.

'They're getting smarter. Not on their own, but because they're thinking together. Probably that sounds crazy, but I think it's more likely than them collecting a big pile of battery-powered FM suitcases to blast us all into loony-land.'

'Telepathic group-think,' Tom said. He mulled it over. Alice watched him do it. Clay, who had already decided she was right, looked out the barn door at the last of the day. He was thinking they needed to stop somewhere and pick up a road-atlas.

Tom was nodding. 'Hey, why not? After all, that's probably what flocking *is*: telepathic group-think.'

'Do you really think so or are you just saying that to make me—'

'I really think so,' he said. He reached out and touched

her hand, which was now squeezing the little sneaker rapidly. 'I really really do. Give that thing a rest, will you?'

She gave him a fleeting, distracted smile. Clay saw it and thought again how beautiful she was, how really beautiful. And how close to breaking. 'That hay looks soft and I'm tired. I think I'll take a nice long nap.'

'Get down with your bad self,' Clay said.

2

Clay dreamed that he and Sharon and Johnny-Gee were having a picnic behind their little house in Kent Pond. Sharon had spread her Navajo blanket on the grass. They were having sandwiches and iced tea. Suddenly the day went dark. Sharon pointed over Clay's shoulder and said, 'Look! Telepaths!' But when he turned that way, he saw nothing but a flock of crows, one so huge it blotted out the sun. Then a tinkling began. It sounded like the Mister Softee truck playing the *Sesame Street* theme song, but he knew it was a ring-tone, and in his dream he was terrified. He turned back and Johnny-Gee was gone. When he asked Sharon where he was – already dreading, already knowing the answer – she said Johnny had gone under the blanket to answer his cell phone. There was a bump in the blanket. Clay dived under, into the overpowering smell of sweet hay, shouting for Johnny not to pick up, not to answer, reaching for him and finding instead only the cold curve of a glass ball: the paperweight he'd bought in Small Treasures, the one with the haze of dandelion fluff floating deep down inside like a pocket fog.

Then Tom was shaking him, telling him it was past nine by his watch, the moon was up, and if they were going to do some more walking they ought to get at it. Clay had never been so glad to wake up. On the whole, he preferred dreams of the Bingo Tent.

Alice was looking at him oddly.

'What?' Clay said, checking to make sure their automatic

weapon was safetied – that was already becoming second nature to him.

'You were talking in your sleep. You were saying, "Don't answer it, don't answer it."'

'*Nobody* should have answered it,' Clay said. 'We all would have been better off.'

'Ah, but who can resist a ringing phone?' Tom asked. 'And there goes your ballgame.'

'Thus spake fuckin Zarathustra,' Clay said. Alice laughed until she cried.

3

With the moon racing in and out of the clouds – like an illustration in a boy's novel of pirates and buried treasure, Clay thought – they left the horse-farm behind and resumed their walk north. That night they began to meet others of their own kind again.

Because this is our time now, Clay thought, shifting the automatic rifle from one hand to the other. Fully loaded, it was damned heavy. *The phone-crazies own the days; when the stars come out, that's us. We're like vampires. We've been banished to the night. Up close we know each other because we can still talk; at a little distance we can be pretty sure of each other by the packs we wear and the guns more and more of us carry; but at a distance, the one sure sign is the waving flashlight beam. Three days ago we not only ruled the earth, we had survivor's guilt about all the other species we'd wiped out on our climb to the nirvana of round-the-clock cable news and microwave popcorn. Now we're the Flashlight People.*

He looked over at Tom. 'Where do they go?' he asked. 'Where do the crazies go after sundown?'

Tom gave him a look. 'North Pole. All the elves died of mad reindeer disease and these guys are helping out until the new crop shows up.'

'Jesus,' Clay said, 'did someone get up on the wrong side of the haystack tonight?'

142

But Tom still wouldn't smile. 'I'm thinking about my cat,' he said. 'Wondering if he's all right. No doubt you think that's quite stupid.'

'No,' Clay said, although, having a son and a wife to worry about, he sort of did.

4

They got a road atlas in a card-and-book shop in the two-stoplight burg of Ballardvale. They were now traveling north, and very glad they had decided to stay in the more-or-less bucolic V between Interstates 93 and 95. The other travelers they met – most moving west, away from I-95 – told of horrendous traffic-jams and terrible wrecks. One of the few pilgrims who was moving east said that a tanker had crashed near the Wakefield exit of I-93 and the resulting fire had caused a chain of explosions that had incinerated nearly a mile of northbound traffic. The stench, he said, was like 'a fish-fry in hell.'

They met more Flashlight People as they trudged through the outskirts of Andover and heard a rumor so persistent it was now repeated with the assurance of fact: the New Hampshire border was closed. New Hampshire State Police and special deputies were shooting first and asking questions afterward. It didn't matter to them whether you were crazy or sane.

'It's just a new version of the fucking motto they've had on their fucking license plates since forever,' said a bitter-faced elderly man with whom they walked for a while. He was wearing a small pack over his expensive topcoat and carrying a long-barreled flashlight. Poking out of his topcoat pocket was the butt of a handgun. 'If you're *in* New Hampshire, you can live free. If you want to *come* to New Hampshire, you can fucking die.'

'That's just . . . really hard to believe,' Alice said.

'Believe what you want, Missy,' said their temporary

companion. 'I met some people who tried to go north like you folks, and they turned back south in a hurry when they saw some people shot out of hand trying to cross into New Hampshire north of Dunstable.'

'When?' Clay asked.

'Last night.'

Clay thought of several other questions, but held his tongue instead. At Andover, the bitter-faced man and most of the other people with whom they had been sharing their vehicle-clogged (but passable) route turned onto Highway 133, toward Lowell and points west. Clay, Tom, and Alice were left on Andover's main street – deserted except for a few flashlight-waving foragers – with a decision to make.

'Do you believe it?' Clay asked Alice.

'No,' she said, and looked at Tom.

Tom shook his head. 'Me either. I thought the guy's story had an alligators-in-the-sewers feel to it.'

Alice was nodding. 'News doesn't travel that fast anymore. Not without phones.'

'Yep,' Tom said. 'Definitely the next-generation urban myth. Still, we *are* talking about what a friend of mine likes to call New Hamster. Which is why I think we should cross the border at the most out-of-the-way spot we can find.'

'Sounds like a plan,' Alice said, and with that they moved on again, using the sidewalk as long as they were in town and there was a sidewalk to use.

5

On the outskirts of Andover, a man with a pair of flashlights rigged in a kind of harness (one light at each temple) stepped out through the broken display window of the IGA. He waved to them in companionable fashion, then picked a course toward them between a jumble of shopping carts, dropping canned goods into what looked like a newsboy's pouch as he walked. He stopped beside a pickup truck lying on its side, introduced himself as Mr Roscoe Handt of Methuen, and asked where they were going. When Clay told them Maine, Handt shook his head.

'New Hampshire border's closed. I met two people not half an hour ago who got turned back. He said they're trying to tell the difference between the phone-crazies and people like us, but they're not trying too hard.'

'Did these two people actually see this with their own eyes?' Tom asked.

Roscoe Handt looked at Tom as though *he* might be crazy. 'You got to trust the word of others, man,' he said. 'I mean, you can't exactly phone someone up and ask for verification, can you?' He paused. 'They're burning the bodies at Salem and Nashua, that's what these folks told me. And it smells like a pig-roast. They told me that, too. I've got a party of five I'm taking west, and we want to make some miles before sunup. The way west is open.'

'That the word you're hearing, is it?' Clay asked.

Handt looked at him with mild contempt. 'That's the word, all right. And a word to the wise is sufficient, my ma used to say. If you really mean to go north, make sure you get to the border in the middle of the night. The crazies don't go out after dark.'

'We know,' Tom said.

The man with the flashlights affixed to the sides of his head ignored Tom and went on talking to Clay. He had pegged Clay as the trio's leader. 'And they don't carry flashlights. Wave your flashlights back and forth. Talk. *Yell.* They don't do those things, either. I doubt the people at the border will let you through, but if you're lucky, they won't shoot you, either.'

'They're getting smarter,' Alice said. 'You know that, don't you, Mr Handt?'

Handt snorted. 'They're traveling in packs and they're not killing each other anymore. I don't know if that makes them smarter or not. But they're still killing *us,* I know that.'

Handt must have seen doubt on Clay's face, because he smiled. His flashlights turned it into something unpleasant.

'I saw them catch a woman out this morning,' he said. 'With my own eyes, okay?'

Clay nodded. 'Okay.'

'I think I know why she was on the street. This was in Topsfield, about ten miles east of here? Me and my people, we were in a Motel 6. She was walking that way. Only not really walking. Hurrying. Almost running. Looking back over her shoulder. I saw her because I couldn't sleep.' He shook his head. 'Getting used to sleeping days is a bitch.'

Clay thought of telling Handt they'd all get used to it, then didn't. He saw Alice was holding her talisman again. He didn't want Alice hearing this and knew there was no way to keep it from her. Partly because it was survival inform- ation (and unlike the stuff about the New Hampshire state line, he was almost positive this was solid information); partly because the world was going to be full of stories like this for a while. If they listened to enough of them, some might eventu- ally begin to line up and make patterns.

'Probably just looking for a better place to stay, you know? No more than that. Saw the Motel 6 and thought, "Hey, a room with a bed. Right up there by the Exxon station. Only a block away." But before she got even halfway, a bunch of them came around the corner. They were walking . . . you know how they walk now?'

Roscoe Handt walked toward them stiffly, like a tin soldier, with his newsboy's bag swinging. That wasn't how the phone-crazies walked, but they knew what he was trying to convey and nodded.

'And she . . .' He leaned back against the overturned truck and scrubbed briefly at his face with his hands. 'This is what I want you to understand, okay? This is why you can't get caught out, can't get fooled that they're getting normal because every now and then one or two of them has lucked into hitting the right controls on a boombox and started a CD playing—'

'You've seen that?' Tom asked. '*Heard* that?'

'Yeah, twice. Second guy I saw was walking along, swinging the thing from side to side so hard in his arms that it was skipping like hell, but yeah, it was playing. So they like music, and sure, they might be retrieving some of their marbles, but that's exactly why you have to be careful, see?'

'What happened to the woman?' Alice asked. 'The one who got caught out?'

'She tried to act like one of them,' Handt said. 'And I thought, standing there at the window of the room where I was, I thought, "Yeah, you go, girl, you might have a chance if you can hang on to that act a little while and then make a break, get inside somewhere." Because they don't like to go inside places, have you noticed that?'

Clay, Tom, and Alice shook their heads.

The man nodded. 'They *will*, I've seen em do it, but they don't like to.'

'How did they get onto her?' Alice asked again.

'I don't exactly know. They smelled her, or something.'

'Or maybe touched her thoughts,' Tom said.

'Or *couldn't* touch them,' Alice said.

'I don't know about any of that,' Handt said, 'but I know they tore her apart in the street. I mean literally tore her to pieces.'

'And this happened when?' Clay asked. He saw Alice was swaying and put an arm around her.

'Nine this morning. In Topsfield. So if you see a bunch of them walking up the Yella Brick Road with a boombox that's playing "Why Can't We Be Friends" . . .' He surveyed them grimly by the glow of the flashlights strapped to the sides of his head. 'I wouldn't go running out yelling *kemo sabe,* that's all.' He paused. 'And I wouldn't go north, either. Even if they don't shoot you at the border, it's a waste of time.'

But after a little consultation at the edge of the IGA parking lot, they went north anyway.

6

They paused near North Andover, standing on a pedestrian overpass above Route 495. The clouds were thickening again, but the moon broke through long enough to show them six lanes of silent traffic. Near the bridge where they stood, in the southbound lanes, an overturned sixteen-wheeler lay like a dead elephant. Orange pylons had been set up around it, showing that someone had made at least a token response, and there were two abandoned police cruisers beyond them, one on its side. The rear half of the truck had been burned black. There was no sign of bodies, not in the momentary moonlight. A few people labored westward in the breakdown lane, but it was slow going even there.

'Kind of makes it all real, doesn't it?' Tom said.

'No,' Alice said. She sounded indifferent. 'To me it looks like a special effect in some big summer movie. Buy a bucket of popcorn and a Coke and watch the end of the world in . . . what do they call it? Computer graphic imaging? CGI? Blue screens? Some fucking thing.' She held up the little sneaker by one lace. 'This is all I need to make it real. Something small enough to hold in my hand. Come on, let's go.'

7

There were plenty of abandoned vehicles on Highway 28, but it was wide-open compared to 495, and by four o'clock they were nearing Methuen, hometown of Mr Roscoe Handt, he of the stereo flashlights. And they believed enough of Handt's story to want to be under cover well before daylight. They chose a motel at the intersection of 28 and 110. A dozen or so cars were parked in front of the various units, but to Clay they had an abandoned feel. And why wouldn't they? The two roads were passable, but only if you were on foot. Clay and Tom stood at the edge of the parking lot, waving their flashlights over their heads.

'We're okay!' Tom called. 'Normal folks! Coming in!'

They waited. There was no response from what the sign identified as the Sweet Valley Inn, Heated Pool, HBO, Group Rates.

'Come on,' Alice said. 'My feet hurt. And it'll be getting light soon, won't it?'

'Look at this,' Clay said. He picked up a CD from the motel's turn-in and shone the beam of his flashlight on it. It was *Love Songs,* by Michael Bolton.

'And you said they were getting smarter,' Tom said.

'Don't be so quick to judge,' Clay said as they started toward the units. 'Whoever had it threw it away, right?'

'More likely just dropped it,' Tom said.

Alice shone her own light on the CD. 'Who *is* this guy?'

'Honeybunch,' Tom said, 'you don't want to know.' He took the CD and tossed it back over his shoulder.

They forced the doors on three adjoining units – as gently as possible, so they could at least shoot the bolts once they were inside – and with beds to sleep in, they slept most of the day away. They were not disturbed, although that evening Alice said she thought she had heard music coming from far away. But, she admitted, it might have been part of a dream she was having.

8

There were maps for sale in the lobby of the Sweet Valley Inn that would offer more detail than their road atlas. They were in a glass display cabinet that had been smashed. Clay took one for Massachusetts and one for New Hampshire, reaching in carefully so as not to cut his hand, and saw a young man lying on the other side of the reception counter as he did so. His eyes glared sightlessly. For a moment Clay thought someone had put an oddly colored corsage in the corpse's mouth. Then he saw the greenish points poking out through the dead man's cheeks and realized they matched the broken glass littering the shelves of the display cabinet. The corpse was wearing a nametag that said MY NAME IS HANK ASK ME ABOUT WEEKLY RATES. Clay thought briefly of Mr Ricardi as he looked at Hank.

Tom and Alice were waiting for him just inside the lobby door. It was quarter of nine, and outside it was full dark. 'How did you do?' Alice asked.

'These may help,' he said. He gave her the maps, then lifted the Coleman lantern so she and Tom could study them, compare them against the road atlas, and plot the night's travel. He was trying to cultivate a sense of fatalism about Johnny and Sharon, trying to keep the bald truth of his current family situation front and center in his mind: what had happened in Kent Pond had happened. His son and his wife were either all right or they weren't. He would either find them or he wouldn't. His success at this sort of semi-magical thinking came and went.

When it started slipping, he told himself he was lucky to be alive, and this was certainly true. What balanced his good luck out was that he'd been in Boston, a hundred miles south of Kent Pond by even the quickest route (which they were definitely *not* taking), when the Pulse happened. And yet he'd fallen in with good people. There was that. People he could think of as friends. He'd seen plenty of others – Beer-Keg Guy and Plump Bible-Toting Lady as well as Mr Roscoe Handt of Methuen – who weren't as lucky.

If he got to you, Share, if Johnny got to you, you better be taking care of him. You just better be.

But suppose he'd had his phone? Suppose he'd taken the red cell phone to school? Might he not have been taking it a little more often lately? Because so many of the other kids took theirs?

Christ.

'Clay? You all right?' Tom asked.

'Sure. Why?'

'I don't know. You looked a little . . . grim.'

'Dead guy behind the counter. He's not pretty.'

'Look here,' Alice said, tracing a thread on the map. It squiggled across the state line and then appeared to join New Hampshire Route 38 a little east of Pelham. 'That looks pretty good to me,' she said. 'If we go west on the highway out there for eight or nine miles —' she pointed at 110, where both the cars and the tar were gleaming faintly in a misty drizzle — 'we should hit it. What do you think?'

'I think that sounds good,' Tom said.

She looked from him to Clay. The little sneaker was put away — probably in her backpack — but Clay could see her wanting to squeeze it. He supposed it was good she wasn't a smoker, she'd be up to four packs a day. 'If they've got the way across guarded—' she began.

'We'll worry about that if we have to,' Clay said, but he wasn't worrying. One way or another, he was getting to Maine. If it meant crawling through some puckerbrush, like an illegal crossing the Canadian border to pick apples in October, he would do it. If Tom and Alice decided to stay behind, that would be too bad. He'd be sorry to leave them . . . but he would go. Because he had to know.

The red squiggle Alice had found on the Sweet Valley maps had a name — Dostie Stream Road — and it was almost wide-open. It was a four-mile hike to the state line, and they came upon no more than five or six abandoned vehicles and only a single wreck. They also passed two houses where they could see lights and hear the roar of generators. They considered stopping at these, but not for long.

'We'd probably get into a firefight with some guy defending his hearth and home,' Clay said. 'Always assuming there's anyone there. Those generators were probably set to come on when the county juice failed, and they'll run until they're out of gas.'

'Even if there are sane people and they let us in, which would hardly be a sane act, what are we going to do?' Tom said. 'Ask to use the phone?'

They discussed stopping somewhere and trying to liberate a vehicle (*liberate* was Tom's word), but in the end decided against that, too. If the state line was being defended by deputies or vigilantes, driving up to it in a Chevy Tahoe might not be the smoothest move.

So they walked, and of course there was nothing at the state line but a billboard (a small one, as befitted a two-lane blacktop road winding through farm country) reading YOU ARE NOW ENTERING NEW HAMPSHIRE and BIENVENUE! There was no sound but the drip of moisture in the woods on either side of them, and an occasional sigh of breeze. Maybe the rustle of an animal. They stopped briefly to read the sign and then walked on, leaving Massachusetts behind.

9

Any sense of being alone ended along with the Dostie Stream Road, at a signpost reading NH ROUTE 38 and MANCHESTER 19 MI. There were still only a few travelers on 38, but when they switched to 128 – a wide, wreck-littered road that headed almost due north – half an hour later, that trickle became part of a steady stream of refugees. They traveled mostly in little groups of three and four, and with what struck Clay as a rather shabby lack of interest in anyone other than themselves.

They encountered a woman of about forty and a man maybe twenty years older pushing shopping carts, each containing a child. The one in the man's cart was a boy, and too big for the conveyance, but he had found a way to curl up inside and fall asleep. While Clay and his party were passing this jackleg family, a wheel came off the man's shopping cart. It tipped sideways, spilling out the boy, who looked about seven. Tom caught him by the shoulder and broke the worst of the kid's fall, but he scraped one knee. And of course he was frightened. Tom picked him up, but the boy didn't know him and struggled to get away, crying harder than ever.

'That's okay, thanks, I've got him,' the man said. He took the child and sat down at the side of the road with him, where he made much of what he called the boo-boo, a term Clay didn't think he'd heard since *he* was seven. The man said, 'Gregory kiss it, make it all better.' He kissed the child's scrape, and the boy laid his head against the man's shoulder. He was already going to sleep again. Gregory smiled at Tom and Clay and nodded. He looked weary almost to death, a man who might have been a trim and Nautilus-toned sixty last week and now looked like a seventy-five-year-old Jew trying to get the hell out of Poland while there was still time.

'We'll be all right,' he said. 'You can go now.'

Clay opened his mouth to say, *Why shouldn't we all go on together? Why don't we hook up? What do you think, Greg?* It was the sort of thing the heroes of the science fiction novels he'd read as a teenager were always saying: *Why don't we hook up?*

'Yeah, go on, what are you waiting for?' the woman asked before he could say that or anything else. In her shopping cart a girl of about five still slept. The woman stood beside the cart protectively, as if she had grabbed some fabulous sale item and was afraid Clay or one of his friends might try to wrest it from her. 'You think we got something you want?'

'Natalie, stop,' Gregory said with tired patience.

But Natalie didn't, and Clay realized what was so dispiriting about this little scene. Not that he was getting his lunch – his *midnight* lunch – fed to him by a woman whose exhaustion and terror had led to paranoia; that was understandable and forgivable. What made his spirits sink to his shoetops was the way people just kept on walking, swinging their flashlights, and talking low among themselves in their own little groups, swapping the occasional suitcase from one hand to the other. Some yob on a pocket-rocket motorbike wove his way up the road between the wrecks and over the litter, and people made way for him, muttering resentfully. Clay thought it would have been the same if the little boy had fallen out of the shopping cart and broken his neck instead of just scraping his knee. He thought it would have been the same if that heavyset guy up there panting along the side of the road with an overloaded duffelbag dropped with a thunder-clap coronary. No one would try to resuscitate him, and of course the days of 911 were done.

No one even bothered to yell *You tell im, lady!* or *Hey dude, why don't you tell her to shut up?* They just went on walking.

'—cause all we got is these *kids*, a responsibility we didn't ask for when we can hardly take care of *ourselfs,* he has a pacemaker, what are we supposed to do when the *baddery* runs out, I'd like to know? And now these kids! You want a kid?' She looked around wildly. '*Hey! Anyone want a kid?'*

The little girl began to stir.

'Natalie, you're disturbing Portia,' Gregory said.

The woman named Natalie began to laugh. 'Well tough *shit*! It's a disturbing-ass world!' Around them, people continued doing the Refugee Walk. No one paid any attention and Clay thought, *So this is how we act. This is how it goes when the bottom drops out. When there are no cameras turning, no buildings burning, no Anderson Cooper saying 'Now back to the CNN studios in Atlanta.' This is how it goes when Homeland Security's been canceled due to lack of sanity.*

'Let me take the boy,' Clay said. 'I'll carry him until you find something better to put him in. That cart's shot.' He looked at Tom. Tom shrugged and nodded.

'Stay away from us,' Natalie said, and all at once there was a gun in her hand. It wasn't a big one, probably only a .22, but even a .22 would do the job if the bullet went in the right place.

Clay heard the sound of guns being drawn on either side of him and knew that Tom and Alice were now pointing the pistols they'd taken from the Nickerson home at the woman named Natalie. This was also how it went, it seemed.

'Put it away, Natalie,' he said. 'We're going to get moving now.'

'You're double-fuckin right you are,' she said, and brushed an errant lock of hair out of her eye with the heel of her free hand. She didn't seem to be aware that the young man and younger woman with Clay were holding guns on her. Now people passing by *did* look, but their only response was to move past the spot of confrontation and potential blood-shed a little faster.

'Come on, Clay,' Alice said quietly. She put her free hand on his wrist. 'Before someone gets shot.'

They started walking again. Alice walked with her hand on Clay's wrist, almost as if he were her boyfriend. *Just a little midnight stroll,* Clay thought, although he had no idea of what time it was and didn't care. His heart was beating hard. Tom walked with them, only until they were around the next curve he walked backward, with his gun still out. Clay supposed Tom wanted to be ready to shoot back if Natalie decided to use her little popgun after all. Because shooting back was also how it went, now that phone service had been interrupted until further notice.

10

In the hours before dawn, walking on Route 102 east of Manchester, they began to hear music, very faint.

'Christ,' Tom said, coming to a stop. 'That's "Baby Elephant Walk."'

'It's *what?*' Alice asked. She sounded amused.

'A big-band instrumental from the age of quarter gas. Les Brown and His Band of Renown, someone like that. My mother had the record.'

Two men pulled even with them and stopped for a blow. They were elderly, but both looked fit. *Like a couple of recently retired postmen hiking the Cotswolds,* Clay thought. *Wherever they are.* One wore a pack – no pussy day-pack, either, but the waist-length kind on a frame – and the other had a ruck-sack hanging from his right shoulder. Hung over the left was what looked like a .30-.30.

Packsack wiped sweat from his seamed forehead with a forearm and said, 'Your mama might have had a version by Les Brown, son, but more likely it was Don Costa or Henry Mancini. Those were the popular ones. That one –' he inclined his head toward the ghostly strains— 'that's Lawrence Welk, as I live and breathe.'

'Lawrence Welk,' Tom breathed, almost in awe.

'Who?' Alice asked.

'Listen to that elephant walk,' Clay said, and laughed. He was tired and feeling goofy. It occurred to him that Johnny would *love* that music.

Packsack gave him a glance of passing contempt, then looked back at Tom. 'That's Lawrence Welk, all right,' he said. 'My eyes aren't half-right anymore, but my ears are fine. My wife and I used to watch his show every fucking Saturday night.'

'Dodge had a good time, too,' Rucksack said. It was his only addition to the conversation, and Clay hadn't the slightest idea what it meant.

'Lawrence Welk and his Champagne Band,' Tom said. 'Think of it.'

'Lawrence Welk and his Champagne *Music Makers,'* Packsack said. 'Jesus *Christ.'*

'Don't forget the Lennon Sisters and the lovely Alice Lon,' Tom said.

In the distance, the ghostly music changed. 'That one's "Calcutta",' Packsack said. He sighed. 'Well, we'll be getting along. Nice passing the time of day with you.'

'Night,' Clay said.

'Nope,' Packsack said. 'These're our days now. Haven't you noticed? Have a good one, boys. You too, little ma'am.'

'Thank you,' the little ma'am standing between Clay and Tom said faintly.

Packsack started along again. Rucksack fell sturdily in beside him. Around them, a steady parade of bobbing flashlight beams led people deeper into New Hampshire. Then Packsack stopped and looked back for a final word.

'You don't want to be on the road more than another hour,' he said. 'Find a house or motel unit and get inside. You know about the shoes, right?'

'What about the shoes?' Tom asked.

Packsack looked at him patiently, the way he'd probably look at anyone who couldn't help being a fool. Far down the road, 'Calcutta' – if that's what it was – had given way to a polka. It sounded insane in the foggy, drizzly night. And now this old man with the big pack on his back was talking about shoes.

'When you go inside a place, you put your shoes out on the stoop,' Packsack said. 'The crazy ones won't take them, don't worry about that, and it tells other people the place is taken and to move along, find another. Saves—' his eyes dropped to the heavy automatic weapon Clay was carrying— 'Saves accidents.'

'Have there been accidents?' Tom asked.

'Oh yes,' Packsack said, with chilling indifference. 'There's always accidents, people being what they are. But there's plenty of places, so there's no need for *you* to have one. Just put out your shoes.'

'How do you know that?' Alice asked.

He gave her a smile that improved his face out of all measure. But it was hard not to smile at Alice; she was young, and even at three in the morning, she was pretty. 'People talk; I listen. I talk, *sometimes* other folks listen. Did you listen?'

'Yes,' Alice said. 'Listening's one of my best things.'

'Then pass it on. Bad enough to have *them* to contend with.' He didn't have to be more specific. 'Too bad to have accidents among ourselves on top of that.'

Clay thought of Natalie pointing the .22. He said, 'You're right. Thank you.'

Tom said, 'That one's "The Beer Barrel Polka", isn't it?'

'That's right, son,' Packsack said. 'Myron Floren on the squeezebox. God rest his soul. You might want to stop in Gaiten. It's a nice little village two miles or so up the road.'

'Is that where you're going to stay?' Alice asked.

'Oh, me and Rolfe might push on a dight further,' he said.

'Why?'

'Because we can, little ma'am, that's all. You have a good day.'

This time they didn't contradict him, and although the two men had to be pushing seventy, they were soon out of sight, following the beam of a single flashlight, which Rucksack – Rolfe – held.

'Lawrence Welk and his Champagne Music Makers,' Tom marveled.

'"Baby Elephant Walk",' Clay said, and laughed.

'Why did Dodge have a good time, too?' Alice wanted to know.

'Because it could, I guess,' Tom said, and burst out laughing at her perplexed expression.

11

The music was coming from Gaiten, the nice little village Packsack had recommended as a place to stop. It was not nearly as loud as the AC/DC concert Clay had gone to in Boston as a teenager – that had left his ears ringing for days – but it was loud enough to make him think of summer band concerts he'd attended in South Berwick with his parents. In fact he had it in his mind that they would discover the source of the music on the Gaiten town common – likely some elderly person, not a phone-crazy but disaster-addled, who had taken it into his head to serenade the ongoing exodus with easy-listening oldies played through a set of battery-powered loudspeakers.

There *was* a Gaiten town common, but it was deserted save for a few people eating either a late supper or an early breakfast by the glow of flashlights and Coleman lanterns. The source of the music was a little farther to the north. By then Lawrence Welk had given way to someone blowing a horn so mellow it was soporific.

'That's Wynton Marsalis, isn't it?' Clay asked. He was ready to call it quits for the night and thought Alice looked done almost to death.

'Him or Kenny G,' Tom said. 'You know what Kenny G said when he got off the elevator, don't you?'

'No,' Clay said, 'but I'm sure you'll tell me.'

'"Man! This place rocks!"'

Clay said, 'That's so funny I think my sense of humour just imploded.'

'I don't get it,' Alice said.

'It's not worth explaining,' Tom said. 'Listen, guys, we've got to call it a night. I'm about kilt.'

'Me too,' Alice said. 'I thought I was in shape from soccer, but I'm really tired.'

'Yeah,' Clay agreed. 'Baby makes three.'

They had already passed through Gaiten's shopping district, and according to the signs, Main Street – which was also Route 102 – had now become Academy Avenue. This was no surprise to Clay, because the sign on the outskirts of town had proclaimed Gaiten home to Historic Gaiten Academy, an institution of which Clay had heard vague rumors. He thought it was one of those New England prep schools for kids who can't quite make it into Exeter or Milton. He supposed the three of them would be back in the land of Burger Kings, muffler-repair shops, and chain motels soon enough, but this part of New Hampshire 102 was lined with very nice-looking homes. The problem was, there were shoes – sometimes as many as four pairs – in front of most of the doors.

The foot-traffic had thinned considerably as other

travelers found shelter for the coming day, but as they passed Academy Grove Citgo and approached the fieldstone pillars flanking Gaiten Academy's entrance drive, they began to catch up to a trio just ahead: two men and a woman, all well into middle age. As these three walked slowly up the sidewalk, they inspected each house for one without shoes placed at the front door. The woman was limping badly, and one of the men had his arm around her waist.

Gaiten Academy was on the left, and Clay realized this was where the music (currently a droning, string-laden version of 'Fly Me to the Moon') was coming from. He noticed two other things. One was that the road-litter here – torn bags, half-eaten vegetables, gnawed bones – was especially heavy, and that most of it turned in at the gravel Academy drive. The other was that two people were standing there. One was an old man hunched over a cane. The other was a boy with a battery-powered lantern parked between his shoes. He looked no more than twelve and was dozing against one of the pillars. He was wearing what looked like a school uniform: gray pants, gray sweater, a maroon jacket with a crest on it.

As the trio ahead of Clay and his friends drew abreast of the Academy drive, the old man – dressed in a tweed jacket with patches on the elbows – spoke to them in a piercing, I-will-be-heard-all-the-way-to-the-back-of-the-lecture-hall voice. 'Hi, there! Hi, I say! Won't you come in here? We can offer you shelter, but more importantly, we have to—'

'We don't have to anything, mister,' the woman said. 'I got four burst blisters, two on each foot, and I can hardly walk.'

'But there's plenty of room—' the old fellow began. The man supporting the woman gave him a look that must have been unpleasant, because the old fellow stopped. The trio went past the drive and the pillars and the sign on old-fashioned iron S-hooks reading **GAITEN ACADEMY EST. 1846** *'A Young Mind Is A Lamp In The Darkness'.*

The old fellow slumped over his cane again, then saw

Clay, Tom, and Alice approaching and straightened up once more. He seemed about to hail them, then apparently decided his lecture-hall approach wasn't working. He poked his companion in the ribs with the tip of his cane instead. The boy straightened up with a wild look as behind them, where brick buildings loomed in the dark along the slope of a mild hill, 'Fly Me to the Moon' gave way to an equally sluggish rendition of something that might once have been 'I Get a Kick out of You'.

'Jordan!' he said. 'Your turn! Ask them in!'

The boy named Jordan started, blinked at the old man, then looked at the new trio of approaching strangers with gloomy mistrust. Clay thought of the March Hare and the Dormouse in *Alice in Wonderland*. Maybe that was wrong – probably it was – but he was very tired. 'Aw, *they* won't be any different, sir,' he said. '*They* won't come in. Nobody will. We'll try again tomorrow night. I'm *sleepy*.'

And Clay knew that, tired or not, they were going to find out what the old man wanted . . . unless Tom and Alice absolutely refused, that was. Partly because the old man's companion reminded him of Johnny, yes, but mostly because the kid had made up his mind that no one was going to help in this not-very-brave new world – he and the one he called *sir* were on their own because that was just how it went. Only if that were true, pretty soon there wouldn't be anything worth saving.

'Go on,' the old man encouraged him. He prodded Jordan with the tip of his cane again, but not hard. Not painfully. 'Tell them we can give them shelter, we have plenty of room, but they ought to see, first. Someone needs to see this. If they also say no, we will indeed give up for the night.'

'All right, sir.'

The old man smiled, exposing a mouthful of large horse-teeth. 'Thank you, Jordan.'

The boy walked toward them with absolutely no relish, his dusty shoes scuffing, his shirttail hanging below the hem of his sweater. He held his lantern in one hand, and it fizzed faintly. There were dark up-all-night circles under his eyes, and his hair badly needed washing.

'Tom?' Clay asked.

'We'll see what he wants,' Tom said, 'because I can see it's what *you* want, but—'

'Sirs? Pardon me, sirs?'

'One second,' Tom said to the boy, then turned back to Clay. His face was grave. 'But it's going to start getting light in an hour. Maybe less. So that old guy better be right about there being a place for us to stay.'

'Oh, yes, sir,' Jordan said. He looked like he didn't want to hope and couldn't help it. 'Lots of places. Hundreds of dorm rooms, not to mention Cheatham Lodge. Tobias Wolff came last year and stayed there. He gave a lecture on his book, *Old School.*'

'I read that,' Alice said, sounding bemused.

'The boys who didn't have cell phones have all run off. The ones who did have them . . .'

'We know about them,' Alice said.

'I'm a scholarship boy. I lived in Holloway. I didn't have a cell phone. I had to use the dorm mother's phone whenever I wanted to call home and the other boys would make fun of me.'

'Looks to me like you got the last laugh there, Jordan,' Tom said.

'Yes, sir,' he said dutifully, but in the light of his fizzing lantern Clay saw no laughter, only woe and weariness. 'Won't you please come and meet the Head?'

And although he had to be very tired himself, Tom responded with complete politeness, as if they had been standing on a sunny veranda – at a Parents' Tea, perhaps – instead of on the trash-littered verge of Academy Avenue at four-fifteen in the morning. 'That would be our pleasure, Jordan,' he said.

12

'The devil's intercoms is what I used to call them,' said Charles Ardai, who had been chairman of Gaiten Academy's English Department for twenty-five years and acting Headmaster of the Academy entire at the time of the Pulse. Now he stumped with surprising rapidity up the hill on his cane, keeping to the sidewalk, avoiding the river of swill that carpeted Academy Drive. Jordan walked watchfully beside him, the other three behind him. Jordan was worried about the old man losing his balance. Clay was worried that the man might have a heart attack, trying to talk and climb a hill – even a relatively mild one like this – at the same time.

'I never really meant it, of course; it was a joke, a jape, a comic exaggeration, but in truth, I never liked the things, especially in an academic environment. I might have moved to keep them out of the school, but naturally I would have been overruled. Might as well try to legislate against the rising of the tide, eh?' He puffed rapidly several times. 'My brother gave me one for my sixty-fifth birthday. I ran the thing flat . . .' Puff, pant. 'And simply never recharged it. They emit radiation, are you aware of this? In minuscule amounts, it's true, but still . . . a source of radiation that close to one's head . . . one's brain . . .'

'Sir, you should wait until we get to Tonney,' Jordan said. He steadied Ardai as the Head's cane slid on a rotten piece of fruit and he listed momentarily (but at an alarming angle) to port.

'Probably a good idea,' Clay said.

'Yes,' the Head agreed. 'Only . . . I never trusted them, this is my point. I was never that way with my computer. Took to that like a duck to water.'

At the top of the hill, the campus's main road split in a Y. The left fork wound its way to buildings that were almost surely dorms. The right one went toward lecture halls, a cluster of administration buildings, and an archway that glimmered white in the dark. The river of garbage and discarded wrappers flowed beneath it. Headmaster Ardai led them that way, skirting as much of the litter as he could, Jordan holding his elbow. The music – now Bette Midler, singing 'Wind Beneath My Wings' – was coming from beyond the arch, and Clay saw dozens of discarded compact discs among the bones and empty potato chip bags. He was starting to get a bad feeling about this.

'Uh, sir? Headmaster? Maybe we should just—'

'We'll be fine,' the Head replied. 'Did you ever play musical chairs as a child? Of course you did. Well, as long as the music doesn't stop, we have nothing to worry about. We'll have a quick peek, and then we'll go over to Cheatham Lodge. That's the Headmaster's residence. Not two hundred yards from Tonney Field. I promise you.'

Clay looked at Tom, who shrugged. Alice nodded.

Jordan happened to be looking back at them (rather anxiously), and he caught this collegial interplay. 'You ought to see it,' he told them. 'The Head's right about that. Until you see it, you don't know.'

'See what, Jordan?' Alice asked.

But Jordan only looked at her – big young eyes in the dark. 'Wait,' he said.

13

'Holy fucking shit,' Clay said. In his mind the words sounded like a full-throated bellow of surprise and horror – with maybe a soupçon of outrage – but what actually emerged was more of a whipped whimper. Part of it might have been that this close the music *was* almost as loud as that long-ago AC/DC concert (although Debby Boone making her sweet schoolgirl way through 'You Light Up My Life' was quite a stretch from 'Hell's Bells', even at full volume), but mostly it was pure shock. He thought that after the Pulse and their subsequent retreat from Boston he'd be prepared for anything, but he was wrong.

He didn't think prep schools like this indulged in anything so plebeian (and so smashmouth) as football, but soccer had apparently been a big deal. The stands stacking up on either side of Tonney Field looked as if they could seat as many as a thousand, and they were decked with bunting that was only now beginning to look bedraggled by the showery weather of the last few days. There was an elaborate scoreboard at the far end of the field with big letters marching along the top. Clay couldn't read the message in the dark and probably wouldn't have taken it in even if it had been daylight. There was enough light to see the field itself, and that was all that mattered.

Every inch of grass was covered with phone-crazies. They were lying on their backs like sardines in a can, leg to leg and hip to hip and shoulder to shoulder. Their faces stared up into the black predawn sky.

'Oh my Lord Jesus,' Tom said. His voice was muffled because one fist was pressed against his mouth.

'Catch the girl!' the Head rapped. 'She's going to faint!'

'No – I'm all right,' Alice said, but when Clay put his arm around her she slumped against him, breathing fast. Her eyes were open but they had a fixed, druggy look.

'They're under the bleachers, too,' Jordan said. He spoke with a studied, almost showy calm that Clay did not believe for a minute. It was the voice of a boy assuring his pals that he's not grossed out by the maggots boiling in a dead cat's eyes . . . just before he leans over and blows his groceries. 'Me and the Head think that's where they put the hurt ones that aren't going to get better.'

'The Head and *I*, Jordan.'

'Sorry, sir.'

Debby Boone achieved poetic catharsis and ceased. There was a pause and then Lawrence Welk's Champagne Music Makers once more began to play 'Baby Elephant Walk'. *Dodge had a good time, too,* Clay thought.

'How many of those boomboxes have they got rigged

together?' he asked Headmaster Ardai. 'And how did they do it? They're *brainless,* for Christ's sake, zombies!' A terrible idea occurred to him, illogical and persuasive at the same time. 'Did *you* do it? To keep them quiet, or . . . I don't know . . .'

'He didn't do it,' Alice said. She spoke quietly from her safe place within the circle of Clay's arm.

'No, and both of your premises are wrong,' the Head told him.

'Both? I don't—'

'They must be dedicated music-lovers,' Tom mused, 'because they don't like to go inside buildings. But that's where the CDs are, right?'

'Not to mention the boomboxes,' Clay said.

'There's no time to explain now. Already the sky has begun to lighten, and . . . tell them, Jordan.'

Jordan replied dutifully, with the air of one who recites a lesson he does not understand, 'All good vampires must be in before cockcrow, sir.'

'That's right – before cockcrow. For now, only look. That's all you need to do. You didn't know there were places like this, did you?'

'Alice knew,' Clay said.

They looked. And because the night *had* begun to wane, Clay realized that the eyes in all those faces were open. He was pretty sure they weren't seeing; they were just . . . open.

Something bad's going on here, he thought. *The flocking was only the beginning of it.*

Looking at the packed bodies and empty faces (mostly white; this was New England, after all) was awful, but the blank eyes turned up to the night sky filled him with unreasoning horror. Somewhere, not too distant, the morning's first bird began to sing. It wasn't a crow, but the Head still jerked, then tottered. This time it was Tom who steadied him.

'Come on,' the Head told them. 'It's only a short walk

to Cheatham Lodge, but we ought to start. The damp has made me stiffer than ever. Take my elbow, Jordan.'

Alice broke free of Clay and went to the old man's other side. He gave her a rather forbidding smile and a shake of his head. 'Jordan can take care of me. We take care of each other now – ay, Jordan?'

'Yes, sir.'

'Jordan?' Tom asked. They were nearing a large (and rather pretentious) Tudor-style dwelling that Clay presumed was Cheatham Lodge.

'Sir?'

'The sign over the scoreboard – I couldn't read it. What did it say?'

'WELCOME ALUMNI TO HOMECOMING WEEKEND.' Jordan almost smiled, then remembered there would be no Homecoming Weekend this year – the bunting on the stands had already begun to tatter – and the brightness left his face. If he hadn't been so tired, he might still have held his composure, but it was very late, almost dawn, and as they made their way up the walk to the Headmaster's residence, the last student at Gaiten Academy, still wearing his colors of maroon and gray, burst into tears.

14

'That was incredible, sir,' Clay said. He had fallen into Jordan's mode of address very naturally. So had Tom and Alice. 'Thank you.'

'Yes,' Alice said. 'Thanks. I've never eaten two burgers in my life – at least not big ones like that.'

It was three o'clock the following afternoon. They were on the back porch of Cheatham Lodge. Charles Ardai – the Head, as Jordan called him – had grilled the hamburgers on a small gas grill. He said the meat was perfectly safe because the generator powering the cafeteria's freezer had run until noon yesterday (and indeed, the patties he took from the cooler Tom and Jordan had carried in from the pantry had still been white with frost and as hard as hockey pucks). He said that *grilling* the meat would probably be safe until five o'clock, although prudence dictated an early meal.

'They'd smell the cooking?' Clay asked.

'Let's just say that we have no desire to find out,' the Head replied. 'Have we, Jordan?'

'No, sir,' Jordan said, and took a bite of his second burger. He was slowing down, but Clay thought he'd manage to do his duty. 'We want to be inside when they wake up, and inside when they come back from town. That's where they go, to town. They're picking it clean, like birds in a field of grain. That's what the Head says.'

'They were flocking back home earlier when we were in Malden,' Alice said. 'Not that we knew where home for them was.' She was eyeing a tray with pudding cups on it. 'Can I have one of those?'

'Yes, indeed.' The Head pushed the tray toward her. 'And another hamburger, if you'd like. What we don't eat soon will just spoil.'

Alice groaned and shook her head, but she took a pudding cup. So did Tom.

'They seem to leave at the same time each morning, but the home-flocking behavior *has* been starting later,' Ardai said thoughtfully. 'Why would that be?'

'Slimmer pickings?' Alice asked.

'Perhaps . . .' He took a final bite of his own hamburger, then covered the remains neatly with a paper napkin. 'There are many flocks, you know. Maybe as many as a dozen within a fifty-mile radius. We know from people going south that there are flocks in Sandown, Fremont, and Candia. They forage about almost aimlessly in the daytime, perhaps for music as well as food, then go back to where they came from.'

'You know this for sure,' Tom said. He finished one pudding cup and reached for another.

Ardai shook his head. 'Nothing is for sure, Mr McCourt.'

His hair, a long white tangle (an English professor's hair for sure, Clay thought), rippled a bit in the mild afternoon breeze. The clouds were gone. The back porch gave them a good view of the campus, and so far it was deserted. Jordan went around the house at regular intervals to scout the hill sloping down to Academy Avenue and reported all quiet there, as well. 'You've not seen any of the other roosting places?'

'Nope,' Tom said.

'But we're traveling in the dark,' Clay reminded him, 'and now the dark is *really* dark.'

'Yes,' the Head agreed. He spoke almost dreamily. 'As in *le moyen âge*. Translation, Jordan?'

'The middle age, sir.'

'Good.' He patted Jordan's shoulder.

'Even big flocks would be easy to miss,' Clay said. 'They wouldn't have to be hiding.'

'No, they're not hiding,' Headmaster Ardai agreed, steepling his fingers. 'Not yet, at any rate. They flock . . . they forage . . . and their group mind may break down a bit *while* they forage . . . but perhaps less. Every day perhaps less.'

'Manchester burned to the ground,' Jordan said suddenly. 'We could see the fire from here, couldn't we, sir?'

'Yes,' the Head agreed. 'It's been very sad and frightening.'

'Is it true that people trying to cross into Massachusetts are being shot at the border?' Jordan asked. 'That's what people are saying. People are saying you have to go to Vermont, only that way is safe.'

'It's a crock,' Clay said. 'We heard the same thing about the New Hampshire border.'

Jordan goggled at him for a moment, then burst out laughing. The sound was clear and beautiful in the still air. Then, in the distance, a gun went off. And closer, someone shouted in either rage or horror.

Jordan stopped laughing.

'Tell us about that weird state they were in last night,'

Alice said quietly. 'And the music. Do all the other flocks listen to music at night?'

The Head looked at Jordan.

'Yes,' the boy said. 'It's all soft stuff, no rock, no country—'

'I should guess nothing classical, either,' the Head put in. 'Not of a challenging nature, at any rate.'

'It's their lullabies,' Jordan said. 'That's what the Head and me think, isn't it, sir?'

'The Head and *I*, Jordan.'

'Head and I, yes, sir.'

'But it is indeed what we think,' the Head agreed. 'Although I suspect there may be more to it than that. Yes, quite a bit more.'

Clay was flummoxed. He hardly knew how to go on. He looked at his friends and saw on their faces what he was feeling – not just puzzlement, but a dreadful reluctance to be enlightened.

Leaning forward, Headmaster Ardai said, 'May I be frank? I *must* be frank; it is the habit of a lifetime. I want you to help us do a terrible thing here. The time to do it is short, I think, and while one such act alone may come to nothing, one never knows, does one? One never knows what sort of communication may flow between these . . . flocks. In any case, I will not stand idly by while these . . . *things* . . . steal away not only my school but the very daylight itself. I might have attempted it already, but I'm old and Jordan is very young. Too young. Whatever they are now, they were human not long ago. I won't let him be a part of this.'

'I can do my share, sir!' Jordan said. He spoke as stoutly, Clay thought, as any Muslim teenager who ever strapped on a suicide belt stuffed with explosives.

'I salute your courage, Jordan,' the Head told him, 'but I think not.' He looked at the boy kindly, but when he returned his gaze to the others, his eyes had hardened considerably. 'You have weapons – good ones – and I have nothing but an old single-shot .22 rifle that may not even work anymore, although the barrel's open – I've looked. Even if it does work, the cartridges I have for it may not fire. But we have a gasoline pump at our little motor-pool, and gasoline might serve to end their lives.'

He must have seen the horror in their faces, because he nodded. To Clay he no longer looked like kindly old Mr Chips; he looked like a Puritan elder in an oil-painting. One who could have sentenced a man to the stocks without batting an eye. Or a woman to be burned at the stake as a witch.

He nodded at Clay in particular. Clay was sure of it. 'I know what I'm saying. I know how it sounds. But it wouldn't be murder, not really; it would be extermination. And I have no power to make you do anything. But in any case . . . whether you help me burn them or not, you must pass on a message.'

'To who?' Alice asked faintly.

'To everyone you meet, Miss Maxwell.' He leaned over the remains of their meal, those hanging-judge eyes sharp and small and burning hot. 'You must tell what's happening to *them* – to the ones who heard the infernal message on their devil's intercoms. You must pass this on. Everyone who has had the daylight robbed away from them must hear, and before it's too late.' He passed a hand over his lower face, and Clay saw the fingers were shaking a little. It would be easy to dismiss that as a sign of the man's age, but he hadn't seen any tremors before. 'We're afraid it soon will be. Aren't we, Jordan?'

'Yes, sir.' Jordan certainly thought he knew something; he looked terrified.

'What? What's happening to them?' Clay asked. 'It's got something to do with the music and those wired-together boomboxes, doesn't it?'

The Head sagged, suddenly looking tired. 'They're *not* wired together,' he said. 'Don't you remember me telling you that both of your premises were wrong?'

171

'Yes, but I don't understand what you m—'

'There's one sound-system with a CD in it, about that you're certainly right. A single compilation disc, Jordan says, which is why the same songs play over and over.'

'Lucky us,' Tom muttered, but Clay barely heard him. He was trying to get the sense of what Ardai had just said – *they're not wired together.* How could that be? It couldn't.

'The sound-systems – the boomboxes, if you like – are placed all around the field,' the Head went on, 'and they're all on. At night you can see their little red power lamps—'

'Yes,' Alice said. 'I did notice some red lights, I just didn't think anything of it.'

'—but there's nothing in them – no compact discs or cassette tapes – and no wires linking them. They're just slaves that pick up the master-disc audio and rebroadcast it.'

'If their mouths are open, the music comes from them, too,' Jordan said. 'It's just little . . . not hardly a whisper . . . but you can hear it.'

'No,' Clay said. 'That's your imagination, kiddo. Gotta be.'

'I haven't heard that myself,' Ardai said, 'but of course my ears aren't what they were back when I was a Gene Vincent and the Blue Caps fan. "Back in the day," Jordan and his friends would say.'

'You're *very* old-school, sir,' Jordan said. He spoke with gentle solemnity and unmistakable affection.

'Yes, Jordan, I am,' the Head agreed. He clapped the boy on the shoulder, then turned his attention to the others. 'If Jordan says he's heard it . . . I believe him.'

'It's not possible,' Clay said. 'Not without a transmitter.'

'*They* are transmitting,' the Head replied. 'It is a skill they seem to have picked up since the Pulse.'

'Wait,' Tom said. He raised one hand like a traffic cop, lowered it, began to speak, raised it again. From his place of dubious shelter at Headmaster Ardai's side, Jordan watched him closely. At last Tom said, 'Are we talking telepathy here?'

'I should guess that's not exactly *le mot juste* for this particular phenomenon,' the Head answered, 'but why stick at technicalities? I would be willing to wager all the frozen hamburgers remaining in my cooler that the word has been used among you before today.'

'You'd win double burgers,' Clay said.

'Well yeah, but the flocking thing is different,' Tom said.

'Because?' The Head raised his tangled brows.

'Well, because . . .' Tom couldn't finish, and Clay knew why. It *wasn't* different. The flocking wasn't human behavior and they'd known it from the moment they'd observed George the mechanic following the woman in the filthy pants suit across Tom's front lawn to Salem Street. He'd been walking so closely behind her that he could have bitten her neck . . . but he hadn't. And why? Because for the phone-crazies, biting was done, flocking had begun.

At least, biting their own kind was done. Unless—

'Professor Ardai, at the beginning they killed everyone . . .'

'Yes,' the Head agreed. 'We were very lucky to escape, weren't we, Jordan?'

Jordan shuddered and nodded. 'The kids ran everywhere. Even some of the teachers. Killing . . . biting . . . babbling nonsense stuff . . . I hid in one of the greenhouses for a while.'

'And I in the attic of this very house,' the Head added. 'I watched out of the small window up there as the campus – the campus I love – literally went to hell.'

Jordan said, 'Most of the ones who didn't die ran away toward downtown. Now a lot of them are back. Over there.' He nodded his head in the general direction of the soccer field.

'All of which leads us to what?' Clay asked.

'I think you know, Mr Riddell.'

'Clay.'

'Clay, fine. I think what's happening now is more than temporary anarchy. I think it's the start of a war. It's going to be a short but extremely nasty one.'

'Don't you think you're overstating—'

'I don't. While I have only my own observations to go on – mine and Jordan's – we've had a very large flock to observe, and we've seen them going and coming as well as . . . *resting,* shall we say. They've stopped killing each other, but they continue to kill the people we would classify as normal. I call that warlike behavior.'

'You've actually seen them killing normals?' Tom asked. Beside him, Alice opened her pack, removed the Baby Nike, and held it in her hand.

The Head looked at him gravely. 'I have. I'm sorry to say that Jordan has, too.'

'We couldn't help,' Jordan said. His eyes were leaking. 'There were too many. It was a man and a woman, see? I don't know what they were doing on campus so close to dark, but they sure couldn't've known about Tonney Field. She was hurt. He was helping her along. They ran into about twenty of *them* on their way back from town. The man tried to carry her.' Jordan's voice began to break. 'On his own he might have gotten away, but with her . . . he only made it as far as Horton Hall. That's a dorm. That's where he fell down and they caught them. *They—*'

Jordan abruptly buried his head against the old man's coat – a charcoal gray number this afternoon. The Head's big hand stroked the back of Jordan's smooth neck.

'They seem to know their enemies,' the Head mused. 'It may well have been part of the original message, don't you think?'

'Maybe,' Clay said. It made a nasty sort of sense.

'As to what they are doing at night as they lie there so still and open-eyed, listening to their music . . .' The Head sighed, took a handkerchief from one of his coat pockets, and wiped the boy's eyes with it in matter-of-fact fashion. Clay saw he was both very frightened and very sure of whatever conclusion he had drawn. 'I think they're rebooting,' he said.

15

'You note the red lamps, don't you?' the Head asked in his carrying I-will-be-heard-all-the-way-to-the-back-of-the-lecture-hall voice. 'I count at least sixty-thr—'

'Hush up!' Tom hissed. He did everything but clap a hand over the old man's mouth.

The Head looked at him calmly. 'Have you forgotten what I said last night about musical chairs, Tom?'

Tom, Clay, and Ardai were standing just beyond the turnstiles, with the Tonney Field archway at their backs. Alice had stayed at Cheatham Lodge with Jordan, by mutual agreement. The music currently drifting up from the prep-school soccer field was a jazz-instrumental version of 'The Girl from Ipanema.' Clay thought it was probably cutting-edge stuff if you were a phone-crazy.

'No,' Tom said. 'As long as the music doesn't stop, we have nothing to worry about. I just don't want to be the guy who gets his throat torn out by an insomniac exception to the rule.'

'You won't.'

'How can you be so positive, sir?' Tom asked.

'Because, to make a small literary pun, we cannot call it sleep. Come.'

He started down the concrete ramp the players once took to reach the field, saw that Tom and Clay were hanging back, and looked at them patiently. 'Little knowledge is gained without risk,' he said, 'and at this point, I would say knowledge is critical, wouldn't you? Come.'

They followed his rapping cane down the ramp toward the field, Clay a little ahead of Tom. Yes, he could see the red power-lamps of the boomboxes circling the field. Sixty or seventy looked about right. Good-sized sound-systems spotted at ten- or fifteen-foot intervals, each one surrounded with bodies. By starlight those bodies were an eye-boggling sight. They weren't stacked – each had his or her own space – but not so much as an inch had been wasted. Even the arms had been interwoven, so that the impression was one of paper dolls carpeting the field, rank on rank, while that music – *Like something you'd hear in a supermarket,* Clay thought – rose in the dark. Something else rose, as well: a sallow smell of dirt and rotting vegetables, with a thicker odour of human waste and putrefaction lingering just beneath.

The Head skirted the goal, which had been pushed aside, overturned, its netting shredded. Here, where the lake of bodies started, lay a young man of about thirty with jagged bite-marks running up one arm to the sleeve of his NASCAR T-shirt. The bites looked infected. In one hand he held a red cap that made Clay think of Alice's pet sneaker. He stared dully up at the stars as Bette Midler once more began singing about the wind beneath her wings.

'Hi!' the Head cried in his rusty, piercing voice. He poked the young man briskly in the middle with the tip of his cane, pushing in until the young man broke wind. 'Hi, I say!'

'Stop it!' Tom almost groaned.

The Head gave him a look of tight-lipped scorn, then worked the tip of his cane into the cap the young man was holding. He flicked it away. The cap sailed about ten feet and landed on the face of a middle-aged woman. Clay watched, fascinated, as it slid partially aside, revealing one rapt and blink-less eye.

The young man reached up with dreamy slowness and clutched the hand that had been holding the cap into a fist. Then he subsided.

'He thinks he's holding it again,' Clay whispered, fascinated.

'Perhaps,' the Head replied, without much interest. He poked the tip of his cane against one of the young man's infected bites. It should have hurt like hell, but the young man didn't react, only went on staring up at the sky as Bette Midler gave way to Dean Martin. 'I could put my cane right through his throat and he wouldn't try to stop me. Nor would

176

those around him spring to his defense, although in the daytime I have no doubt they'd tear me limb from limb.'

Tom was squatting by one of the ghetto blasters. 'There are batteries in this,' he said. 'I can tell by the weight.'

'Yes. In all of them. They do seem to need batteries.' The Head considered, then added something Clay could have done without. 'At least so far.'

'We could wade right in, couldn't we?' Clay said. 'We could wipe them out the way hunters exterminated passenger pigeons back in the 1880s.'

The Head nodded. 'Bashed their little brains out as they sat on the ground, didn't they? Not a bad analogy. But I'd make slow work of it with my cane. You'd make slow work of it even with your automatic weapon, I'm afraid.'

'I don't have enough bullets, in any case. There must be . . .' Clay ran his eye over the packed bodies again. Looking at them made his head hurt. 'There must be six or seven hundred. And that's not even counting the ones under the bleachers.'

'Sir? Mr Ardai?' It was Tom. 'When did you . . . how did you first . . . ?'

'How did I determine the depth of this trance state? Is that what you're asking me?'

Tom nodded.

'I came out the first night to observe. The flock was much smaller then, of course. I was drawn to them out of simple but overwhelming curiosity. Jordan wasn't with me. Switching to a nighttime existence has been rather hard for him, I'm afraid.'

'You risked your life, you know,' Clay said.

'I had little choice,' the Head replied. 'It was like being hypnotized. I quickly grasped the fact that they were unconscious even though their eyes were open, and a few simple experiments with the tip of my cane confirmed the depth of the state.'

Clay thought of the Head's limp, thought of asking

him if he'd considered what would have happened to him if he'd been wrong and they'd come after him, and held his tongue. The Head would no doubt reiterate what he'd already said: no knowledge obtained without risk. Jordan was right – this was one *very* old-school dude. Clay certainly wouldn't have wanted to be fourteen and standing on his disciplinary carpet.

Ardai, meanwhile, was shaking his head at him. 'Six or seven hundred's a very low estimate, Clay. This is a regulation-size soccer field. That's six thousand square yards.'

'How many?'

'The way they're packed together? I should say a thousand at the very least.'

'And they're not really here at all, are they? You're sure of that.'

'I am. And what comes back – a little more each day, Jordan says the same, and he's an acute observer, you may trust me on that – is not what they were. Which is to say, not human.'

'Can we go back to the Lodge now?' Tom asked. He sounded sick.

'Of course,' the Head agreed.

'Just a second,' Clay said. He knelt beside the young man in the NASCAR T-shirt. He didn't want to do it – he couldn't help thinking that the hand which had clutched for the red cap would now clutch at *him* – but he made himself. Down here at ground level the stink was worse. He had believed he was getting used to it, but he had been wrong.

Tom began, 'Clay, what are you—'

'Quiet.' Clay leaned toward the young man's mouth, which was partly open. He hesitated, then made himself lean closer, until he could see the dim shine of spit on the man's lower lip. At first he thought it might only be his imagination, but another two inches – he was now almost close enough to kiss the not-sleeping thing with Ricky Craven on its chest – took care of that.

178

It's just little, Jordan had said. *Not hardly a whisper . . . but you can hear it.*

Clay heard it, the vocal by some trick just a syllable or two ahead of the one coming from the linked boomboxes: Dean Martin singing 'Everybody Loves Somebody Sometime'.

He stood up, nearly screaming at the pistol-shot sound of his own knees cracking. Tom held up his lantern, looking at him, stare-eyed. 'What? *What?* You're not going to say that kid was—'

Clay nodded. 'Come on. Let's go back.'

Halfway up the ramp he grabbed the Head roughly by the shoulder. Ardai turned to face him, seemingly not disturbed to be handled so.

'You're right, sir. We have to get rid of them. As many as we can, and as fast as we can. This may be the only chance we get. Or do you think I'm wrong?'

'No,' the Head replied. 'Unfortunately, I don't. As I said, this is war – or so I believe – and what one does in war is kill one's enemies. Why don't we go back and talk it over? We could have hot chocolate. I like a tiny splash of bourbon in mine, barbarian that I am.'

At the top of the ramp, Clay spared one final look back. Tonney Field was dark, but under strong northern starlight not too dark to make out the carpet of bodies spread from end to end and side to side. He thought you might not know what you were looking at if you just happened to stumble on it, but once you did . . . once you did . . .

His eyes played him a funny trick and for a moment he almost thought he could see them breathing – all eight hundred or a thousand of them – as one organism. That frightened him badly and he turned to catch up to Tom and Headmaster Ardai, almost running.

16

The Head made hot chocolate in the kitchen and they drank it in the formal parlour, by the light of two gas lanterns. Clay thought the old man would suggest they go out to Academy Avenue later on, trolling for more volunteers in Ardai's Army, but he seemed satisfied with what he had.

The gasoline-pump at the motor pool, the Head told them, drew from a four-hundred-gallon overhead tank – all they'd have to do was pull a plug. And there were thirty-gallon sprayers in the greenhouse. At least a dozen. They could load up a pickup truck with them, perhaps, and back it down one of the ramps—

'Wait,' Clay said. 'Before we start talking strategy, if you have a theory about all this, sir, I'd like to hear it.'

'Nothing so formal,' the old man said. 'But Jordan and I have observation, we have intuition, and we have a fair amount of experience between the two of us—'

'I'm a computer geek,' Jordan said over his mug of hot chocolate. Clay found the child's glum assurance oddly charming. 'A total McNerd. Been on em my whole life, just about. Those things're rebooting, all right. They might as well have SOFTWARE INSTALLATION, PLEASE STAND BY blinking on their foreheads.'

'I don't understand you,' Tom said.

'I do,' Alice said. 'Jordan, you think the Pulse really *was* a Pulse, don't you? Everyone who heard it . . . they got their hard drives wiped.'

'Well, *yeah*,' Jordan said. He was too polite to say Well, *duh*.

Tom looked at Alice, perplexed. Only Clay knew Tom wasn't dumb, and he didn't believe Tom was that slow.

'You had a computer,' Alice said. 'I saw it in your little office.'

'Yes—'

'And you've installed software, right?'

180

'Sure, but—' Tom stopped, looking at Alice fixedly. She looked back. 'Their *brains*? You mean their *brains*?'

'What do you think a brain is?' Jordan said. 'A big old hard drive. Organic circuitry. No one knows how many bytes. Say giga to the power of a googolplex. An infinity of bytes.' He put his hands to his ears, which were small and neatly made. 'Right in between here.'

'I don't believe it,' Tom said, but he spoke in a small voice and there was a sick look on his face. Clay thought he *did* believe it. Thinking back to the madness that had convulsed Boston, Clay had to admit the idea was persuasive. It was also terrible: millions, perhaps even billions, of brains all wiped clean at the same time, the way you could wipe an old-fashioned computer disc with a powerful magnet.

He found himself remembering Pixie Dark, the friend of the girl with the peppermint-colored cell phone. *Who are you? What's happening?* Pixie Dark had cried. *Who are you? Who am I?* Then she had smacked herself repeatedly in the forehead with the heel of her hand and had gone running full tilt into a lamppost, not once but twice, smashing her expensive orthodontic work to jagged pieces.

Who are you? Who am I?

It hadn't been *her* cell phone. She had only been listening in and hadn't gotten a full dose.

Clay, who thought in images rather than words a good deal of the time, now got a vivid mental picture of a computer screen filling up with those words: WHO ARE YOU WHO AM I WHO ARE YOU WHO AM I WHO ARE YOU WHO AM I WHO ARE YOU WHO AM I, and finally, at the bottom, as bleak and inarguable as Pixie Dark's fate:

SYSTEM FAILURE.

Pixie Dark as a partially wiped hard drive? It was horrible, but it felt like the stone truth.

'I majored in English, but as a young man I read a great

deal of psychology,' the Head told them. 'I began with Freud, of course, everyone begins with Freud . . . then Jung . . . Adler . . . worked my way around the whole ballfield from there. Lurking behind all theories of how the mind works is a greater theory: Darwin's. In Freud's vocabulary, the idea of survival as the prime directive is expressed by the concept of the id. In Jung's, by the rather grander idea of blood consciousness. Neither man, I think, would argue with the idea that if *all* conscious thought, *all* memory, *all* ratiocinative ability, were to be stripped from a human mind in a moment, what would remain would be pure and terrible.'

He paused, looking around for comment. None of them said anything. The Head nodded as if satisfied and resumed.

'Although neither the Freudians nor the Jungians come right out and say it, they strongly suggest that we *may* have a core, a single basic carrier wave, or – to use language with which Jordan is comfortable – a single line of written code which cannot be stripped.'

'The PD,' Jordan said. 'The prime directive.'

'Yes,' the Head agreed. 'At bottom, you see, we are not *Homo sapiens* at all. Our core is madness. The prime directive is murder. What Darwin was too polite to say, my friends, is that we came to rule the earth not because we were the smartest, or even the meanest, but because we have always been the craziest, most murderous motherfuckers in the jungle. And that is what the Pulse exposed five days ago.'

17

'I refuse to believe that we were lunatics and murderers before we were anything else,' Tom said. 'Christ, man, what about the Parthenon? What about Michelangelo's *David*? What about that plaque on the moon that says, "We came in peace for all mankind"?'

'That plaque also has Richard Nixon's name on it,' Ardai said drily. 'A Quaker, but hardly a man of peace. Mr McCourt

– Tom – I have no interest in handing down an indictment of mankind. If I did, I'd point out that for every Michelangelo there's a Marquis de Sade, for every Gandhi an Eichmann, for every Martin Luther King an Osama bin Laden. Leave it at this: man has come to dominate the planet thanks to two essential traits. One is intelligence. The other has been the absolute willingness to kill anyone and anything that gets in his way.'

He leaned forward, surveying them with his bright eyes.

'Mankind's intelligence finally trumped mankind's killer instinct, and reason came to rule over mankind's maddest impulses. That, too, was survival. I believe the final showdown between the two may have come in October of 1963, over a handful of missiles in Cuba, but that is a discussion for another day. The fact is, most of us had sublimated the worst in us until the Pulse came along and stripped away everything but that red core.'

'Someone let the Tasmanian devil out of its cage,' Alice murmured. 'Who?'

'That need not concern us, either,' the Head replied. 'I suspect they had no idea of what they were doing . . . or how *much* they were doing. Based upon what must have been hurried experiments over a few years – perhaps even months – they may have thought they would unleash a destructive storm of terrorism. Instead they unleashed a tsunami of untold violence, and it's mutating. Horrible as the current days may now seem, we may later view them as a lull between one storm and the next. These days may also be our only chance to make a difference.'

'What do you mean, mutating?' Clay asked.

But the Head didn't answer. Instead he turned to twelve-year-old Jordan. 'If you please, young man.'

'Yes. Well.' Jordan paused to think. 'Your conscious mind only uses a tiny percentage of your brain's capacity. You guys know that, right?'

'Yes,' Tom said, a bit indulgently. 'So I've read.'

Jordan nodded. 'Even when you add in all the autonomic

functions they control, plus the subconscious stuff – dreams, blink-think, the sex drive, all that jazz – our brains are barely ticking over.'

'Holmes, you astound me,' Tom said.

'Don't be a wiseass, Tom!' Alice said, and Jordan gave her a decidedly starry-eyed smile.

'I'm not,' Tom said. 'The kid is good.'

'Indeed he is,' the Headmaster said drily. 'Jordan may have occasional problems with the King's English, but he did not get his scholarship for excelling at tiddlywinks.' He observed the boy's discomfort and gave Jordan's hair an affectionate scruff with his bony fingers. 'Continue, please.'

'Well . . .' Jordan struggled, Clay could see it, and then seemed to find his rhythm again. 'If your brain really *was* a hard drive, the can would be almost empty.' He saw only Alice understood this. 'Put it this way: the info strip would say something like 2 percent in use, 98 percent available. No one has any real idea what that ninety-eight percent is for, but there's plenty of potential there. Stroke victims, for instance . . . they sometimes access previously dormant areas of their brains in order to walk and talk again. It's like their brains wire *around* the blighted area. The lights go on in a similar area of the brain, but on the other side.'

'You study this stuff?' Clay asked.

'It's a natural outgrowth of my interest in computers and cybernetics,' Jordan said, shrugging. 'Also, I read a lot of cyber-punk science fiction. William Gibson, Bruce Sterling, John Shirley—'

'Neal Stephenson?' Alice asked.

Jordan grinned radiantly. 'Neal Stephenson's a *god*.'

'Back on message,' the Head chided . . . but gently.

Jordan shrugged. 'If you wipe a computer hard drive, it can't regenerate spontaneously . . . except maybe in a Greg Bear novel.' He grinned again, but this time it was quick and, Clay thought, rather nervous. Part of it was Alice, who clearly knocked the kid out. 'People are different.'

'But there's a huge leap between learning to walk again after a stroke and being able to power a bunch of boomboxes by telepathy,' Tom said. 'A quantum leap.' He looked around self-consciously as the word *telepathy* came out of his mouth, as if expecting them to laugh. No one did.

'Yeah, but a stroke victim, even someone who has a bad one, is light-years different from what happened to people who were on their cells during the Pulse,' Jordan replied. 'Me and the Head – the Head and *I* – think that in addition to stripping people's brains all the way to that one unerasable line of code, the Pulse also kicked something on. Something that's probably been sitting inside all of us for millions of years, buried in that ninety-eight percent of dormant hard drive.'

Clay's hand stole to the butt of the revolver he had picked up off the floor in Beth Nickerson's kitchen. 'A trigger,' he said.

Jordan lit up. 'Yeah, exactly! A *mutative* trigger. It never could have happened without this, like, total erasure on a grand scale. Because what's emerging, what's building up in those people out there . . . only they're no longer people, what's building up is—'

'It's a single organism,' the Head interrupted. 'This is what we believe.'

'Yes, but more than just a *flock,*' Jordan said. 'Because what they can do with the CD players may only be the start, like a little kid learning to put his shoes on. Think about what they might be able to do in a week. Or a month. Or a year.'

'You could be wrong,' Tom said, but his voice was as dry as a breaking stick.

'He could also be right,' Alice said.

'Oh, I'm sure he's right,' the Head put in. He sipped his spiked hot chocolate. 'Of course, I'm an old man and my time is almost over in any case. I'll abide by any decision you make.' A slight pause. The eyes flicked from Clay to Alice to Tom. 'As long as it's the right one, of course.'

Jordan said: 'The flocks will try to come together, you know. If they don't hear each other already, they will real soon.'

'Crap,' Tom said uneasily. 'Ghost stories.'

'Maybe,' Clay said, 'but here's something to think about. Right now the nights are ours. What if they decide they need less sleep? Or that they're not afraid of the dark?'

No one said anything for several moments. A wind was rising outside. Clay sipped his hot chocolate, which had never been much more than tepid and was now almost cold. When he looked up again, Alice had put hers aside and was holding her Nike talisman instead.

'I want to wipe them out,' she said. 'The ones on the soccer field, I want to wipe them out. I don't say kill them because I think Jordan's right, and I don't want to do it for the human race. I want to do it for my mother and my dad, because he's gone, too. I know he is, I feel it. I want to do it for my friends Vickie and Tess. They were good friends, but they had cell phones, they never went anywhere without them, and I know what they're like now and where they're sleeping: someplace just like that fucking soccer field.' She glanced at the Head, flushing. ''Scuse me, sir.'

The Head waved her apology away.

'Can we do that?' she asked him. 'Can we wipe them out?'

Charles Ardai, who had been winding down his career as Gaiten Academy's interim Headmaster when the world ended, bared his eroded teeth in a grin Clay would have given much to have captured with pen or brush; there was not a single ounce of pity in it.

'Miss Maxwell, we can try,' he said.

18

At four o'clock the next morning, Tom McCourt sat on a picnic table between the two Gaiten Academy greenhouses, which had both sustained serious damage since the Pulse. His feet, now wearing the Reeboks he'd donned back in Malden, were on one of the benches, and his head lay on his arms, which rested on his knees. The wind blew his hair first one way, then the other. Alice sat across from him with her chin propped on her hands and the rays of several flashlights striking angles and shadows across her face. The harsh light made her look pretty in spite of her obvious weariness; at her age, all light was still flattering. The Head, sitting next to her, only looked exhausted. In the closer of the two greenhouses, two Coleman gas-lanterns floated like uneasy spirits.

The Colemans converged at the near end of the greenhouse. Clay and Jordan used the door, although huge holes in the glass paneling had been opened on either side. A moment later, Clay sat down next to Tom and Jordan resumed his usual spot next to the Head. The boy smelled of gasoline and fertilizer, even more strongly of dejection. Clay dropped several sets of keys on the table amid the flashlights. As far as he was concerned, they could stay there until some archaeologist discovered them four millennia from now.

'I'm sorry,' Headmaster Ardai said softly. 'It seemed so simple.'

'Yeah,' Clay said. It *had* seemed simple: fill the greenhouse sprayers with gasoline, load the sprayers into the back of a pickup truck, drive across Tonney Field, wetting down both sides as they went, toss a match. He thought to tell Ardai that George W. Bush's Iraq adventure had probably looked equally simple – load the sprayers, toss a match – and didn't. It would have been pointlessly cruel.

'Tom?' Clay asked. 'You okay?' He had already realised that Tom didn't have great reserves of stamina.

'Yeah, just tired.' He raised his head and gave Clay a smile. 'Not used to the night shift. What do we do now?'

'Go to bed, I guess,' Clay said. 'It'll be dawn in another forty minutes or so.' The sky had already begun to lighten in the east.

'It's not fair,' Alice said. She brushed angrily at her cheeks. 'It's not fair, we tried so *hard*!'

They *had* tried hard, but nothing had come easily. Every small (and ultimately meaningless) victory had been the sort of maddening struggle his mother had called a Bolshie shit-pull. Part of Clay *did* want to blame the Head . . . also himself, for not taking Ardai's sprayer idea with a grain of salt. Part of him now thought that going along with an elderly English teacher's plan to firebomb a soccer field was a little like taking a knife to a gunfight. Still . . . yeah, it had seemed like a good idea.

Until, that was, they discovered the motor pool's gasoline storage tank was inside a locked shed. They'd spent nearly half an hour in the nearby office, scrounging by lantern-light through maddeningly unmarked keys on a board behind the superintendent's desk. It was Jordan who finally found the key that unlocked the shed door.

Then they discovered that *One would only have to pull a plug* was not exactly the case. There was a cap, not a plug. And like the shed in which the tank resided, the cap was locked. Back to the office; another scrounge by lantern-light; finally a key that did indeed seem to fit the cap. It was Alice who pointed out that since the cap was on the bottom of the tank, assuring gravity-feed in case of a power outage, they would have a flood on their hands without a hose or a siphon. They spent an hour looking for a hose that might fit and couldn't find anything that looked even close. Tom found a small funnel, which sent them all into moderate hysterics.

And because none of the truck keys were marked (at least in ways non-motor-pool employees could understand), locating the right set became another process of trial and error. This one went faster, at least, because there were only eight trucks parked behind the garage.

And last, the greenhouses. There they discovered only eight sprayers, not a dozen, with a capacity of not thirty gallons each but ten. They might be able to fill them from the gasoline storage tank, but they would be drenched in the process, and the result would be a mere eighty gallons of usable, sprayable gas. It was the idea of wiping out a thousand phone-crazies with eighty gallons of regular that had driven Tom, Alice, and the Head out to the picnic bench. Clay and Jordan had hung in a while longer, looking for bigger sprayers, but they had found none.

'We found a few little leaf-sprayers, though,' Clay said. 'You know, what they used to call flit-guns.'

'Also,' Jordan said, 'the big sprayers in there are all full of weed-killer or plant-food or something. We'd have to start by dumping them all out, and that would mean putting on masks just to make sure we didn't gas ourselves or something.'

'Reality bites,' Alice said morosely. She looked at her baby sneaker for a moment, then tucked it away in her pocket.

Jordan picked up the keys they had matched to one of the maintenance pickups. 'We could drive downtown,' he said. 'There's a Trustworthy Hardware. *They* must have sprayers.'

Tom shook his head. 'It's over a mile and the main drag's full of wrecks and abandoned vehicles. We might be able to get around some, but not all. And driving over the lawns is out of the question. The houses are just too close together. There are reasons everybody's on foot.' They had seen a few people on bicycles, but not many; even the ones equipped with lights were dangerous if ridden at any speed.

'Would it be possible for a light truck to negotiate the side streets?' the Head asked.

Clay said, 'We could explore the possibility tomorrow night, I suppose. Scout out a path in advance, on foot, then come back for the truck.' He considered. 'They'd probably have all sorts of hose in a hardware store, too.'

'You don't sound exactly jazzed,' Alice said.

Clay sighed. 'It doesn't take much to block little streets. We'd end up doing a lot of donkey-work even if we got luckier than we did tonight. I just don't know. Maybe it'll look better to me after some rest.'

'Of course it will,' the Head agreed, but he sounded hollow. 'To all of us.'

'What about the gas station across from the school?' Jordan asked without much hope.

'What gas station?' Alice asked.

'He's talking about the Citgo,' the Head replied. 'Same problem, Jordan – plenty of gasoline in the tanks under the pumps, but no power. And I doubt if they have much in the way of containers beyond a few two- or five-gallon gasoline cans. I really think—' But he didn't say what he really thought. He broke off. 'What is it, Clay?'

Clay was remembering the trio ahead of them limping past that gas station, one of the men with an arm around the woman's waist. 'Academy Grove Citgo,' he said. 'That's the name, isn't it?'

'Yes—'

'But they didn't just sell gasoline, I think.' He didn't just think, he *knew*. Because of the two trucks parked on the side. He had seen them and hadn't thought anything of them. Not then, he hadn't. No reason to.

'I don't know what you—' the Head began, then stopped. His eyes met Clay's. His eroded teeth once more made their appearance in that singularly pitiless smile. 'Oh,' he said. '*Oh. Oh my. Oh my, yes.*'

Tom was looking between them with mounting perplexity. So was Alice. Jordan merely waited.

'Would you mind telling the rest of us what you two are communing about?' Tom asked.

Clay was ready to – he already saw clearly how it would work, and it was too good not to share – when the music from Tonney Field died away. It didn't click off, as it usually did when they woke up in the morning; it went in a kind of swoop, as if someone had just kicked the source down an elevator shaft.

'They're up early,' Jordan said in a low voice.

Tom gripped Clay's forearm. 'It's not the same,' he said. 'And one of those damned ghetto blasters is still playing . . . I can hear it, very faint.'

The wind was strong, and Clay knew it was blowing from the direction of the soccer field because of the ripe smells it carried: decaying food, decaying flesh, hundreds of unwashed bodies. It also carried the ghostly sound of Lawrence Welk and his Champagne Music Makers playing 'Baby Elephant Walk'.

Then, from somewhere to the northwest – maybe ten miles away, maybe thirty, it was hard to tell how far the wind might have carried it – came a spectral, somehow mothlike moaning sound. There was silence . . . silence . . . and then the not-waking, not-sleeping creatures on the Tonney soccer field answered in kind. Their moan was much louder, a hollow, belling ghost-groan that rose towards the black and starry sky.

Alice had covered her mouth. The baby sneaker jutted upward from her hands. Her eyes bulged on either side of it. Jordan had thrown his arms around the Head's waist and buried his face against the old man's side.

'Look, Clay!' Tom said. He got to his feet and tottered toward the grassy aisle between the two shattered greenhouses, pointing at the sky as he went. 'Do you see? My God, do you see?'

To the northwest, from where the distant groan had risen, a reddish orange glow had bloomed on the horizon. It strengthened as he watched, the wind bore that terrible sound again . . . and once more it was answered with a similar but much louder groan from Tonney Field.

Alice joined them, then the Head, walking with his arm around Jordan's shoulders.

'What's over there?' Clay asked, pointing toward the glow. It had already begun to wane again.

'It might be Glen's Falls,' the Headmaster said. 'Or it might be Littleton.'

'Wherever it is, there's shrimp on the barbie,' Tom said. 'They're burning. And our bunch knows. They heard.'

'Or *felt,*' Alice said. She shuddered, then straightened and bared her teeth. 'I hope they did!'

As if in answer, there was another groan from Tonney Field: many voices raised as one in a cry of sympathy and – perhaps – shared agony. The one boombox – it was the master, Clay assumed, the one with an actual compact disc in it – continued to play. Ten minutes later, the others joined in once more. The music – it now was 'Close to You', by The Carpenters – swooped up, just as it had previously swooped down. By then Headmaster Ardai, limping noticeably on his cane, had led them back to Cheatham Lodge. Not long after that, the music stopped again . . . but this time it simply clicked off, as it had the previous morning. From far away, carried across God alone knew how many miles by the wind, came the faint pop of a gunshot. Then the world was eerily and completely silent, waiting for the dark to give place to the day.

19

As the sun began to spoke its first red rays through the trees on the eastern horizon, they watched the phone-crazies once again begin leaving the soccer field in close-order patterns, headed for downtown Gaiten and the surrounding neigh-borhoods. They fanned out as they went, headed downhill toward Academy Avenue as if nothing untoward had happened near the end of the night. But Clay didn't trust that. He thought they had better do their business at the Citgo station quickly, today, if they intended to do it at all. Going out in the daylight might mean shooting some of *them,* but as long as they only moved en masse at the beginning and end of the day, he was willing to take that risk.

They watched what Alice called 'the dawn of the dead' from the dining room. Afterward, Tom and the Head went into the kitchen. Clay found them sitting at the table in a bar of sunshine and drinking tepid coffee. Before Clay could begin explaining what he wanted to do later in the day, Jordan touched his wrist.

'Some of the crazies are still there,' he said. And, in a lower voice: 'I went to school with some of them.'

Tom said, 'I thought they'd all be shopping Kmart by now, looking for Blue Light Specials.'

'You better check it out,' Alice said from the doorway. 'I'm not sure it's another – what-would-you-call-it, developmental step forward, but it might be. It probably is.'

'Sure it is,' Jordan said gloomily.

The phone-crazies who had stayed behind – Clay thought it was a squad of about a hundred – were removing the dead from beneath the bleachers. At first they simply carried them off into the parking lot south of the field and behind a long low brick building. They came back empty-handed.

'That building's the indoor track,' the Head told them. 'It's also where all the sports gear is stored. There's a steep drop-off on the far side. I imagine they're throwing the bodies over the edge.'

'You bet,' Jordan said. He sounded sick. 'It's all marshy down there. They'll rot.'

'They were rotting anyway, Jordan,' Tom said gently.

'I know,' he said, sounding sicker than ever, 'but they'll rot even faster in the sun.' A pause. 'Sir?'

'Yes, Jordan?'

'I saw Noah Chutsky. From your Drama Reading Club.'

The Head patted the boy's shoulder. He was very pale. 'Never mind.'

'It's hard not to,' Jordan whispered. 'He took my picture once. With his . . . with his you-know.'

Then, a new wrinkle. Two dozen of the worker-bees peeled off from the main group with no pause for discussion and headed for the shattered greenhouses, moving in a V-shape that reminded the watchers of migrating geese. The one Jordan had identified as Noah Chutsky was among these. The rest of the body-removal squad watched them go for a moment, then marched back down the ramps, three abreast, and resumed fishing dead bodies out from under the bleachers.

Twenty minutes later the greenhouse party returned, now spread out in a single line. Some were still empty-handed, but most had acquired wheelbarrows or handcarts of the sort used to transport large bags of lime or fertilizer. Soon the phone-crazies were using the carts and barrows to dispose of the bodies, and their work went faster.

'It's a step forward, all right,' Tom said.

'More than one,' the Head added. 'Cleaning house; using tools to do it.'

Clay said, 'I don't like this.'

Jordan looked up at him, his face pale and tired and far older than its years. 'Join the club,' he said.

20

They slept until one in the afternoon. Then, after confirming that the body detail had finished its work and gone to join the rest of the foragers, they went down to the fieldstone pillars marking the entrance to Gaiten Academy. Alice had scoffed at Clay's idea that he and Tom should do this on their own. 'Never mind that Batman and Robin crap,' she said.

'Oh my, I always wanted to be the Boy Wonder,' Tom said with a trace of a lisp, but when she gave him a humor-less look, her sneaker (now beginning to look a bit tattered) clasped in one hand, he wilted. 'Sorry.'

'You can go across to the gas station on your own,' she said. 'That much makes sense. But the rest of us will stand lookout on the other side.'

The Head had suggested that Jordan should stay behind at the Lodge. Before the boy could respond – and he looked ready to do so hotly – Alice asked, 'How are your eyes, Jordan?'

He had given her a smile, once more accompanied by the slightly starry look. 'Good. Fine.'

'And you've played video games? The ones where you shoot?'

'Sure, a ton.'

She handed him her pistol. Clay could see him quiver slightly, like a tapped tuning fork, when their fingers touched. 'If I tell you to point and shoot − or if Headmaster Ardai tells you − will you do it?'

'Sure.'

Alice had looked at Ardai with a mixture of defiance and apology. 'We need every hand.'

The Head had given in, and now here they were and there was the Academy Grove Citgo, on the other side of the street and just a little way back toward town. From here the other, slightly smaller, sign was easy to read: ACADEMY LP GAS. The single car standing at the pumps with its driver's door open already had a dusty, long-deserted look. The gas station's big plate-glass window was broken. Off to the right, parked in the shade of what had to be one of northern New England's few surviving elm trees, were two trucks shaped like giant propane bottles. Written on the side of each were the words **Academy LP Gas** and **Serving Southern New Hampshire Since 1982.**

There was no sign of foraging phone-crazies on this part of Academy Avenue, and although most of the houses Clay could see had shoes on their front stoops, several did not. The rush of refugees seemed to be drying up. *Too early to tell,* he cautioned himself.

'Sir? Clay? What's that?' Jordan asked. He was pointing to the middle of the Avenue − which of course was still Route 102, although that was easy to forget on this sunny, quiet afternoon where the closest sounds were birds and the rustle of the wind in the leaves. There was something written in bright pink chalk on the asphalt, but from where they were, Clay couldn't make it out. He shook his head.

'Are you ready?' he asked Tom.

'Sure,' Tom said. He was trying to sound casual, but a pulse beat rapidly on the side of his unshaven throat. 'You Batman, me Boy Wonder.'

They trotted across the street, pistols in hand. Clay had left the Russian automatic weapon with Alice, more or less convinced it would spin her around like a top if she actually had to use it.

The message scrawled in pink chalk on the macadam was

KASHWAK=NO-FO

'Does that mean anything to you?' Tom asked.

Clay shook his head. It didn't, and right now he didn't care. All he wanted was to get out of the middle of Academy Avenue, where he felt as exposed as an ant in a bowl of rice. It occurred to him, suddenly and not for the first time, that he would sell his soul just to know that his son was okay, and in a place where people weren't putting guns into the hands of children who were good at video games. It was strange. He'd think he had his priorities settled, that he was dealing with his personal deck one card at a time, and then these thoughts would come, each as fresh and painful as an unsettled grief.

Get out of here, Johnny. You don't belong here. Not your place, not your time.

The propane trucks were empty and locked, but that was all right; today their luck was running the right way. The keys were hanging on a board in the office, below a sign reading **NO TOWING BETWEEN MIDNITE AND 6 AM NO EXEMPTIONS**. A tiny propane bottle dangled from each keychain. Halfway back to the door, Tom touched Clay's shoulder.

Two phone-crazies walked up the middle of the street, side by side but by no means in lockstep. One was eating

Twinkies from a box of them; his face was lathered with cream, crumbs, and frosting. The other, a woman, was holding a coffee-table-sized book out in front of her. To Clay she looked like a choir-member holding an oversize hymnal. On the front there appeared to be a photograph of a collie jumping through a tire swing. The fact that the woman held the book upside down gave Clay some comfort. The vacant, blasted expressions on their faces – and the fact that they were wandering on their own, meaning midday was still a non-flocking time – gave him more.

But he didn't like that book.

No, he didn't like that book at all.

They wandered past the fieldstone pillars, and Clay could see Alice, Jordan, and the Head peering out, wide-eyed. The two crazies walked over the cryptic message chalked in the street – *KASHWAK=NO-FO* – and the woman reached for her companion's Twinkies. The man held the box away from her. The woman cast her book aside (it landed rightside up and Clay saw it was *100 Best Loved Dogs of the World*) and reached again. The man slapped her face hard enough to make her filthy hair fly, the sound very loud in the stillness of the day. All this time they were walking. The woman made a sound: '*Aw!*' The man replied (it sounded to Clay like a reply): '*Eeeen!*' The woman reached for the box of Twinkies. Now they were passing the Citgo. The man punched her in the neck this time, a looping overhand blow, and then dived a hand into his box for another treat. The woman stopped. Looked at him. And a moment later the man stopped. He had pulled a bit ahead, so his back was mostly to her.

Clay felt something in the sunwarmed stillness of the gas station office. *No*, he thought, *not in the office, in me. Shortness of breath, like after you climb a flight of stairs too fast.*

Except maybe it was in the office, too, because—

Tom stood on his toes and whispered in his ear, 'Do you feel that?'

Clay nodded and pointed at the desk. There was no wind,

no discernible draft, but the papers there were fluttering. And in the ashtray, the ashes had begun to circle lazily, like water going down a bathtub drain. There were two butts in there – no, three – and the moving ashes seemed to be pushing them toward the center.

The man turned toward the woman. He looked back at her. She looked at him. They looked at each other. Clay could read no expression on either face, but he could feel the hairs on his arms stirring, and he heard a faint jingling. It was the keys on the board below the **NO TOWING** sign. They were stirring, too – chittering against each other just the tiniest bit.

'*Aw!*' said the woman. She held out her hand.

'*Eeen!*' said the man. He was wearing the fading remains of a suit. On his feet were dull black shoes. Six days ago he might have been a middle manager, a salesman, or an apartment-complex manager. Now the only real estate he cared about was his box of Twinkies. He held it to his chest, his sticky mouth working.

'*Aw!*' the woman insisted. She held out both hands instead of just one, the immemorial gesture signifying *gimme,* and the keys were jingling louder. Overhead there was a *bzzzzt* as a fluorescent light for which there was no power flickered and then went out again. The nozzle fell off the middle gas pump and hit the concrete island with a dead-metal clank.

'*Aw,*' the man said. His shoulders slumped and all the tension went out of him. The tension went out of the air. The keys on the board fell silent. The ashes made one final, slowing circuit of their dented metal reliquary and came to a stop. You would not have known anything had happened, Clay thought, if not for the fallen nozzle out there and the little cluster of cigarette butts in the ashtray on the desk in here.

'*Aw,*' the woman said. She was still holding out her hands. Her companion advanced to within reach of them. She took a Twinkie in each and began to eat them, wrappings and all. Once more Clay was comforted, but only a little. They resumed their slow shuffle toward town, the woman pausing long enough to spit a filling-caked piece of cellophane from the side of her mouth. She showed no interest in *100 Best Loved Dogs of the World*.

'What was *that*?' Tom asked in a low and shaken voice when the two of them were almost out of sight.

'I don't know, but I didn't like it,' Clay said. He had the keys to the propane trucks. He handed one set to Tom. 'Can you drive a standard shift?'

'I *learned* on a standard. Can you?'

Clay smiled patiently. 'I'm straight, Tom. Straight guys know how to drive standards without instruction. It's instinct with us.'

'Very funny.' Tom wasn't really listening. He was looking after the departed odd couple, and that pulse in the side of his throat was going faster than ever. 'End of the world, open season on the queers, why not, right?'

'That's right. It's gonna be open season on straights, too, if they get *that* shit under control. Come on, let's do it.'

He started out the door, but Tom held him back a minute. 'Listen. The others may have felt that over there, or they may not have. If they didn't, maybe we should keep it to ourselves for the time being. What do you think?'

Clay thought about how Jordan wouldn't let the Head out of his sight and how Alice always kept the creepy little sneaker somewhere within reach. He thought about the circles under their eyes, and then about what they were planning to do tonight. Armageddon was probably too strong a word for it, but not by much. Whatever they were now, the phone-crazies had once been human beings, and burning a thousand of them alive was burden enough. Even thinking about it hurt his imagination.

'Fine by me,' he said. 'Go up the hill in low gear, all right?'

'Lowest one I can find,' Tom said. They were walking to the big bottle-shaped trucks now. 'How many gears do you think a truck like that has?'

'One forward should be enough,' Clay said.

'Based on the way they're parked, I think you're going to have to start by finding reverse.'

'Fuck it,' Clay said. 'What good is the end of the world if you can't drive through a goddam board fence?'

And that was what they did.

21

Academy Slope was what Headmaster Ardai and his one remaining pupil called the long, rolling hill that dropped from the campus to the main road. The grass was still bright green and only beginning to be littered with fallen leaves. When afternoon gave way to early evening and Academy Slope was still empty – no sign of returning phone-crazies – Alice began to pace the main hall of Cheatham Lodge, pausing in each circuit only long enough to look out the bay window of the living room. It offered a fine view of the Slope, the two main lecture halls, and Tonney Field. The sneaker was once more tied to her wrist.

The others were in the kitchen, sipping Cokes from cans. 'They're not coming back,' she told them at the end of one of her circuits. 'They got wind of what we were planning – read our minds or something – and they're not coming.'

Two more circuits of the long downstairs hall, each with a pause to look out the big living room window, and then she looked in on them again. 'Or maybe it's a general migration, did you guys ever think of that? Maybe they go south in the winter like the goddam robins.'

She was gone without waiting for a reply. Up the hall and down the hall. Up and down the hall.

'She's like Ahab on the prod for Moby,' the Head remarked.

'Eminem might have been a jerk, but he was right about that guy,' Tom said morosely.

'I beg your pardon, Tom?' the Head asked.

Tom waved it away.

Jordan glanced at his watch. 'They didn't come back last night until almost half an hour later than it is right now,' he said. 'I'll go tell her that, if you want.'

'I don't think it would do any good,' Clay said. 'She's got to work through it, that's all.'

'She's pretty freaked-out, isn't she, sir?'

'Aren't you, Jordan?'

'Yes,' Jordan said in a small voice. 'I'm Freak City.'

The next time Alice came back to the kitchen she said, 'Maybe it's best if they *don't* come back. I don't know if they're rebooting their brains some new way, but for sure there's some bad voodoo going on. I felt it from those two this afternoon. The woman with the book and the man with the Twinkies?' She shook her head. 'Bad voodoo.'

She plunged off on hall patrol again before anyone could reply, the sneaker swinging from her wrist.

The Head looked at Jordan. 'Did you feel anything, son?'

Jordan hesitated, then said, 'I felt *something*. The hair on my neck tried to stand up.'

Now the Head turned his gaze to the men on the other side of the table. 'What about you two? You were far closer.'

Alice saved them from having to answer. She ran into the kitchen, her cheeks flushed, her eyes wide, the soles of her sneakers squeaking on the tiles. 'They're coming,' she said.

22

From the bay window the four of them watched the phone-crazies come up Academy Slope in converging lines, their long shadows making a huge pinwheel shape on the green grass. As they neared what Jordan and the Head called Tonney

Arch, the lines drew together and the pinwheel seemed to spin in the late golden sunlight even as it contracted and solidified.

Alice could no longer stand not holding the sneaker. She had torn it from her wrist and was squeezing it compulsively. 'They'll see what we did and they'll turn around,' she said, speaking low and rapidly. 'They've gotten at least *that* smart, if they're picking up books again, they must have.'

'We'll see,' Clay said. He was almost positive the phone-crazies *would* go onto Tonney Field, even if what they saw there disquieted their strange group mind; it would be dark soon and they had nowhere else to go. A fragment of a lullaby his mother used to sing him floated through his mind: *Little man, you've had a busy day.*

'I hope they go and I hope they stay,' she said, lower than ever. 'I feel like I'm going to explode.' She gave a wild little laugh. 'Only it's *them* that's supposed to explode, isn't it? *Them.*' Tom turned to look at her and she said, 'I'm all right. I'm fine, so just close your mouth.'

'All I was going to say is that it'll be what it is,' he said.

'New Age crap. You sound like my father. The Picture Frame King.' A tear rolled down one cheek and she rubbed it impatiently away with the heel of her hand.

'Just calm down, Alice. Watch.'

'I'll try, okay? I'll try.'

'And stop with the sneaker,' Jordan said – irritably, for him. 'That squelchy sound is making me crazy.'

She looked down at the sneaker, as if surprised, then slipped it around her wrist on its loop again. They watched as the phone-crazies converged at Tonney Arch and passed beneath it with less pushing and confusion than any crowd attending the Homecoming Weekend soccer match could ever have equaled – Clay was sure of that. They watched as the crazies spread out again on the far side, crossing the concourse and filing down the ramps. They waited to see that steady march slow and stop, but it never did. The last

202

stragglers – most of them hurt and helping each other along, but still walking in those close groups – were in long before the reddening sun had passed below the dormitories on the west side of the Gaiten Academy campus. They had returned once more, like homing pigeons to their nests or the swallows to Capistrano. Not five minutes after the evening star became visible in the darkening sky, Dean Martin began singing 'Everybody Loves Somebody Sometime'.

'I was worried for nothing, wasn't I?' Alice said. 'Sometimes I'm a putz. That's what my father says.'

'No,' the Head told her. 'All the putzes had cell phones, dear. That's why they're out there and you're in here, with us.'

Tom said: 'I wonder if Rafe's still making out okay.'

'I wonder if Johnny is,' Clay said. 'Johnny and Sharon.'

23

At ten o'clock on that windy autumn night, under a moon now entering its last quarter, Clay and Tom stood in the band alcove at the home end of the Tonney soccer field. Directly in front of them was a waist-high concrete barrier that had been heavily padded on the playing-field side. On their side were a few rusting music stands and a drift of litter that was ankle-deep; the wind blew the torn bags and scraps of paper in here, and here they came to rest. Behind and above them, back at the turnstiles, Alice and Jordan flanked the Head, a tall figure propped on a slender rod of cane.

Debby Boone's voice rolled across the field in amplified waves of comic majesty. Ordinarily she would be followed by Lee Ann Womack singing 'I Hope You Dance', then back to Lawrence Welk and his Champagne Music Makers, but perhaps not tonight.

The wind was freshening. It brought them the smell of rotting bodies from the marsh behind the indoor-track building and the aroma of dirt and sweat from the living ones packed together on the field beyond the band alcove. *If you can call that living,* Clay thought, and flashed himself a small and bitter inside smile. Rationalization was a great human sport, maybe *the* great human sport, but he would not fool himself tonight: of course they called it living. Whatever they were or whatever they were becoming, they called it living just as he did.

'What are you waiting for?' Tom murmured.

'Nothing,' Clay murmured back. 'Just . . . nothing.'

From the holster Alice had found in the Nickerson basement, Clay drew Beth Nickerson's old-fashioned Colt .45 revolver, now once more fully loaded. Alice had offered him the automatic rifle – which so far they had not even test-fired – and he had refused, saying that if the pistol didn't do the job, probably nothing would.

'I don't know why the auto wouldn't be better, if it squirts thirty or forty bullets a second,' she said. 'You could turn those trucks into cheese-graters.'

He had agreed that this might be so, but reminded Alice that their object tonight was not destruction per se but ignition. Then he'd explained the highly illegal nature of the ammunition Arnie Nickerson had obtained for his wife's .45: fraggers. What had once been called dumdum bullets.

'Okay, but if it doesn't work, you can still try Sir Speedy,' she'd said. 'Unless the guys out there just, you know . . .' She wouldn't actually use the word *attack,* but had made a little walking motion with the fingers of the hand not holding the sneaker. 'In that case, beat feet.'

The wind tore a tattered strip of Homecoming Weekend bunting free of the scoreboard and sent it dancing above the packed sleepers. Around the field, seeming to float in the dark, were the red eyes of the boomboxes, all but one playing without benefit of CDs. The bunting struck the bumper of one of the propane trucks, flapped there several seconds, then slipped free and flew off into the night. The trucks were parked side by side in the middle of the field, rising from the mass of packed forms like weird metal mesas. The phone-crazies slept beneath them and so closely around them that some were crammed up against the wheels. Clay thought again of passenger pigeons, and the way nineteenth-century hunters had brained them on the ground with clubs. The whole species had been wiped out by the beginning of the twentieth . . . but of course they'd only been birds, with little bird-brains, incapable of rebooting.

'Clay?' Tom asked, low. 'Are you sure you want to go through with this?'

'No,' Clay said. Now that he was face-to-face with it, there were too many unanswered questions. What they would do if it went wrong was only one of them. What they would do if it went right was another. Because passenger pigeons were incapable of revenge. Those things out there, on the other hand—

'But I'm going to.'

'Then do it,' Tom said. 'Because, all else aside, "You Light Up My Life" blows dead rats in hell.'

Clay raised the .45 and held his right wrist firmly with his left hand. He centered the gunsight on the tank of the truck on the left. He would fire twice into that one, then twice into the other one. That would leave one more bullet for each, if necessary. If that didn't work, he could try the automatic weapon Alice had taken to calling Sir Speedy.

'Duck if it goes up,' he told Tom.

'Don't worry,' Tom said. His face was drawn into a grimace, anticipating the report of the gun and whatever might follow.

Debby Boone was building to a big finish. It suddenly seemed very important to Clay that he beat her. *If you miss at this range, you're a monkey,* he thought, and pulled the trigger.

There was no chance for a second shot and no need of one. A bright red flower bloomed in the center of the tank, and by its light he saw a deep dent in the previously smooth metal surface. Hell appeared to be inside, and growing. Then the flower was a river, red turning orange-white.

'*Down!*' he shouted, and pushed Tom's shoulder. He fell

on top of the smaller man just as the night became desert noon. There was a huge, whooshing roar followed by a guttering *BANG* that Clay felt in every bone of his body. Shrapnel shot overhead. He thought Tom screamed but he wasn't sure, because there was another of those whooshing roars and suddenly the air was growing hot, hot, hot.

He seized Tom partly by the scruff of the neck and partly by the collar of his shirt and began to drag him backward up the concrete ramp leading to the turnstiles, his eyes slitted almost completely shut against the enormous glare flowing from the center of the soccer field. Something enormous landed in the auxiliary stands to his right. He thought maybe an engine block. He was pretty sure the shattered bits and twists of metal under his feet had once been Gaiten Academy music stands.

Tom was screaming and his glasses were askew, but he was on his feet and he looked intact. The two of them ran up the ramp like escapees from Gomorrah. Clay could see their shadows, long and spider-thin in front of them, and realized objects were falling all around them: arms, legs, a piece of bumper, a woman's head with the hair blazing. From behind them came a second tremendous *BANG* – or maybe it was a third – and this time *he* was the one who screamed. His feet tangled and he went sprawling. The whole world was rapidly building heat and the most incredible light: he felt as if he were standing on God's personal soundstage.

We didn't know what we were doing, he thought, looking at a wad of gum, a tromped Junior Mints box, a blue Pepsi Cola cap. *We didn't have a clue and we're going to pay with our fucking lives.*

'Get up!' That was Tom, and he thought Tom was screaming, but his voice seemed to be coming from a mile away. He felt Tom's delicate, long-fingered hands yanking at his arm. Then Alice was there, too. Alice was yanking on his other arm, and she was *glaring* in the light. He could see the sneaker dancing and bobbing from its string on her wrist.

She was spattered with blood, bits of cloth, and gobbets of smoking flesh.

Clay scrambled up, then went back to one knee, and Alice hauled him up again by main force. From behind them, propane roared like a dragon. And here came Jordan, with the Head tottering along right behind him, his face rosy and every wrinkle running with sweat.

'No, Jordan, no, just get him out of the way!' Tom yelled, and Jordan pulled the Head aside for them, gripping the old man grimly around the waist when he tottered. A burning torso with a ring in its navel landed at Alice's feet and she booted it off the ramp. *Five years of soccer,* Clay remembered her saying. A blazing piece of shirt landed on the back of her head and Clay swept it aside before it could set her hair on fire.

At the top of the ramp, a blazing truck tire with half a sheared-off axle still attached leaned against the last row of reserved seats. If it had landed blocking their way, they might have cooked — the Head almost certainly would have. As it was, they were able to slide past, holding their breath against billows of oily smoke. A moment later they were lurching through the turnstile, Jordan on one side of the Head and Clay on the other, the two of them almost carrying the old man along. Clay had his ear boxed twice by the Head's flailing cane, but thirty seconds after passing the tire they were standing beneath Tonney Arch, looking back at the huge column of fire rising above the bleachers and center press box with identical expressions of stupefied disbelief.

A blazing rag of Homecoming bunting floated down to the pavement next to the main ticket booth, trailing a few sparks before coming to rest.

'Did you know that would happen?' Tom asked. His face was white around the eyes, red across the forehead and cheeks. Half his mustache appeared to have been singed off. Clay could hear his voice, but it sounded distant. Everything did. It was as if his ears had been packed with cotton balls, or the shooter's plugs Beth Nickerson's husband Arnie had no doubt made her wear when he took her to their favorite target-range. Where they'd probably shot with their cell phones clipped to one hip and their pagers to the other.

'*Did you know?*' Tom attempted to shake him, got nothing but a piece of his shirt, and tore it all the way down the front.

'Fuck no, are you insane?' Clay's voice was beyond hoarse, beyond parched; it sounded *baked*. 'You think I would have stood there with a pistol if I'd known? If it hadn't been for that concrete barrier, we would have been cut in two. Or vaporized.'

Incredibly, Tom began to grin. 'I tore your shirt, Batman.'

Clay felt like knocking his head off. Also like hugging and kissing him just because he was still alive.

'I want to go back to the Lodge,' Jordan said. The fear in his voice was unmistakable.

'By all means let us remove to a safe distance,' the Head agreed. He was trembling badly, his eyes fixed on the inferno rising above the Arch and the bleachers. 'Thank God the wind's blowing toward Academy Slope.'

'Can you walk, sir?' Tom asked.

'Thank you, yes. If Jordan will assist me, I'm sure I can walk as far as the Lodge.'

'We got them,' Alice said. She was wiping splatters of gore almost absently from her face, leaving smears of blood. Her eyes were like nothing Clay had ever seen except in a few photographs and some inspired comic art from the 1950s and '60s. He remembered going to a comics convention once, only a kid himself then, and listening to Wallace Wood talk about trying to draw something he called Panic Eye. Now Clay was seeing it in the face of a fifteen-year-old suburban schoolgirl.

'Alice, come on,' he said. 'We have to go back to the Lodge and get our shit together. We have to get out of here.' As soon as the words were out of his mouth, he had to say them again and hear if they had the ring of truth. The second time they sounded more than true; they sounded scared.

She might not have heard. She looked exultant. Stuffed with triumph. Sick with it, like a kid who has eaten too much Halloween candy on the way home. The pupils of her eyes were full of fire. 'Nothing could live through that.'

Tom gripped Clay's arm. It hurt the way a sunburn hurt. 'What's wrong with you?'

'I think we made a mistake,' Clay said.

'Is it like in the gas station?' Tom asked him. Behind his crooked spectacles, his eyes were sharp. 'When the man and woman were fighting over the damn Tw—'

'No, I just think we made a mistake,' Clay said. Actually, it was stronger than that. He *knew* they had made a mistake. 'Come on. We have to go tonight.'

'If you say so, okay,' Tom said. 'Come on, Alice.'

She went with them a little way down the path toward the Lodge, where they had left a pair of gas lanterns burning in the big bay window, then turned back for another look. The press box was on fire now, and the bleachers. The stars over the soccer field were gone; even the moon was nothing but a ghost dancing a wild jig in the heat-haze above that fierce gas-jet. 'They're *dead,* they're *gone,* they're *crispy,*' she said. 'Burn, baby, b—'

That was when the cry rose, only now it wasn't coming from Glen's Falls or Littleton ten miles away. It was coming from right behind them. Nor was there anything spectral or wraithlike about it. It was a cry of agony, the scream of some-thing – a single entity, and *aware,* Clay was certain of it – that had awakened from deep sleep to find it was burning alive.

Alice shrieked and covered her ears, her eyes bulging in the firelight.

'Take it back!' Jordan said, grasping the Head's wrist. 'Sir, we have to take it back!'

'Too late, Jordan,' Ardai said.

24

Their knapsacks were a little plumper as they leaned against the front door of Cheatham Lodge an hour later. There were a couple of shirts in each one, plus bags of trail-mix, juice-boxes, and packets of Slim Jims as well as batteries and spare flashlights. Clay had harried Tom and Alice into sweeping their possessions together as quickly as possible, and now he was the one who kept darting into the living room to steal looks out the big window.

The gas-jet over there was finally starting to burn low, but the bleachers were still blazing and so was the press box. Tonney Arch itself had caught and glared in the night like a horseshoe in a smithy. Nothing that had been on that field could still be alive – Alice had been right about that much, surely – but twice on their return to the Lodge (the Head shambling like an old drunk in spite of their best efforts to support him), they had heard those ghostly cries coming down the wind from other flocks. Clay told himself he didn't hear anger in those cries, it was just his imagination – his guilty imagination, his murderer's imagination, his *mass* murderer's imagination – but he didn't completely believe it.

It had been a mistake, but what else could they have done? He and Tom had felt their gathering power just that afternoon, had *seen* it, and that had been only two of them, just two. How could they have let that go on? Just let it grow?

'Damned if you do, damned if you stand pat,' he said under his breath, and turned from the window. He didn't even know how long he'd been looking at the burning stadium and resisted the urge to check his watch. It would be easy to give in to the panic-rat, he was close to it now, and if he gave in, it would travel to the others quickly. Starting with Alice. Alice had managed to get herself back under some sort of control, but it was thin. *Thin enough to read a newspaper through,* his bingo-playing mother might have said. Although a kid herself, Alice had managed to keep herself shiny-side up mostly for the other kid's sake, so he wouldn't give way entirely.

The other kid. Jordan.

Clay hurried back into the front hall, noted there was still no fourth pack by the door, and saw Tom coming down the stairs. Alone.

'Where's the kid?' Clay asked. His ears had started to clear a little, but his voice still sounded too far away, and like a stranger's. He had an idea that was going to continue for a while. 'You were supposed to be helping him put some stuff together – Ardai said he brought a pack over with him from that dorm of his—'

'He won't come.' Tom rubbed the side of his face. He looked tired, sad, distracted. With half his mustache gone, he looked ludicrous as well.

'*What?*'

'Lower your voice, Clay. I don't make the news, I just report it.'

'Then tell me what you're talking about, for Christ's sake.'

'He won't go without the Head. He said, "You can't make me." And if you're really serious about going tonight, I believe he's right.'

Alice came tearing out of the kitchen. She had washed up, tied her hair back, and put on a new shirt – it hung almost to her knees – but her skin glowed with the same burn Clay felt on his own. He supposed they should count themselves lucky that they weren't popping blisters.

'Alice,' he began, 'I need you to exercise your womanly powers over Jordan. He's being—'

She steamed past as if he hadn't spoken, fell on her knees, seized her pack, and tore it open. He watched, perplexed, as she began to pull out the stuff inside. He looked at Tom and saw an expression of understanding and sympathy dawning on Tom's face.

'What?' Clay asked. '*What,* for chrissake?' He had felt an all too similar exasperated annoyance toward Sharon during the last year they'd actually lived together – had felt it often – and hated himself for having that pop up now, of all times. But *dammit,* another complication was the last thing they needed now. He ran his hands through his hair. *'What?'*

'Look at her wrist,' Tom said.

Clay looked. The dirty piece of shoestring was still there, but the sneaker was gone. He felt an absurd sinking in his stomach. Or maybe it wasn't so absurd. If it mattered to Alice, he supposed it *mattered.* So what if it was just a sneaker?

The spare T-shirt and sweatshirt she had packed (GAITEN BOOSTERS' CLUB printed across the front) went flying. Batteries rolled. Her spare flashlight hit the tile floor and the lens-cover cracked. That was enough to convince Clay. This wasn't a Sharon Riddell tantrum because they were out of hazelnut coffee or Chunky Monkey ice cream; this was unvarnished terror.

He went to Alice, knelt beside her, and took hold of her wrists. He could feel the seconds flying by, turning into minutes they should have been using to put this town behind them, but he could also feel the lightning sprint of her pulse under his fingers. And he could see her eyes. It wasn't panic in them now but agony, and he realized she'd put everything in that sneaker: her mother and father, her friends, Beth Nickerson and her daughter, the Tonney Field inferno, everything.

'It's not in here!' she cried. 'I thought I must have packed it, but I didn't! *I can't find it anywhere!'*

'No, honey, I know.' Clay was still holding her wrists. Now he lifted the one with the shoelace around it. 'Do you see?' He waited until he was sure her eyes had focused, then he flipped the ends beyond the knot, where there had been a second knot.

'It's too long now,' she said. 'It wasn't that long before.'

Clay tried to remember the last time he'd seen the sneaker. He told himself it was impossible to remember a thing like that, given all that had been going on, then realized he could. Very clearly, too. It was when she'd helped Tom pull him up after the second truck had exploded. It had been dancing from its string then. She had been covered with blood, scraps of cloth, and little chunks of flesh, but the sneaker had still been on her wrist. He tried to remember if it was still there when she'd booted the burning torso off the ramp. He didn't think so. Maybe that was hindsight, but he didn't think so.

'It came untied, honey,' he said. 'It came untied and fell off.'

'I *lost* it?' Her eyes, unbelieving. The first tears. 'Are you *sure?*'

'Pretty sure, yeah.'

'It was my luck,' she whispered, the tears spilling over.

'No,' Tom said, and put an arm around her. '*We're* your luck.'

She looked at him. 'How do you know?'

'Because you found us first,' Tom said. 'And we're still here.'

She hugged them both and they stood that way for a while, the three of them, with their arms around each other in the hall with Alice's few possessions scattered around their feet.

25

The fire spread to a lecture building the Head identified as Hackery Hall. Then, around four a.m., the wind dropped away and it spread no further. When the sun came up, the Gaiten campus stank of propane, charred wood, and a great many burnt bodies. The bright sky of a perfect New England morning in October was obscured by a rising column of gray-black smoke. And Cheatham Lodge was still occupied. In the end it had been like dominoes: the Head couldn't travel except by car, car travel was impossible, and Jordan would not go without the Head. Nor was Ardai able to persuade him. Alice, although resigned to the loss of her talisman, refused to go without Jordan. Tom would not go without Alice. And Clay was loath to go without the two of them, although he was horrified to find these newcomers in his life seemed at least temporarily more important than his own son, and although he continued to feel certain that they would pay a high price for what they'd done on Tonney Field if they stayed in Gaiten, let alone at the scene of the crime.

He thought he might feel better about that last at daybreak, but he did not.

The five of them watched and waited at the living room window, but of course nothing came out of the smoldering wreckage, and there was no sound but the low crackle of fire eating deep into the Athletic Department offices and locker rooms even as it finished off the bleachers above-ground. The thousand or so phone-crazies who had been roosting there were, as Alice had said, *crispy*. The smell of them was rich and stick-in-your-throat awful. Clay had vomited once and knew the others had, as well – even the Head.

We made a mistake, he thought again.

'You guys should have gone on,' Jordan said. 'We would have been all right – we were before, weren't we, sir?'

Headmaster Ardai ignored the question. He was studying Clay. 'What happened yesterday when you and Tom were in that service station? I think something happened then to make you look as you do now.'

'Oh? How do I look, sir?'

'Like an animal that smells a trap. Did those two in the street see you?'

'It wasn't exactly that,' Clay said. He didn't love being called an animal, but couldn't deny that was what he was: oxygen and food in, carbon dioxide and shit out, pop goes the weasel.

The Head had begun to rub restlessly at the left side of his midsection with one big hand. Like many of his gestures, Clay thought it had an oddly theatrical quality – not exactly phony, but meant to be seen at the back of the lecture hall. 'Then what exactly *was* it?'

And because protecting the others no longer seemed like an option, Clay told the Head exactly what they'd seen in the office of the Citgo station – a physical struggle over a box of stale treats that had suddenly turned into something else. He told about the fluttering papers, the ashes that had begun circling in the ashtray like water going down a bathtub drain, the keys jingling on the board, the nozzle that fell off the gas-pump.

'I saw that,' Jordan said, and Alice nodded.

Tom mentioned feeling short of breath, and Clay agreed. They both tried to explain the sense of something powerful building in the air. Clay said it was how things felt before a thunderstorm. Tom said the air just felt *fraught,* somehow. Too heavy.

'Then he let her take a couple of the fucking things and it all went away,' Tom said. 'The ashes stopped spinning, the keys stopped jingling, that thundery feeling went out of the air.' He looked to Clay for confirmation. Clay nodded.

Alice said, 'Why didn't you tell us this before?'

'Because it wouldn't have changed anything,' Clay said. 'We were going to burn the nest if we could, regardless.'

'Yes,' Tom said.

Jordan said suddenly, 'You think the phone-crazies are turning into psionics, don't you?'

Tom said, 'I don't know what that word means, Jordan.'

'People who can move things around just by thinking about it, for one thing. Or by accident, if their emotions get out of control. Only psionic abilities like telekinesis and levitation—'

'*Levitation?*' Alice almost barked.

Jordan paid no mind. '—are only branches. The trunk of the psionic tree is telepathy, and that's what you're afraid of, isn't it? The telepathy thing.'

Tom's fingers went to the place above his mouth where half of his mustache was gone and touched the reddened skin there. 'Well, the thought has crossed my mind.' He paused, head cocked. 'That might be witty. I'm not sure.'

Jordan ignored this, as well. 'Say that they are. Getting to be true telepaths, I mean, and not just zombies with a flocking instinct. So what? The Gaiten Academy flock is *dead,* and they died without a clue of who lit em up, because they died in whatever passes for sleep with them, so if you're worrying that they telepathically faxed our names and descriptions to any of their buddies in the surrounding New England states, you can relax.'

'Jordan—' the Head began, then winced. He was still rubbing his midsection.

'Sir? Are you all right?'

'Yes. Fetch my Zantac from the downstairs bathroom, would you? And a bottle of the Poland Spring water. There's a good lad.'

Jordan hurried away on the errand.

'Not an ulcer, is it?' Tom asked.

'No,' the Head replied. 'It's stress. An old . . . one cannot say friend . . . acquaintance?'

'Your heart okay?' Alice asked, speaking in a low voice.

'I suppose,' the Head agreed, and bared his teeth in a smile of disconcerting jollity. 'If the Zantac doesn't work, we may resuppose . . . but so far, the Zantac always has, and one doesn't care to buy trouble when so much of it is on sale. Ah, Jordan, thank you.'

'Quite welcome, sir.' The boy handed him the glass and the pill with his usual smile.

'I think you ought to go with them,' Ardai told him after swallowing the Zantac.

'Sir, with all respect, I'm telling you there's no *way* they could know, no *way.*'

The Head looked a question at Tom and Clay. Tom raised his hands. Clay only shrugged. He could say what he felt right out loud, could articulate what they surely must know he felt – *we made a mistake, and staying here is compounding it* – but saw no point. Jordan's face was set and stubborn on top, scared to death just beneath. They were not going to persuade him. And besides, it was day again. Day was *their* time.

He rumpled the boy's hair. 'If you say so, Jordan. I'm going to catch some winks.'

Jordan looked almost sublimely relieved. 'That sounds like a good idea. I think I will, too.'

'I'm going to have a cup of Cheatham Lodge's world-famous tepid cocoa before I come up,' Tom said. 'And I believe I'll shave off the rest of this mustache. The wailing and lamentation you hear will be mine.'

'Can I watch?' Alice asked. 'I always wanted to watch a grown man wail and lament.'

26

Clay and Tom were sharing a small bedroom on the third floor; Alice had been given the only other. While Clay was taking off his shoes, there was a perfunctory knock on the door, which the Head followed without pause. Two bright spots of color burned high up on his cheekbones. Otherwise his face was deathly pale.

'Are you all right?' Clay asked, standing. 'Is it your heart, after all?'

'I'm glad you asked me that,' the Head replied. 'I wasn't entirely sure I planted the seed, but it seems I did.' He glanced back over his shoulder into the hall, then closed the door with the tip of his cane. 'Listen carefully, Mr Riddell – Clay – and don't ask questions unless you feel you absolutely must. I am going to be found dead in my bed late this afternoon or early this evening, and you will say of course it was my heart after all, that what we did last night must have brought it on. Do you understand?'

Clay nodded. He understood, and he bit back the automatic protest. It might have had a place in the old world, but it had none here. He knew why the Head was proposing what he was proposing.

'If Jordan even suspects I may have taken my own life to free him from what he, in his boyishly admirable way, regards as a sacred obligation, he may take his own. At the very least he would be plunged into what the elders of my own childhood called a black fugue. He will grieve for me deeply as it is, but that is permissible. The thought that I committed suicide to get him out of Gaiten is not. Do you understand *that*?'

'Yes,' Clay said. Then: 'Sir, wait another day. What you're thinking of . . . it may not be necessary. Could be we're going to get away with this.' He didn't believe it, and in any case Ardai meant to do what he said; all the truth Clay needed was in the man's haggard face, tightly pressed lips, and gleaming eyes. Still, he tried again. 'Wait another day. No one may come.'

'You heard those screams,' the Head replied. 'That was rage. They'll come.'

'Maybe, but—'

The Head raised his cane to forestall him. 'And if they do, and if they can read our minds as well as each other's, what will they read in yours, if yours is still here to be read?'

Clay didn't reply, only watched the Head's face.

'Even if they can't read minds,' the Head continued, 'what do you propose? To stay here, day after day and week after week? Until the snow flies? Until I finally expire of old age? My own father lived to the age of ninety-seven. Meanwhile, you have a wife and a child.'

'My wife and boy are either all right or they're not. I've made my peace with that.'

This was a lie, and perhaps Ardai saw it in Clay's face, because he smiled his unsettling smile. 'And do you believe your son has made peace with not knowing if his father is alive, dead, or insane? After only a week?'

'That's a low blow,' Clay said. His voice was not quite steady.

'Really? I didn't know we were fighting. In any case,

218

there's no referee. No one here but us chickens, as they say.'
The Head glanced at the closed door, then looked back at
Clay again. 'The equation is very simple. You can't stay and
I can't go. It's best that Jordan go with you.'

'But to put you down like a horse with a broken leg—'

'No such thing,' the Head interrupted. 'Horses do not
practice euthanasia, but people do.' The door opened, Tom
stepped in, and with hardly a pause for breath the Head went
on, 'And have you ever considered commercial illustration,
Clay? For books, I mean?'

'My style is too flamboyant for most of the commercial
houses,' Clay said. 'I *have* done jackets for some of the small
fantasy presses like Grant and Eulalia. Some of the Edgar Rice
Burroughs Mars books.'

'Barsoom!' the Head cried, and waved his cane vigor-
ously in the air. Then he rubbed his solar plexus and grimaced.
'Damned heartburn! Excuse me, Tom – just came up to have
a natter before lying down a bit myself.'

'Not at all,' Tom said, and watched him go out. When
the sound of the Head's cane had gotten a good distance
down the hall, he turned to Clay and said, 'Is he okay? He's
very pale.'

'I think he's fine.' He pointed at Tom's face. 'I thought
you were going to shave off the other half.'

'I decided against it with Alice hanging around,' Tom
said. 'I like her, but about certain things she can be evil.'

'That's just paranoia.'

'Thanks, Clay, I needed that. It's only been a week and
I'm already missing my analyst.'

'Combined with a persecution complex and delusions
of grandeur.' Clay swung his feet up onto one of the room's
two narrow beds, put his hands behind his head, and looked
at the ceiling.

'You wish we were out of here, don't you?' Tom asked.

'You bet I do.' He spoke in a flat and uninflected mono-
tone.

'It'll be all right, Clay. Really.'

'So you say, but you have a persecution complex and delusions of grandeur.'

'That's true,' Tom said, 'but they're balanced out by poor self-image and ego menstruation at roughly six-week intervals. And in any case—'

'—too late now, at least for today,' Clay finished.

'That's right.'

There was actually a kind of peace in that. Tom said something else, but Clay only caught 'Jordan thinks . . .' and then he was asleep.

27

He woke screaming, or so he thought at first; only a wild look at the other bed, where Tom was still sleeping peacefully with something – a washcloth, maybe – folded over his eyes convinced Clay that the scream had been inside his head. A cry of some sort might have escaped him, but if so it hadn't been enough to wake his roommate.

The room was nowhere near dark – it was midafternoon – but Tom had pulled the shade before corking off himself, and it was at least dim. Clay stayed where he was for a moment, lying on his back, his mouth as dry as woodshavings, his heartbeat rapid in his chest and in his ears, where it sounded like running footsteps muffled in velvet. Otherwise the house was dead still. They might not have made the switchover from days to nights completely yet, but last night had been extraordinarily exhausting, and at this moment he heard no one stirring in the Lodge. Outside a bird called and somewhere quite distant – not in Gaiten, he thought – a stubborn alarm kept on braying.

Had he ever had a worse dream? Maybe one. A month or so after Johnny was born, Clay had dreamed he'd picked the baby up from the crib to change him, and Johnny's chubby little body had simply fallen apart in his hands like a badly put-together dummy. That one he could understand – fear of fatherhood, fear of fucking up. A fear he still lived with, as Headmaster Ardai had seen. What was he to make of this one?

Whatever it meant, he didn't want to lose it, and he knew from experience that you had to act quickly to keep that from happening.

There was a desk in the room, and a ballpoint pen tucked into one pocket of the jeans Clay had left crumpled at the foot of the bed. He took the pen, crossed to the desk in his bare feet, sat down, and opened the drawer above the knee-hole. He found what he was hoping for, a little pile of blank stationery with the heading **GAITEN ACADEMY** and '*A Young Mind Is A Lamp In The Darkness*' on each sheet. He took one of them and placed it on the desk. The light was dim, but would serve. He clicked out the tip of the ballpoint and paused for just a moment, recalling the dream as clearly as he could.

He, Tom, Alice, and Jordan had been lined up in the center of a playing field. Not a soccer field like Tonney – a football field, maybe? There had been some sort of skeletal construction in the background with a blinking red light on it. He had no idea what it was, but he knew the field had been full of people looking at them, people with ruined faces and ripped clothes that he recognized all too well. He and his friends had been . . . had they been in cages? No, on platforms. And they *were* cages, all the same, although there were no bars. Clay didn't know how that could be, but it was. He was losing the details of the dream already.

Tom was on one end of the line. A man had walked to him, a special man, and put a hand over his head. Clay didn't remember how the man could do that since Tom – like Alice, Jordan, and Clay himself – had been on a platform, but he had. And he'd said, '*Ecce homo – insana.*' And the crowd – thousands of them – had roared back, '*DON'T TOUCH!*' in a single voice. The man had gone to Clay and repeated this. With his hand above Alice's head the man had said, *'Ecce femina – insana.'* Above Jordan, *'Ecce puer – insanus.'* Each time the response had been the same: *'DON'T TOUCH!'*

Neither the man – the host? the ringmaster? – or the people in the crowd had opened their mouths during this ritual. The call-and-response had been purely telepathic.

Then, letting his right hand do all the thinking (his hand and the special corner of his brain that ran it), Clay began to stroke an image onto the paper. The entire dream had been terrible – the false accusation of it, the *caughtness* of it – but nothing in it had been so awful as the man who had gone to each of them, placing his open palm-down hand over their heads like an auctioneer preparing to sell livestock at a county fair. Clay felt that if he could catch that man's image on paper, he could catch the terror.

He had been a black man with a noble head and an ascetic's face above a lanky, almost scrawny body. The hair was a tight cap of dark ringlets cut open on one side by an ugly triangular gouge. The shoulders were slight, the hips nearly nonexistent. Below the cap of curls Clay quick-sketched the broad and handsome forehead – a scholar's forehead. Then he marred it with another slash and shaded in the hanging flap of skin that obscured one eyebrow. The man's left cheek had been torn open, possibly by a bite, and the lower lip was also torn on that side, making it droop in a tired sneer. The eyes were a problem. Clay couldn't get them right. In the dream they had been both full of awareness yet somehow dead. After two tries he left them and dropped to the pullover before he lost that: the kind the kids called a hoodie (RED, he printed, with an arrow), with white block letters across the front. It had been too big for the skinny body and a flap of material lay over the top half of the letters, but Clay was pretty sure it said HARVARD. He was starting to print that when the weeping started, soft and muffled, from somewhere below him.

28

It was Jordan: Clay knew at once. He took one look back over his shoulder at Tom as he pulled on his jeans, but Tom hadn't moved. *Out for the count,* Clay thought. He opened the door, slipped through, and closed it behind him.

Alice, wearing a Gaiten Academy T-shirt as a nightgown, was sitting on the second-floor landing with the boy cradled in her arms. Jordan's face was pressed against her shoulder. She looked up at the sound of Clay's bare feet on the stairs and spoke before Clay said something he might have regretted later: *Is it the Head?*

'He had a bad dream,' she said.

Clay said the first thing that came to him. At that moment it seemed vitally important. 'Did *you?*'

Her brow creased. Bare-legged, with her hair pulled back in a ponytail and her face sunburned as if from a day at the beach, she looked like Jordan's eleven-year-old sister. 'What? No. I heard him crying in the hall. I guess I was waking up anyway, and—'

'Just a minute,' Clay said. 'Stay right there.'

He went back to his third-floor room and snatched his sketch off the desk. This time Tom's eyes sprang open. He looked around with a mixture of fright and disorientation, then fixed on Clay and relaxed. 'Back to reality,' he said. Then, rubbing a hand over his face and getting up on one elbow: 'Thank God. Jesus. What time is it?'

'Tom, did you have a dream? A bad dream?'

Tom nodded. 'I think so, yeah. I heard crying. Was that Jordan?'

'Yes. What did you dream? Do you remember?'

'Somebody called us insane,' Tom said, and Clay felt his stomach drop. 'Which we probably are. The rest is gone. Why? Did you—'

Clay didn't wait for any more. He hurried back out and

down the stairs again. Jordan looked around at him with a kind of dazed timidity when Clay sat down. There was no sign of the computer whiz now; if Alice looked eleven with her ponytail and sunburn, Jordan had regressed to nine.

'Jordan,' Clay said. 'Your dream . . . your nightmare. Do you remember it?'

'It's going away now,' Jordan said. 'They had us up on stands. They were looking at us like we were . . . I don't know, wild animals . . . only they said—'

'That we were insane.'

Jordan's eyes widened. 'Yeah!'

Clay heard footfalls behind him as Tom came down the stairs. Clay didn't look around. He showed Jordan his sketch. 'Was this the man in charge?'

Jordan didn't answer. He didn't have to. He winced away from the picture, grabbing for Alice and turning his face against her chest again.

'What is it?' Alice asked, bewildered. She reached for the sketch, but Tom took it first.

'Christ,' he said, and handed it back. 'The dream's almost gone, but I remember the torn cheek.'

'And his lip,' Jordan said, the words muffled against Alice's chest. 'The way his lip hangs down. He was the one showing us to them. To *them*.' He shuddered. Alice rubbed his back, then crossed her hands over his shoulder blades so she could hold him more tightly.

Clay put the picture in front of Alice. 'Ring any bells? Man of your dreams?'

She shook her head and started to say no. Before she could, there was a loud, protracted rattling and a loose series of thuds from outside Cheatham Lodge's front door. Alice screamed. Jordan clutched her tighter, as if he would burrow into her, and cried out. Tom clutched at Clay's shoulder. 'Oh man, what the *fuck*—'

There was more rattling thunder outside the door, long and loud. Alice screamed again.

'Guns!' Clay shouted. *'Guns!'*

For a moment they were all paralyzed there on the sunny landing, and then another of those long, loud rattles came, a sound like rolling bones. Tom bolted for the third floor and Clay followed him, skidding once in his stocking feet and grabbing the banister to regain his balance. Alice pushed Jordan away from her and ran for her own room, the hem of the shirt fluttering around her legs, leaving Jordan to huddle against the newel post, staring down the stairs and into the front hall with huge wet eyes.

29

'Easy,' Clay said. 'Let's just take this easy, okay?'

The three of them stood at the foot of the stairs not two minutes after the first of those long, loose rattling sounds had come from beyond the front door. Tom had the unproven Russian assault rifle they had taken to calling Sir Speedy, Alice was holding a nine-millimeter automatic in each hand, and Clay had Beth Nickerson's .45, which he had somehow managed to hold on to the previous night (although he had no memory of tucking it back into his belt, where he later found it). Jordan still huddled on the landing. Up there he couldn't see the downstairs windows, and Clay thought that was probably a good thing. The afternoon light in Cheatham Lodge was much dimmer than it should have been, and that was most definitely not a good thing.

It was dimmer because there were phone-crazies at every window they could see, crowded up to the glass and peering in at them: dozens, maybe hundreds of those strange blank faces, most marked by the battles they had been through and the wounds they had suffered during the last anarchic week. Clay saw missing eyes and teeth, torn ears, bruises, burns, scorched skin, and hanging wads of blackened flesh. They were silent. There was a kind of haunted avidity about them, and that feeling was back in the air, that breathless sense of

225

some enormous, spinning power barely held in check. Clay kept expecting to see their guns fly out of their hands and begin to fire on their own.

At us, he thought.

'Now I know how the lobsters feel in the tank at Harbor Seafood on Twofer Tuesday,' Tom said in a small, tight voice.

'Just take it easy,' Clay repeated. 'Let them make the first move.'

But there *was* no first move. There was another of those long, rattling thumps – the sound of something being off-loaded on the front porch was what it sounded like to Clay – and then the creatures at the windows drew back, as if at some signal only they could hear. They did this in orderly rows. This wasn't the time of day during which they ordinarily flocked, but things had changed. That seemed obvious.

Clay walked to the bay window in the living room, holding the revolver at his side. Tom and Alice followed. They watched the phone-crazies (who no longer seemed crazy at all to Clay, at least not in any way he understood) retreat, walking backward with eerie, limber ease, each never losing the little envelope of space around him- or herself. They settled to a stop between Cheatham Lodge and the smoking remains of the Tonney soccer stadium, like some raggedy-ass army battalion on a leaf-strewn parade ground. Every not-quite-vacant eye rested upon the Headmaster's residence.

'Why are their hands and feet all smudgy?' a timid voice asked. They looked around. It was Jordan. Clay himself hadn't even noticed the soot and char on the hands of the silent hundreds out there, but before he could say so, Jordan answered his own question. 'They went to see, didn't they? Sure. They went to see what we did to their friends. And they're mad. I can feel it. Can you feel it?'

Clay didn't want to say yes, but of course he could. That heavy, charged feeling in the air, that sense of turning thunder barely contained in a net of electricity: that was rage. He thought about Pixie Light battening on Power Suit Woman's neck and the elderly lady who'd won the Battle of the Boylston Street T Station, the one who'd gone striding off into Boston Common with blood dripping out of her cropped iron-gray hair. The young man, naked except for his sneakers, who had been jabbing a car aerial in each hand as he ran. All that rage – did he think it had just disappeared when they started to flock? Well, think again.

'I feel it,' Tom said. 'Jordan, if they've got psychic powers, why don't they just make us kill ourselves, or each other?'

'Or make our heads explode,' Alice said. Her voice was trembling. 'I saw that in an old movie once.'

'I don't know,' Jordan said. He looked up at Clay. 'Where's the Raggedy Man?'

'Is that what you call him?' Clay looked down at his sketch, which he was still carrying – the torn flesh, the torn sleeve of the pullover, the baggy blue jeans. He supposed that Raggedy Man was not a bad name at all for the fellow in the Harvard hoodie.

'I call him trouble, is what I call him,' Jordan said in a thin voice. He looked out again at the newcomers – three hundred at least, maybe four hundred, recently arrived from God knew which surrounding towns – and then back at Clay. 'Have you seen him?'

'Other than in a bad dream, no.'

Tom shook his head.

'To me he's just a picture on a piece of paper,' Alice said. 'I didn't dream him, and I don't see anyone in a hoodie out there. What were they doing on the soccer field? Do they try to identify their dead, do you think?' She looked doubtful at this. 'And isn't it still hot in there? It must be.'

'What are they waiting for?' Tom asked. 'If they aren't going to charge us or make us stick kitchen knives in each other, what are they waiting for?'

Clay suddenly knew what they were waiting for, and also where Jordan's Raggedy Man was – it was what Mr Devane, his high school algebra teacher, would have called an *aha!* moment. He turned and headed for the front hall.

'Where are you going?' Tom asked.

'To see what they left us,' Clay said.

They hurried after him. Tom caught up first, while Clay's hand was still on the doorknob. 'I don't know if this is a good idea,' Tom said.

'Maybe not, but it's what they're waiting for,' Clay said. 'And you know what? I think if they meant to kill us, we'd be dead already.'

'He's prob'ly right,' Jordan said in a small, wan voice.

Clay opened the door. Cheatham Lodge's long front porch, with its comfortable wicker furniture and its view of Academy Slope rolling down to Academy Avenue, was made for sunny autumn afternoons like this, but at that moment the ambience was the furthest thing from Clay's mind. Standing at the foot of the steps was an arrowhead of phone-crazies: one in front, two behind him, three behind them, then four, five, and six. Twenty-one in all. The one in front was the Raggedy Man from Clay's dream, his sketch come to life. The lettering on the front of the tattered red hoodie did indeed spell out HARVARD. The torn left cheek had been pulled up and secured at the side of the nose with two clumsy white stitches that had torn teardrops in the indifferently mended dark flesh before holding. There were rips where a third and fourth stitch had pulled free. Clay thought the stitching might have been done with fish-line. The sagging lip revealed teeth that looked as if they had been seen to by a good orthodontist not long ago, when the world had been a milder place.

In front of the door, burying the welcome mat and spreading in both directions, was a heap of black, misshapen objects. It could almost have been some half-mad sculptor's idea of art. It took Clay only a moment to realize he was looking at the melted remains of the Tonney Field flock's ghetto blasters.

Then Alice shrieked. A few of the heat-warped boomboxes had fallen over when Clay opened the door, and something that had very likely been balanced on top of the pile had fallen over with them, lodging half in and half out of the pile. She stepped forward before Clay could stop her, dropping one of the automatic pistols and grabbing the thing she had seen. It was the sneaker. She cradled it between her breasts.

Clay looked past her, at Tom. Tom gazed back at him. They weren't telepathic, but in that moment they might as well have been. *Now what?* Tom's eyes asked.

Clay turned his attention back to the Raggedy Man. He wondered if you could feel your mind being read and if his was being read right that second. He put his hands out to the Raggedy Man. The gun was still in one of them, but neither the Raggedy Man nor anyone in his squad seemed to feel threatened by it. Clay held his palms up: *What do you want?*

The Raggedy Man smiled. There was no humor in the smile. Clay thought he could see anger in the dark brown eyes, but he thought it was a surface thing. Underneath there was no spark at all, at least that he could discern. It was almost like watching a doll smile.

The Raggedy Man cocked his head and held up a finger – *Wait.* And from below them on Academy Avenue, as if on cue, came many screams. Screams of people in mortal agony. Accompanying them were a few guttural, predatory cries. Not many.

'What are you doing?' Alice shouted. She stepped forward, squeezing the little sneaker convulsively in her hand. The cords in her forearm stood out strongly enough to make shadows like long straight pencil-strokes on her skin. '*What are you doing to the people down there?*'

As if, Clay thought, there could be any doubt.

She raised the hand that still held a gun. Tom grabbed it and wrestled it away from her before she could pull the trigger. She turned on him, clawing at him with her free hand.

'*Give it back, don't you hear that? Don't you hear?*'

Clay pulled her away from Tom. During all of this Jordan watched from the entryway with wide, terrified eyes and the Raggedy Man stood at the tip of the arrow, smiling from a face where rage underlay humor and beneath the rage was . . . nothing, as far as Clay could tell. Nothing at all.

'Safety was on, anyway,' Tom said after a quick glance. 'Thank the Lord for small favors.' And to Alice: 'Do you want to get us killed?'

'Do you think they're just going to let us *go?*' She was crying so hard it had become difficult to understand her. Snot hung from her nostrils in two clear strings. From below, on the tree-lined avenue that ran past Gaiten Academy, there were screams and shrieks. A woman cried *No, please don't please don't* and then her words were lost in a terrible howl of pain.

'I don't know what they're going to do with us,' Tom said in a voice that strove for calm, 'but if they meant to kill us, they wouldn't be doing that. Look at him, Alice – what's going on down there is for our benefit.'

There were a few gunshots as people tried to defend themselves, but not many. Mostly there were just screams of pain and terrible surprise, all coming from the area directly adjacent to Gaiten Academy, where the flock had been burned. It surely didn't last any longer than ten minutes, but sometimes, Clay thought, time really *was* relative.

It seemed like hours.

30

When the screams finally stopped, Alice stood quietly between Clay and Tom with her head lowered. She had put both automatics on a table meant for briefcases and hats inside the front door. Jordan was holding her hand, looking out at the Raggedy Man and his colleagues standing at the head of the walk. So far the boy hadn't noticed the Head's absence. Clay knew he would soon, and then the next scene of this terrible day would commence.

The Raggedy Man took a step forward and made a little bow with his hands held out to either side, as if to say, *At your service.* Then he looked up and held a hand out toward Academy Slope and the avenue beyond. He looked at the little group clustered in the open door behind the melted boombox sculpture as he did this. To Clay the meaning seemed clear: *The road is yours. Go on and take it.*

'Maybe,' he said. 'In the meantime, let's be clear on one thing. I'm sure you can wipe us out if you choose to, you've obviously got the numbers, but unless you plan to hang back at Command HQ, someone else is going to be in charge of things tomorrow. Because I'll personally make sure you're the first one to go.'

The Raggedy Man put his hands to his cheeks and widened his eyes: *Oh dear!* The others behind him were as expressionless as robots. Clay looked a moment longer, then gently closed the door.

'I'm sorry,' Alice said dully. 'I just couldn't stand listening to them scream.'

'It's okay,' Tom said. 'No harm done. And hey, they brought back Mr Sneaker.'

She looked at it. 'Is this how they found out it was us? Did they smell it, the way a bloodhound smells a scent?'

'No,' Jordan said. He was sitting in a high-backed chair beside the umbrella stand, looking small and haggard and used-up. 'That's just their way of saying they know *you*. At least, that's what I think.'

'Yeah,' Clay said. 'I bet they knew it was us even before they got here. Picked it out of our dreams the way we picked his face out of our dreams.'

'I didn't—' Alice began.

'Because you were waking up,' Tom said. 'You'll be hearing from him in the fullness of time, I imagine.' He paused. 'If he has anything else to say, that is. I don't understand this, Clay. *We* did it. We did it and they *know* we did it, I'm convinced of that.'

'Yes,' Clay said.

'Then why kill a bunch of innocent pilgrims when it would have been just as easy – well, *almost* as easy – to break in here and kill us? I mean, I understand the concept of reprisals, but I don't see the point in this—'

That was when Jordan slid off his chair and, looking around with an expression of suddenly blossoming worry, asked: 'Where's the Head?'

31

Clay caught up with Jordan, but not until the boy had made it all the way to the second-floor landing. 'Hang on, Jordan,' he said.

'*No,*' Jordan said. His face was whiter, shockier, than ever. His hair bushed out around his head, and Clay supposed it was only because the boy needed a cut, but it looked as if it were trying to stand on end. 'With all the commotion, he should have been with us! He *would* have been with us, if he was all right.' His lips began to tremble. 'Remember the way he was rubbing himself? What if that wasn't just his acid reflux stuff?'

'Jordan—'

Jordan paid no attention, and Clay was willing to bet he'd forgotten all about the Raggedy Man and his cohorts, at least for the time being. He yanked free of Clay's hand and went running down the corridor, yelling, 'Sir! *Sir!*' while Heads going back to the nineteenth century frowned down at him from walls.

Clay glanced back down the stairs. Alice was going to be no help – she was sitting at the foot of the staircase with her head bent, staring at that fucking sneaker like it was the skull of Yorick – but Tom started reluctantly up to the second floor. 'How bad is this going to be?' he asked Clay.

'Well . . . Jordan thinks the Head would have joined us if he was all right and I tend to think he's—'

Jordan began to shriek. It was a drilling soprano sound

that went through Clay's head like a spear. It was actually Tom who got moving first; Clay was rooted at the staircase end of the corridor for at least three and perhaps as many as seven seconds, held there by a single thought: *That's not how someone sounds when they've found what looks like a heart attack. The old man must have botched it somehow. Maybe used the wrong kind of pills.* He was halfway down the hall when Tom cried out in shock— 'Oh my God Jordan don't look –' almost as if it were one word.

'Wait!' Alice called from behind him, but Clay didn't. The door to the Head's little upstairs suite was open: the study with its books and its now useless hotplate, the bedroom beyond with the door standing open so the light streamed through. Tom was standing in front of the desk, holding Jordan's head against his stomach. The Head was seated behind his desk. His weight had rocked his swivel chair back on its pivot and he seemed to be staring up at the ceiling with his one remaining eye. His tangled white hair hung down over the chairback. To Clay he looked like a concert pianist who had just played the final chord of a difficult piece.

He heard Alice give a choked cry of horror, but hardly noticed. Feeling like a passenger inside his own body, Clay walked to the desk and looked at the sheet of paper that rested on the blotter. Although it was stained with blood, he could make out the words on it; the Head's cursive had been fine and clear. Old-school to the end, Jordan might have said.

        aliene   geisteskrank
          insano
    elnebajos   vansinnig   fou
      atamagaokashii   gek   dolzinnig
                            hullu

     gila
     meschuge   nebun
     dement

Clay spoke nothing but English and a little high school French, but he knew well enough what this was, and what it meant. The Raggedy Man wanted them to go, and he knew somehow that Headmaster Ardai was too old and too arthritic to go with them. So he had been made to sit at his desk and write the word for *insane* in fourteen different languages. And when he was done, he had been made to plunge the tip of the heavy fountain pen with which he had written into his right eye and from there into the clever old brain behind it.

'They made him kill himself, didn't they?' Alice asked in a breaking voice. 'Why him and not us? *Why him and not us? What do they want?*'

Clay thought of the gesture the Raggedy Man had made toward Academy Avenue – Academy Avenue, which was also New Hampshire Route 102. The phone-crazies who were no longer exactly crazy – or were crazy in some brand-new way – wanted them on the road again. Beyond that he had no idea, and maybe that was good. Maybe that was all for the best. Maybe that was a mercy.

FADING ROSES,
THIS GARDEN'S OVER

1

There were half a dozen fine linen tablecloths in a cabinet at the end of the back hallway, and one of these served as Headmaster Ardai's shroud. Alice volunteered to sew it shut, then collapsed in tears when either her needlework or her nerve did not prove equal to such finality. Tom took over, pulling the tablecloth taut, doubling the seam, and sewing it closed in quick, almost professional overhand strokes. Clay thought it was like watching a boxer work an invisible light bag with his right hand.

'Don't make jokes,' Tom said without looking up. 'I appreciate what you did upstairs – I never could have done that – but I can't take a single joke right now, not even of the inoffensive *Will and Grace* variety. I'm barely holding myself together.'

'All right,' Clay said. Joking was the farthest thing from his mind. As for what he had done upstairs . . . well, the pen had to be removed from the Head's eye. No way were they going to leave that in. So Clay had taken care of it, looking away into the corner of the room as he wrenched it free, trying not to think about what he was doing or why it was stuck so fucking tight, and mostly he had succeeded in not thinking, but the pen had made a grinding sound against the bone of the old man's eyesocket when it finally let go, and there had been a loose, gobbety plopping sound as something fell from the bent tip of the pen's steel nib onto the blotter.

He thought he would remember those sounds forever, but he had succeeded in getting the damn thing out, and that was the important thing.

Outside, nearly a thousand phone-crazies stood on the lawn between the smoking ruins of the soccer field and Cheatham Lodge. They stood there most of the afternoon. Then, around five o'clock, they flocked silently off in the direction of downtown Gaiten. Clay and Tom carried the Head's shrouded body down the back stairs and put it on the back porch. The four survivors gathered in the kitchen and are the meal they had taken to calling breakfast as the shadows began to draw long outside.

Jordan ate surprisingly well. His color was high and his speech was animated. It consisted of reminiscences of his life at Gaiten Academy, and the influence Headmaster Ardai had had on the heart and mind of a friendless, introverted computer geek from Madison, Wisconsin. The brilliant lucidity of the boy's recollections made Clay increasingly uncomfortable, and when he caught first Alice's eyes and then Tom's, he saw they felt the same. Jordan's mind was tottering, but it was hard to know what to do about that; they could hardly send him to a psychiatrist.

At some point, after full dark, Tom suggested that Jordan should rest. Jordan said he would, but not until they had buried the Head. They could put him in the garden behind the Lodge, he said. He told them the Head had called the little vegetable patch his 'victory garden,' although he had never told Jordan why.

'That's the place,' Jordan said, smiling. His cheeks now flamed with color. His eyes, deep in their bruised sockets, sparkled with what could have been inspiration, good cheer, madness, or all three. 'Not only is the ground soft, it's the place he always liked the best . . . outside, I mean. So what do you say? *They're* gone, they still don't come out at night, that hasn't changed, and we can use the gas lanterns to dig by. What do you say?'

After consideration, Tom said, 'Are there shovels?'

'You bet, in the gardening shed. We don't even need to go up to the greenhouses.' And Jordan actually laughed.

'Let's do it,' Alice said. 'Let's bury him and have done with it.'

'And you'll rest afterwards,' Clay said, looking at Jordan.

'Sure, sure!' Jordan cried impatiently. He got up from his chair and began to pace around the room. 'Come on, you guys!' As if he were trying to get up a game of tag.

So they dug the grave in the Head's garden behind the Lodge and buried him among the beans and tomatoes. Tom and Clay lowered the shrouded form into the hole, which was about three feet deep. The exercise kept them warm, and only when they stopped did they notice the night had grown cold, almost frosty. The stars were brilliant overhead, but a heavy ground-mist was rolling up the Slope. Academy Avenue was already submerged in that rising tide of white; only the steeply slanted roofs of the biggest old houses down there broke its surface.

'I wish someone knew some good poetry,' Jordan said. His cheeks were redder than ever, but his eyes had receded into circular caves and he was shivering in spite of the two sweaters he was wearing. His breath came out in little puffs. 'The Head loved poetry, he thought that stuff was the shit. He was . . .' Jordan's voice, which had been strangely gay all night, finally broke. 'He was so *totally* old-school.'

Alice folded him against her. Jordan struggled, then gave in.

'Tell you what,' Tom said, 'let's cover him up nice – cover him against the cold – and then I'll give him some poetry. Would that be okay?'

'Do you really know some?'

'I really do,' Tom said.

'You're so smart, Tom. Thank you.' And Jordan smiled at him with weary, horrible gratitude.

Filling in the grave was quick, although in the end they

had to borrow some earth from the garden's nether parts to bring it up to dead level. By the time they were finished, Clay was sweating again and he could smell himself. It had been a long time between showers.

Alice had tried to keep Jordan from helping, but he broke free of her and pitched in, using his bare hands to toss earth into the hole. By the time Clay finished tamping the ground with the flat of his spade, the boy was glassy-eyed with exhaustion, all but reeling on his feet like a drunk.

Nevertheless, he looked at Tom. 'Go ahead. You promised.' Clay almost expected him to add, *And make it good, señor, or I weel put a boolet in you,* like a homicidal bandido in a Sam Peckinpah western.

Tom stepped to one end of the grave – Clay thought it was the top, but in his weariness could no longer remember. He could not even remember for sure if the Head's first name had been Charles or Robert. Runners of mist curled around Tom's feet and ankles, twined among the dead beanstalks. He removed his baseball cap, and Alice took off hers. Clay reached for his own and remembered he wasn't wearing one.

'That's right!' Jordan cried. He was smiling, frantic with understanding. 'Hats off! Hats off to the Head!' He was bare-headed himself, but mimed taking a hat off just the same – taking it off and flinging it into the air – and Clay once more found himself fearing for the boy's sanity. 'Now the poem! Come on, Tom!'

'All right,' Tom said, 'but you have to be quiet. Show respect.'

Jordan laid a finger across his lips to show he understood, and Clay saw by the brokenhearted eyes above that upraised finger that the boy had not lost his mind yet. His friend, but not his mind.

Clay waited, curious to see how Tom would go on. He expected some Frost, maybe a fragment of Shakespeare (surely the Head would have approved of Shakespeare, even if it had only been *When shall we three meet again*), perhaps even a little extemporaneous Tom McCourt. What he did not expect was what came from Tom's mouth in low, precisely measured lines.

'Do not withhold Your mercy from us, O Lord; may Your love and Your truth always protect us. For troubles without numbers surround us; our sins have overtaken us and we cannot see. Our sins are more than the hairs of our heads, and our hearts fail within us. Be pleased, O Lord, to save us; O Lord, come quickly to help us.'

Alice was holding her sneaker and weeping at the foot of the grave. Her head was bowed. Her sobs were quick and low.

Tom pressed on, holding one hand out over the new grave, palm extended, fingers curled in. 'May all who seek to take our lives as this life was taken be put to shame and confusion; may all who desire our ruin be turned back in disgrace. May those who say to us, "Aha, aha!" be appalled at their own shame. Here lies the dead, dust of the earth—'

'I'm so sorry, Head!' Jordan cried in a breaking treble voice. 'I'm so sorry, it's not right, sir, I'm so sorry you're dead—' His eyes rolled up and he crumpled to the new grave. The mist stole its greedy white fingers over him.

Clay picked him up and felt the pulse in Jordan's neck, strong and regular. 'Just fainted. What is it you're saying, Tom?'

Tom look flustered, embarrassed. 'A rather free adaptation of Psalm Forty. Let's take him inside—'

'No,' Clay said. 'If it's not too long, finish.'

'Yes, please,' Alice said. 'Finish. It's lovely. Like salve on a cut.'

Tom turned and faced the grave again. He seemed to gather himself, or perhaps he was only finding his place. 'Here lies the dead, dust of the earth, and here are we the living, poor and needy; Lord, think of us. You are our help and our deliverer; O my God, do not delay. Amen.'

'Amen,' Clay and Alice said together.

'Let's get the kid inside,' Tom said. 'It's fucking freezing out here.'

'Did you learn that from the holy Hannahs at the First
N.E. Church of Christ the Redeemer?' Clay asked.

'Oh, yes,' Tom said. 'Many psalms by heart, good for
extra desserts. I also learned how to beg on street corners
and leaflet a whole Sears parking lot in just twenty minutes
with *A Million Years in Hell and Not One Drink of Water*. Let's
put this kid to bed. I'm betting he'll sleep through until at
least four tomorrow afternoon and wake up feeling a hell
of a lot better.'

'What if that man with the torn cheek comes and finds
we're still here after he told us to go?' Alice asked.

Clay thought that was a good question, but not one he
needed to spend a lot of time mulling over. Either the Raggedy
Man would give them another day's grace or he wouldn't.
As he took Jordan upstairs to his bed, Clay found he was too
tired to care one way or the other.

2

At around four in the morning, Alice bid Clay and Tom a
foggy goodnight and stumbled off to bed. The two men sat
in the kitchen, drinking iced tea, not talking much. There
seemed nothing to say. Then, just before dawn, another of
those great groans, made ghostly by distance, rode in on the
foggy air from the northeast. It wavered like the cry of a
theremin in an old horror movie, and just as it began to fade,
a much louder answering cry came from Gaiten, where the
Raggedy Man had taken his new, larger flock.

Clay and Tom went out front, pushing aside the barrier
of melted boomboxes to get down the porch steps. They
could see nothing; the whole world was white. They stood
there awhile and went back in.

Neither the death-cry nor the answer from Gaiten woke
Alice and Jordan; they had that much to be grateful for. Their
road atlas, now bent and crumpled at the corners, was on the
kitchen counter. Tom thumbed through it and said, 'That

might have come from Hooksett or Suncook. They're both good-sized towns northeast of here – good-sized for New Hampshire, I mean. I wonder how many they got? And how they did it.'

Clay shook his head.

'I hope it was a lot,' Tom said with a thin and charmless smile. 'I hope it was at least a thousand, and that they slow-cooked them. I find myself thinking of some restaurant chain or other that used to advertise "broasted chicken". Are we going tomorrow night?'

'If the Raggedy Man lets us live through today, I guess we ought to. Don't you think?'

'I don't see any choice,' Tom said, 'but I'll tell you something, Clay – I feel like a cow being driven down a tin chute into the slaughterhouse. I can almost smell the blood of my little moo-brothers.'

Clay had the same feeling, but the same question recurred: If slaughtering was what they had on their group mind, why not do it here? They could have done it yesterday afternoon, instead of leaving melted boomboxes and Alice's pet sneaker on the porch.

Tom yawned. 'Turning in. Are you good for another couple of hours?'

'I could be,' Clay said. In fact, he had never felt less like sleeping. His body was exhausted but his mind kept turning and turning. It would begin to settle a bit, and then he'd recall the sound the pen had made coming out of the Head's eyesocket: the low squall of metal against bone. 'Why?'

'Because if they decide to kill us today, I'd rather go my way than theirs,' Tom said. 'I've seen theirs. You agree?'

Clay thought that if the collective mind which the Raggedy Man represented had really made the Head stick a fountain pen in his eye, the four remaining residents of Cheatham Lodge might find that suicide was no longer among their options. That was no thought to send Tom to bed on, however. So he nodded.

243

'I'll take all the guns upstairs. You've got that big old .45, right?'

'The Beth Nickerson special. Right.'

'Good night, then. And if you see them coming – or *feel* them coming – give a yell.' Tom paused. 'If you have time, that is. And if they let you.'

Clay watched Tom leave the kitchen, thinking Tom had been ahead of him all the time. Thinking how much he liked Tom. Thinking he'd like to get to know him better. Thinking the chances of that weren't good. And Johnny and Sharon? They had never seemed so far away.

3

At eight o'clock that morning, Clay sat on a bench at one end of the Head's victory garden, telling himself that if he weren't so tired, he'd get up off his dead ass and make the old fellow some sort of marker. It wouldn't last long, but the guy deserved it for taking care of his last pupil, if for nothing else. The thing was, he didn't even know if he could get up, totter into the house, and wake Tom to stand a watch.

Soon they would have a chilly, beautiful autumn day – one made for apple-picking, cider-making, and touch-football games in the backyard. For now the fog was still thick, but the morning sun shone strongly through it, turning the tiny world in which Clay sat to a dazzling white. Fine suspended droplets hung in the air, and hundreds of tiny rainbow wheels circulated in front of his heavy eyes.

Something red materialized out of this burning whiteness. For a moment the Raggedy Man's hoodie seemed to float by itself, and then, as it came up the garden toward Clay, its occupant's dark brown face and hands materialized above and below it. This morning the hood was up, framing the smiling disfigurement of the face and those dead-alive eyes.

Broad scholar's forehead, marred with a slash.

Filthy, shapeless jeans, torn at the pockets and worn more than a week now.

HARVARD across the narrow chest.

Beth Nickerson's .45 was in the side-holster on his belt. Clay didn't even touch it. The Raggedy Man stopped about ten feet from him. He – it – was standing on the Head's grave, and Clay believed that was no accident. 'What do you want?' he asked the Raggedy Man, and immediately answered himself: 'To. Tell you.'

He sat staring at the Raggedy Man, mute with surprise. He had expected telepathy or nothing. The Raggedy Man grinned – insofar as he could grin, with that badly split lower lip – and spread his hands as if to say, *Shucks, 't'warn't nuthin.*

'Say what you have to say, then,' Clay told him, and tried to prepare for having his voice hijacked a second time. He discovered it was a thing you couldn't prepare for. It was like being turned into a grinning piece of wood sitting on a ventriloquist's knee.

'Go. Tonight.' Clay concentrated and said, 'Shut up, stop it!'

The Raggedy Man waited, the picture of patience.

'I think I can keep you out if I try hard,' Clay said. 'I'm not sure, but I think I can.'

The Raggedy Man waited, his face saying *Are you done yet?*

'Go ahead,' Clay said, and then said, 'I could bring. More. I came. Alone.'

Clay considered the idea of the Raggedy Man's will joined to that of an entire flock and conceded the point.

'Go. Tonight. North.' Clay waited, and when he was sure the Raggedy Man was done with his voice for the time being, he said, 'Where? Why?'

There were no words this time, but an image suddenly rose before him. It was so clear that he didn't know if it was in his mind or if the Raggedy Man had somehow conjured it on the brilliant screen of the mist. It was what they had seen scrawled in the middle of Academy Avenue in pink chalk:

KASHWAK=NO-FO

'I don't get it,' he said.

But the Raggedy Man was walking away. Clay saw his red hoodie for a moment, once again seeming to float unoccupied against the brilliant mist; then that was gone, too. Clay was left with only the thin consolation of knowing that they had been going north anyway, and that they had been given another day's grace. Which meant there was no need to stand a watch. He decided to go to bed and let the others sleep through, as well.

4

Jordan awoke in his right mind, but his nervy brilliance had departed. He nibbled at half a rock-hard bagel and listened dully as Clay recounted his meeting with the Raggedy Man that morning. When Clay finished, Jordan got their road atlas, consulted the index at the back, and then opened it to the western Maine page. 'There,' he said, pointing to a town above Freyburg. 'This is Kashwak here, to the east, and Little Kashwak to the west, almost on the Maine–New Hampshire state line. I knew I recognized the name. Because of the lake.' He tapped it. 'Almost as big as Sebago.'

Alice leaned closer to read the name on the lake. 'Kash . . . Kashwakamak, I guess it is.'

'It's in an unincorporated area called TR-90,' Jordan said. He tapped this on the map, also. 'Once you know that, Kashwak Equals No-Fo is sort of a no-brainer, wouldn't you say?'

'It's a dead zone, right?' Tom said. 'No cell phone towers, no microwave towers.'

Jordan gave him a wan smile. 'Well, I imagine there are plenty of people with satellite dishes, but otherwise . . . bingo.'

'I don't get it,' Alice said. 'Why would they want to send us to a no-cell zone where everyone should be more or less all right?'

'Might as well ask why they let us live in the first place,' Tom said.

'Maybe they want to turn us into living guided missiles and use us to bomb the joint,' Jordan said. 'Get rid of us *and* them. Two birds with one stone.'

They considered this in silence for a moment.

'Let's go and find out,' Alice said, 'but I'm not bombing *anybody*.'

Jordan eyed her bleakly. 'You saw what they did to the Head. If it comes right down to it, do you think you'll have any choice?'

5

There were still shoes on most of the stoops across from the fieldstone pillars marking the entrance to Gaiten Academy, but the doors of the nice-looking homes either stood open or had been torn off their hinges. A few of the dead they saw littered on those lawns as they once more began their trek north were phone-crazies, but most had been innocent pilgrims who had happened to be in the wrong place at the wrong time. They were the ones with no shoes on their feet, but there was really no need to look as far as their feet; many of the reprisal victims had literally been torn limb from limb.

Beyond the school, where Academy Avenue once more became Route 102, there was carnage on both sides for half a mile. Alice walked with her eyes resolutely closed, allowing Tom to lead her as if she were blind. Clay offered to do the same for Jordan, but he only shook his head and walked stolidly up the centerline, a skinny kid with a pack on his back and too much hair on his head. After a few cursory glances at the kill-off, he looked down at his sneakers.

'There are hundreds,' Tom said once. It was eight o'clock and full dark, but they could still see far more than they wanted to. Lying curled around a stop-sign at the corner of Academy and Spofford was a girl in red pants and a white sailor blouse. She looked no more than nine, and she was shoeless. Twenty yards away stood the open door of the house from which she had probably been dragged, screaming for mercy. *'Hundreds.'*

'Maybe not that many,' Clay said. 'Some of our kind were armed. They shot quite a few of the bastards. Knifed a few more. I even saw one with an arrow sticking out of his—'

'We *caused* this,' Tom said. 'Do you think we *have* a kind anymore?'

This question was answered while they were eating their cold lunch at a roadside picnic spot four hours later. By then they were on Route 156, and according to the sign, this was a Scenic Turnout, offering a view of Historic Flint Hill to the west. Clay imagined the view was good, if you were eating lunch here at noon rather than midnight, with gas lanterns at either end of your picnic table to see by.

They had reached the dessert course − stale Oreos − when a party of half a dozen came toiling along, all of them older folks. Three were pushing shopping carts full of supplies and all were armed. These were the first other travelers they had seen since setting out again.

'Hey!' Tom called, giving them a wave. 'Got another picnic table over here, if you want to sit a spell!'

They looked over. The older of the two women in the party, a grandmotherly type with lots of white, fluffy hair that shone in the starlight, started to wave. Then she stopped.

'That's them,' one of the men said, and Clay did not mistake either the loathing or the fear in the man's voice. 'That's the Gaiten bunch.'

One of the other men said, 'Go to hell, buddy.' They

kept on walking, even moving a little faster, although the grandmotherly type was limping, and the man beside her had to help her past a Subaru that had locked bumpers with somebody's abandoned Saturn.

Alice jumped up, almost knocking over one of the lanterns. Clay grabbed her arm. 'Don't bother, kiddo.'

She ignored him. 'At least we did *something!*' she shouted after them. 'What did *you* do? Just what the fuck did *you* do?'

'Tell you what we didn't do,' one of the men said. The little group was past the scenic turnout now, and he had to look back over his shoulder to talk to her. He could do this because the road was free of abandoned vehicles for a couple of hundred yards here. 'We didn't get a bunch of normies killed. There are more of them than us, in case you didn't notice—'

'Oh bullshit, you don't know if that's true!' Jordan shouted. Clay realized it was the first time the kid had spoken since they'd passed the Gaiten town limits.

'Maybe it is and maybe it isn't,' the man said, 'but they can do some very weird and powerful shit. You gotta buy *that* for a dollar. They say they'll leave us alone if we leave them alone . . . and *you* alone. We say fine.'

'If you believe anything they say – or think at you – then you're an *idiot,*' Alice said.

The man faced forward, raised his hand in the air, shook it in a combined fuck-off/bye-bye gesture, and said no more.

The four of them watched the shopping-cart people out of sight, then gazed at each other across the picnic table with its intaglios of old initials.

'So now we know,' Tom said. 'We're outcasts.'

'Maybe not if the phone people want us to go where the rest of the – what did he call them? – the rest of the normies are going,' Clay said. 'Maybe we're something else.'

'What?' Alice asked.

Clay had an idea, but he didn't like to put it into words.

Not at midnight. 'Right now I'm more interested in Kent Pond,' he said. 'I want – I *need* to see if I can find my wife and son.'

'It's not very likely that they're still there, is it?' Tom asked in his low, kind voice. 'I mean, no matter which way things went for them, normal or phoner, they've probably moved on.'

'If they're all right, they will have left word,' Clay said. 'In any case, it's a place to go.'

And until they got there and that part of it was done, he wouldn't have to consider why the Raggedy Man would send them to a place of safety if the people there hated and feared them.

Or how, if the phone people knew about it, Kashwak No-Fo could be safe at all.

6

They were edging slowly east toward Route 19, a highway that would take them across the state line and into Maine, but they didn't make it that night. All the roads in this part of New Hampshire seemed to pass through the small city of Rochester, and Rochester had burned to the ground. The fire's core was still alive, putting out an almost radioactive glow. Alice took over, leading them around the worst of the fiery ruins in a half-circle to the west. Several times they saw **KASHWAK=NO-FO** scrawled on the sidewalks; once spray-painted on the side of a U.S. mailbox.

'That's a bazillion-dollar fine and life in prison at Guantánamo Bay,' Tom said with a wan smile.

Their course eventually took them through the vast parking lot of the Rochester Mall. Long before they reached it, they could hear the overamplified sound of an uninspired New Age jazz trio playing the sort of stuff Clay thought of as music to shop by. The parking lot was buried in drifts of moldering trash; the remaining cars stood up to their hubcaps in litter. They could smell the blown and fleshy reek of dead bodies on the breeze.

'Flock here somewhere,' Tom commented.

It was in the cemetery next to the mall. Their course was going to take them south and west of it, but when they left the mall parking lot, they were close enough to see the red eyes of the boomboxes through the trees.

'Maybe we ought to do em up,' Alice proposed suddenly as they stepped back onto North Main Street. 'There must be a propane truck that isn't working around here somewhere.'

'Yeah, baby!' Jordan said. He raised his fists to the sides of his head and shook them, looking really alive for the first time since leaving Cheatham Lodge. 'For the Head!'

'I think not,' Tom said.

'Afraid of trying their patience?' Clay asked. He was surprised to find himself actually sort of in favour of Alice's crazy idea. That torching another flock *was* a crazy idea he had no doubt, but . . .

He thought, *I might do it just because that's the absolute worst version of 'Misty' I've ever heard in my life. Twist my fuckin arm.*

'Not that,' Tom said. He seemed to be thinking. 'Do you see that street there?' He was pointing to an avenue that ran between the mall and the cemetery. It was choked with stalled cars. Almost all of them were pointed away from the mall. Clay found it all too easy to imagine those cars full of people trying to get home after the Pulse. People who would want to know what was happening, and if their families were all right. They would have reached for their car phones, their cell phones, without a second thought.

'What about it?' he asked.

'Let us stroll down there a little way,' Tom said. 'Very carefully.'

'What did you see, Tom?'

'I'd rather not say. Maybe nothing. Keep off the sidewalk, stay under the trees. And that was one hell of a traffic jam. There'll be bodies.'

There were dozens rotting their way back into the great scheme of things between Twombley Street and the West Side Cemetery. 'Misty' had given way to a cough-syrup rendition of 'I Left My Heart in San Francisco' by the time they reached the edge of the trees, and they could again see the red eyes of the boombox power lamps. Then Clay saw something else and stopped. 'Jesus,' he whispered. Tom nodded.

'What?' Jordan whispered. *'What?'*

Alice said nothing, but Clay could tell by the direction she was looking and the defeated slump of her shoulders that she'd seen what he had. There were men with rifles standing a perimeter guard around the cemetery. Clay took Jordan's head, turned it, and saw the boy's shoulders also slump.

'Let's go,' the kid whispered. 'The smell's making me sick.'

7

In Melrose Corner, about four miles north of Rochester (they could still see its red glow waxing and waning on the southern horizon), they came to another picnic area, this one with a little stone firepit as well as picnic tables. Clay, Tom, and Jordan picked up dry wood. Alice, who claimed to have been a Girl Scout, proved her skills by making a neat little fire and then heating three cans of what she called 'hobo beans'. As they ate, two little parties of pilgrims passed them by. Both looked; no one in either group waved or spoke.

When the wolf in his belly had quieted a little, Clay said, 'You saw those guys, Tom? All the way from the mall parking lot? I'm thinking of changing your name to Hawkeye.'

Tom shook his head. 'It was pure luck. That and the light from Rochester. You know, the embers?'

Clay nodded. They all did.

'I happened to look over at that cemetery at just the right time and the right angle and saw the shine on a couple of rifle-barrels. I told myself it couldn't be what it looked like, that it was probably iron fence-palings, or something, but . . .' Tom sighed, looked at the rest of his beans, then put them aside. 'There you have it.'

'They were phone-crazies, maybe,' Jordan said, but he didn't believe it. Clay could hear it in his voice.

'Phone-crazies don't do the night shift,' Alice said.

'Maybe they need less sleep now,' Jordan said. 'Maybe that's part of their new programming.'

Hearing him talk that way, as if the phone people were organic computers in some kind of upload cycle, never failed to give Clay a chill.

'They don't do rifles, either, Jordan,' Tom said. 'They don't need them.'

'So now they've got a few collaborators taking care of them while they get their beauty rest,' Alice said. There was brittle contempt on top of her voice, tears just beneath. 'I hope they rot in hell.'

Clay said nothing, but he found himself thinking of the people they had met earlier that night, the ones with the shopping carts – the fear and loathing in the voice of the man who had called them the Gaiten bunch. *He might as well have called us the Dillinger gang,* Clay thought. And then he thought, *I don't think of them as the phone-crazies anymore; now I think of them as the phone-people. Why is that?* The thought that followed was even more uncomfortable: *When does a collaborator stop being a collaborator?* The answer, it seemed to him, was when the collaborators became the clear majority. Then the ones who *weren't* collaborators became . . .

Well, if you were a romantic, you called those people 'the underground'. If you weren't a romantic, you called them fugitives.

Or maybe just criminals.

They pushed on to the village of Hayes Station and stayed the night at a tumbledown motel called Whispering Pines. It was within sight of a sign reading **ROUTE 19, 7**

MI SANFORD THE BERWICKS KENT POND. They didn't leave their shoes outside the doors of the units they chose.

There no longer seemed any need of that.

8

He was standing on a platform in the middle of that damned field again, somehow immobilized, the object of every eye. On the horizon was the skeletal shape with the blinking red light on top. The place was bigger than Foxboro. His friends were lined up with him, but now they weren't alone. Similar platforms ran the length of the open area. On Tom's left stood a pregnant woman in a Harley-Davidson T-shirt with cutoff sleeves. On Clay's right was an elderly gent – not in the Head's league, but getting there – with graying hair pulled back in a ponytail and a frightened frown on his horsey, intelligent face. Beyond him was a younger man wearing a battered Miami Dolphins cap.

Clay saw people that he knew among the thousands and wasn't surprised – wasn't that how things always went in dreams? One minute you were phone-booth-cramming with your first-grade teacher; a minute later you were making out with all three members of Destiny's Child on the observation deck of the Empire State Building.

Destiny's Child wasn't in this dream, but Clay saw the naked young man who had been jabbing the car aerials (now dressed in chinos and a clean white T-shirt), and the guy with the packsack who had called Alice little ma'am, and the limping grandmotherly type. She pointed to Clay and his friends, who were more or less on the fifty-yard line, then spoke to the woman next to her ... who was, Clay observed without surprise, Mr Scottoni's pregnant daughter-in-law. *That's the Gaiten bunch,* the limping grandmotherly type said, and Mr Scottoni's pregnant daughter-in-law lifted her full upper lip in a sneer.

Help me! called the woman on the platform next to Tom's. It was Mr Scottoni's daughter-in-law she was calling to. *I want to have my baby the same as you! Help me!*

You should have thought of that while there was still time, Mr Scottoni's daughter-in-law replied, and Clay realized, as he had in the other dream, that no one was actually talking. This was telepathy.

The Raggedy Man began making his way up the line, putting a hand over the head of each person he came to. He did this as Tom had over the Head's grave: palm extended, fingers curled in. Clay could see some sort of ID bracelet flashing on the Raggedy Man's wrist, maybe one of those medical-alert things, and realized there was power here – the light-towers were blazing. He saw something else, as well. The reason the Raggedy Man could reach above their heads even though they were standing on platforms was because the Raggedy Man wasn't on the ground. He was walking, but on four feet of thin air.

'*Ecce homo – insanus,*' he said. '*Ecce femina – insana.*' And each time the crowd roared back '*DON'T TOUCH!*' in a single voice, both the phone-people and the normies. Because now there was no difference. In Clay's dream they were the same.

9

He awoke in the late afternoon, huddled in a ball and clutching a flat motel pillow. He went outside and saw Alice and Jordan sitting on the curb between the parking lot and the units. Alice had her arm around Jordan. His head was on her shoulder and his arm was around her waist. His hair was sticking up in back. Clay sat down with them. Beyond them, the highway leading to Route 19 and Maine was deserted except for a Federal Express truck sitting dead on the white line with its back doors standing open, and a crashed motorcycle.

Clay sat down with them. 'Did you—'

'*Ecce puer, insanus,*' Jordan said, without lifting his head from Alice's shoulder. 'That's me.'

'And I'm the *femina*,' Alice said. 'Clay, is there some sort of humongous football stadium in Kashwak? Because if there is, I'm not going near the place.'

A door closed behind them. Footsteps approached. 'Me either,' Tom said, sitting down with them. 'I have many issues – I'd be the first to admit it – but a death-wish has never been one of them.'

'I'm not positive, but I don't think there's much more than an elementary school up there,' Clay said. 'The high school kids probably get bused to Tashmore.'

'It's a *virtual* stadium,' Jordan said.

'Huh?' Tom said. 'You mean like in a computer game?'

'I mean like in a computer.' Jordan lifted his head, still staring at the empty road leading to Sanford, the Berwicks, and Kent Pond. 'Never mind that, I don't care about that. If they won't touch us – the phone-people, the normal people – who will touch us?' Clay had never seen such adult pain in a child's eyes. 'Who *will* touch us?'

No one answered.

'Will the Raggedy Man touch us?' Jordan asked, his voice rising a little. 'Will the Raggedy Man touch us? Maybe. Because he's watching, I feel him watching.'

'Jordan, you're getting carried away,' Clay said, but the idea had a certain weird interior logic. If they were being sent this dream – the dream of the platforms – then maybe he *was* watching. You didn't mail a letter if you didn't have an address.

'I don't want to go to Kashwak,' Alice said. 'I don't care if it's a no-phone zone or not. I'd rather go to . . . to Idaho.'

'I'm going to Kent Pond before I go to Kashwak or Idaho or anywhere,' Clay said. 'I can be there in two nights' walk. I wish you guys would come, but if you don't want to – or can't – I'll understand.'

'The man needs closure, let's get him some,' Tom said.

'After that, we can figure out what comes next. Unless someone's got another idea.'

No one did.

10

Route 19 was totally clear on both sides for short stretches, sometimes up to a quarter of a mile, and that encouraged sprinters. This was the term Jordan coined for the semi-suicidal dragsters who would go roaring past at high speeds, usually in the middle of the road, always with their high beams glaring.

Clay and the others would see the approaching lights and get off the pavement in a hurry, right off the shoulder and into the weeds if they had spotted wrecks or stalls up ahead. Jordan took to calling these 'sprinter-reefs'. The sprinter would blow past, the people inside frequently whooping (and almost certainly liquored up). If there was only one stall – a small sprinter-reef – the driver would most likely elect to weave around it. If the road was completely blocked, he might still try to go around, but he and his passengers were more apt to simply abandon their vehicle and resume their east-ward course on foot until they found something else that looked worth sprinting in – which was to say, something fast and temporarily amusing. Clay imagined their course as a series of jerks . . . but then, most of the sprinters were jerks, just one more pain in the ass in what had become a pain-in-the-ass world. That seemed true of Gunner, as well.

He was the fourth sprinter of their first night on Highway 19, spotting them standing at the side of the road in the flare of his headlights. Spotting *Alice*. He leaned out, dark hair streaming back from his face, and yelled *'Suck my rod, you teenybop bitch!'* as he slammed by in a black Cadillac Escalade. His passengers cheered and waved. Someone shouted *'Tell huh!'* To Clay it sounded like absolute ecstasy expressed in a South Boston accent.

'Charming' was Alice's only comment.

'Some people have no—'Tom began, but before he could tell them what some people didn't have, there was a scream of tires from the dark not far ahead, followed by a loud, hollow bang and the tinkle of glass.

'Jesus-*fuck*,' Clay said, and began to run. Before he had gotten twenty yards, Alice blew past him. 'Slow down, they might be dangerous!' he shouted.

Alice held up one of the automatic pistols so Clay could see it and ran on, soon outdistancing him completely.

Tom caught up with Clay, already working for breath. Jordan, running beside him, could have been in a rocking chair.

'What . . . are we going . . . to do . . . if they're badly hurt?' Tom asked. 'Call . . . an ambulance?'

'I don't know,' Clay said, but he was thinking of how Alice had held up one of the automatic pistols. He knew.

11

They caught up with her around the next curve of the highway. She was standing behind the Escalade. It was lying on its side with the airbags deployed. The tale of the accident wasn't hard to read. The Escalade had come steaming around the blind curve at maybe sixty miles an hour and had encountered an abandoned milk tanker dead ahead. The driver, jerk or not, had done well to avoid being totaled. He was walking around the battered SUV in a dazed circle, pushing his hair away from his face. Blood gushed from his nose and a cut in his forehead. Clay walked to the Escalade, sneakers gritting on pebbles of Saf-T-Glas, and looked inside. It was empty. He shone his light around and saw blood on the steering wheel, nowhere else. The passengers had been lively enough to exit the wreck, and all but one had fled the scene, probably out of simple reflex. The one who had stuck with the driver was a shrimpy little postadolescent with bad acne scars, buck teeth, and long, dirty red hair. His steady line of jabber reminded Clay of the little dog who idolized Spike in the Warner Bros. cartoons.

'Ah you all right, Gunnah?' he asked. Clay presumed this was how you pronounced *Gunner* in Southie. 'Holy shit, you're bleedin like a mutha. Fuckin-A, I thought we was dead.' Then, to Clay: 'Whutta *you* lookin at?'

'Shut up,' Clay said – and, under the circumstances, not unkindly.

The redhead pointed at Clay, then turned to his bleeding friend. 'This is one of em, Gunnah! This is a *bunch* of em!'

'Shut up, Harold,' Gunner said. Not kindly at all. Then he looked at Clay, Tom, Alice, and Jordan.

'Let me do something about your forehead,' Alice said. She had reholstered her gun and taken off her pack. Now she was rummaging through it. 'I've got Band-Aids and gauze pads. Also hydrogen peroxide, which will sting, but better a little sting than an infection, am I right?'

'Considering what this young man called you on his way by, you're a better Christian than I was in my prime,' Tom said. He had unslung Sir Speedy and was holding it by the strap as he looked at Gunner and Harold.

Gunner might have been twenty-five. His long black rock-vocalist hair was now matted with blood. He looked at the milk tanker, then at the Escalade, then at Alice, who had a gauze pad in one hand and the bottle of hydrogen peroxide in the other.

'Tommy and Frito and that guy who was always pickin his nose, they took off,' the redheaded shrimp was saying. He expanded what chest he had. 'But I stuck around, Gunnah! Holy fuck, buddy, you're bleedin like a pig.'

Alice put hydrogen peroxide on the gauze pad, then took a step toward Gunner. He immediately took a step back. 'Get away from me. You're poison.'

'It's *them*!' the redhead cried. 'From the dreams! What'd I tellya?'

'Keep away from me,' Gunner said. 'Fuckin bitch. Alla ya.'

Clay felt a sudden urge to shoot him and wasn't surprised. Gunner looked and acted like a dangerous dog backed into a corner, teeth bared and ready to bite, and wasn't that what you did to dangerous dogs when there was no other recourse? Didn't you shoot them? But of course they *did* have recourse, and if Alice could play Good Samaritan to the scumbag who had called her a teenybop bitch, he guessed he could refrain from executing him. But there was something he wanted to find out before he let these two charming fellows go their way.

'These dreams,' he said. 'Do you have a . . . I don't know . . . a kind of spirit guide in them? A guy in a red hoodie, let's say?'

Gunner shrugged. Tore a piece off his shirt and used it to mop the blood on his face. He was coming back a little now, seemed a little more aware of what had happened. 'Harvard, yeah. Right, Harold?'

The little redhead nodded. 'Yeah. Harvard. The black guy. But they ain't dreams. If you don't know, it ain't no fuckin good telling ya. They're fuckin *broadcasts*. Broadcasts in our sleep. If you don't get em, it's because you're poison. Ain't they, Gunnah?'

'You guys fucked up bigtime,' Gunner said in a brooding voice, and mopped his forehead. 'Don't you touch me.'

'We're gonna have our own place,' Harold said. 'Ain't we, Gunnah? Up Maine, fuckin right. Everyone who didn't get Pulsed is goin there, and we're gonna be left alone. Hunt, fish, live off the fuckin land. Harvard says so.'

'And you believe him?' Alice said. She sounded fascinated.

Gunner raised a finger that shook slightly. 'Shut your mouth, bitch.'

'I think you better shut yours,' Jordan said. 'We've got the guns.'

'You better not even *think* about shootin us!' Harold said shrilly. 'Whatcha think Harvard would do to you if you shot us, you fuckin punkass shorty?'

'Nothing,' Clay said.

'You don't—' Gunner began, but before he could get any further, Clay took a step forward and pistol-whipped him across the jaw with Beth Nickerson's .45. The sight at the end of the barrel opened a fresh cut along Gunner's jaw, but Clay hoped that in the end this might prove better medicine than the hydrogen peroxide the man had refused. In this he proved wrong.

Gunner fell back against the side of the abandoned milk tanker, looking at Clay with shocked eyes. Harold took an impulsive step forward. Tom trained Sir Speedy on him and gave his head a single forbidding shake. Harold shrank back and began to gnaw the ends of his dirty fingers. Above them his eyes were huge and wet.

'We're going now,' Clay said. 'I'd advise you stay here at least an hour, because you really don't want to see us again. We're leaving you your lives as a gift. If we see you again, we'll take them away.' He backed toward Tom and the others, still staring into that glowering, unbelieving bloody face. He felt a little like the old-time lion-tamer Frank Buck, trying to do it all by pure force of will. 'One more thing. I don't know why the phone-people want all the "normies" in Kashwak, but I know what a roundup usually means for the cattle. You might think about that the next time you're getting one of your nightly podcasts.'

'Fuck you,' Gunner said, but broke his eyelock with Clay and gazed down at his shoes.

'Come on, Clay,' Tom said. 'Let's go.'

'Don't let us see you again, Gunner,' Clay said, but they did.

12

Gunner and Harold must have gotten ahead of them somehow, maybe by taking a chance and traveling five or ten daylight miles while Clay, Tom, Alice, and Jordan were sleeping in the State Line Motel, which was about two hundred yards into Maine. The pair might have laid up in the Salmon Falls rest area, Gunner hiding his new ride among the half a dozen or so cars that had been abandoned there. It didn't really matter. What mattered was they got ahead of them, waited for them to go by, and then pounced.

Clay barely registered the approaching sound of the engine or Jordan's comment— 'Here comes a sprinter.' This was his home turf, and as they passed each familiar landmark – the Freneau Lobster Pound two miles east of the State Line Motel, Shaky's Tastee Freeze across from it, the statue of General Joshua Chamberlain in the tiny Turnbull town square – he felt more and more like a man having a vivid dream. He didn't realize how little he'd expected to ever reach home again until he saw the big plastic sof'-serv cone towering over Shaky's – it looked both prosaic and as exotic as something from a lunatic's nightmare, hulking its curled tip against the stars.

'Road's pretty littered for a sprinter,' Alice commented.

They walked to the side of the road as headlights brightened on the hill behind them. An overturned pickup truck was lying on the white line. Clay thought there was a good chance the oncoming vehicle would ram it, but the headlights swerved to the left only an instant after they cleared the hilltop; the sprinter avoided the pickup easily, running on the shoulder for a few seconds before regaining the road. Clay surmised later that Gunner and Harold must have gone over this stretch, mapping the sprinter-reefs carefully.

They stood watching, Clay closest to the approaching lights, Alice standing next to him on his left. On her left were

Tom and Jordan. Tom had his arm slung casually around Jordan's shoulders.

'Boy, he's really comin,' Jordan said. There was no alarm in his voice; it was just a remark. Clay felt no alarm, either. He had no premonition of what was going to happen. He had forgotten all about Gunner and Harold.

There was a sports car of some sort, maybe an MG, parked half on and half off the road fifty feet or so west of where they were standing. Harold, who was driving the sprinter vehicle, swerved to avoid it. Just a minor swerve, but perhaps it threw Gunner's aim off. Or perhaps not. Perhaps Clay had never been his target. Perhaps it was Alice he'd meant to hit all along.

Tonight they were in a nondescript Chevrolet sedan. Gunner was kneeling on the backseat, out the window to his waist, holding a ragged chunk of cinderblock in his hands. He gave an inarticulate cry that could have come directly from a balloon in one of the comic books Clay had drawn as a freelance – 'Yahhhhhh!' – and threw the block. It flew a short and lethal course through the dark and struck Alice in the side of the head. Clay never forgot the sound it made. The flashlight she had been holding – which would have made her a perfect target, although they had all been holding them – tumbled from her relaxing hand and sprayed a cone of light across the macadam, picking out pebbles and a piece of taillight glass that glinted like a fake ruby.

Clay fell on his knees beside her, calling her name, but he couldn't hear himself in the sudden roar of Sir Speedy, which was finally getting a trial. Muzzle-flashes strobed the dark, and by their glare he could see blood pouring down the left side of her face – oh God, *what* face – in a torrent.

Then the gunfire stopped. Tom was screaming *'The barrel pulled up, I couldn't hold it down, I think I shot the whole fucking clip into the sky'* and Jordan was screaming *'Is she hurt, did he get her?'* and Clay thought of how she had offered to put hydrogen peroxide on Gunner's forehead and then bandage it. *Better a little sting than an infection, am I right?* she had said, and he had to stop the bleeding. He had to stop it right *now*. He stripped off the jacket he was wearing, then the sweater beneath. He would use the sweater, wrap it around her head like a fucking turban.

Tom's roving flashlight happened on the cinderblock and stopped. It was matted with gore and hair. Jordan saw it and began to shriek. Clay, panting and sweating madly in spite of the chilly evening air, began to wrap the sweater around Alice's head. It soaked through immediately. His hands felt like they were wearing warm wet gloves. Now Tom's light found Alice, her head wrapped in a sweater down to the nose so that she looked like a prisoner of Islamic extremists in an Internet photo, her cheek (the *remains* of her cheek) and her neck drowned in blood, and he also began to scream.

Help me, Clay wanted to say. *Stop that, both of you, and help me with her.* But his voice wouldn't come out and all he could do was press the sopping sweater against the spongy side of her head, remembering that she had been bleeding when they had first met her, thinking she had been okay that time, she had been okay then.

Her hands were twitching aimlessly, the fingers kicking up little sprays of roadside dirt. *Somebody give her that sneaker of hers,* Clay thought, but the sneaker was in her pack and she was lying on her pack. Lying there with the side of her head crushed in by someone who'd had a little score to settle. Her feet were twitching, too, he saw, and he could still feel the blood pouring out of her, through the sweater and over his hands.

Here we are at the end of the world, he thought. He looked up in the sky and saw the evening star.

13

She never really passed out and never fully regained consciousness. Tom got himself under control and helped carry her up the slope on their side of the road. Here were trees – what Clay remembered as an apple orchard. He thought he and

264

Sharon had come here once to pick, back when Johnny had been small. When it had been good between them and there had been no arguments about money and ambitions and the future.

'You're not supposed to move people when they've got bad head-wounds,' Jordan fretted, trailing along behind them and carrying her pack.

'That's nothing we have to worry about,' Clay said. 'She can't live, Jordan. Not like she is. I don't think even a hospital could do much for her.' He saw Jordan's face begin to crumple. There was enough light for that. 'I'm sorry.'

They laid her on the grass. Tom tried to give her water from a Poland Spring bottle with a nipple end, and she actually took some. Jordan gave her the sneaker, the Baby Nike, and she took that, too, squeezing it, leaving smears of blood on it. Then they waited for her to die. They waited all that night.

14

She said, 'Daddy told me I could have the rest, so don't blame *me.*' That was around eleven o'clock. She lay with her head on Tom's pack, which he had stuffed with a motel blanket he'd taken from the Sweet Valley Inn. That had been on the outskirts of Methuen, in what now seemed like another life. A better life, actually. The pack was already soaked with blood. Her one remaining eye stared up at the stars. Her left hand lay open on the grass beside her. It hadn't moved in over an hour. Her right hand squeezed the little sneaker relentlessly. Squeeze . . . and relax. Squeeze . . . and relax.

'Alice,' Clay said. 'Are you thirsty? Do you want some more water?'

She did not answer.

15

Later – quarter of one by Clay's watch – she asked someone if she could go swimming. Ten minutes later she said, 'I don't want those tampons, those tampons are dirty,' and laughed. The sound of her laughter was natural, shocking, and it roused Jordan, who had been dozing. He saw how she was and started to cry. He went off by himself to do it. When Tom tried to sit beside him and comfort him, Jordan screamed for him to go away.

At quarter past two, a large party of normies passed by on the road below them, many flashlights bobbing in the dark. Clay went to the edge of the slope and called down to them. 'You don't have a doctor, do you?' he asked, without much hope.

The flashlights stopped. There was a murmur of consultation from the dark shapes below, and then a woman's voice called up to him, a rather beautiful voice. 'Leave us alone. You're off-limits.'

Tom joined Clay at the edge of the bank. '"And the Levite also passed by on the other side,"' Tom called down. 'That's King James for fuck you, lady.'

Behind them, Alice suddenly spoke in a strong voice. 'The men in the car will be taken care of. Not as a favour to you but as a warning to others. You understand.'

Tom grabbed Clay's wrist with a cold hand. 'Jesus Christ, she sounds like she's awake.'

Clay took Tom's hand in both of his own and held it. 'That's not her. That's the guy in the red hoodie, using her as a . . . as a loudspeaker.'

In the dark Tom's eyes were huge. 'How do you know that?'

'I know,' Clay said.

Below them, the flashlights were moving away. Soon they were gone and Clay was glad. This was their business, it was private.

16

At half past three, in the ditch of the night, Alice said: 'Oh, Mummy, too bad! Fading roses, this garden's over.' Then her tone brightened. 'Will there be snow? We'll make a fort, we'll make a leaf, we'll make a bird, we'll make a bird, we'll make a hand, we'll make a blue one, we'll . . .' She trailed off, looking up at stars that turned on the night like a clock. The night was cold. They had bundled her up. Every breath she exhaled came out in white vapour. The bleeding had finally stopped. Jordan sat next to her, petting her left hand, the one that was already dead and waiting for the rest of her to catch up.

'Play the slinky one I like,' she said. 'The one by Hall and Oates.'

17

At twenty to five, she said, 'It's the loveliest dress ever.' They were all gathered around her. Clay had said he thought she was going.

'What color, Alice?' Clay asked, not expecting an answer – but she *did* answer.

'Green.'

'Where will you wear it?'

'The ladies come to the table,' she said. Her hand still squeezed the sneaker, but more slowly now. The blood on the side of her face had dried to an enamel glaze. 'The ladies come to the table, the ladies come to the table. Mr Ricardi stays at his post and the ladies come to the table.'

'That's right, dear,' Tom said softly. 'Mr Ricardi stayed at his post, didn't he?'

'The ladies come to the table.' Her remaining eye turned to Clay, and for the second time she spoke in that other voice. One he had heard coming from his own mouth. Only four words this time. 'Your son's with us.'

'You lie,' Clay whispered. His fists were clenched, and he had to restrain himself from striking the dying girl. 'You bastard, you lie.'

'The ladies come to the table and we all have tea,' Alice said.

18

The first line of light had begun to show in the east. Tom sat beside Clay, and put a tentative hand on his arm. 'If they read minds,' he said, 'they could have gotten the fact that you have a son and you're worried to death about him as easily as you'd look something up on Google. That guy could be using Alice to fuck with you.'

'I know that,' Clay said. He knew something else: what she'd said in Harvard's voice was all too plausible. 'You know what I keep thinking about?'

Tom shook his head.

'When he was little, three or four – back when Sharon and I still got along and we called him Johnny-Gee – he'd come running every time the phone rang. He'd yell "Fo-fo-me-me?" It knocked us out. And if it was his nana or his PeePop, we'd say "Fo-fo-you-you" and hand it to him. I can still remember how big the fucking thing looked in his little hands . . . and against the side of his face . . .'

'Clay, stop.'

'And now . . . now . . .' He couldn't go on. And didn't have to.

'Come here, you guys!' Jordan called. His voice was agonized. 'Hurry up!'

They went back to where Alice lay. She had come up off the ground in a locked convulsion, her spine a hard, quivering arc. Her remaining eye bulged in its socket; her lips pulled down at the corners. Then, suddenly, everything relaxed. She spoke a name that had no meaning for them – Henry – and squeezed the sneaker one final time. Then the fingers relaxed and it slipped free. There was a sigh and a final white cloud, very thin, from between her parted lips.

Jordan looked from Clay to Tom, then back to Clay again. 'Is she—'

'Yes,' Clay said.

Jordan burst into tears. Clay allowed Alice another few seconds to look at the paling stars, then used the heel of his hand to close her eye.

19

There was a farmhouse not far from the orchard. They found shovels in one of the sheds and buried her under an apple tree, with the little sneaker in her hand. It was, they agreed, what she would have wanted. At Jordan's request, Tom once more recited Psalm Forty, although this time he had difficulty finishing. They each told one thing they remembered about Alice. During this part of the impromptu service, a flock of phone-people – a small one – passed north of them. They were noticed but not bothered. This did not surprise Clay in the slightest. They were insane, not to be touched . . . as he was sure Gunner and Harold would learn to their sorrow.

They slept away most of the daylight hours in the farm-house, then moved on to Kent Pond. Clay no longer really expected to find his son there, but he hadn't given up hope of finding word of Johnny, or perhaps Sharon. Just to know she was alive might lift a little of the sorrow he now felt, a feeling so heavy that it seemed to weigh him down like a cloak lined with lead.

KENT POND

1

His old house – the house where Johnny and Sharon had lived at the time of the Pulse – was on Livery Lane, two blocks north of the dead traffic light that marked the center of Kent Pond. It was the sort of place some real estate ads called a 'fixer-upper' and some a 'starter home'. Clay and Sharon's joke – before the separation – was that their 'starter home' would probably also be their 'retirement home'. And when she'd gotten pregnant, they had talked about naming the baby Olivia if it turned out to be of what Sharon called 'the feminine persuasion'. Then, she said, they'd have the only Livvie of Livery Lane. How they had laughed.

Clay, Tom, and Jordan – a pallid Jordan, a thoughtfully silent Jordan who now usually responded to questions only if asked a second or even a third time – arrived at the intersection of Main and Livery at just past midnight on a windy night during the second week of October. Clay stared wildly at the stop sign on the corner of his old street, where he had come as a visitor for the last four months. *NUCLEAR POWER* was still stenciled there in spray-paint, as it had been before he'd left for Boston. STOP . . . *NUCLEAR POWER.* STOP . . . *NUCLEAR POWER.* He couldn't seem to get the sense of it. It wasn't a question of *meaning,* that was clear enough, just someone's clever little political statement (if he looked he'd probably find the same thing on stop signs all over town, maybe in Springvale and Acton, too), but the sense of how

273

this could be the same when the whole world had changed
– that eluded him. Clay felt somehow that if he stared at
STOP . . . *NUCLEAR POWER* with enough desperate intensity,
a wormhole would open, some kind of sci-fi time-tunnel,
and he'd dive into the past, and all this would be undone. All
this darkness.

'Clay?' Tom asked. 'Are you all right?'

'This is my street,' Clay said, as if that explained everything, and then, without knowing he was going to do it, he
began to run.

Livery Lane was a cul-de-sac, all the streets on this side
of town dead-ending against the flank of Kent's Hill, which
was really an eroded mountain. Oaks overhung it and the
street was full of dead leaves that crackled under his feet.
There were also a lot of stalled cars, and two that were locked
grille to grille in a strenuous mechanical kiss.

'Where's he going?' Jordan called behind him. Clay hated
the fear he heard in Jordan's voice, but he couldn't stop.

'He's all right,' Tom said. 'Let him go.'

Clay wove around the stalled cars, the beam of his flashlight jigging and stabbing in front of him. One of the stabs
caught Mr Kretsky's face. Mr Kretsky always used to have a
Tootsie Pop for Johnny on haircut day when Johnny was
Johnny-Gee, just a little guy who used to yell *fo-fo-me-me*
when the phone rang. Mr Kretsky was lying on the sidewalk
in front of his house, half-buried in fallen oak-leaves, and his
nose appeared to be gone.

I mustn't find them dead. This thought drummed in his
mind, over and over. *Not after Alice. I mustn't find them dead.*
And then, hatefully (but in moments of stress the mind almost
always told the truth): *And if I have to find one of them dead
. . . let it be her.*

Their house was the last one on the left (as he always
used to remind Sharon, with a suitably creepy laugh – long
after the joke had worn thin, actually), and the driveway
slanted up to the refurbished little shed that was just big

enough to park one car. Clay was already out of breath but he didn't slow. He sprinted up the driveway, kicking leaves in front of him, feeling the stitch starting to sink in high up on his right side, tasting copper in the back of his mouth, where his breathing seemed to rasp. He lifted his flashlight and shined it into the garage.

Empty. Question was, was that good or bad?

He turned around, saw Tom's and Jordan's lights bobbing toward him down below, and shone his own on his back door. His heart leaped into the back of his throat at what he saw. He ran up the three steps to the stoop, stumbled, and almost put his hand through the storm door, pulling the note off the glass. It was held by only a corner of Scotch tape; if they'd come along an hour later, maybe even half an hour, the restless night wind would have blown it over the hills and far away. He could kill her for not taking more pains, such carelessness was just so *Sharon,* but at least—

The note wasn't from his wife.

2

Jordan came up the driveway and stood at the foot of the steps with his light trained on Clay. Tom came toiling along behind, breathing hard and making an enormous crackling sound as he scuffed through the leaves. He stopped beside Jordan and put his own light on the scrap of unfolded paper in Clay's hand. He raised the beam slowly to Clay's thunderstruck face.

'I forgot about her mother's fucking diabetes,' Clay said, and handed over the note that had been Scotch-taped to the door. Tom and Jordan read it together.

> *Daddy,*
> *Something bad hapen as you porbly know, I hope your all right & get this. Mitch Steinman and George Gendron are with me, people are going crazy & we think*

its the cell phones. Dad here is the bad part, we came here because I was afraid. I was going to break mine if I was wrong but I wasnt wrong, it was gone. Mom has been taking it because you know nana is sick and she wanted to keep checking. I gotta go Jesus I'm scrared, someone killed Mr Kretsky. All kinds of people are dead & nuts like in a horra movie but we heard people are getting together (NORMAL people) at the Town Hall and thats where we are going. Maybe mom is there but jesus she had my PHONE. Daddy if you get here okay PLEASE COME GET ME.
  Your Son,
  John Gavin Riddell

Tom finished, then spoke in a tone of kindly caution that terrified Clay more thoroughly than the most dire warning could have done. 'You know that any people who gathered at the Town Hall have probably gone many different ways, don't you? It's been ten days, and the world has undergone a terrible convulsion.'

'I know,' Clay said. His eyes were stinging and he could feel his voice beginning to waver. 'And I know his mother is probably . . .' He shrugged and flung an unsteady hand at the dark, sloping-away world beyond his leaf-strewn driveway. 'But Tom, I have to go to the Town Hall and see. They may have left word. *He* may have left word.'

'Yes,' Tom said. 'Of course you do. And when we get there, we can decide what comes next.' He spoke in that same tone of awful kindness. Clay almost wished he'd laugh and say something like *Come on, you poor sap – you don't really think you're going to see him again, do you? Get fucking real.*

Jordan had read the note a second time, maybe a third and fourth. Even in his current state of horror and grief, Clay felt like apologizing to Jordan for Johnny's poor spelling and composition skills – reminding Jordan that his son must have written under terrible stress, crouched on the stoop, scribbling while his friends stood watching chaos swirl below.

Now Jordan lowered the note and said, 'What does your son look like?'

Clay almost asked why, then decided he didn't want to know. At least not yet. 'Johnny's almost a foot shorter than you. Stocky. Dark brown hair.'

'Not skinny. Not blond.'

'No, that sounds like his friend George.'

Jordan and Tom exchanged a look. It was a grave look, but Clay thought there was relief in it, too.

'What?' he asked. '*What?* Tell me.'

'The other side of the street,' Tom said. 'You didn't see because you were running. There's a dead boy about three houses down. Skinny, blond, red backpack—'

'That's George Gendron,' Clay said. He knew George's red backpack as well as he knew Johnny's blue one with the strips of reflecting tape on it. 'He and Johnny made a Puritan village together for their fourth-grade history project. They got an A-plus. George can't be dead.' But he almost certainly was. Clay sat down on the stoop, which gave its old familiar creak under his weight, and put his face in his hands.

3

The Town Hall was at the intersection of Pond and Mill streets, in front of the town common and the body of water that gave the little village its name. The parking lot was almost empty except for the spaces reserved for employees, because both streets leading to the big white Victorian building were jammed with stalled vehicles. People had gotten as close as they could, then walked the rest of the way. For latecomers like Clay, Tom, and Jordan, it was a slow slog. Within two blocks of the Town Hall, not even the lawns were free of cars. Half a dozen houses had burned down. Some were still smoldering.

Clay had covered the body of the boy on Livery Lane – it had indeed been Johnny's friend George – but they could do nothing for the scores of swollen and putrefying dead they encountered as they made their slow way toward the Kent Pond Town Hall. There were hundreds, but in the dark Clay saw none that he recognized. That might have been true even in daylight. The crows had put in a busy week and a half.

His mind kept going back to George Gendron, who had been lying facedown in a clot of bloody leaves. In his note, John had said that George and Mitch, his other good friend this year in the seventh grade, had been with him. So whatever had happened to George must have happened after Johnny taped that note to the storm door and the three of them left the Riddell house. And since only George had been in those bloody leaves, Clay could assume Johnny and Mitch had gotten off Livery Lane alive.

Of course assume makes an ass out of you and *me,* he thought. *The gospel according to Alice Maxwell, may she rest in peace.*

And it was true. George's killer might have chased them and gotten them somewhere else. On Main Street, or Dugway Street, maybe neighboring Laurel Way. Stabbed them with a Swedish butcher knife or a couple of car aerials . . .

They had reached the edge of the Town Hall parking lot. On their left was a pickup truck that had tried to reach it overland and wound up mired in a boggy ditch less than five yards from an acre of civilized (and largely deserted) asphalt. On their right was a woman with her throat torn out and her features pecked away to black holes and bloody ribbons by the birds. She was still wearing her Portland Sea Dogs baseball cap, and her purse was still over her arm.

Killers weren't interested in money anymore.

Tom put a hand on his shoulder, startling him. 'Stop thinking about what might have happened.'

'How did you know—'

'It doesn't take a mind reader. If you find your son –

you probably won't, but if you do – I'm sure he'll tell you the whole story. Otherwise . . . does it matter?'

'No. Of course not. But Tom . . . I *knew* George Gendron. The kids used to call him Connecticut sometimes, because his family moved from there. He ate hot dogs and hamburgers in our backyard. His dad used to come over and watch the Patriots with me.'

'I know,' Tom said. 'I know.' And, to Jordan, sharply: 'Stop looking at her, Jordan, she's not going to get up and walk.'

Jordan ignored him and kept staring at the crow-picked corpse in the Sea Dogs hat. 'The phoners started trying to take care of their own as soon as they got back some base-level programming,' he said. 'Even if it was only fishing them out from under the bleachers and throwing them into the marsh, they tried to do *something*. But they don't take care of ours. They leave ours to rot where they fell.' He turned to face Clay and Tom. 'No matter what they say or what they promise, we can't trust them,' he said fiercely. 'We *can't*, okay?'

'I'm totally down with that,' Tom said.

Clay nodded. 'Me too.'

Tom tipped his head toward the Town Hall, where a few emergency lights with long-life batteries still shone, casting a sickly yellow glow on the employees' cars, which now stood in drifts of leaves. 'Let's go in there and see what they left behind.'

'Yes, let's do it,' Clay said. Johnny would be gone, he had no doubt of that, but some small part of him, some small, childish, never-say-die part, still continued to hope that he would hear a cry of *'Daddy!'* and his son would spring into his arms, a living thing, real weight in the midst of this night-mare.

4

They knew for sure the Town Hall was deserted when they saw what had been painted across the double doors. In the fading glow of the battery-powered emergency lights, the large, sloppy strokes of red paint looked like more dried blood:

KASHWAK=NO-FO

'How far away is this Kashwak place?' Tom asked.

Clay thought about it. 'I'd say eighty miles, almost due north. You'd take Route 160 most of the way, but once you get on the TR, I don't know.'

Jordan asked, 'What exactly is a TR?'

'TR-90's an unincorporated township. There are a couple of little villages, some quarries, and a two-bit Micmac rez up north, but mostly it's just woods, bear, and deer.' Clay tried the door and it opened to his hand. 'I'm going to check this place out. You guys really don't have to come if you don't want to – you can be excused.'

'No, we'll come,' Tom said. 'Won't we, Jordan?'

'Sure.' Jordan sighed like a boy confronted with what may be a difficult chore. Then he smiled. 'Hey, electric lights. Who knows when we'll get to see *them* again.'

5

No Johnny Riddell came hurtling out of a dark room to throw himself into his father's arms, but the Town Hall was still redolent of the cooking that had been done on gas grills and hibachis by the people who'd gathered here following the Pulse. Outside the big main room, on the long bulletin board where notices of town business and upcoming events usually hung, perhaps two hundred notes had been posted. Clay, so tense he was nearly panting, began to study these with the intensity of a scholar who believes he may have found the lost Gospel of Mary Magdalene. He was afraid of what he might find and terrified of what he might not. Tom and Jordan retreated tactfully to the main meeting room, which was still littered with the remains of the refugees who had apparently spent several nights here, waiting for a rescue that had never come.

In the posted notes, Clay saw the survivors had come to believe that they could hope for more than rescue. They believed that salvation awaited them in Kashwak. Why that particular townlet, when probably all of TR-90 (certainly the northern and western quadrants) was dead to cell phone transmission and reception? The notes on the bulletin board weren't clear on that. Most seemed to assume that any readers would understand without needing to be told; it was a case of 'everybody knows, everybody goes'. And even the clearest of the correspondents had obviously been struggling to keep terror and elation balanced and under control; most messages amounted to little more than *follow the Yellow Brick Road to Kashwak and salvation as soon as you can.*

Three-quarters of the way down the board, half-hidden by a note from Iris Nolan, a lady Clay knew quite well (she volunteered at the tiny town library), he saw a sheet with his son's familiar, looping scrawl and thought, *Oh, dear God, thank you. Thank you so much.* He pulled it off the board, being careful not to tear it.

This note was dated: *Oct 3.* Clay tried to remember where he had been on the night of October 3 and couldn't quite do it. Had it been the barn in North Reading, or the Sweet Valley Inn, near Methuen? He thought the barn, but he couldn't be absolutely certain – it all ran together and if he thought too hard about it, it began to seem that the man with the flashlights on the sides of his head had also been the young man jabbing the car aerials, that Mr Ricardi had killed himself by gobbling broken glass instead of hanging himself, and it had been Alice in Tom's garden, eating cucumbers and tomatoes.

'Stop it,' he whispered, and focused on the note. It was better spelled and a little better composed, but there was no mistaking the agony in it.

Oct 3

Dear Dad,

I hope you are alive & get this. Me & Mitch made it okay but Hughie Darden got George, I think he killed him. Me & Mitch just outran faster. I felt like it was my fault but Mitch, he said how could you know he was just a Phoner like the others its not your fault.

Daddy there is worse. Mom is one of them, I saw her with one of the 'flocks' today. (That is what they call them, flocks.) She doesnt look as bad as some but I know if I went out there she wouldnt even no me and would kill me soon as look at me. IF YOU SEE HER DON'T BE FOOLED, I'M SORRY BUT ITS TRUE.

We're going to Kashwak (its up north) tomorrow or next day, Mitch's mom is here I could kill him I'm so ennveous. Daddy I know you dont have a cell phone and everyone knows about Kashwak how it's a safe place. If you get this note PLEASE COME GET ME.

I love you with all my Heart,
Your Son,
John Gavin Riddell

Even after the news about Sharon, Clay was doing all right until he got to *I love you with all my Heart.* Even then he might have been all right if not for that capital *H.* He kissed his twelve-year-old son's signature, looked at the bulletin board through eyes that had become untrustworthy – things doubled, tripled, then shivered completely apart – and let out a hoarse cry of pain. Tom and Jordan came running.

'What, Clay?' Tom said. 'What is it?' He saw the sheet of paper – a ruled yellow page from a legal pad – and slipped it out of Clay's hand. He and Jordan scanned it quickly.

'I'm going to Kashwak,' Clay said hoarsely.

'Clay, that's probably not such a hot idea,' Jordan said cautiously. 'Considering, you know, what we did at Gaiten Academy.'

'I don't care. I'm going to Kashwak. I'm going to find my son.'

6

The refugees who had taken shelter in the Kent Pond Town Hall had left plenty of supplies behind when they decamped, presumably en masse, for TR-90 and Kashwak. Clay, Tom, and Jordan made a meal of canned chicken salad on stale bread, with canned fruit salad for dessert.

As they were finishing, Tom leaned over to Jordan and murmured something. The boy nodded. The two of them got up. 'Would you excuse us for a few minutes, Clay? Jordan and I need to have a little talk.'

Clay nodded. While they were gone, he cracked another fruit salad cup and read Johnny's letter over for the ninth and tenth times. He was already well on the way to having it memorized. He could remember Alice's death just as clearly, but that now seemed to have happened in another life, and to a different version of Clayton Riddell. An earlier draft, as it were.

He finished his meal and stowed the letter away just as Tom and Jordan returned from the hall, where they had held what he supposed lawyers had called a sidebar, back in the days when there *were* lawyers. Tom once more had his arm around Jordan's narrow shoulders. Neither of them looked happy, but both looked composed.

'Clay,' Tom began, 'we've talked it over, and—'

'You don't want to go with me. Perfectly understandable.'

Jordan said, 'I know he's your son and all, but—'

'And you know he's all I've got left. His mother . . .' Clay laughed, a single humorless bark. 'His mother. *Sharon.* It's ironic, really. After all the worry I put in about *Johnny* getting a blast from that goddam little red rattlesnake. If I had to pick one, I would have picked her.' There, it was out. Like a chunk of meat that had been caught in his throat and was threatening to block his windpipe. 'And you know how that makes me feel? Like I offered to make a deal with the devil, and the devil actually came through for me.'

Tom ignored this. When he spoke, he did so carefully, as if he were afraid of setting Clay off like an unexploded land mine. 'They hate us. They started off hating everyone and progressed to just hating us. Whatever's going on up there in Kashwak, if it's their idea, it can't be good.'

'If they're rebooting to some higher level, they may get to a live-and-let-live plane,' Clay said. All of this was point-less, surely they both must see that. He *had* to go.

'I doubt it,' Jordan said. 'Remember that stuff about the chute leading to the slaughterhouse?'

'Clay, we're normies and that's strike one,' Tom said. 'We torched one of their flocks. That's strike two and strike three combined. Live and let live won't apply to us.'

'Why should it?' Jordan added. 'The Raggedy Man says we're insane.'

'And not to be touched,' Clay said. 'So I should be fine, right?'

After that there didn't seem to be any more to say.

7

Tom and Jordan had decided to strike out due west, across New Hampshire and into Vermont, putting **KASHWAK=NO-FO** at their backs – and over the horizon – as soon as possible. Clay said that Route 11, which made an elbow-bend at Kent Pond, would serve them both as a starting-point. 'It'll take me north to 160,' he said, 'and you guys can follow it all the way to Laconia, in the middle of New Hampshire. It's not exactly a direct route, but what the hell – you don't exactly have a plane to catch, have you?'

Jordan dug the heels of his hands into his eyes, rubbed them, then brushed the hair back from his forehead, a gesture

Clay had come to know well – it signaled tiredness and distraction. He would miss it. He would miss Jordan. And Tom even more.

'I wish Alice was still here,' Jordan said. 'She'd talk you out of this.'

'She wouldn't,' Clay said. Still, he wished with all his heart that Alice could have had her chance. He wished with all his heart that Alice could have had her chance at a lot of things. Fifteen was no age at which to die.

'Your current plans remind me of act four in *Julius Caesar*,' Tom said. 'In act five, everyone falls on their swords.' They were now making their way around (and sometimes over) the stalled cars jamming Pond Street. The emergency lights of the Town Hall were slowly receding behind them. Ahead was the dead traffic light marking the center of town, swaying in a slight breeze.

'Don't be such a fucking pessimist,' Clay said. He had promised himself not to become annoyed – he wouldn't part with his friends that way if he could possibly help it – but his resolve was being tried.

'Sorry I'm too tired to cheerlead,' Tom said. He stopped beside a road-sign reading **JCT RT 11 2 MI**. 'And – may I be frank? – too heartsick at losing you.'

'Tom, I'm sorry.'

'If I thought there was one chance in five that you had a happy ending in store . . . hell, one in *fifty* . . . well, never mind.' Tom shone his flashlight at Jordan. 'What about you? Any final arguments against this madness?'

Jordan considered, then shook his head slowly. 'The Head told me something once,' he said. 'Do you want to hear it?'

Tom made an ironic little salute with his flashlight. The beam skipped off the marquee of the Ioka, which had been showing the new Tom Hanks picture, and the pharmacy next door. 'Have at it.'

'He said the mind can calculate, but the spirit yearns, and the heart knows what the heart knows.'

'Amen,' Clay said. He said it very softly.

They walked east on Market Street, which was also Route 19A, for two miles. After the first mile, the sidewalks ended and the farms began. At the end of the second there was another dead stoplight and a sign marking the Route 11 junction. There were three people sitting bundled up to the neck in sleeping bags at the crossroads. Clay recognized one of them as soon as he put the beam of his flashlight on him: an elderly gent with a long, intelligent face and graying hair pulled back in a ponytail. The Miami Dolphins cap the other man was wearing looked familiar, too. Then Tom put his beam on the woman next to Mr Ponytail and said, 'You.'

Clay couldn't tell if she was wearing a Harley-Davidson T-shirt with cutoff sleeves, the sleeping bag was pulled up too high for that, but he knew there was one in the little pile of packs lying near the Route 11 sign if she wasn't. Just as he knew she was pregnant. He had dreamed of these two in the Whispering Pines Motel, two nights before Alice had been killed. He had dreamed of them in the long field, under the lights, standing on the platforms.

The man with the gray hair stood up, letting his sleeping bag slither down his body. There were rifles with their gear, but he raised his hands to show they were empty. The woman did the same, and when the sleeping bag dropped to her feet, there was no doubt about her pregnancy. The guy in the Dolphins cap was tall and about forty. He also raised his hands. The three of them stood that way for a few seconds in the beams of the flashlights, and then the gray-haired man took a pair of black-rimmed spectacles from the breast pocket of his wrinkled shirt and put them on. His breath puffed out white in the chilly night air, rising to the Route 11 sign, where arrows pointed both west and north.

'Well, well,' he said. 'The President of Harvard said you'd probably come this way, and here you are. Smart fellow, the President of Harvard, although a trifle young for the job, and in my opinion he could use some plastic surgery before going out to meet with potential big-ticket donors.'

'Who are you?' Clay asked.

'Get that light out of my face, young man, and I'll be happy to tell you.'

Tom and Jordan lowered their flashlights. Clay also lowered his, but kept one hand on the butt of Beth Nickerson's .45.

'I'm Daniel Hartwick, of Haverhill, Mass,' the gray-haired man said. 'The young lady is Denise Link, also of Haverhill. The gentleman on her right is Ray Huizenga, of Groveland, a neighboring town.'

'Meetcha,' Ray Huizenga said. He made a little bow that was funny, charming, and awkward. Clay let his hand fall off the butt of his gun.

'But our names don't actually matter anymore,' Daniel Hartwick said. 'What matters is what we *are*, at least as far as the phoners are concerned.' He looked at them gravely. 'We are insane. Like you.'

8

Denise and Ray rustled a small meal over a propane cooker ('These canned sausages don't taste too bad if you boil em up ha'aad,' Ray said) while they talked – while Dan talked, mostly. He began by telling them it was twenty past two in the morning, and at three he intended to have his 'brave little band' back on the road. He said he wanted to make as many miles as possible before daylight, when the phoners started moving around.

'Because they do *not* come out at night,' he said. 'We have that much going for us. Later, when their programming is complete, or *nears* completion, they may be able to, but—'

'You agree that's what's happening?' Jordan asked. For the first time since Alice had died, he looked engaged. He grasped Dan's arm. 'You agree that they're rebooting, like computers whose hard drives have been—'

'—wiped, yes, yes,' Dan said, as if this were the most elementary thing in the world.

'Are you – were you – a scientist of some sort?' Tom asked.

Dan gave him a smile. 'I was the entire sociology department at Haverhill Arts and Technical,' he said. 'If the President of Harvard has a worst nightmare, that would be me.'

Dan Hartwick, Denise Link, and Ray Huizenga had destroyed not just one flock but two. The first, in the back lot of a Haverhill auto junkyard, they had stumbled on by accident, when there had been half a dozen in their group and they were trying to find a way out of the city. That had been two days after the onset of the Pulse, when the phone-people had still been the phone-crazies, confused and as apt to kill each other as any wandering normies they encountered. That first had been a small flock, only about seventy-five, and they had used gasoline.

'The second time, in Nashua, we used dynamite from a construction-site shed,' Denise said. 'We'd lost Charlie, Ralph, and Arthur by then. Ralph and Arthur just took off on their own. Charlie – poor old Charlie had a heart attack. Anyhow, Ray knew how to rig the dynamite, from when he worked on a road crew.'

Ray, hunkered over his cooker and stirring the beans next to the sausages, raised his free hand and gave it a flip.

'After that,' Dan Hartwick said, 'we began to see those Kashwak No-Fo signs. Sounded good to us, didn't it, Denni?'

'Yep,' Denise said. 'Olly-olly-in-for-free. We were headed north, same as you, and when we started seeing those signs, we headed north faster. I was the only one who didn't absolutely love the idea, because I lost my husband during the Pulse. Those fucks are the reason my kid's going to grow up not knowing his daddy.' She saw Clay wince and said, 'Sorry. We know your boy's gone to Kashwak.'

Clay gaped.

'Oh yes,' Dan said, taking a plate as Ray began passing

them around. 'The President of Harvard knows all, sees all, has dossiers on all . . . or so he'd like us to believe.' He gave Jordan a wink, and Jordan actually grinned.

'Dan talked me around,' Denise said. 'Some terrorist group – or maybe just a couple of inspired nutcases working in a garage – set this thing off, but no one had any idea it would lead to this. The phoners are just playing out their part in it. They weren't responsible when they were insane, and they aren't really responsible now, because—'

'Because they're in the grip of some group imperative,' Tom said. 'Like migration.'

'It's a group imperative, but it ain't migration,' Ray said, sitting down with his own plate. 'Dan says it's pure survival. I think he's right. Whatever it is, we gotta find a place to get in out of the rain. You know?'

'The dreams started coming after we burned the first flock,' Dan said. 'Powerful dreams. *Ecce homo, insanus* – very Harvard. Then, after we bombed the Nashua flock, the President of Harvard showed up in person with about five hundred of his closest friends.' He ate in quick, neat bites.

'And left a lot of melted boomboxes on your doorstep,' Clay said.

'Some were melted,' Denise said. 'Mostly what we got were bits and pieces.' She smiled. It was a thin smile. 'That was okay. Their taste in music sucks.'

'You call him the President of Harvard, we call him the Raggedy Man,' Tom said. He had set his plate aside and opened his pack. He rummaged and brought out the drawing Clay had made on the day the Head had been forced to kill himself. Denise's eyes got round. She passed the drawing to Ray Huizenga, who whistled.

Dan took it last and looked up at Tom with new respect. 'You drew this?'

Tom pointed to Clay.

'You're very talented,' Dan said.

'I took a course once,' Clay said. 'Draw Fluffy.' He turned

289

to Tom, who also kept their maps in his pack. 'How far is it between Gaiten and Nashua?'

'Thirty miles, tops.'

Clay nodded and turned back to Dan Hartwick. 'And did he speak to you? The guy in the red hoodie?'

Dan looked at Denise and she looked away. Ray turned back to his little cooker – presumably to shut it down and pack it up – and Clay understood. 'Which one of you did he speak *through*?'

'Me,' Dan said. 'It was horrible. Have you experienced it?'

'Yeah. You can stop it from happening, but not if you want to know what's on his mind. Does he do it to show how strong he is, do you think?'

'Probably,' Dan said, 'but I don't think that's all. I don't think they can talk. They can *vocalize,* and I'm sure they think – although not as they did, it would be a terrible mistake to think of them as having human thoughts – but I don't think they can actually speak words.'

'Yet,' Jordan said.

'Yet,' Dan agreed. He glanced at his watch, and that prompted Clay to look at his own. It was already quarter to three.

'He told us to go north,' Ray said. 'He told us Kashwak No-Fo. He said our flock-burnin days were over because they were settin up guards—'

'Yes, we saw some in Rochester,' Tom said.

'And you've seen plenty of Kashwak No-Fo signs.'

They nodded.

'Purely as a sociologist, I began to question those signs,' Dan said. 'Not how they began – I'm sure the first No-Fo signs were posted soon after the Pulse, by survivors who'd decided a place like that, where there was no cell phone coverage, would be the best place on earth to go. What I questioned was how the idea – and the graffiti – could spread so quickly in a catastrophically fragmented society where all normal forms of communication – other than my mouth to your ear, of course – had broken down. The answer seemed clear, once one admitted that a *new* form of communication, available to only one group, had entered the picture.'

'Telepathy.' Jordan almost whispered the word. '*Them*. The phoners. They *want* us to go north to Kashwak.' He turned his frightened eyes to Clay. 'It really *is* a frigging slaughter-house chute. Clay, you *can't* go up there! This is all the Raggedy Man's idea!'

Before Clay could respond, Dan Hartwick was speaking again. He did it with a teacher's natural assumptions: lecturing was his responsibility, interruption his privilege.

'I'm afraid I really must hurry this along, sorry. We have something to show you – something the President of Harvard has *demanded* we show you, actually—'

'In your dreams, or in person?' Tom asked.

'Our dreams,' Denise said quietly. 'We've only seen him once in person since we burned the flock in Nashua, and that was at a distance.'

'Checkin up on us,' Ray said. 'That's what I think.'

Dan waited with a look of exasperated patience for this exchange to conclude. When it had, he resumed. 'We were willing to comply, since this was on our way—'

'You're going north, then?' Clay was the one to inter-rupt this time.

Dan, looking more exasperated now, flicked another quick glance at his watch. 'If you look at that route-sign closely, you'll see that it offers a choice. We intend to go west, not north.'

'Fuckin right,' Ray muttered. 'I may be stupid, but I'm not crazy.'

'What I show you will be for our purposes rather than theirs,' Dan said. 'And by the way, talking about the President of Harvard – or the Raggedy Man, if you prefer – showing up in person is probably a mistake. Maybe a bad one. He's really no more than a pseudopod that the group mind, the overflock, puts out front to do business with ordinary normies and special insane normies like us. I theorize that there are overflocks all over the world now, and each may have put forward such a pseudopod. Maybe even more than one. But don't make the mistake of thinking that when you're talking to your Raggedy Man you're talking to an *actual* man. You're talking to the flock.'

'Why don't you show us what he wants us to see?' Clay asked. He had to work to sound calm. His mind was roaring. The one clear thought in it was that if he could get to his son before Johnny got to Kashwak – and whatever was going on there – he might still have a chance to save him. Rationality told him that Johnny must be in Kashwak already, but another voice (and it wasn't entirely irrational) said something might have held up Johnny and whatever group he was traveling with. Or they might have gotten cold feet. It was possible. It was even possible that nothing more sinister than segregation was going on up there in TR-90, that the phone-people were just creating a rez for normies. In the end, he supposed it went back to what Jordan had said, quoting Headmaster Ardai: the mind could calculate, but the spirit yearned.

'Come this way,' Dan said. 'It's not far.' He produced a flashlight and began walking up the shoulder of Route 11–North with the beam aimed at his feet.

'Pardon me if I don't go,' Denise said. 'I've seen. Once was enough.'

'I think this was supposed to please you, in a way,' Dan said. 'Of course it was also supposed to underline the point – to my little group as well as yours – that the phoners are now the ones with the power, and they are to be obeyed.' He stopped. 'Here we are; in this particular sleep-o-gram, the President of Harvard made very sure we all saw the dog, so we couldn't get the wrong house.' The flashlight beam nailed a roadside mailbox with a collie painted on the side. 'I'm sorry Jordan has to see this, but it's probably best that you know what you're dealing with.' He raised his flashlight higher.

Ray joined his beam to Dan's. They lit up the front of a modest one-story wooden house, sitting neatly on a postage stamp of lawn.

Gunner had been crucified between the living room window and the front door. He was naked except for a pair of bloodstained Joe Boxers. Nails big enough to be railspikes jutted from his hands, feet, forearms, and knees. Maybe they *were* railspikes, Clay thought. Sitting splay-legged at Gunner's feet was Harold. Like Alice when they met her, Harold was wearing a bib of blood, but his hadn't come from his nose. The wedge of glass he'd used to cut his throat after cruci-fying his running buddy still twinkled in one hand.

Hung around Gunner's neck on a loop of string was a piece of cardboard with three words scrawled on it in dark capital letters: **JUSTITIA EST COMMODATUM.**

9

'In case you don't read Latin—' Dan Hartwick began.

'I remember enough from high school to read that,'Tom said. '"Justice is served." This is for killing Alice. For daring to touch one of the untouchables.'

'Right you are,' Dan said, snapping off his light. Ray did the same. 'It also serves as a warning to others. And *they* didn't kill them, although they most certainly could have.'

'We know,' Clay said. 'They took reprisals in Gaiten after we burned their flock.'

'They did the same in Nashua,' Ray said somberly. 'I'll remember the screams until my dyin day. Fuckin horrible. This shit is, too.' He gestured toward the dark shape of the house. 'They got the little one to crucify the big one, and the big one to hold still for it. And when it was done, they got the little one to cut his own throat.'

'It's like with the Head,' Jordan said, and took Clay's hand.

'That's the power of their minds,' Ray said, 'and Dan

thinks that's part of what's sendin everybody north to Kashwak – maybe part of what kept *us* movin north even when we told ourselves it was only to show you this and persuade you to hook up with us. You know?'

Clay said, 'Did the Raggedy Man tell you about my son?'

'No, but if he had I'm sure it would have been that he's with the other normies, and that you and he will have a happy reunion in Kashwak,' Dan said. 'You know, just forget about those dreams of standing on a platform while the President tells the cheering crowd you're insane, that ending's not for you, it can't be for you. I'm sure by now you've thought of all the possible happy-ending scenarios, the chief one being how Kashwak and who knows how many other cell phone dead zones are the normie equivalent of wildlife refuges, places where folks who didn't get a blast on the day of the Pulse will be left alone. I think what your young friend said about the chute leading to the slaughterhouse is far more likely, but even supposing normies *are* to be left alone up there, do you think the phoners will forgive people like us? The flock-killers?'

Clay had no answer for this.

In the dark, Dan looked at his watch again. 'It's gone three,' he said. 'Let's walk back. Denise will have us packed up by now. The time has come when we've either got to part company or decide to go on together.'

But when you talk about going on together, you're asking me to part company from my son, Clay thought. And that he would never do unless he discovered Johnny-Gee was dead.

Or changed.

10

'How can you hope to get west?' Clay asked as they walked back to the junction sign. 'The nights still may be ours for a while, but the days belong to them, and you see what they can do.'

'I'm almost positive we can keep them out of our heads when we're awake,' Dan said. 'It takes a little work, but it can be done. We'll sleep in shifts, at least for a while. A lot depends on keeping away from the flocks.'

'Which means getting into western New Hampshire and then into Vermont as fast as we can,' Ray said. 'Away from built-up areas.' He shone his light on Denise, who was reclining on the sleeping bags. 'We set, darlin?'

'All set,' she said. 'I just wish you'd let me carry something.'

'You're carryin your kid,' Ray said fondly. 'That's enough. And we can leave the sleepin bags.'

Dan said, 'There are places where driving may actually make sense. Ray thinks some of the back roads could be clear for as much as a dozen miles at a stretch. We've got good maps.' He dropped to one knee and shouldered his pack, looking up at Clay with a small and bitter half-smile as he did it. 'I know the chances aren't good; I'm not a fool, in case you wondered. But we wiped out two of their flocks, killed hundreds of them, and I don't want to wind up on one of those platforms.'

'We've got something else going for us,' Tom said. Clay wondered if Tom realized he'd just put himself in the Hartwick camp. Probably. He was far from stupid. 'They want us alive.'

'Right,' Dan said. 'We might really make it. This is still early times for them, Clay – they're still weaving their net, and I'm betting there are plenty of holes in it.'

'Hell, they haven't even changed their clothes yet,' Denise said. Clay admired her. She looked like she was six months along, maybe more, but she was a tough little thing. He wished Alice could have met her.

'We *could* slip through,' Dan said. 'Cross into Canada from Vermont or New York, maybe. Five is better than three, but six would be better than five – three to sleep, three to stand watch in the days, fight off the bad telepathy. Our own little flock. So what do you say?'

Clay shook his head slowly. 'I'm going after my son.'

'Think it over, Clay,' Tom said. *'Please.'*

'Let him alone,' Jordan said. 'He's made up his mind.' He put his arms around Clay and hugged him. 'I hope you find him,' he said. 'But even if you do, I guess you'll never find us again.'

'Sure I will,' Clay said. He kissed Jordan on the cheek, then stood back. 'I'll hogtie me a telepath and use him like a compass. Maybe the Raggedy Man himself.' He turned to Tom and held out his hand.

Tom ignored it and put his arms around Clay. He kissed him first on one cheek, then the other. 'You saved my life,' he whispered into Clay's ear. His breath was hot and ticklish. His cheek rasped against Clay's. 'Let me save yours. Come with us.'

'I can't, Tom. I have to do this.'

Tom stood back and looked at him. 'I know,' he said. 'I know you do.' He wiped his eyes. 'Goddam, I *suck* at good-byes. I couldn't even say goodbye to my fucking *cat*.'

11

Clay stood beside the junction sign and watched their lights dwindle. He kept his eyes fixed on Jordan's, and it was the last to disappear. For a moment or two it was alone at the top of the first hill to the west, a single small spark in the black, as if Jordan had paused there to look back. It seemed to wave. Then it was also gone, and the darkness was complete. Clay sighed – an unsteady, tearful sound – then shouldered his own pack and started walking north along the dirt shoulder of Route 11. Around quarter to four he crossed the North Berwick town line and left Kent Pond behind.

PHONE-BINGO

1

There was no reason not to resume a more normal life and start traveling days; Clay knew the phone-people wouldn't hurt him. He was off-limits and they actually *wanted* him up there in Kashwak. The problem was he'd become habituated to a nighttime existence. *All I need is a coffin and a cape to wrap around myself when I lie down in it,* he thought.

When dawn came up red and cold on the morning after his parting from Tom and Jordan, he was on the outskirts of Springvale. There was a little house, probably a caretaker's cottage, next to the Springvale Logging Museum. It looked cosy. Clay forced the lock on the side door and let himself in. He was delighted to find both a woodstove and a hand-pump in the kitchen. There was also a shipshape little pantry, well stocked and untouched by foragers. He celebrated this find with a large bowl of oatmeal, using powdered milk, adding heaps of sugar, and sprinkling raisins on top.

In the pantry he also found concentrated bacon and eggs in foil packets, stored as neatly on their shelf as paperback books. He cooked one of these and stuffed his pack with the rest. It was a much better meal than he had expected, and once in the back bedroom, Clay fell asleep almost immediately.

2

There were long tents on both sides of the highway.

This wasn't Route 11 with its farms and towns and open fields, with its pump-equipped convenience store every fifteen miles or so, but a highway somewhere out in the williwags. Deep woods crowded all the way up to the roadside ditches. People stood in long lines on both sides of the white center-stripe.

Left and right, an amplified voice was calling. *Left and right, form two lines.*

It sounded a little like the amplified voice of the bingo-caller at the Akron State Fair, but as Clay drew closer, walking up the road's center-stripe, he realized all the amplification was going on in his head. It was the voice of the Raggedy Man. Only the Raggedy Man was just a – what had Dan called him? – just a pseudopod. And what Clay was hearing was the voice of the flock.

Left and right, two lines, that's correct. That's doing it.

Where am I? Why doesn't anybody look at me, say 'Hey buddy, no cutting in front, wait your turn'?

Up ahead the two lines curved off to either side like turnpike exit ramps, one going into the tent on the left side of the road, one going into the tent on the right. They were the kind of long tents caterers put up to shade outdoor buffets on hot afternoons. Clay could see that just before each line reached the tents, the people were splitting into ten or a dozen shorter lines. Those people looked like fans waiting to have their tickets ripped so they could go into a concert venue.

Standing in the middle of the road at the point where the double line split and curved off to the right and the left, still wearing his threadbare red hoodie, was the Raggedy Man himself.

Left and right, ladies and gentlemen. Mouth not moving. Telepathy that was all jacked up, amped by the power of the flock. *Move right along. Everyone gets a chance to call a loved one before you go into the no-fo zone.*

That gave Clay a shock, but it was the shock of the known – like the punchline of a good joke you'd heard for the first time ten or twenty years ago. 'Where is this?' he asked the Raggedy Man. 'What are you doing? What the hell is going on?'

But the Raggedy Man didn't look at him, and of course Clay knew why. This was where Route 160 entered Kashwak, and he was visiting it in a dream. As for what was going on . . .

It's phone-bingo, he thought. *It's phone-bingo, and those are the tents where the game is played.*

Let's keep it moving, ladies and gents, the Raggedy Man sent. *We've got two hours until sunset, and we want to process as many of you as we can before we have to quit for the night.*

Process.

Was this a dream?

Clay followed the line curving toward the pavilion-style tent on the left side of the road, knowing what he was going to see even before he saw it. At the head of each shorter line stood one of the phone-people, those connoisseurs of Lawrence Welk, Dean Martin, and Debby Boone. As each person in line reached the front, the waiting usher – dressed in filthy clothes, often much more horribly disfigured by the survival-struggles of the last eleven days than the Raggedy Man – would hold out a cell phone.

As Clay watched, the man closest to him took the offered phone, punched it three times, then held it eagerly to his ear. 'Hello?' he said. 'Hello, Ma? *Ma?* Are you th—' Then he fell silent. His eyes emptied and slackness loosened his face. The cell sagged away from his ear slightly. The facilitator – that was the best word Clay could think of – took the phone back, gave the man a push to start him forward, and motioned for the next person in line to step forward.

Left and right, the Raggedy Man was calling. *Keep it moving.*

The guy who'd been trying to call his mom plodded out from beneath the pavilion. Beyond it, Clay saw, hundreds of other people were milling around. Sometimes someone would get in someone else's way and there would be a little weak slapping. Nothing like before, however. Because—

Because the signal's been modified.

Left and right, ladies and gentlemen, keep it moving, we've got a lot of you to get through before dark.

Clay saw Johnny. He was wearing jeans, his Little League hat, and his favourite Red Sox T-shirt, the one with Tim Wakefield's name and number on the back. He had just reached the head of the line two stations down from where Clay was standing.

Clay ran for him, but at first his path was blocked. 'Get out of my way!' he shouted, but of course the man in his way, who was shuffling nervously from foot to foot as if he needed to go to the bathroom, couldn't hear him. This was a dream and besides, Clay was a normie – he had no telepathy.

He darted between the restless man and the woman behind him. He pushed through the next line as well, too fixated on reaching Johnny to know if the people he was pushing had substance or not. He reached Johnny just as a woman – he saw with mounting horror that it was Mr Scottoni's daughter-in-law, still pregnant but now missing an eye – handed the boy a Motorola cell phone.

Just dial 911, she said without moving her mouth. *All calls go through 911.*

'No, Johnny, don't!' Clay shouted, and grabbed for the phone as Johnny-Gee began punching in the number, surely one he'd been taught long ago to call if he was ever in trouble. *'Don't do that!'*

Johnny turned to his left, as if to shield his call from the pregnant facilitator's one dully staring eye, and Clay missed. He probably couldn't have stopped Johnny in any case. This was a dream, after all.

302

Johnny finished (punching three keys didn't take long), pushed the SEND button, and put the phone to his ear. 'Hello? Dad? Dad, are you there? Can you hear me? If you can hear me, *please come get m*—' Turned away as he was, Clay could only see one of his son's eyes, but one was enough when you were watching the lights go out. Johnny's shoulders slumped. The phone sagged away from his ear. Mr Scottoni's daughter-in-law snatched the phone from him with a dirty hand, then gave Johnny-Gee an unloving push on the back of the neck to get him moving into Kashwak, along with all the others who had come here to be safe. She motioned for the next person in line to come forward and make his call.

Left and right, form two lines, the Raggedy Man thundered in the middle of Clay's head, and he woke up screaming his son's name in the caretaker's cottage as late-afternoon light streamed in the windows.

3

At midnight Clay reached the little town of North Shapleigh. By then a nasty cold rain that was almost sleet – what Sharon had called 'Slurpee rain' – had begun to fall. He heard oncoming motors and stepped off the highway (still good old Route 11; no dream highway here) onto the tarmac of a 7-Eleven store. When the headlights showed, turning the drizzle to silver lines, it was a pair of sprinters running side by side, actually racing in the dark. Madness. Clay stood behind a gas pump, not exactly hiding but not going out of his way to be seen, either. He watched them fly past like a vision of the gone world, sending up thin sprays of water. One of the racers looked like a vintage Corvette, although with only a single failing emergency light on the corner of the store to see by, it was impossible to tell for sure. The racers shot beneath North Shapleigh's entire traffic-control system (a dead blinker), were neon cherries in the dark for a moment, then were gone.

Clay thought again: *Madness.* And as he swung back onto the shoulder of the road: *You're a fine one to talk about madness.*

True. Because his phone-bingo dream *hadn't* been a dream, or not entirely a dream. He was sure of it. The phoners were using their strengthening telepathic abilities to keep track of as many of the flock-killers as they could. That only made sense. They might have a problem with groups like Dan Hartwick's, ones that actually tried to fight them, but he doubted if they were having any trouble with him. The thing was, the telepathy was also oddly like a phone – it seemed to work both ways. Which made him . . . what? The ghost in the machine? Something like that. While they were keeping an eye on him, he was able to keep an eye on *them.* At least in his sleep. In his dreams.

Were there actual tents at the Kashwak border, with normies lining up to get their brains blasted? Clay thought there were, both in Kashwak and places *like* Kashwak all over the country and the world. Business would be slowing down by now, but the checkpoints – the *changing*-points – might still be there.

The phoners used group-speak telepathy to coax the normies into coming. To *dream* them into coming. Did that make the phoners smart, calculating? Not unless you called a spider smart because it could spin a web, or an alligator calculating because it could lie still and look like a log. Walking north along Route 11 toward Route 160, the road that would take him to Kashwak, Clay thought the telepathic signal the phoners sent out like a low siren-call (or a pulse) must contain at least three separate messages.

Come, and you'll be safe – your struggle to survive can cease.
Come, and you'll be with your own kind, in your own place.
Come, and you can speak to your loved ones.

Come. Yes. Bottom line. And once you got close enough, any choice ceased. That telepathy and the dream of safety just took you over. You lined up. You listened as the Raggedy Man told you to keep it moving, everyone gets to call a loved one but we've got a lot of you to process before the sun goes down and we crank up Bette Midler singing 'The Wind Beneath My Wings'.

And how could they continue doing this, even though the lights had failed and the cities had burned and civilisation had slid into a pit of blood? How could they go on replacing the millions of phoners lost in the original convulsion and in the destruction of the flocks that had followed? They could continue because the Pulse wasn't over. Somewhere – in that outlaw lab or nutcase's garage – some gadget was still running on batteries, some modem was still putting out its squealing, insane signal. Sending it up to the satellites that flew around the globe or to the microwave relay towers that cinched it like a steel belt. And where could you call and be sure your call would still go through, even if the voice answering was only on a battery-powered answering machine?

911, apparently.

And that had almost certainly happened to Johnny-Gee.

He *knew* it had. He was already too late.

So why was he still walking north through the drizzling dark? Up ahead was Newfield, not far, and there he'd leave Route 11 for Route 160, and he had an idea that not too far up Route 160 his days of reading road-signs (or anything else) would be done, so *why*?

But he knew why, just as he knew that distant crash and the short, faint blare of horn he heard ahead of him in the rainy darkness meant that one of the racing sprinters had come to grief. He was going on because of the note on the storm door, held by less than a quarter-inch of tape when he'd rescued it; all the rest had pulled free. He was going on because of the second one he'd found on the Town Hall bulletin board, half-hidden by Iris Nolan's hopeful note to her sister. His son had written the same thing both times, in capital letters: *PLEASE COME GET ME.*

If he was too late to get Johnny, he might not be too

late to see him and tell him he'd tried. He might be able to hold on to enough of himself long enough to do that even if they made him use one of the cell phones.

As for the platforms, and the thousands of watching people—

'There's no football stadium in Kashwak,' he said.

In his mind, Jordan whispered: *It's a* virtual *stadium*.

Clay pushed it aside. Pushed it away. He had made his decision. It was madness, of course, but it was a mad world now, and that put him in perfect sync.

4

At quarter to three that morning, footsore and damp in spite of the hooded parka he had liberated from the caretaker's cottage in Springvale, Clay came to the intersection of Routes 11 and 160. There had been a major pileup at the cross-roads, and the Corvette that had gone racing past him in North Shapleigh was now part of it. The driver hung out the severely compressed window on the left side, head down and arms dangling, and when Clay tried to lift the man's face to see if he was still alive, the top half of his body fell into the road, trailing a meaty coil of guts behind. Clay reeled away to a telephone pole, planted his suddenly hot forehead against the wood, and vomited until there was nothing left.

On the other side of the intersection, where 160 took off into the north country, stood the Newfield Trading Post. A sign in the window promised CANDIES NATIVE SIRUP INDIAN CRAFTS 'NICK-NACKS'. It looked as if it had been trashed as well as looted, but it was shelter from the rain and away from the casual, unexpected horror he had just encountered. Clay went in and sat down with his head lowered until he no longer felt like fainting. There were bodies, he could smell them, but someone had thrown a tarp over all but two, and at least those two weren't in pieces. The joint's beer cooler was smashed and empty, the Coke machine only smashed. He took a ginger ale and drank it in long, slow swallows, pausing to belch. After a while he began to feel a little better.

He missed his friends desperately. The unfortunate out there and whomever he'd been racing were the only sprinters he'd seen all night, and he'd encountered no groups of walking refugees at all. He'd spent the entire night with only his thoughts for company. Maybe the weather was keeping the walkers inside, or maybe now they were traveling days. No reason for them not to, if the phoners had switched from murder to conversion.

He realized he hadn't heard any of what Alice had called *flock-music* tonight. Maybe all the flocks were south of here, except for the big one (he assumed it must be a big one) administering the Kashwak Konversions. Clay didn't much care; even alone as he was, he would still take his vacation from 'I Hope You Dance' and 'The Theme from *A Summer Place*' as a little gift.

He decided to walk another hour at most, then find a hole to crawl into. The cold rain was killing him. He left the Newfield Trading Post, resolutely not looking at the crashed Corvette or the soaked remains lying beside it.

5

He ended up walking until nearly daylight, partly because the rain let up but mostly because there wasn't much in the way of shelter on Route 160, just woods. Then, around four thirty, he passed a bullet-pocked sign reading ENTERING GURLEYVILLE, AN UNINCORPORATED TOWNSHIP. Ten minutes or so after that he passed Gurleyville's raison d'être, such as it was – the Gurleyville Quarry, a huge rock pit with a few sheds, dump trucks, and a garage at the foot of its gouged granite walls. Clay thought briefly about spending the night in one of the equipment sheds, decided he could do better, and pushed on. He had still seen no pilgrims and heard no flock-music, even at a distance. He could have been the last person on earth.

He wasn't. Ten minutes or so after leaving the quarry behind, he topped a hill and saw a little village below. The first building he came to was the Gurleyville Volunteer Fire Department (DON'T FORGET THE HALOWEEN BLOOD DRIVE read the notice board out front; it seemed that no one north of Springvale could spell), and two of the phone-people were standing in the parking lot, facing each other in front of a sad-looking old pumper that might have been new around the time the Korean War ended.

They turned slowly toward Clay when he put his flash-light beam on them, but then they turned away to regard each other again. Both were male, one about twenty-five and the other maybe twice that. There was no doubt they were phoners. Their clothes were filthy and almost falling off. Their faces were cut and scraped. The younger man looked as if he had sustained a serious burn all the way up one arm. The older man's left eye glittered from deep inside folds of badly swollen and probably infected flesh. But how they looked wasn't the main thing. The main thing was what Clay felt in *himself*: that same weird shortness of breath he and Tom had experienced in the office of the Gaiten Citgo, where they'd gone to get the keys to the propane trucks. That sense of some powerful gathering force.

And it was *night*. With the heavy cloud cover, dawn was still just a rumor. What were these guys doing up at *night*?

Clay snapped off his flashlight, drew the Nickerson .45, and watched to see if anything would happen. For several seconds he thought nothing would, that the strange out-of-breath feeling, that sense of something being on the *verge* of happening, was going to be the extent of it. Then he heard a high whining sound, almost like someone vibrating the blade of a saw between his palms. Clay looked up and saw the electrical wires passing in front of the fire station were moving rapidly back and forth, almost too fast to see.

'Go-*way!*' It was the young man, and he seemed to jerk the words out with a tremendous effort. Clay jumped. If his finger had been on the revolver's trigger, he would almost certainly have pulled it. This wasn't *Aw* and *Eeen,* this was actual words. He thought he heard them in his head as well, but faint, faint. Only a dying echo.

'*You!* . . . Go!' the older man replied. He was wearing baggy Bermuda shorts with a huge brown stain on the seat. It might have been mud or shit. He spoke with equal effort, but this time Clay heard no echo in his head. Paradoxically, it made him more sure he'd heard the first one.

They'd forgotten *him* entirely. Of that much he was sure.

'*Mine!*' said the younger man, once more jerking the word out. And he *did* jerk it. His whole body seemed to flail with the effort. Behind him, several small windows in the fire station's wide garage door shattered outward.

There was a long pause. Clay watched, fascinated, Johnny completely out of his mind for the first time since Kent Pond. The older man seemed to be thinking furiously, *struggling* furiously, and what Clay thought he was struggling to do was to express himself as he had before the Pulse had robbed him of speech.

On top of the volunteer fire station, which was nothing but a glorified garage, the siren went off with a brief *WHOOP,* as if a phantom burst of electricity had surged through it. And the lights of the ancient pumper − headlights and red flashers − flicked briefly on, illuminating the two men and briefly scaring up their shadows.

'*Hell!* You say!' the older man managed. He spit the words out like a piece of meat that had been choking him.

'*Mynuck!*' the younger man nearly screamed, and in Clay's mind that same voice whispered, *My truck.* It was simple, really. Instead of Twinkies, they were fighting over the old pumper. Only this was at *night* − the end of it, granted, but still full dark − and they were almost talking again. Hell, they *were* talking.

But the talking was done, it seemed. The young man lowered his head, ran at the older man, and butted him in the chest. The older man went sprawling. The younger man tripped over his legs and went to his knees. *'Hell!'* he cried.

'Fuck!' cried the other. No question about it. You couldn't mistake *fuck*.

They picked themselves up again and stood about fifteen feet apart. Clay could feel their hate. It was in his head; it was pushing at his eyeballs, trying to get out.

The young man said, 'That'n . . . *mynuck!'* And in Clay's head the young man's distant voice whispered, *That one is my truck*.

The older man drew in breath. Jerkily raised one scabbed-over arm. And shot the young man the bird. 'Sit. On this!' he said with perfect clarity.

The two of them lowered their heads and rushed at each other. Their heads met with a thudding crack that made Clay wince. This time all the windows in the garage blew out. The siren on the roof gave a long war-cry before winding down. The fluorescent lights in the station house flashed on, running for perhaps three seconds on pure crazypower. There was a brief burst of music: Britney Spears singing 'Oops! . . . I Did It Again'. Two power-lines snapped with liquid twanging sounds and fell almost in front of Clay, who stepped back from them in a hurry. Probably they were dead, they *should* be dead, but—

The older man dropped to his knees with blood pouring down both sides of his head. *'My truck!'* he said with perfect clarity, then fell on his face.

The younger one turned to Clay, as if to recruit him as witness to his victory. Blood was pouring out of his matted, filthy hair, between his eyes, in a double course around his nose, and over his mouth. His eyes, Clay saw, weren't blank at all. They were insane. Clay understood – all at once, completely and unarguably – that if this was where the cycle led, his son was beyond saving.

'*Mynuck!*' the young man shrieked. '*Mynuck, mynuck!*' The pumper's siren gave a brief, winding growl, as if in agreement. '*MYNU*—'

Clay shot him, then reholstered the .45. *What the hell,* he thought, *they can only put me up on a pedestal once.* Still, he was shaking badly, and when he broke into Gurleyville's only motel on the far side of town, it took him a long time to go to sleep. Instead of the Raggedy Man, it was his son who visited him in his dreams, a dirty, blank-eyed child who responded '*Go-hell, mynuck*' when Clay called his name.

6

He woke from this dream long before dark, but sleep was done for him and he decided to start walking again. And once he'd cleared Gurleyville – what little of Gurleyville there was to clear – he'd drive. There was no reason not to; Route 160 now seemed almost entirely clear and probably had been since the nasty pileup where it crossed Route 11. He simply hadn't noticed it in the dark and the rain.

The Raggedy Man and his friends cleared the way, he thought. *Of course they did, it's the fucking cattle-chute. For me it probably is the chute that leads to the slaughterhouse. Because I'm old business. They'd like to stamp me PAID and stick me in the filing cabinet as soon as possible. Too bad about Tom and Jordan and the other three. I wonder if they found enough back roads to take them into central New Hampshire y—*

He topped a rise and this thought broke off cleanly. Parked in the middle of the road below was a little yellow schoolbus with **MAINE SCHOOL DISTRICT 38 NEWFIELD** printed on the side. Leaning against it were a man and a boy. The man had his arm around the boy's shoulders in a casual gesture of friendship Clay would have known anywhere. As he stood there, frozen, not quite believing his eyes, another man came around the schoolbus's blunt nose. He had long gray hair pulled back in a ponytail. Following him was a pregnant woman in a T-shirt. It was powder blue instead of Harley-Davidson black, but it was Denise, all right.

Jordan saw him and called his name. He pulled free of Tom's arm and started running. Clay ran to meet him. They met about thirty yards in front of the schoolbus.

'Clay!' Jordan shouted. He was hysterical with joy. 'It's really you!'

'It's me,' Clay agreed. He swung Jordan in the air, then kissed him. Jordan wasn't Johnny, but Jordan would do, at least for the time being. He hugged him, then set him down and studied the haggard face, not failing to note the brown circles of weariness under Jordan's eyes. 'How in God's name did you get here?'

Jordan's face clouded. 'We couldn't . . . that is, we only dreamed . . .'

Tom came strolling up. Once again he ignored Clay's outstretched hand and hugged him instead. 'How you doin, van Gogh?' he asked.

'Okay. Fucking delighted to see you guys, but I don't understand—'

Tom gave him a smile. It was both tired and sweet, a white flag of a smile. 'What computer-boy's trying to tell you is that in the end we just didn't have any choice. Come on down to the little yellow bus. Ray says that if the road stays clear – and I'm sure it will – we can be in Kashwak by sundown, even traveling at thirty miles an hour. Ever read *The Haunting of Hill House*?'

Clay shook his head, bewildered. 'Saw the movie.'

'There's a line there that resonates in the current situation – "Journeys end in lovers meeting." Looks like I might get to meet your kid after all.'

They walked down to the schoolbus. Dan Hartwick offered Clay a tin of Altoids with a hand that was not quite steady. Like Jordan and Tom, he looked exhausted. Clay, feeling like a man in a dream, took one. End of the world or not, it was curiously strong.

'Hey, man,' Ray said. He was behind the wheel of the schoolbus, Dolphins cap tipped back, a cigarette smoldering in one hand. He looked pale and drawn. He was staring out through the windshield, not at Clay.

'Hey, Ray, what do you say?' Clay asked.

Ray smiled briefly. 'Say I've heard that one a few times.'

'Sure, probably a few hundred. I'd tell you I'm glad to see you, but under the circumstances, I'm not sure you'd want to hear it.'

Still looking out the windshield, Ray replied, 'There's someone up there you'll *definitely* not be glad to see.'

Clay looked. They all did. A quarter of a mile or so north, Route 160 crested another hill. Standing there and looking at them, his HARVARD hoodie dirtier than ever but still bright against the gray afternoon sky, was the Raggedy Man. Maybe fifty other phoners surrounded him. He saw them looking. He raised his hand and waved at them twice, side to side, like a man wiping a windshield. Then he turned and began to walk away, his entourage (*his flocklet,* Clay thought) falling in to either side of him in a kind of trailing V. Soon they were out of sight.

WORM

1

They stopped at a picnic area a little farther up the road. No one was very hungry, but it was a chance for Clay to ask his questions. Ray didn't eat at all, just sat on the lip of a stone barbecue pit downwind and smoked, listening. He added nothing to the conversation. To Clay he seemed utterly disheartened.

'We *think* we're stopping here,' Dan said, gesturing to the little picnic area with its border of firs and autumn-colored deciduous trees, its babbling brook and its hiking trail with the sign at its head reading IF YOU GO **TAKE A MAP**! 'We probably *are* stopping here, because—' He looked at Jordan. 'Would *you* say we're stopping here, Jordan? You seem to have the clearest perception.'

'Yes,' Jordan said instantly. 'This is real.'

'Yuh,' Ray said, without looking up. 'We're here, all right.' He slapped his hand against the rock of the barbecue pit, and his wedding ring produced a little *tink-tink-tink* sound. 'This is the real deal. We're together again, that's all they wanted.'

'I don't understand,' Clay said.

'Neither do we, completely,' Dan said.

'They're a lot more powerful than I ever would have guessed,' Tom said. 'I understand that much.' He took off his glasses and polished them on his shirt. It was a tired, distracted gesture. He looked ten years older than the man Clay had met in Boston. 'And they messed with our minds. *Hard*. We never had a chance.'

'You look exhausted, all of you,' Clay replied.

Denise laughed. 'Yeah? Well, we come by it honestly. We left you and took off on Route 11 westbound. Walked until we saw light starting to come up in the east. Grabbing wheels didn't seem to make any sense, because the road was a freaking mess. You'd get maybe a quarter of a mile clear, then—'

'Road-reefs, I know,' Clay said.

'Ray said it would be better once we got west of the Spaulding Turnpike, but we decided to spend the day in this place called the Twilight Motel.'

'I've heard of that place,' Clay said. 'On the edge of the Vaughan Woods. It's rather notorious in my part of the world.'

'Yeah? Okay.' She shrugged. 'So we get there, and the kid – Jordan – says, "I'm gonna make you the biggest breakfast you ever ate." And we say dream on, kid – which turned out to be sort of funny, since that's what it was, in a way – but the *power* in the place is on, and he *does*. He makes this huge freakin breakfast. We all chip in. It's the Thanksgiving of breakfasts. Am I telling this right?'

Dan, Tom, and Jordan all nodded. Sitting on the barbecue pit, Ray just lit another cigarette.

According to Denise, they had eaten in the dining room, which Clay found fascinating because he was positive the Twilight didn't *have* a dining room; it had been your basic no-tell motel straddling the Maine–New Hampshire state line. Rumour had it that the only amenities were cold-water showers and hot-running X-ies on the TVs in the crackerbox rooms.

The storey got weirder. There had been a jukebox. No Lawrence Welk and Debby Boone, either; it had been stuffed with hot stuff (including 'Hot Stuff', by Donna Summer), and instead of going directly to bed they had danced – arduously – for two or three hours. Then, before turning in, they had eaten another vast meal, this time with Denise donning the chef's hat. After that, finally, they had crashed.

'And dreamed of walking,' Dan said. He spoke with a beaten bitterness that was unsettling. This wasn't the same man Clay had met two nights ago, the one who'd said *I'm almost positive we can keep them out of our heads when we're awake* and *We might really make it, this is still early times for them.* Now he laughed a little, a sound with no humor in it at all. 'Man, we *should* have dreamed about it, because we *were*. All that day we were walking.'

'Not quite all of it,' Tom said. 'I had a driving-dream . . .'

'Yeah, you drove,' Jordan said quietly. 'Only for an hour or so, but you drove. That was when we also dreamed we were sleeping in that motel. The Twilight place. I dreamed of the driving, too. It was like a dream inside of a dream. Only that one was real.'

'You see?' Tom said, smiling at Clay. He ruffled Jordan's heavy pelt. 'On some level, Jordan knew all along.'

'Virtual reality,' Jordan said. 'That's all it was. Like being in a video game, almost. And it wasn't all that good.' He looked north, in the direction the Raggedy Man had disappeared. In the direction of Kashwak. 'It'll get better if *they* get better.'

'Sons of bitches can't do it at all after dark,' Ray said. 'They have to go fucking beddy-bye.'

'And at the end of the day, so did we,' Dan said. 'That was their purpose. To wear us out so completely that we couldn't figure out what was going on even when night came and their control slipped. During the day the President of Harvard was always close, along with a good-sized flock, sending out that mental force-field of theirs, creating Jordan's virtual reality.'

'Must have been,' Denise said. 'Yeah.'

All this had been going on, Clay calculated, while he had been sleeping in the caretaker's cottage.

'Wearing us out wasn't all they wanted,' Tom said. 'Even turning us back north wasn't all they wanted. They also wanted us all together again.'

The five of them had come to in a tumbledown motel on Route 47 – *Maine* Route 47, not too far south of Great Works. The sense of dislocation, Tom said, had been enormous. The sound of flock-music not too far distant had not helped. They all had a sense of what must have happened, but it was Jordan who had verbalized it, as it had been Jordan who'd pointed out the obvious: their escape attempt had failed. Yes, they could probably slip out of the motel where they found themselves and start west again, but how far would they get this time? They were exhausted. Worse, they were disheartened. It was also Jordan who pointed out that the phoners might even have arranged for a few normie spies to track their nighttime movements.

'We ate,' Denise said, 'because we were starving as well as tired. Then we went to bed for real and slept until the next morning.'

'I was the first one up,' Tom said. 'The Raggedy Man himself was standing in the courtyard. He made a little bow to me and waved his hand at the road.' Clay remembered the gesture well. *The road is yours. Go on and take it.* 'I could have shot him, I suppose – I had Sir Speedy – but what good would that have done?'

Clay shook his head. No good at all.

They had gotten back on the road, first walking up Route 47. Then, Tom said, they'd felt themselves mentally nudged onto an unmarked woods road that actually seemed to meander southeast.

'No visions this morning?' Clay asked. 'No dreams?'

'Nope,' Tom said. 'They knew we'd gotten the point. They can read minds, after all.'

'They heard us yell uncle,' Dan said in that same beaten, bitter tone. 'Ray, do you happen to have an extra cigarette? I quit, but maybe I'll take the habit up again.'

Ray tossed him the pack without a word.

'It's like being nudged by a hand, only inside your brain,' Tom said. 'Not at all nice. Intrusive in a way I can't even

320

begin to describe. And all this time there was the sense of the Raggedy Man and his flock, moving with us. Sometimes we saw a few of them through the trees; most times not.'

'So they're not just flocking early and late now,' Clay said.

'No, all that's changing,' Dan said. 'Jordan's got a theory – interesting, and with some evidence to back it up. Besides, we constitute a special occasion.' He lit his cigarette. Inhaled. Coughed. 'Shit, I knew there was a reason I gave these things up.' And then, with hardly a pause: 'They can float, you know. Levitate. Must be a hell of a handy way to get around with the roads so jammed. Like having a magic carpet.'

A mile or so up the seemingly pointless woods road, the five of them had discovered a cabin with a pickup parked in front. Keys in the truck. Ray drove; Tom and Jordan rode in the truck-bed. None of them was surprised when the woods road eventually bent north again. Just before it petered out, the navigation-beacon in their heads sent them onto another, then a third that was little more than a track with weeds growing up the middle. That one eventually drowned in a boggy patch where the truck mired, but an hour's slog brought them out on Route 11, just south of that highway's junction with 160.

'Couple of dead phoners there,' Tom said. 'Fresh. Downed power-lines, snapped-off poles. The crows were having a banquet.'

Clay thought of telling them what he'd seen at the Gurleyville Volunteer Fire Department, then didn't. If it had any bearing on the present situation, he didn't see it. Besides, there were plenty who weren't fighting with each other, and these had kept forcing Tom and the others onward.

That force hadn't led them to the little yellow bus; Ray had found it as a result of exploring the Newfield Trading Post while the others were scrounging sodas from the very same cooler Clay had raided. Ray saw it through a back window.

They had stopped only once since then, to build a fire on the granite floor of the Gurleyville Quarry and eat a hot meal. They had also changed into fresh footwear from the Newfield Trading Post – their bog-slog had left all of them muddy from the shins down – and had an hour's rest. They must have driven past Clay at the Gurleyville Motel right around the time he was waking up, because they were nudged to a stop shortly after that.

'And here we are,' Tom said. 'Case almost closed.' He swept an arm at the sky, the land, the trees. 'Someday, son, all of this will be yours.'

'That pushing thing has gone out of my head, at least for the time being,' Denise said. 'I'm grateful for that. The first day was the worst, you know? I mean, Jordan had the clearest idea that something was wrong, but I think all of us knew it wasn't . . . you know, really right.'

'Yeah,' Ray said. He rubbed the back of his neck. 'It was like being in a kid's story where the birds and snakes talk. They say stuff like, "You're okay, you're fine, never mind that your legs are so tired, you're deenie-cool." Deenie-cool, that's what we used to say when I was growin up in Lynn.'

'"Lynn, Lynn, city of sin, when you get to heaven, they won't let you in,"' Tom chanted.

'You grew up with the Christers, all right,' Ray said. 'Anyway, the kid knew better, I knew better, I think we *all* knew fuckin better. If you had half a brain and still thought you were gettin away—'

'I believed as long as I could because I wanted to believe,' Dan said, 'but in truth? We never had a chance. Other normies might, but not us, not flock-killers. They mean to have us, no matter what happens to them.'

'What do you think they've got in mind for us?' Clay asked.

'Oh, death,' Tom said, almost without interest. 'At least I'll be able to get some decent sleep.'

Clay's mind finally caught up with a couple of things

and latched on. Earlier in the conversation, Dan had said their normal behavior was changing and Jordan had a theory about it. Just now he'd said *no matter what happens to them.*

'I saw a pair of phoners go at each other not far from here,' Clay finally told them.

'Did you?' Dan said, without much interest.

'At *night*,' he added, and now they all looked at him. 'They were fighting over a fire truck. Like a couple of kids over a toy. I got some of that telepathy from one of them, but they were both talking.'

'Talking?' Denise asked sceptically. 'Like actual words?'

'Actual words. The clarity was in and out, but they were definitely words. How many fresh dead have you guys seen? Just those two?'

Dan said, 'We've probably seen a dozen since we woke up to where we really are.' He looked at the others. Tom, Denise, and Jordan nodded. Ray shrugged and lit another cigarette. 'But it's hard to tell about the cause of death. They *might* be reverting; that fits Jordan's theory, although the talking doesn't seem to. They might've just been corpses the flocks haven't gotten around to getting rid of. Body-disposal isn't a priority with them right now.'

'*We're* their priority, and they'll be moving us along pretty soon,' Tom said. 'I don't think we get the . . . you know, the big stadium treatment until tomorrow, but I'm pretty sure they want us in Kashwak before dark tonight.'

'Jordan, what's your theory?' Clay asked.

Jordan said, 'I think there was a worn in the original program.'

2

'I don't understand,' Clay said, 'but that's par for the course. When it came to computers, I could use Word, Adobe Illustrator, and MacMail. After that I was pretty much illiterate. Johnny had to walk me through the solitaire program that came with my Mac.' Talking about that hurt. Remembering Johnny's hand closing over his on the mouse hurt more.

'But you know what a computer worm is, right?'

'Something that gets into your computer and screws up all the programs, right?'

Jordan rolled his eyes but said, 'Close enough. It can burrow in, corrupting your files and your hard drive as it goes. If it gets into shareware and the stuff you send, even e-mail attachments – and they do – it can go viral and spread. Sometimes a worm has babies. The worm itself is a mutant and sometimes the babies mutate further. Okay?'

'Okay.'

'The Pulse was a computer program sent out by modem – that's the only way it could work. And it's *still* being sent out by modem. Only there was a worm in there, and it's rotting out the program. It's becoming more corrupted every day. GIGO. Do you know GIGO?'

Clay said, 'I don't even know the way to San Jose.'

'Stands for "garbage in, garbage out." We think that there are conversion points where the phoners are changing normies over—'

Clay remembered his dream. 'I'm way ahead of you there.'

'But now they're getting bad programming. Do you see? And it makes sense, because it's the newest phoners who seem to be going down first. Fighting, freaking out, or actually dropping dead.'

'You don't have enough data to say that,' Clay replied at once. He was thinking of Johnny.

Jordan's eyes had been bright. Now they dulled a little. 'That's true.' Then his chin lifted. 'But it's logical. If the premise is right – if it's a worm, something actively burrowing deeper and deeper into the original programming – then it's every bit as logical as the Latin they use. The new phoners are rebooting, but now it's a crazy, uneven reboot. They get the telepathy, but they can still talk. They—'

'Jordan, you *can't* draw that conclusion on just the two *I* saw—'

Jordan was paying no attention. He was really talking to himself now. 'They don't flock like the others, not as *completely*, because the flocking imperative is imperfectly installed. Instead they . . . they stay up late and get up early. They revert to aggression against their own kind. And if it's getting worse . . . don't you see? The *newest* phoners would be the first ones to get messed up!'

'It's like in *War of the Worlds*,' Tom said dreamily.

'Huh?' Denise said. 'I didn't see that movie. It looked too scary.'

'The invaders were killed by microbes *our* bodies tolerate easily,' Tom said. 'Wouldn't it be poetic justice if the phone-crazies all died of a computer-virus?'

'I'd settle for aggression,' Dan said. 'Let them kill each other in one big battle royal.'

Clay was still thinking about Johnny. Sharon too, but mostly Johnny. Johnny who'd written *PLEASE COME GET ME* in those big capital letters and then signed all three names, as if that would somehow add weight to his plea.

Ray Huizenga said, 'Isn't going to do us any good unless it happens tonight.' He stood up and stretched. 'They'll be pushin us on pretty quick. I'm gonna pause to do me a little necessary while I've got the time. Don't go without me.'

'Not in the bus, we won't,' Tom said as Ray started up the hiking trail. 'You've got the keys in your pocket.'

'Hope everything comes out all right, Ray,' Denise said sweetly.

'Nobody loves a smartass, darlin,' Ray said, and disappeared from view.

'What *are* they going to do to us?' Clay asked. 'Any ideas about that?'

Jordan shrugged. 'It may be like a closed-circuit TV hookup, only with a lot of different areas of the country participating. Maybe even the whole world. The size of the stadium makes me think that—'

'And the Latin, of course,' Dan said. 'It's a kind of *lingua franca.*'

'Why do they need one?' Clay asked. 'They're telepaths.'

'But they still think mostly in words,' Tom said. 'At least so far. In any case, they do mean to execute us, Clay – Jordan thinks so, Dan does, and so do I.'

'So do I,' Denise said in a small, morose voice, and caressed the curve of her belly.

Tom said, 'Latin is more than a *lingua franca.* It's the language of justice, and we've seen it used by them before.'

Gunner and Harold. Yes. Clay nodded.

'Jordan has another idea,' Tom said. 'I think you need to hear it, Clay. Just in case. Jordan?'

Jordan shook his head. 'I can't.'

Tom and Dan Hartwick looked at each other.

'Well, *one* of you tell me,' Clay said. 'I mean, Jesus!'

So it was Jordan after all. 'Because they're telepaths, they know who our loved ones are,' he said.

Clay searched for some sinister meaning in this and didn't find it. 'So?'

'I have a brother in Providence,' Tom said. 'If he's one of *them,* he'll be my executioner. If Jordan's right, that is.'

'My sister,' Dan Hartwick said.

'My floor-proctor,' Jordan said. He was very pale. 'The one with the megapixel Nokia phone that shows video downloads.'

'My husband,' Denise said, and burst into tears. 'Unless he's dead. I pray God he's dead.'

For a moment Clay still didn't get it. And then he thought: *John? My Johnny?* He saw the Raggedy Man holding a hand over his head, heard the Raggedy Man pronouncing sentence: *'Ecce homo – insanus.'* And saw his son walking toward him, wearing his Little League cap turned around backwards and his favorite Red Sox shirt, the one with Tim

Wakefield's name and number on it. Johnny, small beneath the eyes of the millions watching via the miracle of closed-circuit, flock-boosted telepathy.

Little Johnny-Gee, smiling. Empty-handed.

Armed with nothing but the teeth in his head.

3

It was Ray who broke the silence, although Ray wasn't even there.

'Ah, *Jesus.*' Coming from a little distance up the hiking trail. '*Fuck.*' Then: 'Yo, Clay!'

'What's up?' Clay called back.

'You've lived up here all your life, right?' Ray didn't sound like a happy camper. Clay looked at the others, who returned only blank stares. Jordan shrugged and flipped his palms outward, for one heartbreaking moment becoming a near-teenager instead of just another refugee from the Phone War.

'Well . . . downstate, but yeah.' Clay stood up. 'What's the problem?'

'So you know what poison ivy and poison oak looks like, right?'

Denise started to break up and clapped both hands over her mouth.

'Yeah,' Clay said. He couldn't help smiling himself, but he knew what it looked like for sure, had warned Johnny and his backyard buddies off enough of it in his time.

'Well get up here and take a look,' Ray said, 'and come on your own.' Then, with hardly a pause: 'Denise, I don't need telepathy to know you're laughin. Put a sock in it, girl.'

Clay left the picnic area, walking past the sign reading IF YOU GO **TAKE A MAP!** and then beside the pretty little brook. Everything in the woods was pretty now, a spectrum of furnace colors mixed with the sturdy, never-changing green of the firs, and he supposed (not for the first time, either) that if men and women owed God a death, there were worse seasons of the year in which to pay up.

He had expected to come upon Ray with his pants loosened or actually around his ankles, but Ray was standing on a carpet of pine needles and his pants were buckled. There were no bushes at all where he was, not poison ivy or anything else. He was as pale as Alice had been when she plunged into the Nickersons' living room to vomit, his skin so white it looked dead. Only his eyes still had life. They burned in his face.

'C'mere,' he said in a prison-yard whisper. Clay could hardly hear him over the noisy chuckle of the brook. 'Quick. We don't have much time.'

'Ray, what the hell—'

'Just listen. Dan and your pal Tom, they're too smart. Jordy too. Sometimes thinking gets in the way. Denise is better, but she's pregnant. Can't trust a pregnant woman. So you're it, Mr Artist. I don't like it because you're still holding on to your kid, but your kid's over. In your heart you know it. Your kid is toast.'

'Everything all right back there, you guys?' Denise called, and numb as he was, Clay could hear the smile in her voice.

'Ray, I don't know what—'

'No, and that's how it's gonna stay. Just *listen*. What that fuck in the red hoodie wants isn't gonna happen, if you don't let it. That's all you need to know.'

Ray reached into the pocket of his chinos and brought out a cell phone and a scrap of paper. The phone was gray with grime, as if it had spent most of its life in a working environment.

'Put it in your pocket. When the time comes, call the number on that slip. You'll know the time. I gotta hope you'll know.'

Clay took the phone. It was either take it or drop it. The little slip of paper escaped his fingers.

'*Get that!*' Ray whispered fiercely.

Clay bent and picked up the scrap of paper. Ten digits were scrawled on it. The first three were the Maine area code. 'Ray, *they read minds!* If I have this—'

Ray's mouth stretched in a terrible parody of a grin. 'Yeah!' he whispered. 'They peek in your head and find out you're thinkin about a fuckin cell phone! What else is anyone thinkin about since October first? Those of us who can still fuckin think, that is?'

Clay looked at the dirty, battered cell phone. There were two DYMO-tape strips on the casing. The top one read **MR FOGARTY**. The bottom one read **PROP. GURLEYVILLE QUARRY DO NOT REMOVE.**

'Put it in your fuckin *pocket!*'

It wasn't the urgency of the command that made him obey. It was the urgency of those desperate eyes. Clay began to put the phone and the scrap of paper in his pocket. He was wearing jeans, which made the pocket a tighter fit than Ray's chinos. He was looking down to open the pocket wider when Ray reached forward and pulled Clay's .45 from its holster. When Clay looked up, Ray already had the barrel under his chin.

'You'll be doin your kid a favour, Clay. Believe it. That's no fuckin way to live.'

'*Ray, no!*'

Ray pulled the trigger. The soft-nosed American Defender round took off the entire top half of his head. Crows rose from the trees in a multitude. Clay hadn't even known they were there, but now they scolded the autumn air with their cries.

For a little while he drowned them out with his own.

4

They had barely started scraping him a grave in the soft dark earth under the firs when the phoners reached into their heads. Clay was feeling that combined power for the first time. It was as Tom had said, like being nudged in the back by a powerful hand. If, that was, both the hand and the back were inside your head. No words. Just that push.

'Let us finish!' he shouted, and immediately responded to himself in a slightly higher register that he recognized at once. 'No. Go. Now.'

'Five minutes!' he said.

This time the flock voice used Denise. 'Go. Now.'

Tom tumbled Ray's body – the remains of the head wrapped in one of the headrest-covers from the bus – into the hole and kicked in some dirt. Then he grabbed the sides of his head, grimacing. 'Okay, okay,' he said, and immediately answered himself, 'Go. Now.'

They walked back down the hiking path to the picnic area, Jordan leading the way. He was very pale, but Clay didn't think he was as pale as Ray had been in the last minute of his life. Not even close. *That's no fuckin way to live*: his final words.

Standing at parade rest across the road, in a line that stretched to both horizon-lines, maybe half a mile in all, were phoners. There had to be four hundred of them, but Clay didn't see the Raggedy Man. He supposed the Raggedy Man had gone on to prepare the way, for in his house there were many mansions.

With a phone extension in every one, Clay thought.

As they trooped toward the minibus, he saw three of the phoners fall out of line. Two of them began biting and fighting and tearing at each other's clothes, snarling what could have been words – Clay thought he heard the phrase *bitch-cake,* but he supposed it might just have been a coincidental occurrence of syllables. The third simply turned and began walking away, hiking down the white line toward Newfield.

'That's right, fall out, sojer!' Denise yelled hysterically. '*All* of you fall out!'

But they didn't, and before the deserter – if that was

what he was – had gotten to the curve where Route 160 swept out of sight to the south, an elderly but powerfully built phoner simply shot out his arms, grasped the hiker's head, and twisted it to one side. The hiker collapsed to the pavement.

'Ray had the keys,' Dan said in a tired voice. Most of his ponytail had come undone, and his hair spilled over his shoulders. 'Somebody will have to go back and—'

'I got them,' Clay said. 'And I'll drive.' He opened the side door of the little bus, feeling that steady beat-beat-beat, push-push-push in his head. There was blood and dirt on his hands. He could feel the weight of the cell phone in his pocket and had a funny thought: maybe Adam and Eve had picked a few apples before being driven out of Eden. A little something to munch while on the long and dusty road to seven hundred television channels and backpack bombs in the London subway system. 'Get in, everybody.'

Tom gave him a look. 'You don't have to sound so goddam cheerful, van Gogh.'

'Why not?' Clay said, smiling. He wondered if his smile looked like Ray's – that awful end-of-life rictus. 'At least I won't have to listen to *your* bullshit much longer. Hop aboard. Next stop, Kashwak-No-Fo.'

But before anyone got on the bus, they were made to throw away their guns.

This didn't come as a mental command, nor was their motor-control overridden by some superior force – Clay didn't have to watch as something made his hand reach down and pluck the .45 from its holster. He didn't think the phoners could do that, at least not yet; they couldn't even do the ventriloquism thing unless they were allowed to. Instead he felt something like an itch, a terrible one, just short of intolerable, inside his head.

'Oh, *Mary!*' Denise cried in a low voice, and threw the little .22 she carried in her belt as far as she could. It landed in the road. Dan threw his own pistol after it, then added his hunting knife for good measure. The knife flew blade-first almost to the far side of Route 160, but none of the phoners standing there flinched.

Jordan dropped the pistol he was carrying to the ground beside the bus. Then, whining and twitching, he tore into his pack and tossed away the one Alice had been carrying. Tom added Sir Speedy.

Clay contributed the .45 to the other weapons beside the bus. It had been unlucky for two people since the Pulse, and he wasn't terribly sorry to see it go.

'There,' he said. He spoke to the watching eyes and dirty faces – many of them mutilated – that were watching from across the road, but it was the Raggedy Man he was visualising. 'That's all of them. Are you satisfied?' And answered himself at once. 'Why. Did. He do it?'

Clay swallowed. It wasn't just the phoners who wanted to know; Dan and the others were watching him, too. Jordan, he saw, was holding on to Tom's belt, as if he feared Clay's answer the way a toddler might fear a busy street. One full of speeding trucks.

'He said your way was no way to live,' Clay said. 'He took my gun and blew his head off before I could stop him.'

Silence, except for the cawing of crows. Then Jordan spoke, flat and declamatory. 'Our way. Is the only way.'

Dan was next. Just as flat. *Unless they feel rage, they feel nothing,* Clay thought. 'Get on. The bus.'

They got on the bus. Clay slid behind the wheel and started the engine. He headed north on Route 160. He had been rolling less than a minute when he became aware of movement on his left. It was the phoners. They were moving north along the shoulder – *above* the shoulder – in a straight line, as if on an invisible conveyor belt running maybe eight inches over the dirt. Then, up ahead, where the road crested, they rose much higher, to perhaps fifteen feet, making a human arch against the dull, mostly cloudy sky. Watching the phoners disappear over the top of the hill was like watching people ride the mild swell of an invisible roller coaster.

Then the graceful symmetry broke. One of the rising figures fell like a bird shot from a duck-blind, dropping at least seven feet to the side of the road. It was a man in the tattered remains of a jogging suit. He spun furiously in the dirt, kicking with one leg, dragging the other. As the bus rolled past him at a steady fifteen miles an hour, Clay saw the man's face was drawn down in a grimace of fury and his mouth was working as he spewed out what was almost surely his dying declaration.

'So now we know,' Tom said hollowly. He was sitting with Jordan on the bench at the back of the bus, in front of the luggage area where their packs were stowed. 'Primates give rise to man, man gives rise to phoners, phoners give rise to levitating telepaths with Tourette's syndrome. Evolution complete.'

Jordan said, 'What's Tourette's syndrome?'

Tom said, 'Fucked if I know, son,' and incredibly, they were all laughing. Soon they were roaring – even Jordan, who didn't know what he was laughing *at* – while the little yellow bus rolled slowly north with the phoners passing it and then rising, rising, in a seemingly endless procession.

KASHWAK

1

An hour after leaving the picnic area where Ray had shot himself with Clay's gun, they passed a sign reading

NORTHERN COUNTIES EXPO
OCTOBER 5–15
COME ONE, COME ALL!!!

VISIT KASHWAKAMAK HALL
AND DON'T FORGET THE UNIQUE
'NORTH END'
*SLOTS (INCLUDING TEXAS HOLD 'EM)
*'INDIAN BINGO'

YOU'LL SAY 'WOW!!!'

'Oh my God,' Clay said. 'The Expo. Kashwakamak Hall. Christ. If there was ever a place for a flock, that's it.'

'What's an expo?' Denise asked.

'Your basic county fair,' Clay said, 'only bigger than most of them and quite a lot wilder, because it's on the TR, which is unincorporated. Also, there's that North End business. Everyone in Maine knows about the North End at the Northern Counties Expo. In its own way, it's as notorious as the Twilight Motel.'

Tom wanted to know what the North End was, but

before Clay could explain, Denise said, 'There's two more. Mary-and-Jesus, I know they're phoners, but it still makes me sick.'

A man and a woman lay in the dust at the side of the road. They had died either in an embrace or a bitter battle, and embracing did not seem to go with the phoner lifestyle. They had passed half a dozen other bodies on their run north, almost certainly casualties from the flock that had come down to get them, and had seen twice that number wandering aimlessly south, sometimes alone, sometimes in pairs. One of the pairs, clearly confused about where they wanted to go, had actually tried to hitchhike the bus as it passed.

'Wouldn't it be nice if they'd all either fall out or drop dead before what they've got planned for us tomorrow?' Tom said.

'Don't count on it,' Dan said. 'For every casualty or deserter we've seen, we've seen twenty or thirty who are still with the program. And God knows how many are waiting in this Kashwacky place.'

'Don't count it out, either,' Jordan said from his place beside Tom. He spoke a little sharply. 'A bug in the program – a worm – is not a small thing. It can start out as a minor pain in the ass and then boom, everything's down. I play this game, Star-Mag? Well, you know – I used to play it – and this sore sport out in California got so mad about losing all the time that he put a worm in the system and it took down all the servers in a week. Almost half a million gamers back to computer cribbage because of that jamhead.'

'We don't have a week, Jordan,' Denise said.

'I know,' he said. 'And I know they're not all apt to go wheels-up overnight . . . but it's *possible*. And I won't stop hoping. I don't want to end up like Ray. He stopped . . . you know, hoping.' A single tear rolled down Jordan's cheek.

Tom gave him a hug. 'You won't end up like Ray,' he said. 'You're going to grow up to be like Bill Gates.'

'I don't want to grow up to be like Bill Gates,' Jordan

338

said morosely. 'I bet Bill Gates had a cell phone. In fact I bet he had a dozen.' He sat up straight. 'One thing I'd give a lot to know is how so many cell phone transmission towers can still be working when the fucking *power's* down.'

'FEMA,' Dan said hollowly.

Tom and Jordan turned to look at him, Tom with a tentative smile on his lips. Even Clay glanced up into the rearview mirror.

'You think I'm joking,' Dan said. 'I wish I was. I read an article about it in a news-magazine while I was in my doctor's office, waiting for that disgusting exam where he puts on a glove and then goes prospecting—'

'Please,' Denise said. 'Things are bad enough. You can skip that part. What did the article say?'

'That after 9/11, FEMA requested and got a sum of money from Congress – I don't remember how much, but it was in the tens of millions – to equip cell phone transmission towers nationwide with long-life emergency generators to make sure the nation's ability to communicate wouldn't go to hell in the event of coordinated terrorist attacks.' Dan paused. 'I guess it worked.'

'FEMA,' Tom said. 'I don't know whether to laugh or cry.'

'I'd tell you to write your congressman, but he's probably insane,' Denise said.

'He was insane well before the Pulse,' Tom answered, but he spoke absently. He was rubbing the back of his neck and looking out the window. 'FEMA,' he said. 'You know, it sort of makes sense. Fucking FEMA.'

Dan said, '*I'd* give a lot just to know why they've made such a business of collaring us and bringing us in.'

'And making sure the rest of us don't follow Ray's example,' Denise said. 'Don't forget that.' She paused. 'Not that I would. Suicide's a sin. They can do whatever they want to me here, but I'm going to heaven with my baby. I believe that.'

'The Latin's the part that gives me the creeps,' Dan said. 'Jordan, is it possible that the phoners could take old stuff – stuff from before the Pulse, I mean – and incorporate it into their new programming? If it fit their . . . mmmm, I don't know . . . their long-term goals?'

'I guess,' Jordan said. 'I don't really know, because we don't know what sort of commands might have been encoded in the Pulse. This isn't like ordinary computer programming in any case. It's self-generating. Organic. Like learning. I guess it *is* learning. "It satisfies the definition," the Head would say. Only they're all learning together, because—'

'Because of the telepathy,' Tom said.

'Right,' Jordan agreed. He looked troubled.

'Why does the Latin give you the creeps?' Clay asked, looking at Dan in the rearview mirror.

'Tom said Latin's the language of justice, and I guess that's true, but this feels much more like vengeance to me.' He leaned forward. Behind his glasses, his eyes were tired and troubled. 'Because, Latin or no Latin, *they can't really think*. I'm convinced of that. Not yet, anyway. What they depend on instead of rational thought is a kind of hive mind born out of pure rage.'

'I object, Your Honor, Freudian speculation!' Tom said, rather merrily.

'Maybe Freud, maybe Lorenz,' Dan said, 'but give me the benefit of the doubt either way. Would it be surprising for such an entity – such a raging entity – to confuse justice and vengeance?'

'Would it matter?' Tom asked.

'It might to us,' Dan said. 'As someone who once taught a block course on vigilantism in America, I can tell you that vengeance usually ends up hurting more.'

2

Not long after this conversation, they came to a place Clay recognized. Which was unsettling, because he had never been in this part of the state before. Except once, in his dream of the mass conversions.

Written across the road in broad strokes of bright green paint was **KASHWAK=NO-FO.** The van rolled over the words at a steady thirty miles an hour as the phoners continued to stream past in their stately, witchy procession on the left.

That was no dream, he thought, looking at the drifts of trash caught in the bushes at the sides of the road, the beer and soda cans in the ditches. Bags that had contained potato chips, Doritos, and Cheez Doodles crackled under the tires of the little bus. *The normies stood here in a double line, eating their snacks and drinking their drinks, feeling that funny itch in their heads, that weird sense of a mental hand pushing on their backs, waiting their turns to call some loved one who got lost in the Pulse. They stood here and listened to the Raggedy Man say 'Left and right, two lines, that's correct, that's doing it, let's keep moving, we've got a lot of you to process before dark.'*

Up ahead the trees drew back on either side of the road. What had been some farmer's hard-won grazeland for cows or sheep had now been flattened and churned down to bare earth by many passing feet. It was almost as though there had been a rock concert here. One of the tents was gone – blown away – but the other had caught on some trees and flapped in the dull early-evening light like a long brown tongue.

'I dreamed of this place,' Jordan said. His voice was tight.

'Did you?' Clay said. 'So did I.'

'The normies followed the Kashwak equals No-Fo signs, and this is what they came to,' Jordan said. 'It was like toll-booths, wasn't it, Clay?'

'Kind of,' Clay said. 'Kind of like tollbooths, yeah.'

'They had big cardboard boxes full of cell phones,' Jordan said. This was a detail Clay didn't remember from his own dream, but he didn't doubt it. 'Heaps and heaps of them. And every normie got to make a call. What a bunch of lucky ducks.'

'When did you dream this, Jordy?' Denise asked.

'Last night.' Jordan's eyes met Clay's in the rearview mirror. 'They knew they weren't going to be talking to the people they wanted to talk to. Down deep they knew. But they did it anyway. They took the phones anyway. Took em and listened. Most of em didn't even put up a fight. Why, Clay?'

'Because they were tired of fighting, I suppose,' Clay said. 'Tired of being different. They wanted to hear "Baby Elephant Walk" with new ears.'

They were past the beaten-down fields where the tents had been. Ahead, a paved byroad split off from the highway. It was broader and smoother than the state road. The phoners were streaming up this byway and disappearing into a slot in the woods. Looming high above the trees half a mile or so farther on was a steel gantrylike structure Clay recognized at once from his dreams. He thought it had to be some sort of amusement attraction, maybe a Parachute Drop. There was a billboard at the junction of the highway and the byroad, showing a laughing family – dad, mom, sonny, and little sis – walking into a wonderland of rides, games, and agricultural exhibits.

NORTHERN COUNTIES EXPO
GALA FIREWORKS SHOW OCTOBER 5TH

VISIT KASHWAKAMAK HALL
THE 'NORTH END' OPEN '24/7' OCTOBER 5–15

YOU'LL SAY 'WOW!!!'

Standing below this billboard was the Raggedy Man. He raised one hand and held it out in a *stop* gesture.

Oh Jesus, Clay thought, and pulled the minibus up beside him. The Raggedy Man's eyes, which Clay hadn't been able to get right in his drawing at Gaiten, looked simultaneously dazed and full of malevolent interest. Clay told himself it was impossible for them to appear both ways at the same time, but they did. Sometimes the dazed dullness was foremost in them; a moment later it seemed to be that weirdly unpleasant avidity.

He can't want to get on with us.

But the Raggedy Man did, it seemed. He lifted his hands to the door with the palms pressed together, then opened them. The gesture was rather pretty – like a man indicating *this bird has flown* – but the hands themselves were black with filth, and the little finger on the left one had been badly broken in what looked like two places.

These are the new people, Clay thought. *Telepaths who don't take baths.*

'Don't let him on,' Denise said. Her voice was trembling.

Clay, who could see that the steady conveyor-movement of phoners to the left of the bus had stopped, shook his head. 'No choice.'

They peek in your head and find out you're thinkin about a fuckin cell phone, Ray had said – had almost snorted. *What else is anyone thinkin about since October first?*

Hope you're right, Ray, he thought, *because it's still an hour and a half until dark. An hour and a half at least.*

He threw the lever that opened the door and the Raggedy Man, torn lower lip drooping in its constant sneer, climbed aboard. He was painfully thin; the filthy red sweatshirt hung on him like a sack. None of the normies on the bus was particularly clean – hygiene hadn't been a priority since the first of October – but the Raggedy Man gave off a ripe and powerful stench that almost made Clay's eyes water. It was the smell of strong cheese left to sweat it out in a hot room.

The Raggedy Man sat down in the seat by the door, the one that faced the driver's seat, and looked at Clay. For a moment there was nothing but the dusty weight of his eyes and that strange grinning curiosity.

Then Tom spoke in a thin, outraged voice Clay had heard him use only once before, when he'd said *That's it, everybody out of the pool* to the plump Bible-toting woman who'd started preaching her End Times sermon to Alice. 'What do you want from us? You have the world, such as it is — what do you want from *us*?'

The Raggedy Man's ruined mouth formed the word even as Jordan said it. Only that one word, flat and emotionless. 'Justice.'

'When it comes to justice,' Dan said, 'I don't think you have a clue.'

The Raggedy Man replied with a gesture, raising one hand to the feeder-road, palm up and index finger pointing: *Get rolling.*

When the bus started to move, most of the phoners started to move again, as well. A few more had fallen to fighting, and in the outside mirror Clay saw others walking back down the expo feeder-road toward the highway.

'You're losing some of your troops,' Clay said.

The Raggedy Man made no reply on behalf of the flock. His eyes, now dull, now curious, now both, remained fixed on Clay, who fancied he could almost feel that gaze walking lightly over his skin. The Raggedy Man's twisted fingers, gray with dirt, lay on the lap of his grimy blue jeans. Then he grinned. Maybe that was answer enough. Dan was right, after all. For every phoner who dropped out — who went wheels-up, in Jordan-speak — there were plenty more. But Clay had no idea how many *plenty more* might entail until half an hour later, when the woods opened up on both sides and they passed beneath the wooden arch reading **WELCOME TO THE NORTHERN COUNTIES EXPO**.

3

'Dear God,' Dan said.

Denise articulated Clay's own feelings better; she gave a low scream.

Sitting across the narrow aisle of the little bus in the first passenger seat, the Raggedy Man only sat and stared at Clay with the half-vacant malevolence of a stupid child about to pull the wings off a few flies. *Do you like it?* his grin seemed to say. *It's quite something, isn't it? The gang's all here!* Of course a grin like that could mean that or anything. It could even mean *I know what you have in your pocket.*

Beyond the arch was a midway and a batch of rides, both still being assembled at the time of the Pulse, from the way things looked. Clay didn't know how many of the carny pitch-tents had been erected, but some had blown away, like the pavilions at the checkpoint six or eight miles back, and only half a dozen or so still stood, their sides seeming to breathe in the evening breeze. The Krazy Kups were half-built, and so was the funhouse across from it (**WE DARE YOU TO** ran across the single piece of façade that had been erected; skeletons danced above the words). Only the Ferris wheel and the Parachute Drop at the far end of what would have been the midway looked complete, and with no electric lights to make them jolly, they looked gruesome to Clay, less like amusement rides than gigantic implements of torture. Yet one light *was* blinking, he saw: a tiny red beacon, surely battery-powered, at the very top of the Parachute Drop.

Well beyond the Drop was a white building with red trim, easily a dozen barn-lengths long. Loose hay had been heaped along the sides. American flags, fluttering in the evening breeze, had been planted in this cheap rural insulation every ten feet or so. The building was draped with swags of patriotic bunting and bore the legend

NORTHERN COUNTIES EXPO
KASHWAKAMAK HALL

in bright blue paint.

But none of this was what had attracted their attention. Between the Parachute Drop and Kashwakamak Hall were several acres of open ground. Clay guessed it was where the big crowds gathered for livestock exhibitions, tractor-pulls, end-of-fair-day concerts, and – of course – the fireworks shows that would both open and close the Expo. It was ringed with light-standards and loudspeaker-poles. Now this broad and grassy mall was crammed with phoners. They stood shoulder to shoulder and hip to hip, their faces turned to watch the arrival of the little yellow bus.

Any hope Clay had harbored of seeing Johnny – or Sharon – was gone in a moment. His first thought was that there had to be five thousand people crowded beneath those dead light-standards. Then he saw they had spilled into the grassy parking lots adjoining the main exhibition area as well and revised his estimate upward. Eight. Eight thousand at least.

The Raggedy Man sat where some Newfield Elementary School third-grader belonged, grinning at Clay with his teeth jutting through the split in his lip. *Do you like it?* that grin seemed to ask, and again Clay had to remind himself that you could read anything into a grin like that.

'So who's playing tonight? Vince Gill? Or did you guys break the bank and get Alan Jackson?' That was Tom. He was trying to be funny and Clay gave him high marks for that, but Tom only sounded scared.

The Raggedy Man was still looking at Clay, and a little vertical crease had appeared in the middle of his brow, as if something puzzled him.

Clay drove the minibus slowly up the center of the midway, toward the Parachute Drop and the silent multitude beyond. There were more bodies here; they reminded Clay of how you sometimes found heaps of dead bugs on the windowsills after a sudden cold snap. He concentrated on keeping his hands loose. He didn't want the Raggedy Man to see his knuckles turn white on the wheel.

And go slow. Nice and easy does it. He's only looking at you. As for cell phones, what else has anyone been thinking about since October first?

The Raggedy Man raised a hand and pointed one twisted,

badly used finger at Clay. 'No-fo, you,' Clay said in that other voice. *'Insanus.'*

'Yeah, no-fo-me-me, no-fo none of us, we're all bozos on this bus,' Clay said. 'But you'll fix that, right?'

The Raggedy Man grinned, as if to say that *was* right . . . but the little vertical line was still there. As if something still puzzled him. Maybe something rolling and tumbling around in Clay Riddell's mind.

Clay looked up into the rearview mirror as they neared the end of the midway. 'Tom, you asked me what the North End was,' he said.

'Forgive me, Clay, but my interest seems to have waned,' Tom said. 'Maybe it's the size of the welcoming committee.'

'No, but this is interesting,' Clay said, a little feverishly.

'Okay, what is it?' Jordan asked. God bless Jordan. Curious to the end.

'The Northern Counties Expo was never a big deal in the twentieth century,' Clay said. 'Just your standard little shitpot aggie fair with arts, crafts, produce, and animals over there in Kashwakamak Hall . . . which is where they're going to put us, from the look of things.'

He glanced at the Raggedy Man, but the Raggedy Man neither confirmed nor denied. The Raggedy Man only grinned. The little vertical line had disappeared from his forehead.

'Clay, look out,' Denise said in a tight, controlled voice.

He looked back through the windshield and stepped on the brake. An elderly woman with infected lacerations on both legs came swaying out of the silent crowd. She skirted the edge of the Parachute Drop, trampled over several prefab pieces of the funhouse that had been laid out but not erected at the time of the Pulse, then broke into a shambling run aimed directly at the schoolbus. When she reached it, she began to hammer slowly on the windshield with filthy, arthritis-twisted hands. What Clay saw in this woman's face wasn't the avid blankness he'd come to associate with the phoners but terrified disorientation. And it was familiar. *Who are you?* Pixie Dark had asked. Pixie Dark, who hadn't gotten a direct blast of the Pulse. *Who am I?*

Nine phoners in a neat moving square came after the elderly woman, whose frantic face was less than five feet from Clay's own. Her mouth moved, and he heard four words, both with his ears and with his mind: *'Take me with you.'*

We're not going anywhere you want to go, lady, Clay thought.

Then the phoners grabbed her and took her back toward the multitude on the grassy mall. She struggled to get away, but they were relentless. Clay caught one flash of her eyes and thought they were the eyes of a woman who was in purgatory only if she was lucky. More likely it was hell.

Once more the Raggedy Man held out his hand, palm-up and index finger pointing: *Roll.*

The elderly woman had left a handprint, ghostly but visible, on the windshield. Clay looked through it and got rolling.

4

'Anyhow,' he said, 'until 1999, the Expo was no big deal. If you lived in this part of the world and wanted rides and games – carny stuff – you had to go down to the Fryeburg Fair.' He heard his own voice running as if on a tape loop. Talk for the sake of talk. It made him think of the drivers on the Duck Boat tours in Boston, pointing out the various sights. 'Then, just before the turn of the century, the State Bureau of Indian Affairs did a land-survey. Everybody knew the Expo grounds were right next door to the Sockabasin Rez; what that land-survey showed was that the north end of Kashwakamak Hall was actually on reservation land. Technically, it was in Micmac Indian territory. The people running the Expo were no dummies, and neither were the ones on the Micmac tribal council. They agreed to clean out the little shops from the north end of the hall and put in slots. All at once the Northern Counties Expo was Maine's biggest fall fair.'

They had reached the Parachute Drop. Clay started to jog left and guide the little bus between the ride and the half-constructed funhouse, but the Raggedy Man patted his hands on the air, palms-down. Clay stopped. The Raggedy Man stood up and turned to the door. Clay threw the lever and the Raggedy Man stepped off. Then he turned to Clay and made a kind of sweeping, bowing gesture.

'What's he doing now?' Denise asked. She couldn't see from where she was sitting. None of them could.

'He wants us to get off,' Clay said. He stood up. He could feel the cell phone Ray had given him lying hard along his upper thigh. If he looked down, he would see its outline against the blue denim of his jeans. He pulled down the T-shirt he was wearing, trying to cover it. *A cell phone, so what, everybody's thinking about them.*

'Are we going to?' Jordan asked. He sounded scared.

'Not much choice,' Clay said. 'Come on, you guys, let's go to the fair.'

5

The Raggedy Man led them toward the silent multitude. It opened for them, leaving a narrow aisle – not much more than a throat – from the back of the Parachute Drop to the double doors of Kashwakamak Hall. Clay and the others passed a parking area filled with trucks (NEW ENGLAND AMUSE-MENT CORP. was printed on the sides, along with a roller-coaster logo). Then the crowd swallowed them.

That walk seemed endless to Clay. The smell was nearly insupportable, wild and ferocious even with the freshening breeze to carry the top layer away. He was aware of his legs moving, he was aware of the Raggedy Man's red hoodie ahead of him, but the hall's double doors with their swags of red, white, and blue bunting seemed to get no closer. He smelled

dirt and blood, urine and shit. He smelled fermenting infec-
tions, burned flesh, the spoiled eggwhite aroma of oozing pus.
He smelled clothes that were rotting on the bodies they draped.
He smelled something else, as well – some new thing. Calling
it madness would have been too easy.

*I think it's the smell of telepathy. And if it is, we're not ready
for it. It's too strong for us. It burns the brain, somehow, the way
too much current will burn out the electrical system in a car or a—*

'Help me with her!' Jordan yelled from behind him. 'Help
me with her, she's fainting!'

He turned and saw that Denise had gone down on all
fours. Jordan was on all fours beside her and had one of her
arms over his neck, but she was too heavy for him. Tom and
Dan couldn't get forward enough to help. The corridor cutting
through the mass of phoners was too narrow. Denise raised
her head, and for a moment her eyes met Clay's. The look
was one of dazed incomprehension, the eyes those of a slugged
steer. She vomited a thin gruel onto the grass and her head
dropped down again. Her hair fell around her face like a
curtain.

'Help me!' Jordan shouted again. He began to cry.

Clay went back and started elbowing phoners in order
to get on Denise's other side. 'Get out of the way!' he shouted.
'Get out of the way, she's pregnant, can't you fools see she's
preg—'

It was the blouse he recognized first. The high-necked,
white silk blouse that he had always called Sharon's doctor
shirt. In some ways he thought it was the sexiest garment she
owned, partly because of that high, prim neck. He liked her
bare, but he liked to touch and squeeze her breasts through
that high-necked, white silk blouse even more. He liked to
bring her nipples up until he could see them poking the
cloth.

Now Sharon's doctor shirt was streaked black with dirt
in some places and maroon with dried blood in others. It
was torn under the arm. *She doesnt look as bad as some,* Johnny

had written, but she didn't look good; she certainly wasn't the Sharon Riddell who had gone off to school in her doctor shirt and her dark red skirt while her estranged husband was in Boston, about to make a deal that would put an end to their financial worries and make her realize that all her carping about his 'expensive hobby' had been so much fear and bad faith (that, anyway, had been his semi-resentful dream). Her dark blond hair hung in lank strings. Her face had been cut in a number of places, and one of her ears looked torn half-off; where it had been, a clotted hole bored into the side of her head. Something she had eaten, something dark, clung in curds to the corners of the mouth he had kissed almost every day for almost fifteen years. She stared at him, through him, with that idiotic half-grin they sometimes wore.

'*Clay help me!*' Jordan almost sobbed.

Clay snapped back. Sharon wasn't here, that was the thing to remember. Sharon hadn't been here for almost two weeks now. Not since trying to make a call on Johnny's little red cell phone on the day of the Pulse.

'Give me some room, you bitch,' he said, and pushed aside the woman who'd been his wife. Before she could rebound, he slid into her place. 'This woman's pregnant, so give me some fucking room.' Then he bent, slipped Denise's other arm over his neck, and got her up.

'Go on ahead,' Tom said to Jordan. 'Let me in, I've got her.'

Jordan held up Denise's arm long enough for Tom to slip it over his own neck. He and Clay carried her that way the final ninety yards to the doors of Kashwakamak Hall, where the Raggedy Man stood waiting. By then Denise was muttering that they could let her go, she could walk, she was all right, but Tom wouldn't. Neither would Clay. If he let her go, he might look back for Sharon. He didn't want to do that.

The Raggedy Man grinned at Clay, and this time that grin seemed to have more focus. It really was as though the two of them shared a joke. *Sharon?* he wondered. *Is Sharon the joke?*

It seemed not, because the Raggedy Man made a gesture that would have seemed very familiar to Clay in the old world but seemed eerily out of place here: right hand to the right side of his face, right thumb to ear, pinkie finger to mouth. The phone-mime.

'No-fo-you-you,' Denise said, and then, in her own voice: 'Don't do that, I hate it when you do that!'

The Raggedy Man paid her no mind. He went on holding his right hand in the phone-gesture, thumb to ear and pinkie to mouth, staring at Clay. For one moment Clay was sure he also glanced down at the pocket where the cell phone was stowed. Then Denise said it again, that horrible parody of his old routine with Johnny-Gee: 'No-fo-you-you.' The Raggedy Man mimed laughing, and his ruined mouth made it grue- some. From behind him, Clay felt the eyes of the flock like a physical weight.

Then the double doors of Kashwakamak Hall opened on their own, and the mingled odors that came out, although faint – olfactory ghosts of other years – were still an anodyne to the stink of the flock: spices, jams, hay, and livestock. It wasn't completely dark, either; the battery-powered emer- gency lights were dim, but hadn't yet given out entirely. Clay thought that was pretty amazing, unless they had been saved especially for their arrival, and he doubted that. The Raggedy Man wasn't telling. He only smiled and gestured with his hands for them to go in.

'It'll be a pleasure, you freak,' Tom said. 'Denise, are you sure you can walk on your own?'

'Yes. I've just got one tiny bit of business first.' She drew in breath, then spit in the Raggedy Man's face. 'There. Take that back to Hah-vud with you, fuckface.'

The Raggedy Man said nothing. He only grinned at Clay. Just two fellows sharing a secret joke.

6

No one brought them any food, but there were snack machines galore and Dan found a crowbar in the maintenance closet at the huge building's south end. The others were standing around and watching him pry open the candy machine – *Of course we're insane,* Clay thought, *we eat Baby Ruths for dinner and tomorrow we'll have PayDays for breakfast* – when the music started. And it wasn't 'You Light Up My Life' or 'Baby Elephant Walk' coming out of the big speakers ringing the grassy mall outside, not this time. It was something slow and stately that Clay had heard before, although not for years. It filled him with sadness and made gooseflesh run up the soft insides of his arms.

'Oh my God,' Dan said softly. 'I think it's Albinoni.'

'No,' Tom said. 'That's Pachelbel. It's the Canon in D Major.'

'Of course it is,' Dan said, sounding embarrassed.

'It's as if . . .' Denise began, then stopped. She looked down at her shoes.

'What?' Clay asked. 'Go on, say it. You're among friends.'

'It's like the sound of memories,' she said. 'As if it's all they have.'

'Yes,' Dan said. 'I suppose—'

'You guys!' Jordan called. He was looking out one of the small windows. They were quite high, but by standing on his tiptoes, he could just manage. 'Come look at this!'

They lined up and looked out at the wide mall. It was almost full dark. The speakers and the light-standards loomed, black sentinels against the dead sky. Beyond was the gantry shape of the Parachute Drop with its one lonely blinking light. And ahead, directly ahead, thousands of phoners had gone to their knees like Muslims about to pray while Johann Pachelbel filled the air with what could have been a substitute for memory. And when they lay down they lay as one, producing a great soft swoop of noise and a fluttering

353

displacement of air that sent empty bags and flattened soda cups twirling into the air.

'Bedtime for the whole brain-damaged army,' Clay said. 'If we're going to do something, it's got to be tonight.'

'Do? What are we going to do?' Tom asked. 'The two doors I tried are both locked. I'm sure that's true of the others, as well.'

Dan held up the crowbar.

'Don't think so,' Clay said. 'That thing may work just fine on the vending machines, but remember, this place used to be a casino.' He pointed to the north end of the hall, which was lushly carpeted and filled with rows of one-armed bandits, their chrome muted in the glow of the failing emergency lights. 'I think you'll find the doors are crowbar-resistant.'

'The windows?' Dan asked, then took a closer look and answered his own question. 'Jordan, maybe.'

'Let's have something to eat,' Clay said. 'Then let's just sit down and be quiet for a little while. There hasn't been enough of that.'

'And do what?' Denise asked.

'Well, you guys can do what you want,' Clay said. 'I haven't done any drawing in almost two weeks, and I've been missing it. I think I'll draw.'

'You don't have any paper,' Jordan objected.

Clay smiled. 'When I don't have any paper, I draw in my head.'

Jordan looked at him uncertainly, trying to ascertain whether his leg was being pulled. When he decided it wasn't, he said, 'That can't be as good as drawing on paper, can it?'

'In some ways it's better. Instead of erasing, I just rethink.'

There was a loud clank and the door of the candy machine swung open. 'Bingo!' Dan cried, and lifted his crowbar above his head. 'Who said college professors were good for nothing in the real world?'

'Look,' Denise said greedily, ignoring Dan. 'A whole rack of Junior Mints!' She dug in.

'Clay?' Tom asked.

'Hmmm?'

'I don't suppose you saw your little boy, did you? Or your wife? Sandra?'

'Sharon,' Clay said. 'I didn't see either of them.' He looked around Denise's ample hip. 'Are those Butterfingers?'

7

Half an hour later they had eaten their fill of candy and raided the soda machine. They had tried the other doors and found them all locked. Dan tried his crowbar and couldn't get purchase even at the bottom. Tom was of the opinion that, although the doors looked like wood, they were very likely equipped with steel cores.

'Probably alarmed, too,' Clay said. 'Screw around with them too much and the reservation police will come and take you away.'

Now the other four sat in a little circle on the soft casino carpeting among the slot machines. Clay sat on the concrete, with his back against the double doors through which the Raggedy Man had ushered them with that mocking gesture of his – *After you, see you in the morning.*

Clay's thoughts wanted to return to that other mocking gesture – the thumb-and-pinkie phone-mime – but he wouldn't let them, at least not directly. He knew from long experience that the best way to go after such things was by the back door. So he leaned his head against the wood with the steel core hiding inside, and closed his eyes, and visualized a comic splash-page. Not a page from *Dark Wanderer* – *Dark Wanderer* was kaput and nobody knew it better than him – but from a new comic. Call it *Cell*, for want of a better title, a thrilling end-of-the-world saga of the phoner hordes versus the last few normies—

Except that couldn't be right. It *looked* right if you glanced at it fast, the way the doors in this place looked like wood but weren't. The ranks of the phoners had to be seriously depleted – *had* to be. How many of them had been lost in the violence immediately following the Pulse? Half? He recalled the fury of that violence and thought, *Maybe more. Maybe sixty or even seventy percent.* Then attrition due to serious wounds, infection, exposure, further fighting, and just plain stupidity. Plus, of course, the flock-killers; how many had *they* taken out? How many big flocks like this one were actually left?

Clay thought they might find out tomorrow, if the ones remaining all hooked up for one big execute-the-insane extravaganza. Much good the knowledge would do them.

Never mind. Boil it down. If you wanted backstory on the splash, the situation had to be boiled down enough to fit on a single narrative panel. It was an unwritten rule. The phoners' situation could be summed up in two words: bad losses. They looked like a lot – hell, like a damned *multitude* – but probably the passenger pigeons had looked like a lot right up until the end. Because they traveled in sky-darkening flocks right up to the end. What nobody noticed was that there were fewer and fewer of those giant flocks. Until, that was, they were all gone. Extinct. Finito. Buh-bye.

Plus, he thought, *they've got this other problem now, this bad-programming thing. This worm. What about that? All in all, these guys could have a shorter run than the dinosaurs, telepathy, levitation, and all.*

Okay, enough backstory. What's your illo? What's your damn *picture,* the one that's going to hook them and draw them in? Why, Clay Riddell and Ray Huizenga, that's what. They're standing in the woods. Ray's got the Beth Nickerson .45 with the barrel under his chin and Clay's holding . . .

A cell phone, of course. The one Ray lifted from the Gurleyville Quarry.

CLAY (terrified): **Ray, STOP! This is pointless! Don't you remember? Kashwak's a CELL DEAD Z—**

No good! **KA-POW!** in jagged yellow capitals across the

foreground of the splash, and this one really *is* a splash, because Arnie Nickerson has thoughtfully provided his wife with the kind of softnosed rounds they sell on the Internet at the American Paranoia sites, and the top of Ray's head is a red geyser. In the background – one of those detailed touches for which Clay Riddell might have become famous in a world where the Pulse never happened – a single terrified crow is lifting off from a pine branch.

A damn good splash page, Clay thought. Gory, sure – it would never have passed muster in the old Comics Code days – but instantly involving. And although Clay had never said that thing about cell phones not working beyond the conversion point, he would've if he'd thought of it in time. Only time had run out. Ray had killed himself so that the Raggedy Man and his phoner friends wouldn't see that phone in his mind, which was bitterly ironic. The Raggedy Man had known all about the cell whose existence Ray had died to protect. He knew it was in Clay's pocket . . . and he didn't care.

Standing at the double doors to Kashwakamak Hall. The Raggedy Man making that gesture – thumb to ear, curled fingers next to his torn and stubbly cheek, pinkie in front of his mouth. Using Denise to say it again, to drive the point home: *No-fo-you-you.*

That's right. Because Kashwak=No-Fo.

Ray had died for nothing . . . so why didn't that upset him now?

Clay was aware he was dozing as he often did when he drew inside his head. Coming uncoupled. And that was all right. Because he felt the way he always did just before picture and story became welded into one – happy, like people before an anticipated homecoming. Before journeys end in lovers meeting. He had absolutely no reason to feel that way, but he did.

Ray Huizenga had died for a useless cell phone.

Or was it more than one? Now Clay saw another panel.

This one was a flashback panel, you could tell by the scalloped edges.

CU on RAY'S hand, holding the grimy cell phone and a slip of paper with a telephone number scrawled on it. RAY'S thumb obscures everything but the Maine area code.

RAY (O.S.): **When the time comes, call the number on that slip. You'll know the time. I gotta hope you'll know.**

Can't call anybody from a cell in Kashwakamak, Ray, because Kashwak=No-Fo. Just ask the President of Hah-vud.

And to drive the point home, here's another flashback panel with those scalloped edges. It's Route 160. In the foreground is the little yellow bus with **MAINE SCHOOL DISTRICT 38 NEWFIELD** printed on the side. In the middle distance, painted across the road, is **KASHWAK=NO-FO**. Once again the detail-work is terrific: empty soda cans lying in the ditch, a discarded T-shirt caught on a bush, and in the distance, a tent flapping from a tree like a long brown tongue. Above the minibus are four voice-over balloons. These weren't the things they actually said (even his dozing mind knew it), but that wasn't the point. *Storymaking* wasn't the point, not now.

He thought he might know the point when he came to it.

DENISE (V.O.): **Is this where they—?**

TOM (V.O.): **Where they did the conversions, correct. Get into line a normie, make your call, and when you head on up to the Expo flock, you're one of THEM. What a deal.**

DAN (V.O.): **Why here? Why not on the Expo grounds?**

CLAY (V.O.): **Don't you remember? Kashwak=No-Fo. They lined 'em up at the far edge of cell coverage. Beyond here, nothing. Nada. Zip. Zero bars.**

Another panel. Close-up on the Raggedy Man in all his pestiferous glory. Grinning with his mutilated mouth and summing everything up with one gesture. *Ray had some bright idea that depended on making a cell phone call. It was so bright he completely forgot there's no coverage up here. I'd probably have to go to Quebec to get a bar on that phone he gave me. That's funny, but what's even funnier? I took it! What a sap!*

So whatever Ray had died for was pointless? Maybe, but here was another picture forming. Outside, Pachelbel had given way to Fauré, and Fauré had given way to Vivaldi. Pouring from speakers instead of boomboxes. Black speakers against a dead sky, with the half-constructed amusement rides in the background; in the foreground Kashwakamak Hall with its bunting and cheap hay insulation. And as the final touch, the little piece of detail-work for which Clay Riddell was already becoming known—

He opened his eyes and sat up. The others were still in their circle on the carpet at the north end. Clay didn't know how long he'd been sitting against the door, but it had been long enough for his ass to go numb.

You guys, he tried to say, but at first no sound would come out. His mouth was dry. His heart was pumping hard. He cleared his throat and tried again. 'You guys!' he said, and they looked around. Something in his voice made Jordan scramble to his feet, and Tom wasn't far behind.

Clay walked toward them on legs that didn't feel like his own – they were half-asleep. He took the cell phone out of his pocket as he walked. The one Ray had died for because in the heat of the moment he had forgotten the most salient fact about Kashwakamak: up here at the Northern Counties Expo, these things didn't work.

8

'If it won't work, what good is it?' Dan asked. He had been excited by Clay's excitement, but deflated in a hurry when he saw the object in Clay's hand wasn't a Get Out of Jail Free card but only another goddam cell phone. A dirty old Motorola with a cracked casing. The others looked at it with a mixture of fear and curiosity.

'Bear with me,' Clay said. 'Would you do that?'

'We've got all night,' Dan said. He took off his glasses and began to polish them. 'Got to spin it away somehow.'

'You stopped at that Newfield Trading Post for something to eat and drink,' Clay said, 'and you found the little yellow schoolbus.'

'That seems like a zillion years ago,' Denise said. She stuck out her lower lip and blew hair off her forehead.

'*Ray* found the little bus,' Clay said. 'Seats about twelve—'

'Sixteen, actually,' Dan said. 'It's written on the dashboard. Man, they must have *teensy* schools up here.'

'Seats sixteen, with space behind the rear seat for packs, or a little light luggage for field trips. Then you moved on. And when you got to the Gurleyville Quarry, I bet it was Ray's idea that you should stop there.'

'You know, it was,' Tom said. 'He thought we could use a hot meal and a rest. How'd you know that, Clay?'

'I knew it because I drew it,' Clay said, and this was close to true – he was seeing it as he spoke. 'Dan, you and Denise and Ray wiped out two flocks. The first with gasoline, but on the second you used dynamite. Ray knew how because he'd used it working highway jobs.'

'Fuck,' Tom breathed. 'He got dynamite in that quarry, didn't he? While we were sleeping. And he *could* have – we slept like the dead.'

'Ray was the one who woke us up,' Denise said.

Clay said, 'I don't know if it was dynamite or some other explosive, but I'm almost positive he turned that little yellow bus into a rolling bomb while you were sleeping.'

'It's in back,' Jordan said. 'In the luggage compartment.' Clay nodded.

Jordan's hands were clenched into fists. 'How much, do you think?'

'No way of knowing until it goes up,' Clay said.

'Let me see if I'm following this,' Tom said. Outside, Vivaldi gave way to Mozart – *A Little Night Music*. The phoners had definitely evolved past Debby Boone. 'He stowed

360

a bomb in the back of the bus . . . then somehow rigged a cell phone as a detonator?'

Clay nodded. 'That's what I believe. I think he found two cells in the quarry office. For all I know, there could have been half a dozen, for crew use − God knows they're cheap enough nowadays. Anyway, he rigged one to a detonator on the explosives. It's how the insurgents used to set off roadside bombs in Iraq.'

'He did all that while we were sleeping?' Denise asked. 'And didn't tell us?'

Clay said, 'He kept it from you so it wouldn't be in your minds.'

'And killed himself so it wouldn't be in his,' Dan said. Then he uttered a burst of bitter laughter. 'Okay, he's a goddam hero! The only thing he forgot is that cell phones don't work beyond the place where they put up their goddam conversion tents! I bet they barely worked there!'

'Right,' Clay said. He was smiling. 'That's why the Raggedy Man let me keep this phone. He didn't know what I wanted it for − I'm not sure they exactly think, anyway—'

'Not like us, they don't,' Jordan said. 'And they never will.'

'—but he didn't care, because he knew it wouldn't work. I couldn't even Pulse myself with it, because Kashwak equals no-fo. No-fo-me-me.'

'Then why the smile?' Denise asked.

'Because I know something he doesn't,' Clay said. 'Something *they* don't.' He turned to Jordan. 'Can you drive?'

Jordan looked startled. 'Hey, I'm twelve. I mean, hello?'

'You've never driven a go-kart? An ATV? A snowmobile?'

'Well, sure . . . there's a dirt go-kart track at this pitch-n-putt place outside Nashua, and once or twice . . .'

'That'll work. We're not talking about very far. Assuming, that is, they left the bus at the Parachute Drop. And I bet they did. I don't think they know how to drive any more than they know how to think.'

Tom said, 'Clay, have you lost your mind?'

'No,' he said. 'They may hold their mass flock-killer executions in that virtual stadium of theirs tomorrow, but *we're* not going to be part of it. We're getting out of here.'

9

The little windows were thick, but Dan's crowbar was a match for the glass. He, Tom, and Clay took turns with it, working until all the shards were knocked out. Then Denise took the sweater she'd been wearing and laid it over the bottom of the frame.

'You okay with this, Jordan?' Tom asked.

Jordan nodded. He was frightened – there was no color in his lips at all – but seemed composed. Outside, the phoners' lullaby music had cycled around to Pachelbel's Canon again – what Denise had called the sound of memories.

'I'm okay,' Jordan said. 'I will be, anyway. I think. Once I get going.'

Clay said, 'Tom might be able to squeeze through—'

Behind Jordan's shoulder, Tom looked at the small window, no more than eighteen inches wide, and shook his head.

'I'll be okay,' Jordan said.

'All right. Tell it to me again.'

'Go around and look in the back of the bus. Make sure there's explosives, but don't touch any of it. Look for the other cell phone.'

'Right. Make sure it's on. And if it's not on—'

'I know, *turn* it on.' Jordan gave Clay an I'm-no-dummy look. 'Then start the motor—'

'No, don't get ahead of yourself—'

'Pull the driving seat forward so I can reach the pedals, *then* start the motor.'

'Right.'

'Drive between the Parachute Drop and the funhouse. Go superslow. I'll run over some pieces of the funhouse and they may break – snap under the tires – but don't let that stop me.'

'Right on.'

'Get as close to them as I can.'

'Yes, that's right. Then come around back again, to this window. So the hall is between you and the explosion.'

'What we *hope* will be an explosion,' Dan said.

Clay could have done without this, but let it pass. He stooped and kissed Jordan on the cheek. 'I love you, you know,' he said.

Jordan hugged him briefly, fiercely. Then Tom. Then Denise.

Dan put out his hand, then said, 'Oh, what the hell,' and enfolded Jordan in a bearhug. Clay, who had never warmed very much to Dan Hartwick, liked him better for that.

10

Clay made a step with his hands and boosted Jordan up. 'Remember,' he said, 'it's going to be like a dive, only into hay instead of water. Hands up and out.'

Jordan put his hands over his head, extending them through the broken window and into the night. His face underneath his thick fall of hair was paler than ever; the first red blemishes of adolescence stood out there like tiny burns. He was scared, and Clay didn't blame him. He was in for a ten-foot drop, and even with the hay, the landing was apt to be hard. Clay hoped Jordan would remember to keep his hands out and his head tucked; he'd do none of them any good lying beside Kashwakamak Hall with a broken neck.

'You want me to count three, Jordan?' he asked.

'Fuck, no! Just do it before I pee myself!'

'Then keep your hands out, *go!*' Clay cried, and thrust

his locked hands upward. Jordan shot through the window and disappeared. Clay didn't hear him land; the music was too loud.

The others crowded up to the window, which was just above their heads. 'Jordan?' Tom called. 'Jordan, you there?'

For a moment there was nothing, and Clay was sure Jordan really had broken his neck. Then he said shakily, 'I'm here. *Jeez,* that hurts. I croggled my elbow. The left one. That arm's all weird. Wait a minute . . .'

They waited. Denise took Clay's hand and squeezed it hard.

'It moves,' Jordan said. 'It's okay, I guess, but maybe I ought to see the school nurse.'

They all laughed too hard.

Tom had tied the bus's ignition key to a double line of thread from his shirt, and the thread to the buckle of his belt. Now Clay laced his fingers together again and Tom stepped up. 'I'm going to lower the key to you, Jordan. Ready?'

'Yeah.'

Tom gripped the edge of the window, looked down, and then lowered his belt. 'Okay, you got it,' he said. 'Now listen to me. All we ask is do it if you can. If you can't, no penalty minutes. Got that?'

'Yes.'

'Go on, then. Scat.' He watched a moment, then said, 'He's on his way. God help him, he's a brave kid. Put me down.'

11

Jordan had gone out on the side of the building away from the roosting flock. Clay, Tom, Denise, and Dan crossed the room to the midway side. The three men tipped the already vandalized snack machine over on its side and shoved it against the wall. Clay and Dan could easily see out the high windows by standing on it, Tom by standing on tiptoes. Clay added a crate so Denise could also see, praying she wouldn't topple off it and go into labor.

They saw Jordan cross to the edge of the sleeping multitude, stand there a minute as if debating, and then move off to his left. Clay thought he continued seeing movement long after his rational mind told him that Jordan must be gone, skirting the edge of the massive flock.

'How long will it take him to get back, do you think?' Tom asked.

Clay shook his head. He didn't know. It depended on so many variables – the size of the flock was only one of them.

'What if they looked in the back of the bus?' Denise asked.

'What if *Jordy* looks in the back of the bus and there's nothing there?' Dan asked, and Clay had to restrain himself from telling the man to keep his negative vibe to himself.

Time passed, giving itself up by inches. The little red light on the tip of the Parachute Drop blinked. Pachelbel once more gave way to Fauré and Fauré to Vivaldi. Clay found himself remembering the sleeping boy who had come spilling out of the shopping cart, how the man with him – probably not his father – had sat down with him at the side of the road and said *Gregory kiss it, make it all better.* He remembered the man with the rucksack listening to 'Baby Elephant Walk' and saying *Dodge had a good time, too.* He remembered how, in the bingo tents of his childhood, the man with the microphone would invariably exclaim *It's the sunshine vitamin!* when he pulled B-12 out of the hopper with the dancing Ping-Pong balls inside. Even though the sunshine vitamin was D.

The time now gave itself up in what seemed quarter-inches, and Clay began losing hope. If they were going to hear the sound of the bus's engine, they should have heard it by now.

'It's gone wrong somehow,' Tom said in a low voice.

'Maybe not,' Clay said. He tried to keep his heart's heaviness out of his voice.

'No, Tommy's right,' Denise said. She was on the verge of tears. 'I love him to death, and he was ballsier than Lord Satan on his first night in hell, but if he was coming, he'd be on his way by now.'

Dan's take was surprisingly positive. 'We don't know what he might have run into. Just take a deep breath and try to put your imaginations on hold.'

Clay tried that and failed. Now the seconds *dripped* by. Schubert's 'Ave Maria' boomed through the big concert speakers. He thought, *I would sell my soul for some honest rock and roll – Chuck Berry doing 'Oh, Carol', U2 doing 'When Love Comes to Town'* . . .

Outside, nothing but dark, and stars, and that one tiny red battery-driven light.

'Boost me up over there,' Tom said, hopping down from the snack machine. 'I'll squeeze through that window somehow and see if I can't go get him.'

Clay began, 'Tom, if I was wrong about there being explosives in the back of the bus—'

'Fuck the back of the bus and fuck the explosives!' Tom said, distraught. 'I just want to find Jor—'

'Hey!' Dan shouted, and then: *'Hey, all right! BABY-NOW!'* He slammed one fist against the wall beside the window.

Clay turned and saw headlights had bloomed in the dark. A mist had begun to rise from the blanket of comatose bodies on the acres of mall, and the bus's headlights seemed to be shining through smoke. They flicked bright, then dim, then bright again, and Clay could see Jordan with brilliant clarity, sitting in the driver's seat of the minibus and trying to figure out which controls did which.

Now the headlights began to creep forward. High beams.

'Yeah, honey,' Denise breathed. '*Do* it, my sweetheart.' Standing on her crate, she grabbed Dan's hand on one side and Clay's on the other. 'You're beautiful, just keep on coming.'

The headlights jogged away from them, now illuminating the trees far to the left of the open space with its carpet of phoners.

'What's he doing?' Tom almost moaned.

'That's where the side of the funhouse takes a jog,' Clay said. 'It's all right.' He hesitated. 'I think it's all right.' *If his foot doesn't slip. If he doesn't mix up the brake and the accelerator, run the bus into the side of the damn funhouse, and stick it there.*

They waited, and the headlights swung back, spearing the side of Kashwakamak Hall on the dead level. And in the glare of the high beams, Clay saw why it had taken Jordan so long. Not all of the phoners were down. Dozens of them – the ones with bad programming, he assumed – were up and moving. They walked aimlessly toward any and every point of the compass, black silhouettes moving outward in expanding ripples, struggling to make their way over the bodies of the sleepers, stumbling, falling, getting up and walking on again while Schubert's 'Ave' filled the night. One of them, a young man with a long red gash running across the middle of his forehead like a worry line, reached the Hall and felt his way along the side like a blind man.

'That's far enough, Jordan,' Clay murmured as the head-lights neared the speaker-standards on the far side of the open area. 'Park it and get your ass back here.'

It seemed that Jordan heard him. The headlights came to a stop. For a moment the only things moving out there were the restless shapes of the wakeful phoners and the mist rising from the warm bodies of the others. Then they heard the bus's engine rev – even over the music they heard it – and the headlights leaped forward.

'No, Jordan, what are you doing?' Tom screamed.

Denise recoiled and would have tumbled off her crate if Clay hadn't caught her around the waist.

The bus jounced into the sleeping flock. *Onto* the sleeping flock. The headlights began to pogo up and down, now pointing at them, now lifting briefly upward, now coming back to dead level again. The bus slewed left, came back on course, then slewed right. For a moment one of the night-walkers was illuminated in its four glaring high beams as clearly as something cut from black construction paper. Clay saw the phoner's arms go up, as if it wanted to signal a successful field goal, and then it was borne under the bus's charging grille.

Jordan drove the bus into the middle of them and there it stopped, headlights glaring, grille dripping. By raising a hand to block the worst of the shine, Clay was able to see a small dark form – distinguishable from the rest by its agility and purpose – emerge from the side door of the bus and begin making its way toward Kaskwakamak Hall. Then Jordan fell and Clay thought he was gone. A moment later Dan rapped, 'There he is, *there!*' and Clay picked him up again, ten yards closer and considerably to the left of where he'd lost sight of the kid. Jordan must have crawled for some distance over the sleeping bodies before trying his feet again.

When Jordan came back into the hazy cone of radiance thrown by the bus's headlights, tacked to the end of a forty-foot shadow, they could see him clearly for the first time. Not his face, because of the backlighting, but the crazy-graceful way he was running over the bodies of the phoners. The ones who were down were still dead to the world. The ones who were awake but not close to Jordan paid no attention. Several of those who *were* close, however, made grabs at him. Jordan dodged two of these, but the third, a woman, got him by the tangled mop of his hair.

'*Let him alone!*' Clay roared. He couldn't see her, but he was insanely positive it was the woman who had once been his wife. '*Let him go!*'

She didn't, but Jordan grabbed her wrist, twisted it, went to one knee, and scrambled past. The woman made another grab, just missed the back of his shirt, and then tottered off in her own direction.

Many of the infected phoners, Clay saw, were gathering around the bus. The headlights seemed to be drawing them.

Clay leaped off the snack machine (this time it was Dan Hartwick who saved Denise from a tumble) and grabbed the crowbar. He leaped back up and smashed out the window he'd been looking through.

'Jordan!' he bawled. *'Around back! Get around back!'*

Jordan looked up at the sound of Clay's voice and tripped over something – a leg, an arm, maybe a neck. As he was getting back up, a hand came out of the breathing darkness and clutched the kid's throat.

'Please God, no,' Tom whispered.

Jordan lunged forward like a fullback trying for a first down, pistoning with his legs, and broke the hand's grip. He stumbled onward. Clay could see his staring eyes and the way his chest was heaving. As he neared the hall, Clay could hear Jordan's sobbing gasps for air.

Never make it, he thought. *Never. And he's so close now, so close.*

But Jordan did make it. The two phoners currently staggering along the side of the building showed no interest in him at all as he lunged past them and around to the far side. The four of them were off the snack machine at once and racing across the hall like a relay team, Denise and her belly in the lead.

'Jordan!' she cried, bouncing up and down on her toe-tips. 'Jordan, Jordy, are you there? For chrissake, kid, tell us you're there!'

'I'm—' he tore a great gasp of breath out of the air – 'here.' Another whooping gasp. Clay was distantly aware of Tom laughing and pounding him on the back. 'Never knew—' *Whooo-oooop!* '—running over people was so . . . hard.'

'What did you think you were doing?' Clay shouted. It was killing him not to be able to grab the kid, first to embrace him, then shake him, then kiss him all over his stupid brave face. Killing him to not even be able to see him. 'I said get *close* to them, not drive right the fuck *into* them!'

'I did it—' *Whoo-ooop!* '—for the Head.' There was defiance as well as breathlessness in Jordan's voice now. 'They killed the Head. Them and their Raggedy Man. Them and their stupid President of Harvard. I wanted to make them pay. I want *him* to pay.'

'What took you so long to get going?' Denise asked. 'We waited and waited!'

'There are dozens of them up and around,' Jordan said. 'Maybe hundreds. Whatever's wrong with them . . . or right . . . or just changing . . . it's spreading really fast now. They're walking every which way, like totally lost. I had to keep changing course. I ended up coming to the bus from halfway down the midway. Then—' He laughed breathlessly. *'It wouldn't start!* Do you believe it? I turned the key and turned the key and got nothing but a click every time. I just about freaked, but I wouldn't let myself. Because I knew the Head would be disappointed if I did that.'

'Ah, Jordy . . .' Tom breathed.

'You know what it was? I had to buckle the stupid *seatbelt.* You don't need em for the passenger seats, but the bus won't start unless the driver's wearing his. Anyway, I'm sorry it took me so long, but here I am.'

'And may we assume that the luggage compartment wasn't empty?' Dan asked.

'You can assume the shit out of that. It's full of what look like red bricks. Stacks and stacks of them.' Jordan was getting his breath back now. 'They're under a blanket. There's a cell phone lying on top of them. Ray attached it to a couple of those bricks with an elastic strap, like a bungee cord. The phone's on, and it's the kind with a port, like for a fax or so you can download data to a computer. The power-cord runs down into the bricks. I didn't see it, but I bet the detonator's in the middle.' He grabbed another deep breath. 'And there were bars on the phone. Three bars.'

Clay nodded. He'd been right. Kashwakamak was supposed to be a cell dead zone once you got beyond the feeder-road leading to the Northern Counties Expo. The phoners had plucked that knowledge from the heads of certain normies and had used it. The Kashwak=No-Fo graffiti had spread like smallpox. But had any of the phoners actually tried making a cell-call from the Expo fairgrounds? Of course not. Why would they? When you were telepathic, phones were obsolete. And when you were one member of the flock – one part of the whole – they became doubly obsolete, if such a thing was possible.

But cell phones *did* work within this one small area, and why? Because the carnies were setting up, that was why – carnies working for an outfit called the New England Amusement Corporation. And in the twenty-first century, carnies – like rock-concert roadies, touring stage productions, and movie crews on location – depended on cell phones, especially in isolated places where landlines were in short supply. Were there no cell phone towers to relay signals onward and upward? Fine, they would pirate the necessary software and install one of their own. Illegal? Of course, but judging by the three bars Jordan was reporting, it had been workable, and because it was battery-powered, it was *still* workable. They had installed it on the Expo's highest point.

They had installed it on the tip of the Parachute Drop.

12

Dan recrossed the hall, got up on the snack machine, and looked out. 'They're three deep around the bus,' he reported. 'Four deep in front of the headlights. It's like they think there's some big pop star hiding inside. The ones they're standing on must be getting crushed.' He turned to Clay and nodded at the dirty Motorola cell phone Clay was now holding. 'If you're going to try this, I suggest you try it now, before one of them decides to get in and try driving the damn bus away.'

'I should have turned it off, but I thought the headlights would go out if I did,' Jordan said. 'And I wanted them to see by.'

'It's okay, Jordan,' Clay said. 'No harm done. I'm going to—'

But there was nothing in the pocket from which he'd taken the cell phone. The scrap of paper with the telephone number on it was gone.

13

Clay and Tom were looking for it on the floor – *frantically* looking for it on the floor – and Dan was dolefully reporting from atop the snack machine that the first phoner had just stumbled on board the bus when Denise bellowed, *'Stop! SHUT UP!'*

They all stopped what they were doing and looked at her. Clay's heart was fluttering high in his throat. He couldn't believe his own carelessness. *Ray died for that, you stupid shit!* part of him kept shouting at the rest of him. *He died for it and you lost it!*

Denise closed her eyes and put her hands together over her bowed head. Then, very rapidly, she chanted, 'Tony, Tony, come around, something's lost that can't be found.'

'What the fuck is *that*?' Dan asked. He sounded astonished.

'A prayer to St Anthony,' she said calmly. 'I learned it in parochial school. It always works.'

'Give me a break,' Tom almost groaned.

She ignored him, focusing all her attention on Clay. 'It's not on the floor, is it?'

'I don't think so, no.'

'Another two just got on the bus,' Dan reported. 'And the turn signals are going. So one of them must be sitting at the—'

'Will you please shut up, Dan,' Denise said. She was still

372

looking at Clay. Still calm. 'And if you lost it on the bus, or outside somewhere, it's lost for good, right?'

'Yes,' he said heavily.

'So we know it's not in either of those places.'

'Why do we know that?'

'Because God wouldn't let it be.'

'I think . . . my head's going to explode,' Tom said in a strangely calm voice.

Again she ignored him. 'So which pocket haven't you checked?'

'I checked *every*—' Clay began, then stopped. Without taking his eyes from Denise's, he investigated the small watch-pocket sewn into the larger right front pocket of his jeans. And the slip of paper was there. He didn't remember putting it there, but it was there. He pulled it out. Scrawled on it in the dead man's laborious printing was the number: 207-919-9811.

'Thank St Anthony for me,' he said.

'If this works,' she said, 'I'll ask St Anthony to thank God.'

'Deni?' Tom said.

She turned to him.

'Thank Him for me, too,' he said.

14

The four of them sat together against the double doors through which they had entered, counting on the steel cores to protect them. Jordan was crouched down in back of the building, below the broken window through which he had escaped.

'What are we going to do if the explosion doesn't blow any holes in the side of this place?' Tom asked.

'We'll think of something,' Clay said.

'And if Ray's bomb doesn't go off?' Dan asked.

'Drop back twenty yards and punt,' Denise said. 'Go on, Clay. Don't wait for the theme-music.'

He opened the cell phone, looked at the dark LED

readout, and realized he should have checked for bars on this one before sending Jordan out. He hadn't thought of it. None of them had thought of it. Stupid. Almost as stupid as forgetting he'd put the scrap of paper with the number written on it in his watch pocket. He pushed the power button now. The phone beeped. For a moment there was nothing, and then three bars appeared, bright and clear. He punched in the number, then settled his thumb lightly on the button marked CALL.

'Jordan, you ready back there?'

'Yes!'

'What about you guys?' Clay asked.

'Just do it before I have a heart attack,' Tom said.

An image rose in Clay's mind, nightmarish in its clarity: Johnny-Gee lying almost directly beneath the place where the explosives-laden bus had come to rest. Lying on his back with his eyes open and his hands clasped on the chest of his Red Sox T-shirt, listening to the music while his mind rebuilt itself in some strange new way.

He swept it aside.

'Tony, Tony, come around,' he said for no reason whatever, and then pushed the button that called the cell phone in the back of the minibus.

There was time for him to count *Mississippi ONE* and *Mississippi TWO* before the entire world outside Kashwakamak Hall seemed to blow up, the roar swallowing Tomaso Albinoni's 'Adagio' in a hungry blast. All the small windows lining the flock side of the building blew in. Brilliant crimson light shone through the holes, then the entire south end of the building tore away in a hail of boards, glass, and swirling hay. The doors they were leaning against seemed to bend backward. Denise wrapped protective arms around her belly. From outside a terrible hurt screaming began. For a moment this sound ripped through Clay's head like the blade of a buzzsaw. Then it was gone. The screaming in his ears went on. It was the sound of people roasting in hell.

Something landed on the roof. It was heavy enough to make the whole building shudder. Clay pulled Denise to her feet. She looked at him wildly, as if no longer sure who he was. *'Come on!'* He was shouting but could hardly hear his own voice. It seemed to be seeping through wads of cotton. *'Come on, let's get out!'*

Tom was up. Dan made it halfway, fell back, tried again, and managed it the second time. He grabbed Tom's hand. Tom grabbed Denise's. Linked three-across, they shuffled to the gaping hole at the end of the Hall. There they found Jordan standing next to a litter of burning hay and staring out at what a single phone call had done.

15

The giant's foot that had seemed to stamp the roof of Kashwakamak Hall had been a large chunk of schoolbus. The shingles were burning. Directly in front of them, beyond the little pile of blazing hay, were a pair of upside-down seats, also burning. Their steel frames had been shredded into spaghetti. Clothes floated out of the sky like big snow: shirts, hats, pants, shorts, an athletic supporter, a blazing bra. Clay saw that the hay insulation piled along the bottom of the hall was going to be a moat of fire before very long; they were getting out just in time.

Patches of fire dotted the mall area where concerts, outdoor dances, and various competitions had been held, but the chunks of the exploding bus had swept farther than that. Clay saw flames burning high in trees that had to be at least three hundred yards away. Dead south of their position, the funhouse had started to burn and he could see something – he thought it was probably a human torso – blazing halfway up the strutwork of the Parachute Drop.

The flock itself had become a raw meatloaf of dead and dying phoners. Their telepathy had broken down (although little currents of that strange psychic force occasionally tugged at him, making his hair rise and his flesh crawl), but the survivors could still scream, and they filled the night with their cries. Clay would have gone ahead even if he'd been able to imagine how bad it was going to be – even in the first few seconds he made no effort to mislead himself on that score – but this was beyond imagining.

The firelight was just enough to show them more than they wanted to see. The mutilations and decapitations were bad – the pools of blood, the littered limbs – but the scattered clothes and shoes with nobody inside them were somehow worse, as if the explosion had been fierce enough to actually vaporize part of the flock. A man walked toward them with his hands to his throat in an effort to stem the flow of blood pouring over and between his fingers – it looked orange in the growing glow of the Hall's burning roof – while his intestines swung back and forth at the level of his crotch. More wet loops came sliding out as he walked past them, his eyes wide and unseeing.

Jordan was saying something. Clay couldn't hear it over the screams, the wails, and the growing crackle of fire from behind him, so he leaned closer.

'We had to do it, it was all we could do,' Jordan said. He looked at a headless woman, a legless man, at something so torn open it had become a flesh canoe filled with blood. Beyond it, two more bus seats lay on a pair of burning women who had died in each other's arms. 'We had to do it, it was all we could do. We had to do it, it was all we could do.'

'That's right, honey, put your face against me and walk like that,' Clay said, and Jordan immediately buried his face in Clay's side. Walking that way was uncomfortable, but it could be done.

They skirted the edge of the flock's campground, moving toward the back of what would have been a completed midway and amusement arcade if the Pulse hadn't intervened. As they went, Kashwakamak Hall burned brighter, casting more light on the mall. Dark shapes – many naked or almost naked, the clothes blown right off them – staggered and sham-bled. Clay had no idea how many. The few that passed close by their little group showed no interest in them; they either continued on toward the midway area or plunged into the woods west of the Expo grounds, where Clay was quite sure they would die of exposure unless they could reestablish some sort of flock consciousness. He didn't think they could. Partly because of the virus, but mostly because of Jordan's decision to drive the bus right into the middle of them and achieve a maximum kill-zone, as they had with the propane trucks.

If they'd ever known snuffing one old man could lead to this . . . Clay thought, and then he thought, *But how could they?*

They reached the dirt lot where the carnies had parked their trucks and campers. Here the ground was thick with snaking electrical cables, and the spaces between the campers were filled with the accessories of families who lived on the road: barbecues, gas grills, lawn chairs, a hammock, a little laundry whirligig with clothes that had probably been hanging there for almost two weeks.

'Let's find something with the keys in it and get the hell out of here,' Dan said. 'They cleared the feeder road, and if we're careful I bet we can go north on 160 as far as we want.' He pointed. 'Up there it's just about *all* no-fo.'

Clay had spotted a panel truck with LEM'S PAINTING AND PLUMBING on the back. He tried the doors and they opened. The inside was filled with milk-crates, most crammed with various plumbing supplies, but in one he found what he wanted: paint in spray-cans. He took four of these after checking to make sure they were full or almost full.

'What are those for?' Tom asked.

'Tell you later,' Clay said.

'Let's get out of here, *please,*' Denise said. 'I can't stand this. My pants are soaked with blood.' She began to cry.

They came onto the midway between the Krazy Kups and a half-constructed kiddie ride called Charlie the Choo-Choo. 'Look,' Tom said, pointing.

'Oh . . . my . . . *God,*' Dan said softly.

Lying draped across the peak of the train ride's ticket booth was the remains of a charred and smoking red sweatshirt – the kind sometimes called a hoodie. A large splotch of blood matted the front around a hole probably made by a chunk of flying schoolbus. Before the blood took over, covering the rest, Clay could make out three letters, the Raggedy Man's last laugh: HAR.

16

'There's nobody in the fucking thing, and judging by the size of the hole, he had open-heart surgery without benefit of anesthetic,' Denise said, 'so when you're tired of looking—'

'There's another little parking lot down at the south end of the midway,' Tom said. 'Nice-looking cars in that one. Boss-type cars. We might get lucky.'

They did, but not with a nice-looking car. A small van with TYCO WATER PURIFICATION EXPERTS was parked behind a number of the nice-looking cars, effectively blocking them in. The Tyco man had considerately left his keys in the ignition, probably for that very reason, and Clay drove them away from the fire, the carnage, and the screams, rolling with slow care down the feeder road to the junction marked by the billboard showing the sort of happy family that no longer existed (if it ever had). There Clay stopped and put the gearshift lever in park.

'One of you guys has to take over now,' he said.

'Why, Clay?' Jordan asked, but Clay knew from the boy's voice that Jordan already knew.

'Because this is where I get out,' he said.

'No!'

'Yes. I'm going to look for my boy.'

Tom said, 'He's almost certainly dead back there. I'm not meaning to be a hardass, only realistic.'

'I know that, Tom. I also know there's a chance he's not,

and so do you. Jordan said they were walking every which way, like they were totally lost.'

Denise said, 'Clay ... honey ... even if he's alive, he could be wandering around in the woods with half his head blown off. I hate to say that, but you know it's true.'

Clay nodded. 'I also know he could have gotten out earlier, while we were locked up, and started down the road to Gurleyville. A couple of others made it that far; I saw them. And I saw others on the way. So did you.'

'No arguing with the artistic mind, is there?' Tom asked sadly.

'No,' Clay said, 'but I wonder if you and Jordan would step outside with me for a minute.'

Tom sighed. 'Why not?' he said.

17

Several phoners, looking lost and bewildered, walked past them as they stood by the side of the little water purification van. Clay, Tom, and Jordan paid no attention to them, and the phoners returned the favor. To the northwest the horizon was a brightening red-orange as Kashwakamak Hall shared its fire with the forest behind it.

'No big goodbyes this time,' Clay said, affecting not to see the tears in Jordan's eyes. 'I'm expecting to see you again. Here, Tom. Take this.' He held out the cell phone he'd used to set off the blast. Tom took it. 'Go north from here. Keep checking that thing for bars. If you come to road-reefs, abandon what you're driving, walk until the road's clear, then take another car or truck and drive again. You'll probably get cell transmission bars around the Rangeley area – that was boating in the summer, hunting in the fall, skiing in the winter – but beyond there you should be in the clear, and the days should be safe.'

'I bet they're safe now,' Jordan said, wiping his eyes.

Clay nodded. 'You might be right. Anyway, use your

judgment. When you get a hundred or so miles north of Rangeley, find a cabin or a lodge or something, fill it with supplies, and lay up for the winter. You know what the winter's going to do to these things, don't you?'

'If the flock mind falls apart and they don't migrate, almost all of them will die,' Tom said. 'Those north of the Mason-Dixon Line, at least.'

'I think so, yeah. I put those cans of spray-paint in the center console. Every twenty miles or so, spray T-J-D on the road, nice and big. Got it?'

'T-J-D,' Jordan said. 'For Tom, Jordan, Dan, and Denise.'

'Right. Make sure you spray it extra big, with an arrow, if you change roads. If you take a dirt road, spray it on trees, always on the right-hand side of the road. That's where I'll be looking. Have you got that?'

'Always on the right,' Tom said. 'Come with us, Clay. Please.'

'No. Don't make this harder for me than it already is. Every time you have to abandon a vehicle, leave it in the middle of the road and spray it T-J-D. Okay?'

'Okay,' Jordan said. 'You better find us.'

'I will. This is going to be a dangerous world for a while, but not quite as dangerous as it's been. Jordan, I need to ask you something.'

'All right.'

'If I find Johnny and the worst that's happened to him is a trip through their conversion-point, what should I do?'

Jordan gaped. 'How would *I* know? Jesus, Clay! I mean . . . *Jesus!*'

'You knew they were rebooting,' Clay said.

'I made a *guess!*'

Clay knew it had been a lot more than that. A lot *better* than that. He also knew Jordan was exhausted and terrified. He dropped to one knee in front of the boy and took his hand. 'Don't be afraid. It can't be any worse for him than it already is. God knows it can't.'

'Clay, I . . .' Jordan looked at Tom. 'People aren't like computers, Tom! Tell him!'

'But computers are like people, aren't they?' Tom said. 'Because we build what we know. You knew about the reboot and you knew about the worm. So tell him what you think. He probably won't find the kid, anyway. If he does . . .' Tom shrugged. 'Like he said. How much worse can it be?'

Jordan thought about this, biting his lip. He looked terribly tired, and there was blood on his shirt.

'Are you guys coming?' Dan called.

'Give us another minute,' Tom said. And then, in a softer tone: 'Jordan?'

Jordan was quiet a moment longer. Then he looked at Clay and said, 'You'd need another cell phone. And you'd need to take him to a place where there's coverage . . .'

SAVE TO SYSTEM

1

Clay stood in the middle of Route 160, in what would have been the billboard's shadow on a sunny day, and watched the taillights until they were out of sight. He couldn't shake the idea that he would never see Tom and Jordan again (*fading roses,* his mind whispered), but he refused to let it grow into a premonition. They had come together twice, after all, and didn't people say the third time was the charm?

A passing phoner bumped him. It was a man with blood congealing on one side of his face – the first injured refugee from the Northern Counties Expo that he'd seen. He would see more if he didn't stay ahead of them, so he set off along Route 160, heading south again. He had no real reason to think his kid had gone south, but hoped that some vestige of Johnny's mind – his old mind – told him home lay in that direction. And it was a direction Clay knew, at least.

About half a mile south of the feeder road he encountered another phoner, this one a woman, who was pacing rapidly back and forth across the highway like a captain on the foredeck of her ship. She looked around at Clay with such sharp regard that he raised his hands, ready to grapple with her if she attacked him.

She didn't. 'Who fa–Da?' she asked, and in his mind, quite clearly, he heard: *Who fell? Daddy, who fell?*

'I don't know,' he said, easing past her. 'I didn't see.'

'Where na?' she asked, pacing more furiously than ever,

and in his mind he heard: *Where am I now?* This he made no attempt to answer, but in his mind he thought of Pixie Dark asking, *Who are you? Who am I?*

Clay walked faster, but not quite fast enough. The pacing woman called after him, chilling him: 'Who Pih' Da'?'

And in his mind, he heard this question echo with chilling clarity. *Who is Pixie Dark?*

2

There was no gun in the first house he broke into, but there was a long-barreled flashlight, and he shone it on every straggling phoner he encountered, always asking the same question, trying simultaneously to throw it with his mind like a magic-lantern slide on a screen: *Have you seen a boy?* He got no answers and heard only fading fragments of thought in his head.

At the second house there was a nice Dodge Ram in the driveway, but Clay didn't dare take it. If Johnny was on this road, he'd be walking. If Clay was driving, he might miss his boy even if he was driving slow. In the pantry he found a Daisy canned ham, which he unzipped with the attached key and munched as he hit the road again. He was about to throw the balance into the weeds after he'd eaten his fill when he saw an elderly phoner standing beside a mailbox, watching him with a sad and hungry eye. Clay held out the ham and the old man took it. Then, speaking slowly and clearly, trying to picture Johnny in his mind, Clay said: 'Have you seen a boy?'

The old man chewed ham. Swallowed. Appeared to consider. Said: 'Ganna the wishy.'

'The wishy,' Clay said. 'Right. Thanks.' He walked on.

In the third house, a mile or so farther south, he found a .30–30 in the basement, along with three boxes of shells. In the kitchen he found a cell phone sitting in its charging cradle on the counter. The charger was dead – of course – but when he pushed the button on the phone, it beeped and powered up immediately. He only got a single bar, but this didn't surprise him. The phoners' conversion-point had been at the edge of the grid.

He started for the door with the loaded rifle in one hand, the flashlight in the other, and the cell phone clipped to his belt when simple exhaustion overwhelmed him. He staggered sideways, as if struck by the head of a padded hammer. He wanted to go on, but such sense as his tired mind was able to muster told him he had to sleep now, and maybe sleep even made sense. If Johnny was out here, the chances were good *he* was sleeping, too.

'Switch over to the day shift, Clayton,' he muttered. 'You're not going to find jackshit in the middle of the night with a flashlight.'

It was a small house – the home of an elderly couple, he thought, judging by the pictures in the living room and the single bedroom and the rails surrounding the toilet in the single bathroom. The bed was neatly made. He lay down on it without opening the covers, only taking off his shoes. And once he was down, the exhaustion seemed to settle on him like a weight. He could not imagine getting up for anything. There was a smell in the room, some old woman's sachet, he thought. A grandmotherly smell. It seemed almost as tired as he felt. Lying here in this silence, the carnage at the Expo grounds seemed distant and unreal, like an idea for a comic he would never write. Too gruesome. *Stick with* Dark Wanderer, Sharon might have said – his old, sweet Sharon. *Stick with your apocalypse cowboys.*

His mind seemed to rise and float above his body. It returned – lazily, without hurry – to the three of them standing beside the Tyco Water Purification van, just before Tom and Jordan had climbed back aboard. Jordan had repeated what he'd said back at Gaiten, about how human brains were really just big old hard drives, and the Pulse had wiped them clean. Jordan said the Pulse had acted on human brains like an EMP.

Nothing left but the core, Jordan had said. *And the core was murder. But because brains are* organic *hard drives, they started to build themselves back up again. To reboot. Only there was a glitch in the signal-code. I don't have proof, but I'm positive that the flocking behavior, the telepathy, the levitation . . . all that came from the glitch. The glitch was there from the start, so it became part of the reboot. Are you following this?*

Clay had nodded. Tom had, too. The boy looking at them, his blood-smeared face tired and earnest.

But meanwhile, the Pulse keeps on pulsing, right? Because somewhere there's a computer running on battery power, and it keeps running that program. The program's rotten, so the glitch in it continues to mutate. Eventually the signal may quit or the program may get so rotten it'll shut down. In the meantime, though . . . you might be able to use it. I say might, *you got that? It all depends on whether or not brains do what seriously protected computers do when they're hit with an EMP.*

Tom had asked what that was. And Jordan had given him a wan smile.

They save to system. All data. If that happens with people, and if you could wipe the phoner program, the old programming might eventually reboot.

'He meant the human programming,' Clay murmured in the dark bedroom, smelling that sweet, faint aroma of sachet. 'The human programming, saved somewhere way down deep. All of it.' He was going now, drifting off. If he was going to dream, he hoped it would not be of the carnage at the Northern Counties Expo.

His last thought before sleep took him was that maybe in the long run, the phoners would have been better. Yes, they had been born in violence and in horror, but birth was usually difficult, often violent, and sometimes horrible. Once they had begun flocking and mind-melding, the violence had subsided. So far as he knew, they *hadn't* actually made war on the normies, unless one considered forcible conversion an act of war; the reprisals following the destruction of their flocks had been gruesome but perfectly understandable. If left alone, they might eventually have turned out to be better custodians of the earth than the so-called normies. They certainly wouldn't have been falling all over themselves to buy gas-guzzling SUVs, not with their levitation skills (or with their rather primitive consumer appetites, for that matter). Hell, even their taste in music had been improving at the end.

But what choice did we have? Clay thought. *Survival is like love. Both are blind.*

Sleep took him then, and he didn't dream of the slaughter at the Expo. He dreamed he was in a bingo tent, and as the caller announced B-12 – *It's the sunshine vitamin!* – he felt a tug on the leg of his pants. He looked under the table. Johnny was there, smiling up at him. And somewhere a phone was ringing.

3

Not all of the rage had gone out of the phoner refugees, nor had the wild talents entirely departed, either. Around noon of the next day, which was cold and raw, with a foretaste of November in the air, Clay stopped to watch two of them fighting furiously on the shoulder of the road. They punched, then clawed, then finally grappled together, butting heads and biting at each other's cheeks and necks. As they did, they began to rise slowly off the road. Clay watched, mouth hanging open, as they attained a height of approximately ten feet, still fighting, their feet apart and braced, as if standing on an invisible floor. Then one of them sank his teeth into the nose of his opponent, who was wearing a ragged, blood-stained T-shirt with the words **HEAVY FUEL** printed across the front. Nose-Biter pushed **HEAVY FUEL** backward. **HEAVY FUEL** staggered, then dropped like a rock down a well. Blood streamed upward from his ruptured nose as he fell. Nose-Biter looked down, seemed to realize for the first time that he was a second story's height above the road, and went down himself. *Like Dumbo losing his magic feather,* Clay thought. Nose-Biter wrenched his knee and lay in the dust, lips pulled back from his bloodstained teeth, snarling at Clay as he passed.

Yet these two were an exception. Most of the phoners Clay passed (he saw no normies at all that day or all the following week) seemed lost and bewildered with no flock mind to support them. Clay thought again and again of something Jordan had said before getting back in the van and heading into the north woods where there was no cell phone coverage: *If the worm's continuing to mutate, their newest conversions aren't going to be either phoners or normies, not really.*

Clay thought that meant like Pixie Dark, only a little further gone. *Who are you? Who am I?* He could see these questions in their eyes, and he suspected – no, he *knew* – it was these questions they were trying to ask when they spouted their gibberish.

He continued to ask *Have you seen a boy* and to try to send Johnny's picture, but he had no hope of an answer that made sense now. Most times he got no answer at all. He stayed the next night in a trailer about five miles north of Gurleyville, and the next morning at a little past nine he spied a small figure sitting on the curb outside the Gurleyville Café, in the middle of the town's one-block business district.

It can't be, he thought, but he began to walk faster, and when he got a little closer – close enough to be almost sure that the figure was that of a child and not just a small adult – he began to run. His new pack began to bounce up and down on his back. His feet found the place where Gurleyville's short length of sidewalk commenced and began clapping on the concrete.

It was a boy.

A very skinny boy with long hair almost down to the shoulders of his Red Sox T-shirt.

'Johnny!' Clay shouted. 'Johnny, Johnny-Gee!'

The boy turned toward the sound of the shout, startled.

His mouth hung open in a vacant gawp. There was nothing in his eyes but vague alarm. He looked as if he was thinking about running, but before he could even begin to put his legs in gear, Clay had swept him up and was covering his grimy, unresponsive face and slack mouth with kisses.

'Johnny,' Clay said. 'Johnny, I came for you. I did. I came for you. I came for you.'

And at some point – perhaps only because the man holding him had begun to swing him around in a circle – the child put his hands around Clay's neck and hung on. He said something, as well. Clay refused to believe it was empty vocalisation, as meaningless as wind blowing across the mouth of an empty pop-bottle. It was a *word*. It might have been *tieey*, as if the boy was trying to say *tired*.

Or it might have been *Dieey*, which was the way he had, as a sixteen-month-old, first named his father.

Clay chose to hang on to that. To believe the pallid, dirty, malnourished child clinging to his neck had called him Daddy.

4

It was little enough to hang on to, he thought a week later. One sound that might have been a word, one word that might have been *Daddy*.

Now the boy was sleeping on a cot in a bedroom closet, because Johnny would settle there and because Clay was tired of fishing him out from under the bed. The almost womb-like confines of the closet seemed to comfort him. Perhaps it was part of the conversion he and the others had been through. Some conversion. The phoners at Kashwak had turned his son into a haunted moron without even a flock for comfort.

Outside, under a gray evening sky, snow was spitting down. A cold wind sent it up Springvale's lightless Main Street in undulating snakes. It seemed too early for snow, but of course it wasn't, especially this far north. When it came before Thanksgiving you always griped, and when it came before

Halloween you griped double, and then somebody reminded you that you were living in Maine, not on the isle of Capri.

He wondered where Tom, Jordan, Dan, and Denise were tonight. He wondered how Denise would do when it came time to have her baby. He thought she'd probably do okay – tough as a boiled owl, that one. He wondered if Tom and Jordan thought about him as often as he thought about them, and if they missed him as much as he missed them – Jordan's solemn eyes, Tom's ironic smile. He hadn't seen half enough of that smile; what they'd been through hadn't been all that funny.

He wondered if this last week with his broken son had been the loneliest of his life. He thought the answer to that was yes.

Clay looked down at the cell phone in his hand. More than anything else, he wondered about that. Whether to make one more call. There were bars on its little panel when he powered up, three good bars, but the charge wouldn't last forever, and he knew it. Nor could he count on the Pulse to continue forever. The batteries sending the signal up to the comsatellites (if that was what was happening, and if it *was* still happening) might give out. Or the Pulse might mutate into no more than a simple carrier wave, an idiot hum or the kind of high-pitched shriek you used to get when you called someone's fax line by mistake.

Snow. Snow on the twenty-first of October. *Was* it the twenty-first? He'd lost track of the days. One thing he knew for sure was that the phoners would be dying out there, more every night. Johnny would have been one of them, if Clay hadn't searched and found him.

The question was, what had he found?

What had he saved?

Dieey.

Daddy?

Maybe.

Certainly the kid hadn't said anything even remotely resembling a word since then. He had been willing to walk with Clay . . . but he'd also been prone to wandering off in his own direction. When he did that, Clay had to grab him again, the way you grabbed a tot who tried to take off in a supermarket parking lot. Each time Clay did this he couldn't help thinking of a windup robot he'd had when he was a kid, and how it would always find its way into a corner and stand there marching its feet uselessly up and down until you turned it back toward the middle of the room again.

Johnny had put up a brief, panicky fight when Clay had found a car with the key in it, but once he got the boy buckled and locked in and got the car rolling, Johnny had quieted again and seemed to become almost hypnotized. He even found the button that unrolled the window and let the wind blow on his face, closing his eyes and lifting his head slightly. Clay watched the wind blowing back his son's long, dirty hair and thought, *God help me, it's like riding with a dog.*

When they came to a road-reef they couldn't get around and Clay helped Johnny from the car, he discovered his son had wet his pants. *He's lost his toilet training along with his language,* he had thought dismally. *Christ on a crutch.* And that turned out to be true, but the consequences weren't as complicated or dire as Clay thought they might be. Johnny was no longer toilet-trained, but if you stopped and led him into a field, he would urinate if he had to. Or if he had to squat, he'd do that, looking dreamily up at the sky while he emptied his bowels. Perhaps tracing the courses of the birds that flew there. Perhaps not.

Not toilet-trained, but housebroken. Again, Clay was helpless not to think of dogs he had owned.

Only dogs did not wake up and scream for fifteen minutes in the middle of each night.

5

That first night they had stayed in a house not far from the Newfield Trading Post, and when the screaming started, Clay had thought Johnny was dying. And although the boy had fallen asleep in his arms, he was gone when Clay snapped awake. Johnny was no longer in the bed but under it. Clay crawled underneath, into a choking cavern of dust-kitties with the bottom of the box spring only an inch above his head, and clutched a slender body that was like an iron rail. The boy's shrieks were bigger than such small lungs could produce, and Clay understood that he was hearing them amplified in his head. All of Clay's hair, even his pubic hair, seemed to be standing up straight and stiff.

Johnny had shrieked for nearly fifteen minutes there under the bed, then ceased as abruptly as he had begun. His body went limp. Clay had to press his head against Johnny's side (one of the boy's arms somehow squeezed over his neck in the impossibly small space) to make sure he was breathing.

He had dragged Johnny out, limp as a mailsack, and had gotten the dusty, dirty body back onto the bed. Had lain awake beside him almost an hour before falling soddenly asleep himself. In the morning, the bed had been his alone again. Johnny had crawled underneath once more. Like a beaten dog, seeking the smallest shelter it could find. Quite the opposite of previous phoner behavior, it seemed . . . but of course, Johnny wasn't like them. Johnny was a new thing, God help him.

6

Now they were in the cosy caretaker's cottage next to the Springvale Logging Museum. There was plenty to eat, there was a woodstove, there was fresh water from the hand-pump. There was even a chemical toilet (although Johnny wouldn't use it; Johnny used the backyard). All mod cons, circa 1908.

It had been a quiet time, except for Johnny's nightly screaming fit. There had been time to think, and now, standing here by the living room window and watching snow skirl up the street while his son slept in his little closet hidey-hole, there was time to realize that the time for thinking was done. Nothing was going to change unless he changed it.

You'd need another cell phone, Jordan had said. *And you'd need to take him to a place where there's coverage.*

There was coverage here. Still coverage. He had the bars on the cell phone to prove it.

How much worse can it be? Tom had asked. And shrugged. But of course he *could* shrug, couldn't he? Johnny wasn't Tom's kid, Tom had his own kid now.

It all depends on whether or not brains do what seriously protected computers do when they're hit with an EMP, Jordan had said. *They save to system.*

Save to system. A phrase of some power.

But you'd have to wipe the phoner program first to make space for such a highly theoretical second reboot, and Jordan's idea – to hit Johnny with the Pulse yet *again,* like lighting a backfire – seemed so spooky, so off-the-wall dangerous, given the fact that Clay had no way of knowing what sort of program the Pulse had mutated into by now . . . assuming (makes an ass out of you *and* me, yeah, yeah, yeah) it was still up and running at all . . .

'Save to system,' Clay whispered. Outside the light was almost gone; the skirling snow looked more ghostly than ever.

The Pulse *was* different now, he was sure of that. He remembered the first phoners he'd come upon who were up at night, the ones at the Gurleyville Volunteer Fire Department. They had been fighting over the old pumper, but they had been doing more than that; they had been talking. Not just making phantom vocalisations that might have been words, *talking.* It hadn't been much, not brilliant cocktail-party chatter, but actual talk, just the same. *Go away. You go. Hell you say.* And the always popular *Mynuck.* Those two had been different from the original phoners – the phoners of the Raggedy Man Era – and Johnny was different from those two. Why? Because the worm was still munching, the Pulse program was still mutating? Probably.

The last thing Jordan had said before kissing him goodbye and heading north was *If you set a new version of the program against the one Johnny and the others got at the checkpoint, they might eat each other up. Because that's what worms do. They eat.*

And then, if the old programming was there . . . if it was saved to the system . . .

Clay found his troubled mind turning to Alice – Alice who had lost her mother, Alice who had found a way to be brave by transferring her fears to a child's sneaker. Four hours or so out of Gaiten, on Route 156, Tom had asked another group of normies if they'd like to share their picnic site by the side of the road. *That's them,* one of the men had said. *That's the Gaiten bunch.* Another had told Tom he could go to hell. And Alice had jumped up. Jumped up and said—

'She said at least we did something,' Clay said as he looked out into the darkening street. 'Then she asked them, "Just what the fuck did *you* do?"'

So there was his answer, courtesy of a dead girl. Johnny-Gee wasn't getting better. Clay's choices came down to two: stick with what he had, or try to make a change while there was still time. If there was.

Clay used a battery-powered lamp to light his way into the bedroom. The closet door was ajar, and he could see Johnny's face. In sleep, lying with his cheek on one hand and his hair tousled across his forehead, he looked almost exactly like the boy Clay had kissed goodbye before setting out for Boston with his *Dark Wanderer* portfolio a thousand years ago. A little thinner; otherwise pretty much the same. It was only when he was awake that you saw the differences. The slack mouth and the empty eyes. The slumped shoulders and dangling hands.

Clay opened the closet door all the way and knelt in front of the cot. Johnny stirred a little when the light of the lantern struck his face, then settled again. Clay was not a praying man, and events of the last few weeks had not greatly increased his faith in God, but he *had* found his son, there was that, so he sent a prayer up to whatever might be listening. It was short and to the point: *Tony, Tony, come around, something's lost that can't be found.*

He flipped open the cell and pushed the power button. It beeped softly. The amber light in the window came on. Three bars. He hesitated for a moment, but when it came to placing the call, there was only one sure shot: the one the Raggedy Man and his friends had taken.

When the three digits were entered, he reached out and shook Johnny's shoulder. The boy didn't want to wake up. He groaned and tried to pull away. Then he tried to turn over. Clay wouldn't let him do either.

'Johnny! Johnny-Gee! Wake up!' He shook harder and kept on shaking until the boy finally opened his empty eyes and looked at him with wariness but no human curiosity. It was the sort of look you got from a badly treated dog, and it broke Clay's heart every time he saw it.

Last chance, he thought. *Do you really mean to do this? The odds can't be one in ten.*

But what had the odds been on his finding Johnny in the first place? Of Johnny leaving the Kashwakamak flock before the explosion, for that matter? One in a thousand? In ten thousand? Was he going to live with that wary yet incurious look as Johnny turned thirteen, then fifteen, then twenty-one? While his son slept in the closet and shat in the backyard?

At least we did something, Alice Maxwell had said.

He looked in the window above the keypad. There the numbers 911 stood out as bright and black as some declared destiny.

Johnny's eyes were drooping. Clay gave him another brisk shake to keep him from falling asleep again. He did this with his left hand. With the thumb of his right he pushed the phone's CALL button. There was time to count *Mississippi ONE* and *Mississippi TWO* before CALLING in the phone's little lighted window changed to CONNECTED. When that happened, Clayton Riddell didn't allow himself time to think.

'Hey, Johnny-Gee,' he said. 'Fo-fo-you-you.' And pressed the cell against his son's ear.

December 30, 2004 – October 17, 2005

Center Lovell, Maine

Chuck Verrill edited the book and did a great job. Thanks, Chuck.

Robin Furth did research on cell phones and provided various theories on what may lie at the core of the human psyche. Good info is hers; errors in understanding are mine. Thanks, Robin.

My wife read the first-draft manuscript and said encouraging things. Thanks, Tabby.

Bostonians and northern New Englanders will know I took certain geographical liberties. What can I say? It goes with the territory (to make a small pun).

To the best of my knowledge, FEMA hasn't appropriated any money to provide backup generators for cell telephone transmission towers, but I should note that many transmission towers *do* have generator backup in case of power outages.

S.K.

Stephen King lives in Maine with his wife, the novelist Tabitha King. He does not own a cell phone.

On the following pages is an excerpt – in the author's hand – from the forthcoming novel *Lisey's Story*, which Hodder will publish in October 2006

LISEY'S STORY

Stephen King

PART 1: BOOL HUNT

Chapter I: Lisey and Amanda
(Everything the Same)

1

To the public eye, the spouses of well-known writers are all but invisible, and no one knew it better than Lisey Landon. Her husband had won the Pulitzer and the National Book Award, but Lisey had only given one interview in her life. This was for the well-known women's magazine that publishes the column "Yes, I'm Married To _Him!_" She spent roughly half of its five-hundred-word length explaining that her nickname rhymed with "CeeCee." Most of the other half had to do with her recipe for slow-cooked roast beef. Lisey's sister Amanda said that the picture accompanying the interview made Lisey look fat.

None of Lisey's sisters were immune to the pleasures of setting the cat among the pigeons ("stirring up a stink" had been their father's phrase for it), or having a good natter about someone else's dirty laundry, but the only one Lisey had a hard time liking was this same Amanda. Eldest (and oddest) of the one-time Debusher girls of Lisbon Falls, Amanda currently lived alone, in a house Lisey had provided, a small, weather-tight place not too far from Castle View where Lisey, Darla, and Cantata could keep an eye on her. Lisey had bought it for her seven years ago, five before Scott died. Died Young. Died Before His Time, as the saying was. Lisey still had trouble believing he'd been gone for two years. It seemed both longer and the blink of an eye.

When Lisey finally got around to making a start at cleaning out his office suite, a long and beautifully lit series of rooms that had once been no more than the loft above a country barn, Amanda had shown up on the third day, after Lisey had finished her inventory of all the foreign editions (there were hundreds) but before she could do more than start listing the furniture, with little stars next to the pieces she thought she ought to keep. She waited for Amanda to ask her why

She wasn't moving _faster_, for heaven's sake, but Amanda asked no questions. While Lisey moved from the furniture question to a listless (and day-long) consideration of the cardboard boxes of correspondence stacked in the main closet, Amanda's focus seemed to remain on the impressive stacks and piles of memorabilia which ran the length of the study's south wall. She worked her way back and forth along this snakelike accretion, saying little or nothing but jotting frequently in a little notebook she kept near to hand.

What Lisey didn't say was _What are you looking for?_ or _What are you writing down?_ As Scott had pointed out on more than one occasion, Lisey had what was surely among the rarest of human talents: she was a business-minder who did not mind too much if you didn't mind yours. As long as you weren't making explosives to throw at someone, that was, and in Amanda's case, explosives were always a possibility. She was the sort of woman who couldn't help prying, the sort of woman who _would_ open her mouth sooner or later.

Her husband had headed south from Rumford,

where they had been living ("like a couple of wolverines caught in a drainpipe," Scott said after a visit he vowed never to repeat) in 1985. Her one child, named Intermezzo and called Metzie for short, had gone north to Canada (with a long-haul trucker for a beau) in 1989. "One flew north, one flew south, one couldn't shut her everlasting mouth." That had been their father's rhyme when they were kids, and the one of Dandy Dave Debusher's girls who could never shut her everlasting mouth was surely Manda, first fired by her husband and then dumped by her daughter. Boo! the end, Scott would have said. Probably with a laugh, and probably Lisey would have laughed with him. With Scott she had always laughed a lot.

Hard to like as Amanda sometimes was, Lisey hadn't wanted her down there in Rumford on her own; didn't trust her on her own, if it came to that, and although they'd never said so aloud, Lisey was sure Darla and Cantata felt the same. So she'd had a talk with Scott, and found the little Cape Cod, which could be had for ninety-seven thousand dollars, cash on the nail. Amanda had moved up within easy checking range soon after.

Now Scott was dead and Lisey had finally gotten around to the business of cleaning out his writing quarters. Halfway through the fourth day, the foreign editions were boxed up, the correspondence was marked and in some sort of order, and she had a good idea of what furniture was going and what was staying. So why did it feel that she had done so little? She'd known from the outset that this was a job that couldn't be hurried. Never mind all the importuning letters and phone-calls she'd gotten since Scott's death (and more than a few visits, too). She supposed that in the end, the people who were interested in Scott's unpublished writing would get what they wanted, but not until she was ready to give it to them. They hadn't been clear on that at first; they weren't down with it, as the saying was. Now she thought most of them were.

There were lots of words for the stuff Scott had left behind. The only one she completely understood was memorabilia, but there was another one, a funny one, that sounded like incuncabilla. That was what the

impatient people wanted, the wheedlers, the angry ones — Scott's
incuncabilla. Lisey began to think of them as Incunks.

2

What she felt most of all, especially after Amanda showed up,
was discouraged, as if she'd either underestimated the task
itself or overestimated (wildly) her ability to see it through
to its inevitable conclusion — the saved furniture stored in
the barn below, the rugs rolled up and taped shut, the
yellow Ryder van in the driveway, throwing its shadow on
the board fence between her yard and the Galloways'
next door.

Oh, and don't forget the sad heart of this place,
the three desktop computers (there had been four, but the
one in Scott's memory nook was now gone, thanks to Lisey
herself). Each was newer and lighter than the last, but even
the newest was still a big desktop model and all of them
still worked. They were password-protected, too, and she didn't
know what the passwords were. She'd never asked, and had no
idea what kind of electro-litter might be sleeping on the
computers' hard drives. Grocery lists? Poems? Erotica? She

was sure he'd been connected to the internet, but had no idea where he visited when he was there. Amazon? Drudge? Hank Williams Lives? Madam Cruella's Golden Showers & Tower of Power? She tended not to think anything like that last, to think she would have seen the bills, except of course that was really bullshit. Or billshit, if you wanted to be punny about it. If Scott had wanted to hide a thousand a month from her, he could have done so. And the passwords? The joke was, he might have told her. She forgot stuff like that, that was all. She reminded herself to try her own name. Maybe after Amanda had taken herself home for the day. Which didn't look like happening anytime soon.

Lisey sat back and blew the hair off her forehead. *I won't get to the manuscripts until July at this rate,* she thought. *The Incunks would go nuts if they saw the way I'm crawling along. Especially that last one.*

The last one — five months ago, this had been — had managed not to blow up, had managed to keep a very civil tongue about him until she'd begun to think he might be different. Lisey told him that Scott's writing suite had been sitting empty for almost a year and a

half at that time, but she'd almost mustered the energy and resolve to go up there and start the work of cleaning the rooms
and setting the place to rights.

Her visitor's name had been Professor Joseph Woodbody, of the University of Pittsburgh English Department. Pitt was
Scott's alma mater, and Woodbody's Scott Landon and the American Myth lecture class was extremely popular and extremely
large. He also had four graduate students doing Scott
Landon theses this year, and so it was probably inevitable
that the Incunk warrior should come to the fore when Lisey
spoke in such vague terms as sooner rather than later
and almost certainly sometime this summer. But it wasn't
until she assured him that she would give him a call
"when the dust settles" that Woodbody really began to give
way.

He said the fact that she had shared a great
American writer's bed did not qualify her to serve as
his literary executor. That, he said, was a job for an ex-
pert, and he understood that Mrs. Landon had no college
degree at all. He reminded her of the years already gone
since Scott Landon's death, and of the rumors that con-

tinued to grow. Supposedly there were piles of unpublished Landon fiction — short stories, even novels. Could she not let him into the study for even a little while? Let him prospect a bit in the file cabinets and desk drawers, if only to set the most outrageous rumors at rest? She could stay with him the whole time, of course — that went without saying.

"No," she'd said, showing Professor Woodbody the door. "I'm not ready just yet." Overlooking the man's lower blows — trying to, at least — because he was obviously as crazy as the rest of them. He'd just hidden it better, and for a little longer. "And when I am, I'll want to look at everything, not just the manuscripts."

"But —"

She had nodded seriously at him. "Everything the same."

"I don't understand what you mean by that."

Of course he didn't. It had been part of her marriage's inner language. How many times had Scott come breezing in, calling "Hey, Lisey, I'm home — everything the same?" Meaning is everything all right, is everything cool. But like most phrases of power

(Scott had explained this once to her, but Lisey had already known it), it had an inside meaning. A man like Woodbody could never grasp the inside meaning of <u>everything the same</u>. Lisey could explain all day and he still wouldn't get it. Why? Because he was an Incunk, and when it came to Scott Landon only one thing interested the Incunks.

"It doesn't matter," was what she'd said to Professor Woodbody on that day five months ago. "<u>Scott</u> would have understood."

3

If Amanda had asked Lisey where Scott's "memory nook" things had been stored — the awards and plaques, stuff like that — Lisey would have lied (a thing she did tolerably well for one who did it seldom) and said "a U-Store-It in Mechanic Falls." Amanda did not ask, however. She just paged ever more ostentatiously through her little notebook, surely trying to get her younger sister to broach the subject with the proper question, but Lisey also did not ask. She was thinking of how empty this corner was, how empty and <u>uninteresting</u>, with so many of Scott's mementos gone. Either destroyed (as she had destroyed the computer monitor) or too badly scratched and dented to be shown; such an exhibit would raise more questions than it could ever answer.

At last Amanda gave in and opened her notebook. "Look at this," she said. "Just look."

Manda was holding out the first page. Written on the blue lines, crammed in from the little wire loops on the left to the edge of the sheet on the right (<u>like a coded message</u> <u>from one of those street-crazies</u> you're always running into in New York because there's not enough money for the publicly funded mental institutions anymore, Lisey thought wearily)), were numbers. Most had been circled. A very few had been enclosed in squares. Manda turned the page and now here were <u>two</u> pages filled with more of the same. On the following page, the numbers stopped halfway down. The final one appeared to be 856.

Amanda gave her the sidelong, red-cheeked, and some—how hilarious expression of hauteur that had meant, when she was twelve and little Lisey only two, that Manda had gone and Taken Something On Herself; tears for someone would follow. Amanda herself, more often than not. Lisey found her-self waiting with some interest (and a touch of dread) to see what that expression might mean this time. Amanda had been acting nutty ever since turning up...